Praise for *The Miraculous True History of Nomi Ali*

"Part of the beauty of Khan's writing stems from the fact that she does not need to actively portray racism, she makes virtually all her characters live it . . . Khan writes with quietly restrained but powerful passion." —*Dawn*

"Khan is adept at creating worlds that are at once magical and terrifying. She creates a universe out of a footnote of history." —*Indian Express*

"A richly imagined universe . . . If we are to strive for a more just world, we need to hear the stories." —*The Hindu*

"This fiction is the new truth we need to know." —*New Indian Express*

"A magnificent, rebellious, and moving story. [It] is striking on several levels: as a historical novel, as testimony . . . as a story of hope, friendship, and love that can survive even in the most terrible circumstances." —*Svenska Dagbladet*, Sweden

Praise for *Thinner Than Skin*

WINNER: FRENCH EMBASSY PRIZE FOR BEST FICTION, KARACHI LITERATURE FESTIVAL 2014

LONG-LISTED: DSC PRIZE FOR SOUTH ASIAN FICTION 2014

LONG-LISTED: MAN ASIAN LITERARY PRIZE 2012

"Smart, fierce, and poignant: perhaps the most exciting novel yet by this very talented writer." —Mohsin Hamid

"There is power, serenity and grace in the writing of this literary daughter of the great Pakistani poet Faiz Ahmed Faiz." —*Le Monde*, France

"In (a) magnificent landscape—where anthropomorphic glaciers are born of mating ice—a chance meeting with a young nomad will change lives. *Thinner Than Skin* is a work of piercing beauty and intelligence, and an urgent novel for our times." —Man Asian Jury Prize

Praise for *The Geometry of God*

"Khan's urgent defense of free thought and action—often galvanized by strong-minded, sensuous women—courses through every page of this gorgeously complex book; but what really draws the reader in is the way Mehwish taste-tests the words she hears, as if they were pieces of fruit, and probes the meaning of human connection in a culture of intolerance, but also of stubborn hope."
—Cathleen Medwick, *Oprah* Magazine

"The characters, the poetry and the philosophical questions she raises are rendered with a power and beauty that make this novel linger in the mind and heart." —*Kirkus Reviews*, starred review

"Elegant, sensuous and fiercely intelligent, a wonderfully inventive story that pits science against politics and the freedom of women against the insecurities of men." —Kamila Shamsie

The Miraculous True History of Nomi Ali

Uzma Aslam Khan

DEEP VELLUM PUBLISHING

DALLAS, TEXAS

Deep Vellum Publishing
3000 Commerce St., Dallas, Texas 75226
deepvellum.org · @deepvellum

Deep Vellum is a 501c3 nonprofit literary arts organization
founded in 2013 with the mission to bring
the world into conversation through literature.

Support for this publication has been provided in part by the National
Endowment for the Arts.

ISBNs:
978-1-64605-164-9 (hardcover)
978-1-64605-165-6 (ebook)

LIBRARY OF CONGRESS CONTROL NUMBER: 2021950238

Cover design by Bhavi Mehta
Cover image: detail from *Asakusa Ricefields and Torinomachi Festival, No. 101,
One Hundred Famous Views of Edo, 1857,* by Utagawa Hiroshige (Ando).

Interior Layout and Typesetting by KGT

Printed in the United States of America

For Abbu
(1935–2009)

'You've gone so far.'

'It is when they become westernised that one doesn't feel at home with them.'
—Sir Reginald Maxwell, *The Maxwell Papers*

'Untie the knot from my tongue, that they may hear me speak.'
—Surah Taha, verse 25–28

ONE

The Night They Took Zee
1942

THE SOLDIERS ARRIVED ON A MORNING in spring when the sea was unswollen and everyone said they were here to save them.

'They are Asian, like us,' said the father of Nomi and Zee, because he was like everyone.

Zee did not believe him. 'Nobody cares about us.'

'The British have left. We are free.'

'We are not free. We are now under the Japanese.'

They argued till Zee left the village in a sulk and Nomi followed him.

The soldiers were everywhere, just standing around, carrying long guns and small satchels. When the children reached the jetty, Zee said, 'There is nothing new here, there never is.' Pretending to study the sea, he tried to sound casual, but she knew him as well as he knew her. There was plenty new here. There were bombers in the sky and battleships in the sea. Nomi's nose was full with black snot. The sirens had stopped.

'Let's go up the mountain,' announced Zee.

'Don't be stupid,' she said.

'Are you a coward like—'

'Shut up!'

A soldier looked at her and yawned.

Nomi thought it strange that even the Indians who had worked for the British were now gone.

'Why would they leave, if something bad wasn't going to happen?' Zee had asked, during one of his fights with their father.

'Wait and see,' their father had repeated. 'The Japanese are here to help.' To their mother he said that the price of raising a family on a prison island was that the children would never know trust.

Their father was a settled convict. He had been arrested in India, long ago, for reasons the children were never told, and sent here to South Andaman Island, to the jail that looked like a starfish. After serving out his term, he had been given a ticket of leave and the hut where they now lived. Nomi and Zee were born on the island. They were the Local Borns.

Earlier this morning, Nomi had heard their mother say that the first thing the Japanese did after they arrived was release the prisoners, and now look, terrible men were wandering about stealing chickens and bothering women. She told Nomi to stay close to her, and to keep the hen, Priya, close too.

Now, as Zee pulled Nomi away from the jetty, towards the mountain, she wanted to tell her brother.

He knew her as well as she knew him. 'Don't be afraid.'

'I'm afraid for Priya.'

'The Japanese like fish, not chicken.' He laughed at his own joke, he always did.

'That's not what I mean. Mama says there are freed convicts who are savages.'

'What if Baba was still a prisoner? Would you call him that?'

'I'm just telling you what she said.'

'Mama is usually wrong.'

'No, she isn't.'

'Yes, she is.'

'What about what Baba says?'

'Always wrong.'

'I want to go back.'

'No, you don't.'

'Yes, I do.'

'They can't both be right.'

'About what?'

'Mama sides with the British, Baba with the Japanese, whose side are you on?'

She was stumped. What sort of question was this? Their mother would not be here if not for the British, she had been forced, it was called transportation for life, just because Zee was already in her stomach when Baba did what he did. Her family said she was with his child now and belonged to him. Nomi had heard their mother say this, sometimes holding Nomi while Nomi held Priya—it was one of the important things she had to discuss with Zee.

But he was confusing her. She was twelve—only a year younger than their mother when she got married—yet, with Zee, Nomi felt like a child. Maybe this was why Priya grew muddled and went where she should not. One of the other chickens was saying stupid things.

'That makes no sense,' she decided.

He laughed. 'You're on nobody's side, okay? Because nobody's on our side.'

He looked at her. She looked at him.

And she has wondered ever since, ever since, why she did not think to ask, What's our side, Zee?

They started climbing. Their mother never allowed them up the mountain that Nomi called Mount Top, but Nomi had been here once before. It was their secret, hers and Zee's.

There were no Indian guards telling them not to go up. There were only the Japanese, some lying in the grass with their boots off and long guns to the sky. They said things hard to understand, but did not stop Nomi and Zee from continuing. For a few steps it was just the two of them, then more olive-green uniforms, different up here against the bushes than down there against the sea. And again Zee gripped her arm, and again she wanted to be home, but they kept climbing. There was the lake they had been to before. Then, a little further, through the padauk trees on the summit of the next hill, they saw it. The jail.

Shaped like a starfish and the colour of a wound, its seven arms severed by the tall, tall trees.

This was as far as she had ever come. The higher up Zee took her, the more the ocean flew through the trees, and she tried to focus on this because it was beautiful.

From up here she could finally see where she lived. Where she had always lived. Zee had told her that the Andaman Islands were the tip of a submerged mountain range. Below the surface of the sea, there were many Mount Tops, far taller than the one on which they now stood. If Nomi shut her eyes and listened closely, she could hear a rhythmic rumbling all around her. The islands were breathing. The whole universe seemed to sing. The sea was so many greens and blues, all glassy and glittering. The surf rolled sweetly along the white beaches, though she had never known a beach to be white, a surf to be sweet. The sky was absolutely clear, and there was just enough of a breeze to kiss the sweat from her arms, but not the terrible kind that said a storm was coming and they would be wet for days.

There was another story about how these islands were made. Lord Rama had created them, perhaps on a day such as this, as a bridge to cross the sea. His wife Sita had been abducted by a demon, and he wished for a way to retrieve her. He did recover Sita, but finding the islands too forested for his feet, Rama fled, in search of a softer landing. He soon forgot about this corner of the world.

But on this afternoon, the islands appeared soft to Nomi. She wanted to pull them to her, all the soft corners of the world.

Zee was pointing to the purest of sands below, where palm trees swayed in prayer. Nearby were strict rows of coconut palms, a whole army of them. These were the plantations where some women worked. From this height, the other islands were just dots, and now Zee was pointing to the one where there had been a sawmill and elephants to clear the forests. When the Japanese bombed it, the cry of elephants could be heard even over the sirens, and some people reported seeing monstrous globes of fire charging into the sea. According to Zee, the black snot in Nomi's nose was scorched elephant flesh.

She could hear no elephants now. And though she had not

climbed all the way to the top of the mountain, already she had seen the world, already she had grown older.

'We don't have to keep going up if you're tired,' said Zee. He seemed happy with her now that she had stopped wanting to go back. 'Let's sit here.'

He pulled her through a loop of padauk trees, the tallest tree-loop she had seen, and a wide, wide fig tree with a mesh of vines in its endless loving arms. A flock of yellow parrots fluttered far into the dazzling sky. There was a bench with curly etching. *Harriett Tytler, brave and beloved wife of Colonel Robert Tytler.* Nomi did not like the smell of the bench but when Zee sat down, so did she.

He released her arm. 'Are you still afraid?'

'No,' she lied. The smell was familiar. She did not know why.

'You don't need to be. I have this.' From somewhere under his shirt, he pulled out a small gun. 'It's an air pistol,' he added, as if this meant something.

She was horrified. 'Baba will be angry.'

'Pish!'

'Where did you get it?'

'From Mr Campbell, before he left.'

Mr Campbell had been their school teacher. 'He gave it to you?'

'I found it in his office drawer.'

'You stole it?'

'So? What would he do—transport me?' Again he laughed at his own joke. 'Anyway, he's gone. Maybe he thought I should have it.'

Zee was staring ahead, a smile around his lips. He was not happy with her but with himself. His hair had grown again. As the wind blew, the hair lifted off his forehead, where he had a rash. The rash was all over his body. He had to always keep dry and clean, which was hard on a wet island, with only three shirts. Many children at school had what their mother called 'the itchiness.' Nomi checked her skin for the itchiness often.

This is how she will always see him, her brother, Zeeshan Haider Ali. Gazing at the sea, always at the sea, with a tuft of hair pointing to the sky, like the comb of a rooster. His cheek is red and covered in dark bristles because shaving irritates his skin. So do mosquitoes. He slaps his cheek to move them away, killing one. It hangs from his bristles. He says shaving is the worst part of growing up. His voice has become the best part, since it stopped changing. It is now deep and warm, it is why she follows him. His eyes are light brown, like their mother's. His brows are thick and folded with a deep hollow in the middle, like their father's.

When she flicked the dead mosquito off his cheek, a spot of blood hung on her finger.

'Instead of teaching us to read,' said Zee, 'don't you wish they'd taught us to swim?' He was stroking the gun and still staring ahead, at the everlasting blue below.

The smell was closer now. She could almost touch it, almost name it. Then she heard something.

The bench rested on a level patch of ground, a few feet before the mountain began to descend. There were bushes all around, cupping them. The fig tree had as many roots as arms, and the grass was high. The sound could have come from anywhere. Slowly, Zee began to hide the gun under his shirt. Then he grabbed her arm again, a finger of the free hand firmly to his lips.

It happened again. A shift in the bushes to their right. Zee's hand grew so tight the mark would stay with her for the rest of the day. But she did not feel it, not till later.

From out of the air sprang a toddy cat.

Nomi exhaled.

She had seen one before, at school. The boys pulled its long tail, cheering till the teacher came outside and said to leave it. This civet was smaller, with a hiss that was louder. There was a white spot beneath each brown eye. A white band swept across the forehead, as though it lived inside a worried mask. The tail whipped the air twice before the cat raced over the mountain. They both knew it was time to do as the civet had shown, and go back down.

Instead, Nomi looked behind her. That smell again.

A soldier was pissing in the bushes, the sprinkles brushing her arm. Another crouched and farted. Others emerged from the tall grass, zipping up pants, tucking in shirts. This was their latrine and this was the smell: of the camp of prisoner families before prisoners served out their term and were given a hut. Nomi was born in a camp. She had never wanted to smell that smell again.

Zee pulled her past them, quickly. The soldiers began to yell and whistle and seemed to be everywhere now, shirts off, boots off, kicking at grass. There was a restlessness in the air, she could feel it. It had taken hold of them in the time since they started climbing. They were surrounded by mosquitoes and gnats, the drone filled the heat-haze, the breeze was dead. The white vests under their uniforms were soaked in sweat and mud. They looked at her the way boys in the camp looked at girls. The way boys at school did too, except at her, because she was the sister of Zee. These men were irritated and bored, and their mother always said the bored ones made trouble.

'Wait!' shouted a soldier in English. He had a caterpillar moustache and round glasses.

'Keep walking,' Zee hissed. And then he was dragging her down the mountain so fast she stopped feeling the grass beneath her feet, there was only the sea, all glassy and glittering, they were floating, Nomi and Zee, while behind them, the soldiers laughed.

That night their friend Aye came to their hut. He was Burmese, older than Nomi and Zee, and also a Local Born. Earlier today, Aye said, the soldiers had entered the homes of a village near his own, and everyone should be careful.

'Why would they come to our huts?' asked their father, stooping through the door.

Aye answered in whispers.

Nomi looked at Zee, who put a finger to his lips. She had not told their mother where they were today. She said, 'I went with Zee to the empty school to look for more books but it was empty,' and their mother raised one eyebrow.

The door shut. Their parents talked softly. Then their father shuffled to the neighbour's hut, to repeat what Aye had said. The neighbour went to the next hut, and so on, till someone arrived at the house where an escaped prisoner, a woman known as the one who got away, was once seen. Afterwards, people began saying that no one could escape the island, not even a ghost.

Soon, everyone who lived around Aberdeen Square had spread the word about the soldiers coming to a nearby village, and then their father was back in bed, with a drink.

Priya the chicken lay in her corner, next to where Nomi slept. She was behaving well and did not go out when the door was opened to Aye. From the way she breathed, Nomi could tell she was sleepy. Zee was reading *She* by candlelight. Their teacher had lent him the book and Zee had read it many times, he just liked turning the pages.

'The soldiers must be hungry,' their father whispered.

'They have more food than we do,' their mother said, loudly.

'Why don't you keep some ready, in case they come?' His voice was calm.

'They should be feeding us if they are here to help!'

Zee turned a page.

'Anyway,' she continued, 'what food do we have? You know there's no more fishing, since they put mines in the water. I can't imagine they like tinday ki bhujiya.'

Nomi giggled. Zee kicked her under the table, but his face in the candlelight was so red, she knew he was also laughing. She could feel the mark around her arm, where he had grabbed her on the mountain, reminding her of their father's neck mark.

Nomi had heard the stories. Maybe they started with the neighbours, soft sounds that were picked up the way the swiftlets that lived in mountain caves would pick up soft sounds, till everybody could hear them. Their father had tried to run away before she was born, when Zee was a baby. He was caught and punished as an example to other prisoners. There was a long burn mark around his neck, as thick as a rope, and those welts down his back were not only from being flogged for refusing to grind the mill.

She kept feeling the imprint on her skin.

'Go to sleep, both of you,' snapped their mother.

'One more chapter,' said Zee.

'How long is a chapter?' asked their father.

'Pish!' said Zee.

Nomi left the table and slipped under the sheet next to Priya, who clucked happily when Nomi stroked her back, and Zee turned another page.

Next evening, they came. Their father was outside in the toilet, their mother with him. Zee was standing near a shop with two boys from school. There were chickens milling about and no one noticed, not even the village women complaining about rising prices while their daughters ran in circles. The doors of many huts were open. It was cooler this way.

Their father returned from the toilet, coughing. Their mother left the door open. Through it, Nomi could see five soldiers enter the square. Priya ran for the door. Nomi grabbed her. Priya flapped her wings. The boys stopped talking. The girls stopped playing. The soldiers entered the shop without a sound, coming back out with the shopkeeper and glasses full of icy sharbat. They kept walking. As the sun set, the sky turned the same vivid colour as the drink in their hands.

Priya screeched. Never before had she made so panicked a sound, so Nomi dropped her. Priya ran into the square. Nomi followed. Another hen, white with a droopy comb, began running between a soldier's boots. He bent to pick her up, his sharbat falling down her back. Now her feathers matched the sky. When she hopped out of his arms, the soldier followed her through the open door of a hut. The chicken ran under the bed and over the chair and behind the stove and between his legs. Over the bed and onto a window and down again. Other soldiers came inside. They threw away their drinks and joined the chase. The neighbour's home was littered in feathers and dirt and glass. Finally, a soldier caught the sharbat-pink hen. He put her in his satchel. Her owner tried to explain that she gave his family eggs. They walked past him, chasing other chickens till only three were left, including Priya.

Zee and the other boys were telling the soldiers to stop. 'Oh ho! Oh ho!' they begged. One boy tried to pull a hen out of a satchel. The soldier made a strange sound, almost a bark, and the boy moved aside. But the owner of the hen continued objecting, 'They are not yours, please give them back,' and someone added, 'A chicken that size costs five rupees!'

Nomi couldn't catch Priya. The chicken was in her muddled state, going where she should not, pecking at a soldier's boots, making everyone as nervous as herself. Maybe she was trying to protect them. Maybe she thought she could. She flapped aside then raced back, to strike the soldier's shoulder. Normally, she could barely snag a worm. Her final attack was aimed at his ear. The soldier swiped her face. When she fell backward, the shot was fired. It happened before she could even sit back up, dazed.

It was Zee. He had fired Mr Campbell's gun into the air. All five soldiers were unarmed, three with chickens in their satchels. They talked angrily amongst themselves. Before leaving, the one who had slapped Priya looked at Zee and ran a finger across his neck.

Everyone knew the Japanese would be back. Though Nomi also knew, only later would she understand the meaning of loss to exist somewhere in that moment when first a chicken and then a boy could cause grown men to look foolish. That single moment, it was racing ahead, farther and farther than the ocean that she and Zee had gazed upon together, just yesterday, and she would spend her life trying to catch up with it. But that life, it had not yet begun.

Their father moved quickly. They did not know he could. With left hand to hunched back, he waddled from door to door, seeking help in hiding Zee. Before leaving, he told their mother to find a disguise. She moved quickly. They knew she could. She found a sari, green like the forest, and tore it in half so Zee would not trip as he ran. Priya was in her corner, quiet. Zee was at the table, not turning pages, also quiet. Nomi packed *She* and the sulphur cream for his skin. Their mother packed lassi, bread, water and three golden eggs. She packed the soap and matches made by prisoners.

Their father returned with his friend Dr Singh, who asked if Zee still had the gun. When Zee said yes, Nomi wondered why no one had said anything angry about it. If Zee had not taken the gun, she would have lost Priya, but she would not lose Zee.

When she ran to him, he held her, his rough cheek to her own, his thick hair full with fear. The mark around her arm, where he held her on the mountain, had vanished. As he slipped into the night the green sari billowed behind him. It would lift him into the clouds, helping him to rise, rise, like the island that had come up for air. She could tell. She knew him and he knew Nomi.

Arrival of the S.S. *Noor*
1936

SIX YEARS BEFORE ZEE FLED THE Japanese, Nomi would see the prisoner who would come to be known as the one who got away arrive on South Andaman Island. It was February, and Nomi was six years old. Though the winter monsoons had been fierce, that day the rain was soft and a lean sun scattered across the water.

An hour before the prison ship docked, Nomi was at school with Zee, her mind on monsoon winds. She had seen a shrew spiral backward into the sea. She wanted a pet. A chicken, or a dog. Something to keep her from blowing away before the storms started up again.

The teacher, Mr Campbell, was trying to convince Zee to re-read *The Milly-Molly-Mandy Storybook*. 'Your sister likes it,' he said, looking briefly from Zee to Nomi.

She could tell Zee wanted something new. Books came to the island many years too late, and he often complained that his choices were limited. He liked *Just William*, but Mr Campbell said it incited restlessness and adventure, impulses that had to be tamed.

Through the half-door she could hear their friend Aye in the corridor, changing the light bulb. Like Zee, Aye was always hungry for real news. The kind Mr Campbell never spoke of. The kind whispered most often on the island: the freedom movement on the mainland. The teacher would say there was a civil war in Spain and a Depression in America and pretend nothing was happening in India.

'What is a civil war?'

'Where is America?'

'Chain!'

'Brain!'

And Nomi would search privately for rhyme words that came so easily to them.

She and Zee were happy to stay after school, to help Mr Campbell with tasks. Aye fixed bulbs, Zee put chairs upside down on the desks, and she helped Zee empty out the bowls scattered everywhere on the floor to catch the rain. Besides, Mr Campbell, who was unmarried, was often in need of company. At the right moment, he would speak to them, if not about the world, at least about the island.

The rain that day began soon after dawn and was slowing to a drizzle and the sky turned slate grey. The single electric bulb dangling from the ceiling from a long black wire flickered on and off. The ceiling leaked from several points that Nomi had memorised like constellations in wood. Every now and then, a new star was born.

The swinging half-door leading to the corridor creaked. Aye stepped inside to say he had replaced the bulb. Mr Campbell asked him to replace this one too, but there were no more bulbs. He muttered something about needing to put the order in place or the place in order, please remind him. His King Charles Spaniel, Georgina, was at his feet. The half-door kept groaning. 'Why can I never grow accustomed to this ghastly climate?' He loosened his shirt collar and stashed *The Milly-Molly-Mandy Storybook* (twice rejected) in his drawer.

Zee stood watch over Nomi as she stood watch over a bowl, expecting it to overflow at any moment. New stars were the leakiest.

Earlier today, she had learned the names of as many bodies of water as drops in the bowl. The Arabian Sea. The Andaman Sea. The Bay of Bengal, which was not a sea but part of a sea. The Indian Ocean, with too many bays to name. The Pacific Ocean, around the corner. She recited these names again. Nomi was the keeper of seas that flowed into each other, into her bowl. Bodies of land, on the other hand, did not flow into each other, she could not collect them. Though, sand carried on wind. Ants carried dirt here and there. These she could collect. But what about Kala Paani, Black Water, the prisoners' name for exile? Was Black Water a body of water or a body of land?

'May I be excused, sir?' asked Aye of Mr Campbell. 'I am, er, late for work.'

'What? Oh, yes. Yes, yes.'

Aye thanked the teacher, cast Zee a meaningful glance—one that said *If he tells you anything about anything, tell me*—and left.

'Do it,' Zee whispered in Nomi's ear. She picked up the bowl, ran outside to empty it in the sand, without spilling, and returned just in time to catch the next drip.

Mr Campbell put down his pen. 'I think that will be all for today.' His mouth fell slightly open while his hand stroked Georgina's pelt.

The drizzle had almost ceased. Only a few drops fell from the ceiling, like frog song. When one called, after the count of two, another answered. Within a few minutes, the gaps began to increase.

Interrupting the composition, Mr Campbell tapped a test book on his desk. 'Well done, my boy. You have written a most successful essay. It is purposeful, accurate, and has only one spelling mistake. Do you know, if you were not a convict's son, I would recommend you for study in England?'

Zee's rash turned bright pink.

'Perhaps it is time for a drink,' continued Mr Campbell. Georgina sat up, wagging her feathery tail.

The rain stopped. If it did not start again till tomorrow, the bowls would no more overflow. Zee left his post to help Mr Campbell pack his leather briefcase. It was tan in colour and properly stiff, as though still new, with three smooth sections inside: one for papers, one for books, and a third for items Zee could not touch. There was also the 'Big Red,' a red-capped Parker pen with a gold nib that was prized by the teacher almost as much as his dog, who bounced beside Nomi.

'Georgina, *down*,' commanded Mr Campbell.

The dog sat.

'May I play with her, sir?' Nomi asked.

'Not now. You children always make her dirty.' He leashed the dog and started to walk with Zee to Browning Club, the European club at the corner of Aberdeen Square.

Nomi followed close behind, watching her brother tilt to his left as he carried the heavy briefcase with both hands. The sea was to their right and the waves rose and fell, like a row of schoolchildren moving along. Aberdeen, the village where Nomi and Zee lived, lay ahead. It was named after a place in Scotland, because the British, though they came willingly, were always homesick. Beyond Aberdeen was the summit with the red starfish jail.

The path was slippery but the rain did not start up again. Nomi's white uniform would not get too muddy. After school, she had little to do. While Zee did extra homework, she sometimes played with the neighbours. Other times, the Japanese dentist, Susumu Adachi, would give her and other children rides on his bicycle, or she went up to the Female Factory where their mother worked, or she hovered outside the shop where their father and other men would drink. She used to look for Aye, but lately he had been going to the European farm to be with White Paula, so she looked for him less.

The two hornbills that always appeared around this time flew to the papaya tree at the top of the street. Zee always said they had a nose like Nomi's. He said even when she was a baby, her nose was too big for her face, and her arms too long and bony, like chicken legs. As they walked down the street, the hornbills were chattering. The whole neighbourhood was chattering, but it was different from the noise at the camp, where they lived till just last year with other prisoner families. This chatter faded when doors were shut, when it was time to sleep. At the camp, there were no doors. Families lived in tents and talked all night and many children were never taught to go outside to do their business. They would do it in the tents, even on the tents.

They passed the shop of the Japanese taxidermist who kept stuffed birds in the window. Two doors away was the dentist Susumu Adachi's clinic. He gave children tin toys after fixing their teeth and they were to call him Susumu San.

Outside the dental clinic Mr Campbell looked over his shoulder and handed Georgina's leash to Nomi. He had trusted Zee with it, but this was his first time trusting Nomi.

She took the leash. Immediately, a living warmth pulsed through it. She wanted never to reach the club. In this way, Georgina would forever walk beside her, black nose to wet soil. When the rain returned, they would keep each other from tossing into the sea.

They reached the club. She returned Georgina to the teacher, who took his briefcase from Zee and disappeared inside the building.

Zee looked at her closely. 'You don't have to go to the factory today. I'll tell Mama we got late at school. It's even true.'

She could still feel the round of Georgina's soft stomach against the leather, and the force of her will as she sniffed the ground and took her time.

'Come with me to the jetty,' said Zee.

'Why?'

'A ship is coming. Didn't you hear Mr Campbell?'

'But where's Aye?'

'Collecting nests.'

'Let's wait.'

'The ship will not wait for him, silly.'

The children were not the only ones come to witness a new batch of prisoners arrive. As the *S.S. Noor* heaved into the harbour, the jetty was crowded.

It happened nine times a year and they were always there, to watch the giant ship dock sullenly and sluggishly after a four-day trek from Calcutta. It took longer if she stopped to pick up prisoners in Madras and Rangoon along the way. She wore black, as though always in mourning. She was the namesake of the *Darya-e-Noor*, the Sea of Light, the first ship to carry prisoners to the colony, and herself a namesake. The Darya-e-Noor was one of the largest cut diamonds in the world, and was last seen on King George V, just before his death. Unable to part from the diamond even in the next life, he swallowed it, or so people said. The ship was shrouded in no less mystery. On her return from the islands to Calcutta one day, she disappeared, leaving no trace of herself, or her crew.

The S.S. *Noor* carried a heavy burden. Not only did she transport men and women to a life unknown, but she followed in the wake of a haunted ship and fatal gem. No wonder she moaned and swayed and looked the other way.

Zee liked to tell Nomi that one day someone would find pieces of the vanished *Darya-e-Noor* and that someone would be him. 'You can't swim,' she always replied, to which he countered, 'Pish!'

Now Zee rolled on the balls of his feet, hands scrunched in pockets, while she inspected the mob. Aye and White Paula were not there. Nor were her parents. They never came. Their father said he could not bear to watch others being sent to an island where no god watched over them, only men did.

As the prisoners disembarked, the only European doctor of the settlement, who was really a horse doctor, pushed through the crowd. He was followed by the only European nurse, who wore a blond ponytail that swung. They examined each prisoner briefly before hurrying away.

Next, they waited for the special police.

'There are women,' said Zee.

Nomi had also noticed.

'Look at that fat one,' he said. 'Chained to the skinny one.'

The skinny one had the most difficulty standing upright. Her eyes were mostly shut and already she looked like a ghost.

'She will get the fever first,' said Zee.

'That's mean.'

'You'll see.'

The special police arrived, led by the superintendent of the jail, Mr Howard, for whom Aye worked. A steady whisper extended through the crowd as the prisoners frogmarched up the hill to the jail, a mat rolled on each head and an iron bowl on each mat. Too many who watched had never stopped living it, the climb to the hill's summit to one of the 693 cells, the days and nights creeping from one end to the next, 13½' x 7', a smallness buried deep in the folds of the brain, where it grew, oh it grew. Then the sound of the heavy grill door as it slammed shut, and the three-step snap of a latch system to puzzle even the niftiest thief. Equally dreadful was the *un*snap, for then it might be the jailor, the terrible Cillian, who was born to never die. And even before all of this, at the entrance to the jail, the high wall garlanded with manacles, shackles, iron belts and implements of torture impossible to name, each warped into figures more gruesome than the next. They could not forget the day this sight was first encountered, when the science of bondage dangled inches ahead: to pass through the gates meant to never return the same. In the midst of all the twisted metal hung a plaque bearing the words of the designer of the jail, whose name was never learned but whose words were tattooed even on the hearts of those who could not read. *A mill for grinding rogues honest.* Because it was true, they had been ground, and when they witnessed the grinding of others, they were ground again. Everyone who once lived in the jail now lived in a time when all times were simultaneously present.

Sooner or later, their children would come to know.

But today, Nomi had come to the jetty to observe a spectacle, not to understand why her father was the way he was.

'218 D,' Zee whispered, as the row of prisoners passed them, a wooden tag dangling beneath each chin. 'D for dangerous. She must have killed someone.'

'The fat one?' Nomi whispered back.

'No.' He shook his head. 'You'll see.'

Prisoner 218 D was gathering the heavy chains around her like a skirt. How did she get here? Nomi wondered. And even as she thought it, Nomi was sure of it, she would always be sure of it, the prisoner turned her head and looked straight at her.

FILE COPY.

FRB/DT.   (59 groups)   2877

DECYPHER OF TELEGRAM

(COPIES   From Government of India, Home Department,
CIRCULATED)   to secretary of state for India.
         Dated Simla, 3rd June, 1935
         Received 2:30 p.m., 3rd June, 1935
         _____ X

IMPORTANT
1329. FIRST OF FIVE PARTS.
Home Department.

We have for some time had under discussion
proposals to remove to Andamans persons including
women convicted of offences in connection with
terrorist crime. Local Governments regard this as
essential part of programme against terrorism owing
to increased difficulties of maintaining discipline in
local jails and urgent necessity of deterrent measures.
Chief Commissioner, Andamans, reports that with
certain structural alterations to cellular jail, proposal
is (?, omitted) feasible. Prisoners removed would be
segregated in 2 wings of the jail, kept separate from
the other prisoners, and entirely out of contact with
the settlement.

_____

RECEIVED P.&J. DEPT
6-JUNE 1935
INDIA OFFICE

The Long Walk
1936

THE LONG WALK UP TO THE jail is the prisoner's hardest one yet. Like buffalo herders, the police brandish their batons, smacking the dirt and the hides of prisoners who fall behind. Prisoner 218 D counts every step.

Step one. She is on trial in Lahore, on the British Indian mainland. Two months ago, perhaps?

Step two. Men had come to her, after her arrest, all in black hats with wide black bands. The words they spoke to each other hang heavier than the chains she gathers now, on her way to the jail. '*The women are of a more criminal type than the men. They are murderers of the most abandoned nature and obviously addicted to lustful excesses. There is a distinction between the murder committed by the woman and the murder committed by the man.*'

Step three. Before the *S.S. Noor*, she is tossed in an airless enclosure. Her hands find refuge in the cracks of cold brick, where the clay is soft. Her mother had eaten clay when pregnant with her, believing it would make the delivery easier. As the prisoner waits for her own sentence, she wonders whether eating this soil, her soil, would ease the delivery? She tries to laugh, but finds no appetite for clay or comedy.

Step four. How small the revolver had felt in her hands!

Step five. She is charged with conspiracy to wage war against the King, and awarded the maximum penalty: transportation. Before leaving, she licks the brick.

Step six. Step ten. The prisoner is being weighed. By law, she can only be transported if her weight is acceptable. The warden who pushes her onto the scales checks twice before pushing her off, with a grunt. Next the warden pushes into her hands a blunt pencil and two sheets of paper, saying that if she needs to write any letters, she should do so now.

Step seventeen.

Step twenty.

How long is now?

She wants to cherish those who love her still, to give them perfect words. In the courthouse had sat her mother, with a face like a cloud on the morning after a heavy rain. The prisoner has spent her life following the sun behind it. If she is never to see the face again, what is there to see?

Two sheets of paper, rough and unlined, for the most important words ever said.

Step thirty-eight. The warden returns with a striped uniform and two blankets. She takes away the pages. 'One word!' cries the prisoner. 'Let me write just one!' But she has missed her chance, and is forced into a courtyard where several men and three women stand in file, all carrying the same two blankets and striped clothes. Their ankles are bound in iron fetters. They are handcuffed in pairs. They are each given a string with a wooden tag. Hers says 218 D.

Step fifty. Women are put with men in the train. There is singing. The lyrics are by poets her father loved. Bismil, Majaz, Akhtar Shirani. For her father, every funeral, festival, or summer rain was an occasion to recite poetry. She can hear his voice, and in this way he is still alive, and in this way so is she.

Step sixty. Step seventy.

There are always eyes at the window of the train, watching convicts cross the country. A man outside lifts an arm over his head, she thinks it is to wave goodbye, but instead the arm unwinds a turban, pulling from within its folds the chaos around him, faster, faster still.

Step eighty-five. A week passes in Calcutta jail as more prisoners arrive from across India. When they walk four miles to the port before being thrown into the lower hold of the *S.S. Noor*, the prisoner is shackled to a woman who hums.

The woman has tried to embrace her, whispering, 'My child.' Though it shames the prisoner to think it, truth is, the woman stinks. Before the journey is over she fears she will end up hating those whose dignity she tried to secure when free. The voiceless and faceless. Sick and forgotten. She will hate them, all.

She is startled by her mistake. Were this a journey, she could return.

Step: How long is now?

She feels her own flesh, tracing the contours of her own mouth, her own cheek.

She tries to listen to the sea. She tries to let herself be rocked by the foul stranger and her twin, the foul sea. She tries to remember colours, sunlight, the breezes that tease the crops of open fields. She tries to catch new rain on her tongue. She tries to remember the song of the koel. She tries to forget what she has left. This effort to remember and to forget comes like the waves she cannot hear but can feel, they are there, under her chains.

If she could look outside, just once.

The men in the hold have discovered a small hole. They have been taking turns standing before it since before the ship even left the port, watching the shoreline dissolve. There are whispers that a fisherman in a tiny boat is following their ship from the clock tower all the way out to the open sea. The fisherman is their size and struggle, their weakness and will. When he disappears, a few men cry.

The woman she is shackled to refuses to budge, so the two lie together on the floor. A feathery light falls on the woman's profile and there is pus on her face. Still she hums, a songbird with boils.

The door to the hold opens. Garish light washes over them. Those who are not political prisoners are escorted up to the deck for air. The woman she is bound to is not a political prisoner, but because of her, they both must stay. Perhaps it is for this reason that she drags her more frequently down a step behind them, to a shallow pit. The latrine on the train to Calcutta was a wild rose, by comparison.

The food is always the same. Stale rice, dry beans, a rock of sugar. When the songbird sucks the sugar she purrs more loudly, and now the prisoner longs to lay her head on the bunk of that fat neck. What a delicious nest the filthy folds of her skin would make! Instead, the prisoner cocks her head and listens.

'Na ro puttar, sajna.'

The prisoner concentrates, willing this kind, repulsive creature to say it again.

'Na ro puttar, sajna.'

The prisoner begins to hear the cadences of Aunty Hanan, her neighbour in Lahore. Many lifetimes ago, Aunty Hanan played a tambura after morning prayers. Ma-sa-sa-SA. She would face the rising sun through her ceiling-to-floor window, resting her chin upon the instrument's long neck. After she had plucked the fourth and most resonant string, a koel would answer, always from the same branch of a laburnum tree.

Step one hundred and—Who was that girl who looked at her as she made her way to this summit? That poor child, she looked just like herself!

Prisoner 218 D takes a step back. She can see them, the gates through which she must pass.

Surely the wall will crumble beneath the weight of all that grotesque metal? Surely no man could have envisioned such monstrosity?

A keening starts to rise from the prisoners ahead and behind her.

Na ro puttar, sajna. Don't cry child, beloved one.

Ma-sa-sa-SA. It was an old tambura with a gold pattern down the long neck and four languid, sky-opening notes.

Muhammad's Web
1936

AS THE YEAR PROGRESSED, after school Nomi came more often to the Female Factory, where their mother worked. Zee was writing the perfect essay, hoping Mr Campbell would change his mind and recommend him for study in England. She left him to it.

The factory was full of spiders. Their mother said it was a good thing or there would be more mosquitoes, and once you get malaria, you always get malaria. Besides, the Prophet Muhammad liked spiders. Long ago, as he and a faithful companion fled dangerous men from Mecca, the two took shelter in a cave. As they hid, a spider began to spin her web across the cave's entrance. When the men from Mecca arrived, they saw only the web and a few nesting birds and kept going.

The factory was built by women. At one time, they laboured alongside male prisoners, clearing the jungle and building roads. Now they were kept indoors. Their mother was the overseer of the section with sewing machines and looms. Their neighbour, Aunty Madhu, supervised the back area, with the grinding stone and dirty clothes. As the prisoners worked, the two neighbours met in the middle. Nomi was given a piece of string from one of the sewing machines to play with, but had to put it back afterwards or she would be a thief. Also, if any thread went missing, it was their mother who had to pay for it. 'Do not waste thread,' she said. 'And if the prisoners do, *tell me.*'

Some prisoners were widows. Or had killed children, including their own, or done something terrible, like robbed a train or made a bomb. The ratio of men to women in the jail was at most ten to one. It was why women were kept inside. From their mother's chatter, Nomi had learned about Criminal Lines, which got more tangled than those she made when playing cat's cradle with the string she had to return. Mr Campbell, who sometimes played cat's cradle with Zee (making other children jealous), had told Zee (who told Nomi) that the game was very old, and practiced as far as Hawaii (which was also a group of islands).

Her string today was green. She slid the middle finger through one end then walked through the factory holding both hands out, inside the cradle.

The prisoner who had stared directly at Nomi on her way up to the jail was still wearing the wooden tag 218 D. She sat at one end of a table, sewing. Except, she was not doing very much. She did not look at Nomi now. She did not look anywhere. She was a political prisoner, not an ordinary one, which meant she had done something terrible to the British. Nomi tried to imagine her running after a train, like the one in *My Book of Trains*, but the prisoner looked so tired it was hard to believe she could run after anything.

There were mostly two Criminal Lines. One line divided ordinary prisoners from political prisoners. Another divided men from women. But because women political prisoners were not normally brought to the island, this one had been put with ordinary women prisoners. There was to be no mingling, or their mother would swing her cane.

Ordinary women prisoners were brought here to marry men. The British took a tour of women's prisons on the mainland, looking for prisoner brides. It was what their mother and Aunty Madhu talked about at the prisoner camp, and though they had their own huts now, the talk had not changed. When the British went from prison to prison, they were careful not to call what they were asking for *transportation*, because that would have been frightening. Instead, they said to become a bride, a woman only had to volunteer to be 'sent down.' Once she fulfilled her prison term, she could marry and 'settle down.' So then there was a third line: the one between prisoner brides who volunteered to come, and wives who were not prisoners accompanying prisoner husbands. Nomi's mother and Aunty Madhu were in the last group. They were 'imported women.' When a husband was released from jail, he was given a small plot of land as part of the terms of his release, so that he and his family could develop the settlement.

But it was not so simple, and her mother and Aunty Madhu often gossiped about the other women, the ones who never left the camp.

This too was not so simple, because some of those women were good. For instance, the one who had slept in their tent. She often cooed to her baby while stroking his hair, one end of her tunic pulled high, a thin line of milk stretching from her large brown nipple to the boy's pink mouth. Sometimes, in the middle of the night, a man would pull her away from the thin line of milk to take her somewhere else, and the baby cried. Nomi would comfort him till his mother returned.

She still thought of the woman at night, when she couldn't sleep. She thought of the toilet smell of the camp, of the baby's soft curls and fluttering wet lips. Zee had also liked to watch. Their mother would cover his eyes because she did not like him watching naked women.

Now their mother was saying, 'There are still too many grooms for too few brides, and you know what that means.'

'Every woman who crosses the sea is fallen, Fehmida,' said Aunty Madhu.

'I am no fallen woman, and neither are you. Nor will our daughters be, nor our daughters-in-law.'

'Yes, but you know it, and so do I. If a day comes when we are free to go home, no one in India will know the difference.'

'See what your father did to us,' said their mother, pulling Nomi to herself, and Nomi raised her arms to keep the cat's cradle in place.

The grilled windows of the factory were dusty and high up on one wall, so no one could escape. The ceiling was more slanted than at school but still leaked when it rained. Though it had not rained today, the sound of running water came from the area behind them, where clothes were slapped on rock. Once, a prisoner had refused to do the work. She said she did not come from the dhobi caste. Her hair was cropped, like that of the other prisoners. When their mother dragged her out to the heap of dirty clothes, she needed the help of two male guards. One of the guards said he was unclean now that he had touched the prisoner. She would have to wash his uniform twice. Nomi never saw the woman again.

Now she noticed that one of the windows was screened by a spider web which caught pink light that flickered if she turned her head just so.

The movement reminded her of something.

Lately, at night, when their father thought his children were asleep, he had started sliding towards them on the floor mat. This was hard for him, because his back was so bent that when he stood up, you could lay an egg on him. It happened because for years he was chained to the oil mill in the courtyard of the jail, grinding mustard seed, and the sad part was that their mother still soothed his wounds with mustard oil. When their father came to them at night, Nomi would watch from the corner of her eye, the way she now watched the beautiful pink light at the window. His breath smelled of rum, and his lips fluttered, as though in prayer. He stroked first Nomi's hair, never rushing, and then Zee's. His fingers were wide and rough from the coir ropes he made from coconut husks, after he stopped turning the mill. There was just enough pressure on her scalp to make her sleepy, though Nomi pretended to sleep, breathing deeply. When his focus switched to Zee, a small smile hovered at the corner of his lips. He kept stroking, slowly, because love was the opposite of haste.

At the table in the factory, Prisoner 218 D was still not sewing. Their mother was still talking to Aunty Madhu, and Nomi was still wedged between them, hands extended.

The Many Mistakes of Haider Ali
1936–37

HAIDER ALI, THE FATHER OF Nomi and Zee, had a way of lighting the stove. Puckering his lips, he would blow into a narrow pipe, gently waving a hand-held fan. Nomi loved to watch. It was like he was putting a child to sleep. But tonight, after dinner, as the fire in the wood stove burned low, it was Haider Ali's hour to observe his family.

His wife Fehmida wiped the dishes and Nomi stood beside her, waiting to speak. He could guess that she wanted a pet. The other children had chickens. Nomi wanted one too. A hundred expressions crossed her sweet face as she wondered if it was the right time to ask, if it was ever the right time to ask. She was like him. She weighed her words, even at so young an age. Zee had taken after their mother, all fire and righteous fury.

There was much he longed to convey to the son who sat icily by candlelight each night, trying to put distance between himself and his father. Zee looked instead to his teacher, an Englishman. It was always Mr Campbell this, Mr Campbell that. Haider Ali could not read or write English, and every night, he was tormented by the same thought: it was not books and pencils but rope, made by him, that anchored his family. It was blood that ran through the rope, carrying love and terrible pain from the veins of the father to the veins of the children. Zee would have to learn, soon enough. He would have to see the wrong in believing in those that wronged them.

Somehow, Nomi kept a cooler head. There was always one that waited without a sound, without requiring more. In his family's case, the daughter. Nomi was not only like himself, but also his own mother, a slight woman with a calm demeanour who did not cry when Haider Ali was sent here, not for want of love but for want of hate. Fleeting purity, in an impure world.

Nomi had his mother's mouth, like a jasmine bud, and keen, vaguely close-set eyes. Even their gestures were alike. She too waited patiently for the right moment to speak, hands folded, tilting back her head like a sunbird after a refreshing drink.

The next time the neighbour Mr Bimal's hen laid, Haider Ali decided, he would ask him for a chick. Haider Ali's back ached a little less when he imagined placing the warm bundle in Nomi's hands.

Fehmida kept drying the dishes with a series of quick, effective sweeps, having wasted neither soap nor water, without acknowledging their child. She was at her best when she could see the good she did. But then, who wasn't?

Out of the corner of his eye, he could see Fehmida's prison uniform dangling from a hook on the wall. The British had weakened him till he could work no more, and now he had to live off his wife. Zee loathed him for it, for being without honour.

His fingers slid up to his kurta collar, grazing the mark around his neck, and the action was repeated because he was anxious. The secrets he harboured oppressed him. Yes, it was true, he had tried to escape once, ten years ago. He had not seen the faces of the Andamanese who caught him—they never let him turn around—but he could never stop hearing their call. *Lululululu*. A lullaby made of needles. And then the rope around his neck and the blade at his back, though he was close, *so close*, to almost making it out. Had he succeeded, Fehmida and Zee would have been left behind, and Nomi would never have been born.

He rubbed the mark around his neck, watching the daughter who loved him, and the son who scorned him. He was aware that a ship had arrived just today and that, along with nearly everyone else on the island, his children were at the jetty to receive it. He did not know what they gained from witnessing those awful moments when prisoners first encountered the truth of their eternal exile. Did they not understand that no Indian, not even one who had never been inside a jail, was free?

He asked little of his children, but perhaps he ought to ask that they stop going to the jetty when a ship pulled in, because each time they did, the scar around his neck came to life.

There was a knock at the door.

It was Dr Singh, dressed impeccably as always in a crisp white shalwar kameez and cobalt blue turban. His beard was combed and mostly white. The two men embraced and Dr Singh settled on a low-legged straw chair. Haider Ali settled back on his cot, apologising for his scruffy appearance.

The doctor laughed. 'If we cannot be ourselves at home, why call it home?'

Fehmida told Zee to sit with the men. Reluctantly, he shut his book.

'And how is my santri?' the doctor asked, as Nomi handed him tea. With his free arm, he pulled her close and her fingers found his steel bracelet. The doctor called her santri because it was a holy colour for Sikhs, and because it was the colour for courage and bliss. As she played with the bangle, he said, 'You are a lucky man, Haider Ali.'

The doctor did not have children, or a wife. He did not come here a prisoner. After he joined the Medical Corps of the Indian Army, the British transferred him first to Rangoon and then to these islands, and now twelve years had passed. Haider Ali often wished to ask him what it was like, living in the service of a foreign government in a foreign land inhabited mostly by prisoners and native tribes. He must have known that some prisoners had done terrible things. Yet, the good doctor abided by the rule amongst settled convicts: never ask what they did.

Six years from now, on the night Haider Ali begged the neighbours to conceal his son from the Japanese, he would turn most of all to Dr Singh, who would help him. By the following year, Haider Ali would make the mistake of telling the doctor what he had done—losing his only son, and his only friend.

Why did he never learn from his mistakes?

Tonight, he kept fingering the mark around his neck, and Fehmida must have noticed, because she raised one eyebrow, urging him to stop.

'That I am, that I am,' said Haider Ali. 'A lucky man.'

'And how is your health, my friend?' asked the doctor.

'I am well, very well.'

Fehmida snorted.

'I can hear your chest from here,' the doctor answered gently. 'Let me help. I have medicine, and ointment for your back.'

Haider Ali wiped his mouth with the back of his hand and spoke of other things. The small plot behind the hut had yielded tomatoes and cucumbers. The doctor must join them for a meal because Fehmida's raita was especially delicious, thanks to the new crop. The kari patta was also doing well, despite the heavy rains.

The doctor was too kind to shift the conversation back to his friend's health. He said, 'Thank you, Fehmida,' when she placed a dozen or so leaves of kari patta in his hands. When he smiled, his beard danced up and down.

Zee slurped his tea, looking bored.

'Still first in class?' the doctor asked.

'Yes,' answered Zee.

'And how many books have you read this week?'

'Seven.'

'Well done!' The doctor laughed, and Fehmida kissed Zee's head.

Then the doctor grew serious. He spoke of a new project, a gurdwara, the construction of which the government would allow, provided it had the support of a local committee. 'I am asking you to be on the committee, my friend.'

'Me?' Haider Ali raised his hands.

'Is something wrong?'

'No, of course not. I am honoured. Yes. Very honoured.'

'It will be the first of its kind.' Again the doctor's beard danced. The committee members would represent the many faiths of the island. He had already received the support of another Muslim. He was confident of being joined also by Hindus and Christians. After a while, the doctor declared, 'Let us enjoy the only freedom we have on this rock. The freedom of no caste or creed.'

Haider Ali stood up and took the doctor's free hand in both his own. 'It is a great honour, my friend. Of course I agree.' His eyes were wet.

'And you, santri, do you agree?'

Nomi smiled, still playing with his bracelet.

Before leaving, the doctor told her why he wore the bracelet. It was the Guru's way of urging him to use his hands well. 'As will you, one day, my santri. As will you.'

In the middle of the night, Fehmida whispered to Haider Ali, 'He would not blame you.'

'And you, can you forget? Have you stopped blaming me?'

She was silent. He had pushed her away with his memories.

He listened for the breathing of his children. They slept on the floor mat, and there was a pattern to the air that moved around them. Zee had allergies. His lungs wheezed. Nomi was healthier. Her breathing was deep. She was the one he could hear. Zee was holding his breath. Awake. He had almost certainly heard them speak of it before, how they came here not because Haider Ali was a freedom fighter, or a brave man in any way. Haider Ali just made a mistake. A terrible mistake.

He left the bed, whispering to Fehmida that he could make it to the toilet himself.

Outside, through a ladder of clouds appeared the cold rim of the moon, reminding him of Dr Singh's bracelet. He himself had not been able to bring a single possession with him to the island. Except for his wife, and the son she was carrying in her womb, everything he owned had to be left behind. The crops behind their hut filled him with emotions he could not explain. The fact was, those tomatoes, the ones he pretended to take pride in, they were not his. Worse, they reminded him of what he had no choice in. He *had to* settle this rock in the middle of the vast sea for those who took away his home. This was the condition of his 'release.'

He moved towards the vines. It was his fingers, and Nomi's,

that affixed the trellis upon which they hung. He plucked a tomato. In Jalandhar, where he was born, tomatoes were a strong, bold red, oblong in shape, and the juice was revitalising. Here the tomatoes were round and the skin was pulled too tight even when the crop ripened. The colour was pale. The juice was not plentiful. The taste did not awaken his senses. This was not how he imagined growing old.

His thoughts were interrupted by the chime of the Japanese dentist's bicycle bell. It was a comforting sound, like the whistle of the night watchman in Jalandhar.

The image of his mother's white dupatta in the Punjab dust rose before him. 'It is easier to hate those who wrong us than to love those we wrong,' she would say, adding, 'Living is a graceful task.'

His hand tensed around the tomato. He wanted to love it, but he could not.

When construction of the gurdwara began the following year, Dr Singh had the support of everyone he asked to join him. Eleven Sikhs, six Hindus, five Muslims, two Christians, one Buddhist. Except for Dr Singh, all were former convicts. As the twenty-five men took turns blessing the soil, Haider Ali joked that if any Parsi ever broke a law, he would be most welcome among them.

They knew of no temple like this on the mainland. Each man pledged that, regardless of caste or creed, he would cherish what they had together helped to build. No one could question to which god or guru a prayer was uttered under its roof.

Around them lay scattered a small pile of the same red brick used to make the jail, though the temple was to be built primarily of wood. It would not be fireproof, which was a risk worth taking. The temple could not resemble the jail.

After the ceremony, Dr Singh walked Haider Ali partway back to his hut.

'Your cough is getting worse,' said the doctor.

'It cannot be denied,' said Haider Ali, coughing.

'Let me help,' insisted Dr Singh. 'This will not go away by itself.'

'The gurdwara should be named after you,' said Haider Ali, changing the subject. 'It is your faith that brought us together today.'

'No, it should assume no mortal name. Besides, have you and the others been apart?'

Haider Ali laughed. 'There is no "apart" in prison, the great equaliser.'

Dr Singh's beard danced up and down, and the two men were alone in their thoughts.

When Dr Singh spoke again, it was about events that were strangely far away, and yet too close. 'The Japanese are advancing quickly through China.'

'So I hear. What have you been told?'

'Tianjin and Beiping have fallen. The war is coming to Southeast Asia, this much is clear. The British seem to consider these hidden islands the safest place to be.'

'For whom?' Haider Ali coughed again, more violently.

'You should rest,' said the doctor. 'We can discuss this another time.'

'Well, why would the Japanese come here?'

'That is as much as the British say. They are looking everywhere but here.'

'It is their habit, no?'

Dr Singh uttered quietly, 'I understand.'

'And you? What do you say?'

Dr Singh combed his lush beard with the top row of his teeth. Today he wore a royal blue turban that made him look especially distinguished. Yet, Haider Ali wondered, royal or loyal?

'I do not know,' the doctor answered at last. 'But I fear the nationalists who align themselves with Japan are either looking too far, or not far enough.'

Loyal, decided Haider Ali.

The two men separated and Haider Ali entered Aberdeen. The store was open. He bought a drink, with his wife's money. Guilt only heightened his thirst.

From the store, he could see the starfish jail. The man in the central tower was there, looking at him with all one hundred eyes.

With a bottle of rum in his hands, he walks alone to the jetty, where the *S.S. Noor* is moored. Though he will not watch a new batch of prisoners arrive, at night, when he thinks his children are asleep, Haider Ali comes here to look upon the ship.

He reaches down to touch the rope that anchors her, each tine entering his palm. When he was in jail, the warders said making rope was an easy task, compared to the godforsaken mill. Picking oakum, they called it, while turning the mill was called kolu. He had only to separate the fruit from the shell of two thousand coconuts each day. There are still marks on his palms from those sinful threads.

Haider Ali was used to handling plants in the Punjab, but not coconuts. Then again, it is plants that got him into trouble in the first place.

From the jetty, he can see the gurdwara. He decides to walk towards its god.

When he arrives, Haider Ali sits cross-legged on the pile of dirt that was blessed earlier that day. Though the temple will take a year or so to build, already he can envision the tranquil blue of its large and airy interior.

He asks the guru's forgiveness for not having anything to ask.

He is here merely to talk, from his soul, where he has hidden things for too long.

When he was in jail, Haider Ali saw things. He was put to the mill like a bullock, to extract thirty pounds of mustard oil each day. His back began to bend, he often had a fever. He was accused of feigning sickness. It is not what brings him here tonight.

This is: Haider Ali has seen men so desperate to be spared long hours in the sun that they would opt for anything instead. Anything. Having lost the capacity to differentiate between one humiliation and the next, they let the guards lead them to the forest, only to fall forward on their hands, spread their legs and permit the ultimate disgrace. Later, the guards would call them special names. Girl names.

He has not come here to ask, *how could you let that happen?* He has come instead to envision a god being strapped to a mill and caned for giving only twenty-five pounds of oil. He has come to hear a god scream when the millstone breaks his body, when another god pushes inside him. He has come to envision a god dying to escape. He has come to confess that he has learned something he wishes no one to learn and what he has learned is this. There is nothing more hurtful than hope.

The day he saw his chance to escape: the man tied next to him was in the woods with the only guard on duty. Not the ogre Cillian, who was running a high fever (that he was not accused of feigning), but his second in command at the time, a Baloch and a Muslim. And no, he has not come to ask why it was that the ones who pray to the same god and have the same dark skin and know what it is to be treated like an animal also treated him like an animal, though the question is a good one. Point is, the Baloch and the poor prisoner were away when the third man tied to the mill fainted. Nobody cared, least of all Haider Ali. Without looking up, he slipped the straps off his back. Oh, glory! Heaven itself called out to him: *Do it, and be returned a free man.*

So Haider Ali began to walk. There was the tiniest sliver of a moon. Leaves rustled. Onward.

It rained hard that night. He lay in the cool earth under a canopy of trees, the leeches biting into him, and when the rain subsided, the frogs chirped. The sun that rose the next morning was fragile as a crescent moon, reminding him of apricots and loquats, fruits he might never taste again. Where was he to go? He had taken shelter in the forest to bide his time, believing the guards more likely to search the coast and the prisoner camps, but perhaps it was the wrong choice. How many nights could he hide before being assumed dead? Nor did he have a plan for Fehmida and his baby son. How could he leave without them?

He told himself to keep the hope alive. He looked at the sky. The light was soft and graceful and so was the island. If he could find in his heart a way to allow this, he might be guided to the right place, from where he might find materials to build a raft, and a path to reach his wife. The sea below swayed, tossing with it delicate hues of pink and gold. The colours she wore on their wedding day.

Haider Ali was still gazing at the sea when he felt the rope around his neck. *Lululululu*. The knot tightened, and then he was dragged on all fours, all the way back to jail.

If he were Zee, he might think, hope rhymes with rope.

But now in his belly a subtle warmth, fragile as the sun that morning, has begun to swell. It began when Dr Singh suggested the Japanese might come here. He has no way of knowing just how many Indian nationalists are aligned with them, but what if they are of significant number? Surely they will lead the Japanese army to this island, so that ordinary prisoners, past and present, can be restored their pride. The mere thought makes him want to sing one moment, cry the next, for this swelling in his stomach, it is mixed with fear. What if Dr Singh is wrong, and the Japanese overlook this rock?

On the other hand, if Britain's eyes are turned away from Asia, then maybe the eyes of the man in the tower will do the same. And they will come, his Asian brothers, his liberators, while the British are finally the ones made to crawl on all fours.

He shuts his eyes. He had come to the temple with nothing to ask. But if a god will allow it, he would like to change his mind, and ask a few things.

He wants his children to have a heart expansive enough to hold the sky. He wants birds of every vibrant colour to fly within the limitless confines of their heart. He wants each bird to carry in its beak a precious gift. In one, love. In another, laughter. In a third, hope. In a fourth, a bracelet for using their hands well. In a fifth, the bond between siblings. And so on. He wants his children to never be hurt by any of these gifts, because they are *gifts*. He bows west, towards his home in the Punjab. He says A'meen and Aum Shanti and Waheguru Ji Ka Khalsa Waheguru Ji Ki Fateh and forgets what should come next or if even this is correct and asks for forgiveness if it is not.

He walks home.

Priya
1937

THE THREE CHILDREN WERE AT the beach. Nomi, Zee and Aye. As Nomi watched Aye's feet wiggle in the sand, hers did the same. In the painting that hung in her classroom, Christ's feet were slender, with prominent veins. She had not noticed before, in all the time that Aye had been their friend, but now she did. Aye had the feet of Christ.

Zee stood on her other side, also facing the sea. His feet were short and wide. He was still trying to write the perfect essay, without any spelling mistakes.

She wondered whether she could ever tell Aye that, though he had been acting very strange, his feet were beautiful. He stepped on her, twice, when skipping over the surf. The soles were rough.

Though she could not see Christ's soles in the painting at school, she could see the high arches and hairless toes. One toe was missing. It would have been the longest on the right foot because the left was fairly long in the same place. Their mother's second toes were also long, but hairy. She told Nomi to lip-say the Lord's Prayer, but each morning the preacher Mr Lothian put his hairy ear to her lips to make sure she was really praying. She knew the Lord's Prayer as well as she knew the first kalima, which their mother said all Muslims must recite, but which their father called the Lord's Forgotten Prayer. When he said this, their mother warned them about hell, which was a pit of fire. She asked if in her heart Nomi recited the kalima at school, and Nomi always lied, which meant she committed two wrongs and would be first in hell.

Even after the Lord's Prayer, Nomi stared at the feet in the painting. The feet seemed to fly towards her. And now she knew why. Aye
had the feet of Christ, and the feet had stopped flying. They had
landed softly on the beach with both middle toes intact and were playing in the water, and beside them, so did Nomi's, and beside them, so
did Zee's.

Aye worked up at the starfish jail with Mr Howard, the jail's superintendent. At school, they called Aye Mr Howard's pet and Zee was
Mr Campbell's pet and Nomi wanted a pet.

She had heard men at the shop say that up in the jail, there was
once again a hunger strike. At the Female Factory, Nomi's mother was
to make sure that women prisoners did not join the strike. Some of
them, especially Prisoner 218 D, were very thin. When they lined up
to wash by the tank behind the factory, Prisoner 218 D moaned as sea
water was poured over her head. It was the only sound she made. Her
ribs were like fish on the beach after birds had pulled out the meat.

The last time the strike happened, children at school had copied
the hunger strikers, falling in a faint, force feeding each other with the
vines that wrapped around the bodies of giant padauk trees.

The men at the shop also spoke of the boycott of British cloth
happening in India, in support of the freedom movement. Like the
hunger strikes, the boycott was not new, but they were not meant to
openly speak of Indians on the mainland spinning their own cloth.
On the island, it was the women in the factory who spun and sewed,
mostly hankies for settlers and uniforms for jailors.

Though Aye worked up at the jail, he would not speak of the
strike. Aye would not even speak of White Paula, the girl he loved,
and this was a good thing. But he did not look well. Nomi wondered if
Zee had noticed. The two no longer talked to each other the way their
mother talked to her friends or their father to his. Maybe they were
also on a hunger strike. Maybe she could join them.

Zee said, 'I want to learn how to swim. You promised you would
teach me.'

She looked to her right, at Zee, and then to her left, at Aye. Silence,
still.

The beach was scattered with small bones. In the surf hovered a single seed, shaped like a boat. Further ahead were the twin islands of Neill and Havelock, named after two generals from long ago. The generals had not gotten along. Yet the rocks, which stood side by side, had been named after them. It was God's way, Mr Lothian said. Sooner or later, we all must face each other.

She looked again from Aye to Zee and back. Did they not like each other anymore?

She pressed her toes deep into the sand. She skipped over the surf, strewing sand.

'Stop,' said Zee, irritated. Then he said to Aye, 'At least take us to another beach, where the sand is soft and white, not like this one.'

'What's wrong with this one?' asked Nomi.

'We're not allowed anywhere.' Zee scowled.

'We're allowed here,' said Nomi.

'I wasn't talking to you,' said Zee. 'Aye is allowed everywhere. Mr Howard's pet!'

Aye's feet stopped wiggling in the sand. The boat-shaped seed passed gently by.

There were coins underwater, wavering like God weaving dreams. When Nomi dipped her hand the silver scattered, and it was like losing a dream. She dipped again and scooped the scum of moments ago: sand, stone.

The surf started to swell so she swung around, but Aye said, 'Never have your back to the sea.' He swivelled her till she faced the water again. And now the game was that they stay at the water's edge even when it broke higher up the shore.

Aye said to Zee, 'I will take you to the lake. It is their swimming pool.' When he said *their*, his mouth turned in a way Nomi had not seen before.

Rushing towards Aye, Zee gave him a friendly slap. 'The lake on the mountain? Now?'

'Yes. Now.'

'We are not allowed at the top,' said Nomi.

'You can go home,' said Zee.

Though she had promised never to go up Mount Top and would have to tell their mother another lie, she raced after them.

They climbed for a while before reaching the path where the first Indian guard was stationed. Aye put a finger to his lips and gestured for them to go a different way, while he took the path. Nomi could hear him talking to the guard. She kept her eyes lowered so as not to trip on roots, or on shrews with pink tails.

Within moments, Aye was somehow far ahead, never looking down at his feet but at the tops of bushes, and further away, on the summit of another hill, at the starfish jail. The trees would sometimes hide it but she knew it was there, watching the island with one hundred eyes. Beside it lay the Female Factory, ordinary in shape and much smaller.

'When will we stop?' she whispered.

Surprisingly, Zee did not tell her to shut up. 'It is not far now, promise.'

Aye turned around, motioning for them to crouch low to the ground. Lower. There was a second Indian guard. Zee pushed her onto her stomach. After Aye left, they waited a while before standing up again. The grass came up to her cheeks, but from watching Zee she learned to hold a few blades in each hand, take two steps, and slowly release them. The scratches were not too deep.

They found Aye standing behind a screen of bamboo trees. Through the screen, Nomi could see a lake. It was not empty. To her astonishment, instead of swimming, the two people in the lake were riding around on inflated goat skins, or trying to.

Goat skins were normally used for carrying water in Aberdeen. Now they were bobbing around like balloons in the middle of the lake, and the two people were making so much noise that Aye considered it safe to say, though still in a whisper, that one of them was the European nurse. Nomi looked closely. Miss Mattie! Gone was the pretty, swinging ponytail. Instead, her hair dripped over her shoulders as she threw herself onto the balloons, missed, and tumbled, head first, back into the water. She was dressed in a black skirt and when she fell, layers of frilly undergarments could be seen. Miss Mattie! When Zee started laughing, Aye pinched his arm, telling him to be careful.

The nurse had a clip on her nose, to keep water out. It made her voice peculiar. 'Awn gond avens! Awn Martin!' The man called Martin did not attempt to land on the bulging goat skins as often as Miss Mattie.

There were other bathers, including a woman in a clingy sleeveless top over shorts halfway down her fat thighs. Nomi had seen her before, near the European club. She was the wife of the chief commissioner, and it was at their house on Ross Island, where the Europeans lived, that the biggest parties were held, filling all the skies with the click-click-click of croquet balls.

The commissioner's wife had a long cigarette holder in one hand. She stepped into the lake in her clingy bathing suit, and a man who was not the commissioner followed her in. They began to swim towards two more inflated goat skins. This couple did not try to ride them. They swirled around, giggling, as the woman's cigarette got wet.

Two older women sat on the banks of the lake, dressed in skirts, not shorts. Near a picnic basket were scattered empty bottles of wine and books and clothes. It was like a painting, and Nomi was transfixed.

Miss Mattie and Mr Martin stepped out of the water. 'Bloody refreshing!' he said. His sand-coloured hair was thinning. It dripped down his back and made him look foolish. Miss Mattie's thighs jiggled and Nomi was embarrassed for her, especially when he handed her a towel that she rubbed over her legs. The skin grew pink in patches, yet in other parts, there was no colour at all. The feet were round, like globs of milk. The eyes were red from the water, and the cheeks a shade that was somewhere between her eyes and thighs. As she bent, the breasts shuddered, and then she wrapped herself in the towel, as though also embarrassed. She stepped behind a bush to get dressed and Mr Martin stepped behind another. Their game had changed.

In the centre of the lake, the commissioner's wife did not seem embarrassed. She was stroking the head of the man who was not the commissioner, and the way he looked at her! It was not the way boys looked at girls in the camps of prisoner families. It was not scary. If the woman told the man to float all the way to India, he would.

The two older women, Miss Mattie and Mr Martin were now all dressed and packing the picnic basket. Before heading for the road on the other side of the lake, the older women cast disapproving glances at the couple circling each other in the water. It was similar to the way older Indian women examined young Indian girls.

After the sound of a car's engine receded, Zee pinched Nomi's arm, drawing her attention to a small clearing behind a cluster of white orchids. There, on the ground, were the clothes that belonged to the couple still in the lake. He pulled her towards them. Aye did not move. His body was rigid as he looked up at the treetops, at the sky. As Nomi followed Zee, she thought she could hear Aye mumble, 'There is someone else here.'

Hers were a pink lacy pantie, stiff bodice and long crepe gown. The gown had pretty, colourful beads all across the front and sides in patterns that resembled egrets and coconut palms. There was also a long string of pearls and a pair of silver sandals. Aye now joined them, and though still distracted, he examined the seal on her clothes. Next, he inspected the man's clothes. Grey trousers, a hat with a white satin sash and a linen shirt with a torn label at the collar. The part of the label they could read said *lo Company, Made in France.* Zee tied the pearls around himself and Nomi threw the gown around her shoulders. They twirled around each other, twirled around the orchids, danced higher up the hill and floated back down to the clearing, like swans.

Aye was still looking over his shoulder. The man in the lake was still dying for the woman.

When Nomi took off the gown, to her horror, one side had torn. Zee examined the tear and shrugged. He pulled the pearls off himself, then tore the gown to pieces. All the little egret beads came apart and rolled onto the grass and the coconut palms were dismantled. Nomi joined him. So lost were they in reducing the gown to tinier pieces that even she did not hear the sounds they made.

'You bloody rascals!' shouted the man, swimming to shore. 'I will thrash you girls till you wish you had never set foot on the island!'

Nomi and Zee started to race back down the hill, but Aye tried to stop them. 'Not this way,' he hissed, 'remember the guard!'

They did not listen, and now the woman's voice rose towards them. 'It could not have been girls. Coloured girls are flimsy as vapour, but the boys—the boys are all thieves!'

Racing straight for the guard, they confronted another astonishing sight. A man, neither British, Indian nor Burmese, stepped in front of them. It was the Japanese dentist, Susumu Adachi, fully dressed, and very neatly, too. They did not expect to see him here, so no one said a word. When the guard arrived, Susumu San was the first to speak. Apologising for the intrusion, he explained that he had been granted permission to collect specimens for the taxidermists, and could not contain his excitement at one of his finds. He opened his palm to reveal what looked like a tired and quite ordinary ant. The children were helping him, he added, when the guard examined them.

The guard left, and Susumu San smiled. 'How is the tooth?' he said to Zee, who answered with a nod. 'You should come to the clinic.' Zee nodded again.

Susumu San looked at Aye. Then he looked at Nomi. 'Well, excuse me.' He walked higher up the mountain, away from the pond, the ant still in his fist.

For a time, they did not know what to say. Finally, Nomi asked Zee about the tooth.

'He came to our class, to check us.'

'Did it hurt?'

Zee shrugged.

'He was watching us,' said Aye.

'But he helped us,' said Zee. 'Do you think he'll tell?'

Aye looked up at the sky. 'No.'

They descended Mount Top safely.

The piece of gown in Nomi's fist was the neck with a label that read, mysteriously, *Monge*. She carried it all the way to Aberdeen, while Zee laughed from fear and excitement.

'They might look for you, you know,' said Aye.

'They didn't see us,' answered Zee. 'And you said Susu won't tell.'

'The guard saw you.'

'His name is Susumu San,' said Nomi.

Zee giggled. 'Susu did a susu!'

'What if your parents find it?' asked Aye.

'We'll hide it,' answered Zee.

'Where?'

Zee shrugged. 'We'll throw it in the sea.'

'I don't want to throw it,' said Nomi.

'You can't keep it,' said Aye.

'What can they do?' said Zee.

'They can do a lot.'

'What? Transport us?'

Nomi looked up at Aye. '*Please.*'

Aye hesitated. 'I know what we can do instead.'

So they left the village and followed Aye and did not ask where he was taking them. They were far from the beach where they had started off today, the one from where the twin islands Neill and Havelock could be seen. The sky was blue as a kingfisher's wing. The sea was lilac, with hints of jade. If they passed familiar faces along the way, no one guessed what Nomi carried. They also passed an Andamanese woman feeding a baby. Her eyes were white in her dark face, but when they came closer, the eyes became red, like Miss Mattie's coming out of the water. Her breasts were exposed, though the preacher said they should be covered. Only Aye greeted her and she greeted only him. Nomi wondered if the couple were still circling each other in the lake. What would the woman wear when she came out? Only then did she realise that the woman would have no clothes. She covered her mouth in horror.

'Toothache?' said Zee, grinning.

'He called you a girl.'

Zee flinched, just barely, but she saw it and knew she had him.

'She called you a boy,' said Zee.

'I *am* a boy!' Nomi decided.

'Where are we going?' said Zee, rolling his eyes.

'To Paula's farm,' answered Aye.

Nomi stared at Aye. Why was he taking them there? White Paula used big words and put on an accent. She talked a lot, especially about her pigs. They eat everything, she boasted, from pumpkin peel to the crinkly skin of bitter gourd. One time, she heard Mr Campbell say to White Paula, 'Do you know that gilt is a young female pig?' After this White Paula began boasting that her favourite gilt had a dark grey stain in the shape of Bengal on her right ear. Another time, she asked Nomi, 'If your religion forbids you from eating them, does it also forbid you from liking them? Will you go to hell if you scratch a pig's ear?'

Nomi followed Aye unhappily.

When they arrived at the farm, White Paula and a boy from school, Fuad, both came out of her hut, which was more than twice the size of Nomi's hut. They walked to the back, where the animals were. White Paula started petting Silky, the gilt with the map of Bengal on her right ear. Aye teased the other ear. Fuad lit a cigarette.

Was it forbidden to scratch a pig's ear? The question haunted Nomi. Zee did not step forward, but Fuad smacked the pig's behind, which was branded with a capital G. All the pigs had the same letter. White Paula explained it meant 'property of Gomez Farms,' because an animal was like crockery, it had value only with a seal. 'The English love marks,' she declared. 'Notice how they look at the backs of plates for their value. They do the same with *everything*. We have the best pigs and they know because of that mark.' She poked Silky's bottom and Silky looked sideways at Nomi.

'You won't touch her, will you?' continued White Paula. 'You might have better luck with the fowl, who are awfully tall with lots of feathers on their legs. They peck at everything, though, and never let us tickle them, so I much prefer the pigs.'

Fuad gave Aye a cigarette and Aye inhaled deeply.

Then Aye said, 'Nomi, show them.'

With horror, she realised he wanted her to hand over the slip of gown. She shook her head.

Zee forced open her fist, and showed White Paula.

She squealed with delight. 'Oh, a *seal*. How did you get this?'

And Zee started to talk, about the lake and inflated goat skins and nose clips and picnic baskets. As he kept trying to impress her, White Paula tied the silk scrap around Silky's head like a bonnet. The pig pranced around her pen primly and White Paula said she would feed her a prawn.

But she didn't go inside for a prawn. She kept standing there. And the cloth had touched a pig.

When they were all done cheering for Silky, who was instead fed a coral hibiscus, White Paula said not to worry, the bonnet would never be found. She tore it off the gilt's head and dropped it to the ground and Silky began chewing and snorting loudly.

'She eats everything,' boasted White Paula. 'She will even eat the beads.'

And Fuad said, 'Boycott foreign cloth!'

And Nomi was too shocked to cry.

And Aye said, 'Goodbye, Paula.'

And Paula said, 'Goodbye, Aye. Come and see me some time.'

And Fuad said, '*Ooooh!*'

And they left.

On the way back, Zee whispered, 'She's pretty.'

And Aye said to Nomi, 'I did it to help.'

She was looking at the ground. Then the word was out: 'Liar.'

And she would never again look at his feet the same way, not till he lost one of them.

In the evening, when Zee was pretending to read *She* by candlelight but really dreaming of the girl, their father pulled a small box from under his cot and a chick, small and loud, hopped onto the floor. He asked, 'What will you name her?'

And she did not know why or where the name came from, but like the soft ball in her hands, which she could touch, which was not forbidden like a prayer or a pig or a beach or a mountain or a lake, the name was just there, and always was, the name was hers.

'Priya.'

Islands Apart
1937

THE DENTIST, SUSUMU ADACHI, HOPPED onto his bicycle after leaving his clinic in Aberdeen Square. The children made fun of him. Whenever he passed, they whispered, *Susu did a susu.* To them, he was small and funny. He was aware of this. There were times when he wanted to show them who he was, but their laughter was his best camouflage. Besides, among them were the good children, those that called him Susumu San, and if they ran after him on his bicycle, it was because they had come to associate the sound of its bell with his magical tin toys.

He had brought the toys with him to the island, supposing, correctly, that their effect on a child who stayed till the end of a treatment would always be the same, even a child with no nation. Later today, he had one appointment. A filling for the boy Zee, who would likely come accompanied by his sister, who would never let her teeth be examined. He chuckled. At her age, he was the same.

Along with toys, the dentist had brought with him a knowledge of Urdu, Hindi and English. And he had done his homework. He knew the history of these islands, and learned more of their geography each day. On a cloudless afternoon such as this, he could see the entire archipelago simply by closing his eyes: the shape of a spinal column, with ten times more bones than a human vertebra. At last count, there were 330 islands, some as small as his cottage. A modest number when compared to the Empire of Japan, but considerable when compared to the British Isles.

If what he had learned was correct—and he knew the records

were likely incomplete—among the island's earliest explorers were Malay pirates. They had landed, as the British would later, on South Andaman Island, the lower spine of the chain, in a small inlet close to where Susumu San's bicycle now scratched fresh tracks.

The Malay pirates had captured the aborigines and sold them as slaves in the courts of Siam and Cambodia. They spread tales of fierce cannibal tribes. Yet, their stories did not deter travellers. *And I assure you*, wrote Marco Polo, *all the men of Angamanain have heads like dogs, and teeth and eyes likewise; in fact, in the face they are all just like big mastiff dogs!*

The Malays ruled the islands till the mid-eighteenth century, when the East India Company came in search of an outpost for their fleets. The man they sent, a lieutenant of the Royal Navy, Archibald Blair, was to obtain information about the aborigines; make a detailed survey of the three main land masses; examine the soil for possible cultivation; collect samples of flora and fauna; and gauge the depths of the waters. Like Susumu San, Archibald Blair was good at what he did.

Susumu San now hopped off his bike and started walking it towards an inlet, where he was going to meet Japanese fishermen. He looked around, wondering if he was being watched. The Andamanese were exceptionally light on their feet, especially the one who did not wear clay and dressed in ratty trousers. Susumu San had seen this man at the creek, tending his basket of grubs or tethering his canoe under the mangrove tree. Always, they watched each other in silence, and waited. Susumu San could not see him today, but decided he was being watched. He continued on his way, regardless.

Yes, he thought to himself again, what Blair had been sent to do in 1788 was quite the same as what he was to do now, in 1937. A century and a half divided them, as did the vast oceans, but if there was one white man Susumu San would admit to having respect for, it was Lieutenant Archibald Blair.

Blair set sail twice. On the first mission, he located a site on South Andaman Island suitable for a harbour. He described the aborigines as fierce but not dog-headed or cannibalistic. He said they could be cultivated but did not say how. On the second mission, he brought with him three hundred men and women. Among the former were soldiers, masons and farmers. Among the latter were a small number of English wives, as well as women from prisons in India, Burma, Ceylon, Mauritius and Benkulen who were prostitutes before they arrived and would be prostitutes after they left.

The group stayed almost a year. The forest was partly cleared and a few structures were built, such as the jetty in Aberdeen, the barracks and crude cottages like the one assigned to Susumu San. During the year, the settlers tried to approach the aborigines with offerings of biscuits and knives. It worked, at times. If not, depending on the overseer, the aborigines were left alone, shot, or taken to Calcutta as slaves.

For the next four years, the settlement continued to thrive. Then a new Governor General sent a different group to survey the islands, this time headed by his own brother, Commodore Cornwallis. The commodore declared the location Blair had developed unsuitable for a large fleet. He wished to leave his own stamp on the islands, and led an expedition to North Andaman Island. The settlement he founded was called Port Cornwallis, the older one, Port Blair. But the forests of North Andaman Island proved too dense to clear. Workers began to die of dysentery, malaria and scurvy. Prostitutes grew scarce. Aboriginal women were captured and brought to the ships and when their men came for them, muskets were fired. One diplomat left a written account of his time on a ship where the women were kept in a cabin. At night, their songs could be heard over the endless sheet of dark water, '*sometimes in melancholy recitative,*' wrote the diplomat, '*at others, in a lively key.*'

In time, Port Cornwallis too was abandoned. The British would not return to these shores till soon after the Indian Mutiny of 1857, to build a penal colony.

Susumu San sat on the beach, waiting for the Japanese fishermen. If theft were an art, he thought, the British, a most unaesthetic race, had somehow come close to mastering it. However, safekeeping was also an art, and the British had failed at this.

From what he had discovered, security on these islands was not at all as expected. It had not taken long to scout out the very few

British Army and Navy bases here. If they suspected him, or the other Japanese on the island, they remained too cocky to believe themselves under threat. And if the aborigines were paid to keep an eye on him, how could they, without understanding Japanese? Like Lieutenant Archibald Blair, he had made careful calculations of the island's dimensions, and had also, thanks to the taxidermist's wife, gathered data on the flora, fauna and mineral reserves (only a modest amount of copper, compared with the timber, fish and exotic birds). Gradually, his dossier on each administrator was growing thick. (He had much to say, for instance, about Mr Howard, the superintendent, who spent more time running a side business in opium and bird nests than in running the jail.) He was free to pass on this information to the fishermen, who were already surveying the coastlines, and in return, the fishermen passed on to him news of the world.

The fishermen were issued valid licences by the British Administration. This amazed him. If on paper everything was as should be, white men could not read. It did not occur to them that the Japanese were particularly focused on those the British had marginalised—which, on this island, was just about everybody.

A European did not see. An Asian did.

When a breeze ruffled the creek, the colours that surfaced were turquoise and teal. Colours to soothe the eye. Susumu San thought of the other Japanese on the island. At the time of his arrival, including himself, there had been four. The photographer had died of dysentery, but not before photographing every village. The taxidermist and his wife were soon to leave the island, but they had done what they set out to do. Their maps were the most meticulous he had ever seen.

He was here, the Andamanese with ratty trousers and no clay markings. Susumu San did not turn his head but could see from the corner of his eye that the man was settling a few feet away.

He had tried to speak with him, twice, in English and Hindi. The man would not answer. If it was gifts he wanted, Susumu San could match any offer made by anyone to have set foot on these shores. He had alcohol. The man would not take it from him. He had opium. The man would not take it from him. Iron, used to tip their arrows, was highly prized. His brother-in-law had an enormous share in an iron mine in Malaya. Yes, most of all, Susumu San had iron. The man would not take it from him.

Susumu San turned now to face him. 'Good afternoon,' he said, in English.

Still sharpening his arrow, the man returned the gaze, and said nothing.

Why would aborigines accept bribes from white settlers, but not from him? Susumu San knew in his heart that if he had no answer, he should change the question. But he could not help himself, for the fact was, including the early settlements of Blair and Cornwallis, the British had robbed, raped and murdered the islanders for one hundred and fifty years. Their surveillance might be weak, but all across Asia, their influence was strong. *Why?*

He looked to his left, towards the jail, remembering that their influence was waning. The hunger strikers too were strong. And in India and Burma, alliances with Japan were strengthening. This was how they would fall. Conceit, the white man's defeat.

There came another disturbance on the water. The fishermen were here. He approached them, speaking in low tones. Aside from the occasional bird song, the only sound punctuating the exchange was the sharpening of the arrowhead a few feet away. The fishermen had distressing news from Hawaii. They seemed to enjoy its effect on him. As reparation, they presented him with a spectacular fish that he could not wait to prepare.

When they had gone, he walked his bicycle away from the inlet, nodding at the man who still met his gaze. He needed the help of at least one aborigine if he was to inspect the other islands. He thought, the Malay pirates were here for even longer than the British. Could it be, could it just be, that somewhere in the long memory that was handed down from one generation to the next, he, Susumu San, looked to them like a Malay? Only this would explain their stupidity. They were, after all, *black*.

He had just enough time to return to his cottage with the fish before his appointment at the clinic. There was a small veranda, and on this he built the fire. His meals were often eaten out here in the open, despite the mosquitoes. The taxidermist and his wife lived nearby and sometimes they asked him to join them and sometimes he asked them. Not today.

He waved a paper fan over the flames. The fan was a gift from the taxidermist's wife, and her scent wafted through the air. It was a white fish, smooth and meaty. He watched the skin curl, the juice trickle. The smell was intoxicating.

Susumu San had not been to Marriagetown yet, where the prostitutes lived. His time here had been very alone.

The fire leaped above him, towards the wooden beams of the hut. How easily the island could catch fire! When the skin of the fish coiled off the meat, he browned the other side. Then he took a small bite. It had a generous fat content. In the home he had left behind, he would need to wait for the cooler months before he could afford a fish of this size. He took a few more bites, then wrapped the rest reluctantly in a cloth, hoping the fishermen would offer him another soon—this fish would make a phenomenal soup.

He returned to Aberdeen, ringing his bell. Children called after him for toys. He said they must be patient, and left his bicycle propped against the clinic's brick wall. The children asked for rides. He promised this, too. 'It is coming!' he said. 'It is coming!'

Zee arrived, Nomi with him. She stood aside, hands patiently behind her back, while he sat Zee down in the dentist chair. It was not easy, for the boy was delighted with the way the chair bounced. Eventually, he settled down, and did not cry upon seeing the metal syringe that would numb his gums with a shot of cocaine. When told to spit in the funnel beside the chair, Zee spat.

From the other children, he had learned that Zee was the brightest boy in school, and had a special attachment to his teacher, Mr Campbell. There it was again. *Influence.* Not to be confused with loyalty. A key difference. After all, this was the same boy who had trampled, with ease and even relish, the clothes of his rulers that day on the mountain! Every rebellion against theft began with theft. How glad he was to have been there that day to help! (A common ant could become exotic, a tin toy a magic trick!) The Local Born children did not know loyalty, not yet. Loyalty was something encoded, and could not be felt by the son of a convict any more than by an aborigine. It could only be felt by the free.

Zee was bouncing again in the chair. Susumu San said to sit still, or the filling would fall out. The chair had moved, very slightly. From his first day on the island, Susumu San had arranged it to face the direction of the imperial palace in Tokyo. He corrected its position. Before the filling was complete, Nomi asked if he could do that thing with his hands, when he made a tin toy appear from inside his shirt sleeve. Susumu San smiled. 'It is coming!' he reassured her. 'It is coming!'

TWO

The Winds of Aye
1942

ZEE'S LAST NIGHT WAS SPENT with Aye.

Before meeting his friend, Aye was in his village, listening. There had not been a downpour since Japanese bombers began circling the island two months ago, in January. The rain fell, but he could not name the winds or the silences that accompanied it.

Till the war began, the island had been full of sounds. The click of bamboo, the bicker of parakeets, the edginess of the sea. He had names for each wind, and one day, he would teach Nomi. The yellow angel. The praying mantis. The father. The friend. But with the sirens had come the vertigo wind, or that which made the telegraph wires hum. This new wind had destroyed the others—so what, then, rustled in the rain tonight?

As he stepped outside his hut, a cold wind followed him. This, at least, was familiar. The father wind, counting how many days he had left.

It seemed everyone was awake tonight. Women smoked in doorways, his mother among them. His father rested on a rock some distance between the huts and the Temple of the Buddha, murmuring to himself. When Aye greeted his father, he did not look up.

Nearby, Aye's grandfather sat cross-legged on the ground, whittling by starlight. He kept a second knife, for Aye, who bent down to plant a kiss on the old man's cheek.

'Can't sleep?'

'No, Ah-pay.' Aye had always called him father, and supposed it had once been his grandfather's choice.

'Be with me.' The old man patted the space beside him.

Each knife was made of bamboo, a thin blade wedged into one end of the stalk. When the blade came loose, there was an art to pushing it back in place with the forefinger till a few drops of foam surfaced and the blade could be pushed no deeper. After a minute or so of uninterrupted whittling, the blade came loose again. During this uninterrupted minute, Aye dwelled upon the changes on the island.

When rumours began that the British would be leaving, he had not believed the islands could keep existing without them. There were also rumours that ships of the Royal Indian Navy were being sunk by the Japanese, and children ran around, hoping to see one blown apart. After the *HMIS Sophie Marie* was destroyed off the island's southern tip, and people swore they saw it happen, the whole island was forbidden from talking about any losses to the British side. When a ship came from Ceylon to lay down the mines, followed by the parachutes that dropped them from the air, even Aye's grandfather, who liked to talk, had said nothing. He gave Aye a knife and told him to whittle.

Then one day a different sort of ship arrived. It did not lay mines and did not transport prisoners or goods. When it anchored at Aberdeen jetty, one thousand Gurkha troops disembarked. They were from Nepal, yet Nepal did not belong to the British. Something was about to happen.

The first bombs fell on the first of February. They exploded in the sea.

'What if they hadn't missed?' said Dr Singh, who, like everyone else, had come down to the jetty to see the debris.

'The Japanese have a plan, my friend,' said Haider Ali, the father of Nomi and Zee. 'It does not include killing us.'

Dr Singh scratched his beard with his teeth. 'Then why do they target the jetty?'

'Will you be leaving, too?' Haider Ali snapped.

'Of course not,' Dr Singh snapped back.

'But you are with the British.'

'I am Indian,' said Dr Singh, steel in his voice.

Two weeks later, the Japanese dropped bombs for sixty-five

minutes. Two Gurkha soldiers were injured. More people wondered which way the wings of those planes tilted, away from or towards them. There were blackouts too. Though their huts did not have electricity, they had grown accustomed to the brightness of the British villas. Now, across the sea, Ross Island was shrouded in darkness.

Worst of all were the sirens.

The first time Aye heard one, the horizon was tinted a queer shade of yellow, while directly above, the sky remained blue. As he watched, the colour deepened to a brilliant gold. It went rolling over his head and then the sun departed and the world glowered like a leaden ball. Every wind halted; trees tensed. The siren sounded again and it was coming, the wind that made the telegraph wires hum. It was a slight movement, barely decipherable, but with that terrible hum, the wind was upon him.

When the vertigo hit, earth became sky, and the water his mother moistened his lips with tasted of quinine. He could not lift his chin. If he tried to move, his stomach heaved and a volley of bullets assaulted his left ear. He lay very still, waiting till the world crawled back onto its axis.

And now it seemed to him, as he whittled beside his grandfather, that balance was never restored. His capacity to hear the island had changed because of those sirens. The world kept tilting and the speed of the rotation had not slowed, even though the British had left and the sirens had stopped.

His grandfather worked the stem in his hands with poise. Aye tried to do the same. He was whittling for Nomi, as he had done since the day her scrap of a lady's gown was fed to a pig. It had been his idea, and he knew it. She was the closest thing he had to a sister, and he wanted to make her happy. He kept whittling.

His grandfather talked. It was when Rangoon fell that the British had started packing. Did Aye know—Rangoon had fallen to the Japanese? Yes, Ah-pay, Aye replied. The British ran from Singapore and Rangoon, said his grandfather, then they ran from these shores.

His voice was a deep rumble and Aye loved it, the cadences of warmth and wisdom that flew as untidily as his beard, and without cease. The old man pointed in the direction of Phoenix Bay, at the silhouette of the Temple of the Buddha. He was remembering that, before the British left, they had entered the temple with their shoes and hats on. The Japanese were saying they wanted an Asia for Asians, an Asia for Buddhists. 'But,' asked his grandfather, 'do they take their shoes off before entering our pagodas?'

'I do not know, Ah-pay.'

'I have no memory of Rangoon. Like you, I grew up here. This is all I know.'

They were quiet for some time. The rain had stopped; Aye did not hear it leave.

The talk shifted to Aye's great-grandfather, who was among the first prisoners shipped to these shores, soon after the Indian Mutiny. He had cleared the forests and swamps to build this village, and, upon his release, the village had continued to grow around him. It was where some of the most fertile soil on the colony was farmed. It was also where malaria had caused the most deaths. The clearings had brought the mosquitoes, the mosquitoes had brought the quinine, and the experiments.

Aye looked towards his father, who still sat apart, mumbling on a rock.

But today's story was not about the medical tests, or captivity. It was about magic. His grandfather was saying that when Aye's great-grandfather first came to the islands, two things saved him. The bamboo and the moon. It was the same moon that shone over Rangoon, fat and festive, and the same bamboo that covered Burma's hills. So when the British gave him this plot of land on lease, on moonlit nights, Aye's great-grandfather began to whittle. At first, he wished also for coloured paper, for no festival in Burma was complete without it. Then he decided that coloured paper only created an illusion of magic. If he whittled the bamboo into elephants and jugglers, lanterns and priests, with the help of the moon, the illusion would still be there.

Aye smiled. 'His figurines were the best.'

'Do not forget, it is Burmese hands that carved all the wood on this island. That Mr Howard of yours, the stairwell in his villa was made by one of us.'

'I do not forget.'

'Did you see the one in the chief commissioner's house?'

'Of course, Ah-pay. I went there often with Mr Howard.'

'Was it as beautiful as they say?'

'More beautiful.'

'Your great-grandfather taught me the same tricks, and you will know them too.'

Aye smiled again.

'Tricks can skip a generation.' Pointing his knife at Aye's father, the old man chuckled and elbowed Aye, but Aye never chuckled about his father.

The blade almost slipped away, almost sliced his finger.

'Where are you?' his grandfather asked.

'Tell me about it again.'

'What?'

'The quinine.'

'You already know.'

'I want to know again.'

'Look at him,' he again pointed his knife at Aye's father, 'and you will know.'

Aye whittled fiercely now. He did not want to bring these feelings into his gift for Nomi, but he could not help that it was a small island. What was felt here was felt there.

'Do not carry it,' his grandfather was saying. 'Do not take in the poison. I lost him but I still have you.' He was shaving paper-thin curls away from a single bamboo stalk and the curls met at the top. He made a series of these as clouds drifted across the stars and the women went back into their huts. 'There goes the girl you used to like.'

Thiri. Aye's neighbour, who he had long ago decided was too good for him.

'What's wrong with her?'

'Nothing's wrong with her, Ah-pay.'

The old man grunted.

Aye was making Nomi a fish, a paper-thin tendril for the fin. He had seen a fish just like it in the sea, and he had swum in the sea because Mr Howard had taught him how, in the chief commissioner's pool. 'Breathe,' the superintendent of the jail had said, when Aye began to panic. And Aye's body had begun to drift comfortably in the water with Mr Howard. He was glad that in return, he had helped Mr Howard relax in the bath each morning. It was what he had never been able to do for his own father, whose cheek he had never shaved, whose scalp he had never massaged, and whose mind was a swamp because of men like Mr Howard.

'You have good hands,' his grandfather said, pointing to the emerging fish.

Aye wished, more than anything else, that everyone would stop saying this.

The old man stood up, to fill his bamboo lanterns with fireflies. Aye watched as the fireflies pulsed within the rib cage of their new home.

'What do you think will happen down in Aberdeen?' his grandfather mused idly.

'What do you mean?' asked Aye.

'Did you not hear about the Japanese soldiers? Your friend fired a gun at them.'

'What?'

'Your friend. Zee. I heard there was trouble. I thought you knew.'

Aye was hurrying out of his village towards Aberdeen, the knife still in his hands and the fish tossed somewhere in the dirt, before his grandfather could finish talking. Why hadn't he heard? Why had the island stopped telling him things?

In Aberdeen Square, he found Haider Ali going from one hut to the next, Dr Singh beside him, to find a safe haven for Zee. Aye only knew what his grandfather had told him, and there was no time to find out more. But it seemed to him that no one in Aberdeen had any understanding of the island's geography. They had not lived here as long as his own family. Aye told Haider Ali that he could help. He added that no place along the southeastern coast was safe, especially not Aberdeen, Corbyn's Cove and Rangachang, the three points where the Japanese had landed.

'Where is safe?' asked Haider Ali.

Possibly nowhere, Aye thought, but he could not say this to a broken father. Instead, he offered, 'It has to be inland, and you cannot walk that far.'

When Haider Ali began to cough, Dr Singh looked at Aye and all three knew. Even if a sickly old man were to survive the hike, his cough would give away his son.

'My son is not a prisoner,' said Haider Ali.

'Uncle, I know,' said Aye.

'But you will hide him as you would a prisoner.'

Aye tensed, thinking the comment strange. 'I cannot take him off the island,' he said. 'There are mines in the sea. It has to be inland,' he repeated.

'How will I tell you when it is safe to return him?' asked Haider Ali.

'You will have to stand on the road to Haddo and give me a sign.'

Aye waited while the two men brought Zee. Nomi did not see Aye in the shadows when she came outside. Aye watched them embrace, remembering the fish he had been whittling.

The road to Haddo cut through forests that were almost as sinister as Haddo itself, the place to which the British had banished prisoners who lost their minds.

Aye did not know how much of the island's past the Japanese were familiar with. Curiously, their Army Headquarters were at Haddo. Since the departure of the British, the asylum now held only three men, all Indian inmates long past the point of distinguishing one uniform from another. Because most of the forces were stationed at different points along the eastern coast, Aye was gambling that the Headquarters would be relatively unguarded. He knew the risk but could think of no other plan. The mountain was crawling with soldiers.

Marriagetown was worse. Points on the craggy west coast were too far by foot for the boy in the green sari, who already walked too slowly.

There was only one person who could save Zee. An Andamanese by the name of Loka. But Aye knew he could not reach him. Aye, alone, would have to do his best.

The night grew heavy with clouds and no stars could be seen. At least they had this. And this: the soldiers they slinked past were so irritated by insects and leeches that their watch was spent grumbling. Once, a soldier screamed. A centipede or a snake, Aye supposed. Before fleeing the island, the British had said that though the Japanese had read pamphlets on how to survive war in the tropics, they could not have read a single one on the terrain of the Andamans as not a single one had been written.

The boys reached the Haddo agricultural station, where the sugarcane grew to the height of three men. Behind it lay the pond where Aye's father sometimes lingered, muttering to himself. They walked in silence, one boy with his life in the hands of the other. *You have good hands*, his grandfather had said, just this evening.

There was no one at the pond. No movement, no wind. Had Aye not been here before, he would have seen only the reeds and walked straight into the water. They settled behind what was possibly the largest padauk tree to ever exist, Zee leaning into it, resting for the first time since leaving his hut. He carried a bag with the gun and the items packed by his mother and sister. He gave the bag to Aye, telling him to help himself.

Aye glanced again at the water's edge. Still nothing. He peeled one of Priya's eggs. He took a bite and gave the rest to Zee.

Zee shook his head.

After a while, Zee started to laugh. 'Do you remember the pond on the mountain? When we took the gown and you fed it to the pig?'

'Shh!' whispered Aye. 'Paula fed it to the pig.'

'Did your Mr Howard ever find out?' asked Zee, lowering his voice.

'No. But he never liked the chief commissioner's wife, or her dresses.'

Zee laughed again, softly this time. 'It was five years ago.'

To Aye, Zee sounded old. He said, 'Do you know what Mr Howard told me before leaving?'

'No.'

'He said, "The right sort of chap can turn his hand to anything."'

Zee did not stir.

'Who gave you the gun?'

'Mr Campbell. He left it.'

'I used to hear Mr Howard and the chief commissioner talk. Many political prisoners never practiced firing a gun before using it.'

'Am I a political prisoner?'

'I don't know.'

They drank water.

'I never showed you how to swim, that day.' Aye was pulling off his clothes. 'I can't, with you in a sari.'

'Who will help me put it back on?'

The two boys laughed without making a sound.

Moments later, they were standing naked on the muddy bank. Aye, eighteen years old, with long and sinewy legs from all the climbing he had done, and Zee, fifteen and shorter, scrawnier. The water was up to their ankles and unexpectedly cold. Zee inhaled sharply. Aye reminded him that sound carried over water. Together, they waited for the soft current, the viscid foothold, and the finger-like reeds to feel safe. Then Aye waded in deeper, pulling Zee with him.

'Kick,' he whispered, 'but don't splash.'

Zee tipped his head back into Aye's chest. He lifted his legs. He swallowed water. 'It tastes like poison!'

'*Shh!*'

They tried again. Zee was surprisingly heavy, and Aye wondered if he too had been heavy when falling back into the arms of Mr Howard in the chief commissioner's swimming pool. He tried to take his mind off everything—his father, Mr Howard, the troops beyond the trees, the weight of what he had been entrusted with. Slowly, his body became habituated to Zee's. The two began to glide. A single night became one long and graceful movement.

When the boys came back to shore, languid and cleansed, they each took a corner of the ragged sari to dry themselves. A star shone through the migrating clouds.

Gazing up at the star, Zee said, 'I saw her arrive, you know.'

'Who?'

'The one who got away.'

'I did too.'

'You did?'

'Yes. I saw you, down on the jetty. But I had the nests to deliver.'

'If she could escape, so can I.'

Still without a sound, Aye sighed. 'She did get away,' he whispered. 'I am sure of it.'

It would only occur to him later, much later, that he was the last person to hold Zee's whole body.

A Matter of Bones
1936

ON THE AFTERNOON OF PRISONER 218 D's arrival on the island, after leaving Nomi and Zee at school, Aye walked to the caves, to collect swiftlet nests for Mr Howard.

He looked across the sea, at the *S.S. Noor* drawing close. Either that, or there were to be visitors, coming to photograph the Andamanese and take souvenirs back with them.

It was the Andamanese who first showed Aye the location of the nests, in exchange for opium. They used the Hindi word for it. Chandu Bhai. Large quantities were brought in by the crew of the *S.S. Noor*. Mr Howard was a licensed vendor; a long line of aboriginal men and women came to his villa daily, waiting beneath his fig trees with tortoise shells. Three tortoise shells for two pounds of Chandu Bhai. Those with cowries or a lump of honey received only a little dross.

On the day the Andamanese had shown him the nests, a sweet smell wafted to Mr Howard's kitchen door, where Aye waited. There had been four men, each rewarded with four pounds of Chandu Bhai for agreeing to take him to the cave. They had approached him while smoking, two with bows and arrows and faces washed in white clay. Their eyes had been red and golden orioles had danced above their heads, as though transporting the sweet scent to Aye's nose. He had called the aroma-infused air the yellow angel.

'Your name?' one man had asked.

'Aye. Yours?'

'What they always say. Jack.'

'What they always say,' another had said. 'Jack. Or Jumbo.'

The remaining two, who seemed younger, had been quiet.

It was not their real name, just the one they had been given. The first Jack had worn three thick stripes across his forehead. The second had worn two, with three lighter marks across his cheek. Aye had thought of his great-grandfather, whose forehead was tattooed against his will. The Andamanese before him had worn marks that were not given, but kept.

The men had taken Aye to the cave.

Now Aye glanced again in the direction of the sea, at the darkness drawing close. Definitely the *S.S. Noor*, he decided. Fallen frangipanis lined his path, fresh from the rain. He told himself to pluck one from the wet earth for his mother on his return.

The island was split into sheer, narrow caves that housed the birds and could be reached from a steep, secret trail. As he started the climb, he examined the sky. It was empty of swiftlets, which would make it harder to collect the nests, but collect them he must. It was one of many tasks he did for Mr Howard, who sold the nests to the Chinese in Malaya, who boiled them in soup.

With Mr Howard, Aye had been inside the jail. Political prisoners in particular were arriving in great numbers since the growing freedom movement on the mainland, about which news did reach them, even if Mr Campbell refused to speak of it. The prisoners were on a hunger strike, and Aye could never forget the one called Kirpal and the verge of a smile on his slit and bloody lips as he told Aye that the islands were not evil, even when what happened on them was. The islands, according to Kirpal, were born of the god Rama's desire for a bridge between India and Malaya. Ever since, many gods had come to these islands, and like Rama, they too would leave.

Aye paused, almost at the top. His feet felt no thorns. They feared no forests.

He continued climbing.

When he reached the top of the trail, the clouds parted and three sharp blades of light fell near the mouth of the cave. The sandstone beneath his feet turned pink, the sea far below glistened like a mirror.

There was no breeze. The cliffs were still slick from the storm and he could hear a gentle stream in the chasm, but he was not afraid.

It was here, at the edge of the abyss, more than at the Temple of the Buddha, that he had found a kind of ritual. The repetition of dates of a forgotten past, a past not taught at school. He recited them as a prayer before descending into the cave, perhaps to keep from slipping through time.

When his great-grandfather arrived: 1858.

When the jail was built: 1906.

When his father lost his mind: 1910.

When Aye was born: 1924.

He looked around. The face of the island had never been more illuminated. He hurled himself into the abyss.

His feet could see more intimately than his eyes, tracing an incline that could support his weight. Every ridge was a rib that had to be memorised, for not all would hold him, and he grew bigger each day. Lower now, to a rock that swooped like the hip of his neighbour, Thiri. If his right foot tipped outward, just so, he could rest long enough to feel with his left foot for the other hip, the one like a boy's. There. He grabbed the pigtails, the thick curly roots of a tree that cast long shadows in his mind. The stream was closer. Hungry prisoners slurping soup. Birds fidgeted. The stench of guano fouled the air. He leaped. Quickly, from one slick rock to the next. If he paused, fear would engulf him. It was too dark to see even his nose, and the air was cold here. The father wind. Now his hands. They could unmap the grooves of time. Along this ledge and that they had always guided him, ever since the day the two Jacks first demonstrated, to the prize.

The birds began to circle him. One click two click high-pitched call. When disturbed, the Andamanese had warned him, the swiftlets would speak in the voice of demons. The walls started to swirl. He tried to focus. Once the eggs hatched, the nests were sullied. They had to be harvested today. Only the ones made by white-nest swiftlets. Those of black-nest swiftlets had the wrong shape and colour, and fetched a poor price.

Aye could not see white from black but it was a chance he had to take. His free hand skittered along each ledge and a few nests tumbled without a sound, down to the bottom of the world. The birds were pulling his flesh between their beaks. He kept his eyes shut, they could not take his eyes. More nests slipped away and more demons came as he filled the sack tied to his neck. He was coated in blood, guano and feathers as he began the ascent back to the cave's mouth.

Exiting the cave, he tossed the sack onto a smooth tree limb and spread his still tremulous limbs on the now mostly dry sandstone. The light had softened to a tawny glow. There was a wind that was just so, a wind with no name. It was good to breathe.

A few swiftlets followed him, still invoking calamity and destruction, as he snaked his way down the secret trail. A frangipani was at his ear, bright yellow with pink edges. His mother's favourite colours. He could see Mr Howard snake his way down to the sea, towards the ship.

A large crowd was heading for the jetty, to watch the prisoners disembark. He supposed Mr Howard would be at the jail this evening, with the new prisoners. He would have to wait to show him the nests. The sack was in his hands, secured with a tight knot. The air grew pungent.

He wanted Mr Howard to say he had done well, but what lay inside would not please the superintendent. Before leaving the caves, he had examined the nests. Too few were made by white-nest swiftlets, and too many had broken shells of hatched chicks still caught inside. The bag was mostly filled with dark and crooked fluff-glued cups that would never concoct an edible soup.

The knuckles of his right hand were swollen and bloody. When he sucked them, the salt was a relief. His nose was severely cut; he could see the puffed-up ridge without bringing his eyes together. His scalp was sticky and when the hand pulled away, it carried blue feathers.

What should he do? He could wait on the jetty for the ferry to Ross Island, where Mr Howard lived. The superintendent would be done with the prisoners by dinner time.

But then his mother would not get the flower. He removed it from his ear. It was already beginning to droop, and the pink edges were smeared with his blood.

He was still debating what to do when he heard a whistle. He looked around. It sounded again. There were no more people rushing past him towards the jetty. Who called? When it happened a third time, Aye started back up the trail. He did not get very far before a man dressed in shirt and trousers approached him. He had a bow and arrow but no clay markings. They stared at each other a long time.

'Recognise me,' the man finally spoke. His trousers were held in place with a rope. The shirt too was oversized, with sleeves bunched around the elbows of pencil-thin arms. The frizzy hair lifted off the top of his head like vines.

'Jack?' asked Aye.

The man laughed. 'We give you.' He pointed to the sack.

Aye had rarely seen an Andamanese fully dressed before. He might have come from one of the Andaman Homes, about which all Local Born children had been taught at school (typically, after the Lord's Prayer and just before Mr Lothian said to have a thankful heart for Jesus). Aye's great-grandfather, who had witnessed their construction, said the Homes were built to confine and improve the islanders, the way the jail was built to confine and improve the convicts. With a few differences. In exchange for being baptised and clothed, the late keeper of the Homes, Reverend Corbyn, had offered the aborigines gifts of iron and pork, and lessons in Scripture and English. There had also been other gifts, opium and alcohol, in exchange for Andamanese women.

The Homes were also where escaped convicts were returned to the settlers by the Andamanese who hunted them down with ropes and knives. Aye's great-grandfather had warned him against those who appeared loyal to Corbyn: they had blood on their hands.

'Why afraid,' the man said.

'I am not afraid,' answered Aye.

'Then come, friend. Sit here.'

He led Aye off the path and through a coconut grove till they arrived at a clearing where a canoe was tied to a tall mangrove tree. There were mangroves all around, with spindly legs. Beyond was a creek. They sat in the canoe under the tree, just the two of them. One with a halo of glossy feathers, the other preoccupied with his arrow.

From out of his trouser pocket, the man pulled a piece of paper wrapped around a powder of dried leaves. He reached under the seat of the canoe for a cloth and untied it, revealing a large, fresh leaf. He rolled the powder inside and lit the leaf. He inhaled, then offered it to Aye.

'Not your drug,' said the man, watching Aye hesitate.

'You are not Jack,' said Aye, taking the leaf. The flavour on his tongue was neither sweet nor bitter.

'I am not Jack.'

'What is your name?'

'What they always say. Loka.'

He had not heard the name before, but there was much he had not heard.

As the smoke filled his lungs, Aye's pain left him. The creek was singing and the mangroves had legs without knees. Red legs in blue shoes. He could remember swimming through them once, with fish like bats and leaves like fish. He was glad he could swim. Zee could read big books, but Aye could swim.

Loka talked. He had been one of the four, that time Aye was shown the nests. Younger, and without markings. Yes, Aye remembered now. He returned the leaf and shut his eyes, but Loka nudged him awake.

Loka began to tell him the most astonishing story. 'Men from far come to this creek.'

'You mean, from the North Andamans?' Aye leaned forward in the bow of the canoe. It was filled with twigs and other scampering things. Spiders, maybe, or one of those stick insects that shifted from orange to green.

'No, far. From the cold sea.'

'There are cold seas?'

'Men whiter than you, like the dentist, like the ones who fill birds. They come in boats, taking shellfish and shells. It is not why they come.'

Aye looked out at the water. No one there.

'Mr Howard tells us to watch them, the Japanese.'

'Japanese?'

'Yes. Why repeat.' He turned his head to the left and spat onto the sand.

It occurred to Aye that Loka did not ask questions. He liked this. Why ask questions? Then he realised that this was a question, and started to laugh.

'Why laugh.' Loka turned his head, right this time, spat again.

But that was also a question-not-question. Aye opened his mouth wide and laughed a greater laugh. 'Why laugh!' Aye repeated. 'Why repeat!'

When the laughter came less frequently and the cough that replaced it subsided, Aye examined the sky. He had to take the ferry to Ross Island before it became dark.

'Why did you bring me here?' he asked. More questions, then. He stood up, but sat back down when his stomach heaved into his throat.

Loka was telling him why. Because people did this. They poured their stories into him. They saw him as quiet by nature, and men and women, old and young, free and fettered, together made the quietude they placed in him an invitation to heal their souls. When they told him things, his mind could get so crowded he wished to cover himself in dirt and leaves, listening for the soft footsteps of the toddy cat, the wind he called friend, waiting, waiting, for the noise in his head to stop. It could take hours. It could take weeks.

Loka was telling him about bones. His sister had been wearing her dead husband's skull down her back, to keep him from becoming a malicious spirit. Mr Howard took the skull away by force, for a visitor. She would not stop crying. It had happened before, many times. The visitors would even raid Andamanese burial sites for ancestor bones. In conclusion, Loka told Aye, the Andamanese, who were called the most favoured of all the tribes, did many things. They returned escaped convicts, discovered caves and shipwrecks, and watched for Japanese spies. Now they asked for one thing. They wanted the skull back.

Above them, the clouds were streaked with delicate tendrils of gold. The leaf in Loka's hand was turning to ash.

Aye said, 'You are loyal. You wear clothes.'

Loka crushed the last embers in the sand, close to Aye's feet. 'You are loyal. You take nests.'

'Why are you telling me this?'

'Help us and ask for anything. One thing, friend.'

'What will you do if you do not get it back?'

A single tear ran down the cheek of Loka, who stood up from the canoe with his bow and arrow and soundlessly walked away.

'Why are you telling me this?' Aye asked again. 'I just work for Mr Howard.'

He could not even find the man's footsteps in the sand.

By the time Aye reached the path where he had heard the whistle, a long procession of prisoners was making its way up to the jail, while down by the jetty, the crowd was beginning to disperse. He spotted Shakuntala, the mother of White Paula, as well as Nomi and Zee. But they were too far away to call. The prisoners hung their heads, whether under the weight of their only possessions—a single mat, a single bowl—or of something else, only they could know. Mr Howard was among them, but if he saw a boy covered in crusted blood and feathers, he did not show it.

A few prisoners shook their shoulders and adjusted their burden. There were a handful of women, and Aye glanced at a frail and vaporous form whose striped uniform hung from her hips the way Loka's trousers had done, and whose sleeves were also bunched at her elbows. A wooden ticket around her neck read Prisoner 218 D. Perhaps it was the drug, but something stirred in him, a slender, inscrutable wind too easily missed, one that had not visited in a while. The praying mantis. The wind pointed him to something he recognised in the girl, as though she also wanted to cover herself with leaves and twigs and put a frangipani at her ear. He felt he would have liked to give her these things. And even as he thought it, Aye was sure of it, he would always be sure of it, the prisoner turned her head and looked straight at him.

Every Detail Is Story
1936

ONCE INSIDE HER CELL, THE prisoner's body begins to quake. When she is rooted by memory, every detail is story, but the cell is her present and the cell is without detail. There is a mat she has carried since Calcutta. The same bowl, the same uniform. The items from before the ship. They are all that is hers, but they are not hers. There is a terrible man whose name she has not been told, with a metal-tipped lathi in one hand and a cigar in the other, who locks her in. The door bangs shut. There is nothing to pull her away from herself, not even the awful woman she was chained to first on the train and then the ship and even on the walk to this jail, the one who sang to her, whose urine lingers on her skin, whose wet chin she would gladly rest beneath.

She tries to remember just this. The woman's welcoming flesh.

On the ship, she asked her what she had done, but the woman kept singing. *Na ro puttar, sajna.* Don't cry child, beloved one. Someone shouted that she was a bride, coming to the island willingly. The prisoner did not believe it. 'She is choosing this?' she called back.

Laughter.

And the woman kept singing, and now she is gone.

The prisoner clutches herself but her body will not stop shaking. She stands against the wall, as she had done in Lahore—far, far away Lahore—while waiting for the verdict. How long ago? She cannot remember. There is a small barred window high above. When she slouches to the floor, her back still against the wall, she is looking up at the window and will look nowhere else.

If she could find the missing details, they might absorb her, at least for a while.

The floor she sits upon is 22,000 cubic feet of stone cut by prisoners. The wall she leans against has 3,000,000 bricks laid by prisoners. The concrete came from Burma. The iron grills, fetters, shackles, flogging stands and chains, from England. Outside her door runs a long corridor with an iron railing that faces the backs of other cells in other wings. The jail has three levels and 693 cells along seven corridors—or limbs, to those who see the jail as a starfish—radiating from a central watchtower. Inside the watchtower is a single sentry who can observe each inmate like a god.

Thus each prisoner begins to live in a permanent state of self-correction.

Outside the window above her head are the gallows where, in a single moment, three prisoners can swing. But she cannot see outside, and perhaps it is just as well.

The prisoner looks away from the grate and notices two items in the cell. A slat bed and a black pot. She also notices the wooden ticket around her neck. Prisoner 218 D. She has not put her chin to the indent below her throat to check it in some days.

She is thirsty.

If she drinks water she will have to use the black pot by the opposite wall. She knows it is the pisspot. She wonders how many have used it, and if it has ever been washed. She cannot remember a single day when the white toilet in her house did not shine. Her mother taught her that it is never right if it is not your own. She looks around but finds no water, not even to drink.

When the light outside recedes, the cell grows even smaller. Mosquitoes besiege her. She crawls to the wooden bed and lies flat on her back, straightening her legs the way she was unable to do on the ship. A pain shoots down her thighs. They have forgotten what it is to move. She rolls onto her side, bringing first one leg up towards her stomach, then the other. The legs are swollen, the skin pulled tight around the shins. There are sores and some are open. She does not want to know her body anymore.

When sleep does not come, she scratches the wall with a fingernail, still unable to find a single word.

A Private Woman
1936

SHAKUNTALA, THE MOTHER OF White Paula, walked back to her farm from the jetty. Earlier, as the prisoners disembarked, it was not upon 218 D that her eye had fallen, but the one chained to her. The large one with boils. Shakuntala guessed this woman to be one of the brides, the women who came here voluntarily, or so the British said, to marry. It was likely that the woman would come to work for her.

Each time she witnessed a batch of prisoners arrive, Shakuntala remembered her own strange journey to these shores, as the wife of an Englishman. Though a widow now, Indian women still gossiped about how lucky she was. She had not come here as a prisoner bride but a settler bride—the only Indian one on the island. And she was very dark. Why had an Englishman picked her, they wondered, when he could have had any white woman instead? After his death, when she continued wearing blazingly bright saris with her own casual kind of flair, showing off those mud-brown curves, they began to call her a public woman.

She walked back to her farm from the jetty, missing Thomas.

They had been married for a year and were living in Chittagong when Thomas came to her one day with a map. He had been offered the post of deputy chief commissioner of the Andaman Islands. 'We might be happier there,' he said, without needing to add, *away from your family, and mine.*

'On a prison island?' she replied.

The sun was streaming through his nostrils, turning them translucent and rose. She found a tenderness there, as they sat in his library.

How straight the nose, how straight everything about him—the hair, the fingers resting on his lap, the spine aligned like the bookshelves behind them.

'I must give my answer soon, Shakuntala,' said Thomas. 'Should we move to the Andamans?'

Before she could answer him, there was a knock on the door. The maid said he had a visitor. He stood up, tapping a point on the map he now placed on her knee. The islands were a straight line south from Chittagong. When she measured the distance with her forefinger and thumb, it was precisely the width of her wrist. *Imagine,* she thought, *even exile can be so close.* Could she escape to a place from which prisoners, Indians like her, could never escape, because of Englishmen like him? Was this what their families had done, hers and Thomas's?

After he left the room, she began tracing with her fingers all the things she might soon be leaving. *The Sign of Four,* a book with a character from the Andamans, though she had never realised it till just now. The photographs of this mansion, when it had belonged to an official of the East India Company. The house still wore a stark, whitewashed finish, but a swooping colonnade of Doric columns had been added to the front by Thomas's family. She'd be leaving the house and, quite possibly, the photographs.

Shakuntala stepped out onto the veranda, to look down at the driveway bordered by pillars of trees that never grew tall enough to drop their fruit on the porch. From here she could see the two houses she had already left behind.

The first was her father's, at the bottom of the hill. The second was the house to which she and her mother had moved after her father's death, her maternal grandfather Abilio Vaz's house, higher up the hill. They were a Catholic family, descended from the first Portuguese to arrive in Chittagong, in 1577, or so they said. Her father had been a Hindu. When she moved to her grandfather's house, it was as though she could only look down at her past. She had been Shakuntala Das, but now she was to take one finger and wipe away two letters, replacing them with two new letters to make: Shakuntala Vaz.

In her grandfather's house, there were three unspoken subjects that intrigued her. First, the British, who lived higher up the hill than Abilio Vaz, never invited him to their parties. He called himself European; they called him black Portuguese. Second, she was not to invite any black Portuguese to their home. They were as not-good-enough for them as Abilio Vaz was not-good-enough for the British. Third, she was also rejected by the Hindu and Muslim girls at school. She might always have been, but only felt it now, with her father gone. Abilio Vaz's house was a sad little island waging a sad little contest. The more it calculated who was looking down on who and making sure it was not them, the more it was them. It grew damaged from all quarters: British, Muslim, Hindu, and the Portuguese-Indian families who laughed at hers for thinking they were better.

The only place where Shakuntala did not feel divided was her maternal grandmother's farm, which had for generations bred pigs and Chittagong fowl. After school, she would go there, to Gomez Farms. Thomas Best came there one day, to pick up a delivery. He did not send a servant, and this amazed her. When her grandmother offered him a rusgulla, he accepted. That an Englishman would eat an Indian dessert amazed her too.

Later, when he said he wanted to marry her, she was terrified most of all of his mother. 'I will work on her,' he insisted.

One day, when his mother visited from Calcutta, he asked Shakuntala to wait outside the drawing room. When the time was right, he would call her inside. As Shakuntala waited, she could hear his mother through the door. 'If you will not put an end to your relations, you would not be the first to have an Indian mistress. But your wife must be English.'

It was the wintriness that shook Shakuntala. His mother might as well have been telling the cook to bake the custard.

Thomas's sister, Vicky, was also inside. Shakuntala could hear her contribution. 'You must not let yourself succumb to their flirty ways! It is the climate, the food—'

'Oh, do be quiet,' their mother snapped. 'An English wife, or you will find yourself deteriorating like the Portuguese, whose blue blood turned black in running downstream.'

She knew Shakuntala was listening.

To save Thomas from the embarrassment she hoped he was feeling, she never brought it up with him. He'd never speak of it either, though he might say that in refusing to abide by his mother's rules, and marrying Shakuntala, he did speak. 'Not all of us are horrid,' he told her once. 'Not all of us think of all Indians as our subjects.' *All* Indians? *Us*? She did not know how to explain that she had never trusted these words and did not know what was worse, being a part of *all* or not, as it seemed the decision had never been hers to make. Nor did she know how to explain that it was not a question of what one or two might think. It had more to do with the patterns inherited, the lies inhabited, though she could not find the words, and so she said nothing, except, in answer to his proposal, 'Yes.' She was to take one finger and wipe away three letters, replacing them with four new letters to make, not Shakuntala Das nor Shakuntala Vaz, but Shakuntala Best.

And now, as she looked down at her previous two houses from Thomas's veranda at the very top of the hill, and as he re-entered the library, she said it again. 'Yes.' She would go with him to the Andamans. She would leave all three houses behind, without knowing who she was to become next.

On the island, Shakuntala had told Thomas that she wanted a farm like her grandmother's in Chittagong. She too would raise pigs and poultry. As the new deputy chief commissioner, Thomas was expected to live at the Government House on Ross Island, but Shakuntala knew she would never be accepted by the white settlers. Thomas could only secure land for the farm on South Andaman Island, which meant that if he lived on Ross Island, they would live apart. They had already travelled far enough when they married. They were not about to let two rocks on the eastern edge of the Bay of Bengal separate them. And so, he broke with convention to live with her on the farm, and this time she would acknowledge that, yes, he did speak.

This house they built together had an open layout, with no inner doors. Curtains hung between sections. It was similar to the house she had lived in with her father, who had believed in the healing benefits of circulating air. Her grandfather Abilio Vaz's house, higher up the hill, had inner doors. Thomas's house, at the very top of the hill, also did, though they were added; the original had none.

She planted trees, including the golden rain tree with red pods like fat lanterns, similar to the one in her father's house. How far those seeds had travelled, to lodge themselves on this rock!

As the tree began to swoop down into the pig pen, and her belly swelled with Paula, Thomas would share things whispered between the island's administrators. For instance, in the early years of the settlement, women were so scarce that they had been allowed marriage parades. It was true, he insisted, men had lined up like chattel, as women examined or rejected them. The women lost leverage after a greater number began to be sent down from Indian jails. First they were put in Randi Barrik, the Barracks of Whores, to separate them from the men, and the parades were abolished. Then, once the jail was built, they were transferred out of the Barracks, and confined almost entirely to their cells. The male prison guards had no overseers, further diminishing the power, and value, of convict women.

By the 1920s, 'public women' were being shipped from the mainland, for the guards. The women were kept in Shadipur, or Marriagetown, with the families of prisoners.

Though Randi Barrik was now abandoned, most people had come to believe that shadi sounded very well with randi. Thus Shadipur became the new Barracks of Whores.

Lately, in the morning, while Shakuntala was still in bed, her daughter had taken to bringing her a cup of tea and two fried eggs. It was good to be pampered.

While eating, Shakuntala watched her daughter get ready for school. White Paula, the children called her, and stopped to stare at her light brown eyes and hair. Mothers sent proposals, hoping for fair-skinned grandchildren. Paula was only thirteen. She already spent a lot of time gazing in the mirror. Something in the way Paula pursed her mouth reminded Shakuntala of Thomas's sister. Paula was one half starchy Vicky, while the other half tossed back her hair, as if to enhance her Flirty Ways.

When her daughter was dressed, Shakuntala sat up and kissed her goodbye. The farm workers would soon be arriving, so she came outside. It was during these few quiet moments to herself that she missed Thomas most.

This penal settlement was the only place where they had been free to love, but how short-lived it had been. The day she stood on the veranda of his mansion in Chittagong, resolving to leave behind her past, it had never occurred to her what she was to become next: a widow. Thomas had died of snakebite under that very tree they planted together, the one hanging over the pig pen, when Paula was five.

Her workers were here, replenishing the water in the trough. Pigs did not sweat, not even in the tropics, and needed to stay hydrated and cool. They also needed room to roam, but not too much, or excess muscle would toughen the meat. The pen was the right size, and as the farmhands moved inside, the leggy Chittagong fowl that ambled nearby regarded them with interest.

Most of the workers came from Shadipur, and Shakuntala had discovered a curious illness among the girl children who accompanied their mothers to work. In Shadipur, families lived so close together that they had to consult one another before turning over in their sleep. These girls who came with their mothers were rarely consulted, and were terrified of being suffocated to death as they slept. It had happened. In the middle of the night, an arm would cover a mouth or a chest would fold over a smaller one and the child would be pinned. In the morning, she was found beneath a pile of flesh. The British even had a name for it. Death by walrus. They said it happened in the wild. The dead girls were dropped in the sea, after being tied to a weight.

Shakuntala had attempted different ways of helping girls who carried the fear of death by walrus. She had asked that they sleep inside her house, where no one would touch them, but they were equally terrified of too much space, and cried if they lost sight of their mothers. Shakuntala had discovered a better tactic. She gave the girls Paula's old clothes, the ones that were a little large. Tight, restrictive clothing was something all these children rejected, yet they also rejected a size that was too loose, as though it afforded them no attachments at all. In the right clothes, the girls, like fragile roots in potted plants, grew less anxious, though there were also those who never entirely grew out of their fear and continued to believe that they were being crushed.

After Shakuntala greeted all her workers, she remembered that she was to have a visitor today. Andrew Gallagher, Jr, Senior Officer of Indian Police. She knew why he came, even if he engaged her in conversation instead. He would tell her about Japan's creeping colonisation of Southeast Asia and his belief that with Britain's assistance, China was on its way to becoming Christian and free. He would tell her that he should have been made deputy commissioner, instead of Mr Martin, as though her marriage to a former deputy commissioner qualified her to recognise him as such. She would ply him with tea and biscuits before saying that she had to tend to her farm. He would leave, gallantly enough, though with a chafed look in his eye that asked why she was not like all the other Indian women: grateful to have the attention of an Englishman. She would meet the look in his eye with one of her own: she was a private woman.

Six years from now, as the British evacuated the island, Andrew Gallagher, Jr would come to her with a proposal. Not of marriage, but of a way to change the course of history. But today, as Shakuntala remembered Andrew and missed Thomas and watched over her farm, she noticed that a child had fallen asleep in the middle of the pen. She walked to the fence, to carry the girl to the shade of the golden rain tree. The girl shifted, and began to cry. Shakuntala pointed to her mother at the trough, to show the girl that, from here, she could see all that she needed. From here, she could breathe. There was to be no death by walrus on her farm. Under her care, no child would be tossed into the sea.

Soon the girl was so sound asleep that nothing could disturb her, not even the animals.

Absolute Nature
1937

'The amenities and conditions of life and health of the terrorist prisoners
in the Andamans are superior to those obtaining in the Indian jails . . .
The punishment is not imprisonment but only banishment from home.
It is a prisoner paradise.'
—Sir Henry Craik, Home Secretary to the Government of India.

1

FOR THE SECOND YEAR IN a row, Aye waited for the ferry to Ross
Island, to present to Mr Howard a bag of sour swiftlet nests. The sea
was flat and wore a slippery sheen. The sky was overcast. There was no
thunder, yet. The breeze felt like White Paula's lips.

He hoped Mr Howard would ask for a shave. It relaxed him.

He boarded the ferry. It was called *Jarawa*, after a tribe considered
hostile, and run by another Burmese family. Aye and the boy at the
helm knew each other so well that when they arrived on Ross Island,
Aye hopped out with only a nod, and the boy, who had his back to
Aye, nodded in return.

Ross Island was less than a mile in area and shaped like a butterfly's
wing. At its centre was Government House and in its shadow lay Mr
Howard's villa. As Aye approached the kitchen, he passed the Indian
gardener and his assistant, an Andamanese child named Robinson
Crusoe. A group of aborigines was with them, including Robinson
Crusoe's mother, to whom he clung. They had come to discuss the
case of the woman whose husband's skull had been taken from her by

force last year. The woman was sick. They wanted the skull back. Mr Howard's Indian bodyguard Balaraj was holding out a packet. He said to leave with Chandu Bhai or leave without it.

Inside the kitchen, the cook Khan Baz was arranging the breakfast tray with a fresh hibiscus flower, a small pot of raspberry jelly, whorls of butter, chestnut cream, toast and an omelette. There was also a pot of tea with sugar and cream. The napkin was moulded into a banana flower. 'Should I take it up to him?' asked Aye.

The cook grimaced at the stench of the nests. 'You will go outside with that.'

'But it is for him.'

'Out!'

'Tell him I am here with this year's harvest.'

The cook made another face before picking up the tray.

Aye waited outside for over an hour. Once the Andamanese adults had left, all he could hear was the snapping of the gardener's shears. When he was told to meet the superintendent in the front lawn, he was surprised to find him sitting beneath the shade of an umbrella, still in his dressing gown and bedroom slippers, reading a newspaper.

'Did you collect the nests?' Mr Howard asked, without looking up.

'Yes, sir.'

'Are they any good?'

Silence.

'Let's have a look.'

Aye stepped forward.

Mr Howard tied a napkin around his mouth and nose before looking inside. When he was done, he told Aye to tie up the bag. Ahead, through a cluster of mango and pyinma trees framing the lawn, was an opening. Beyond, a view of the sea. It was towards this that the superintendent's gaze drifted.

Aye shifted. There was a scab behind his ear that he wished to scratch, from his attack in the caves. It was in the same place as one of last year's cuts. While waiting outside the kitchen, he had been picking at it, and it had started to ooze.

There was a jug of lemonade on the table and an empty glass beside it. The moisture had condensed around the jug and one ice cube remained inside.

'Last year was also a disaster,' said Mr Howard, his face turning red.

There was something that happened to the air when a man got angry, thought Aye. Something like the heat the birds generated in the cave. It was a wind that said, *Leave. You are in my home.* The settler wind.

Still looking through the gap in the trees, where the silver sea was no longer flat but furrowed, Mr Howard said, 'When I first came to the islands, I was struck most of all by the shadows. There is no darkness to match the one that falls in the tropics. It struck me then as it strikes me now.'

Aye knew he had not been forgiven for the nests. Should he shave him, here in the lawn? Should he ask?

'How I feel it, pressing down on me, that dreary sky!'

It was getting late, yet here Mr Howard sat, in his dressing gown. It would take but a moment to get the water, the towels, the blade.

'Colour is not an emotion. Remember that. The sky burns blue when God wills it.'

'Yes, sir.'

Two drops of coconut oil, for the massage. Though Mr Howard was scornful of hair oil, he liked to have his scalp invigorated.

Mr Howard was saying he had too many meetings this afternoon. This was Aye's chance. 'Permission to ask a question, sir.'

'What's that?'

'Please, sir.'

'Go on then.'

'Would you like a shave, sir?'

Mr Howard laughed.

'And a massage?'

Mr Howard was back in the gap.

'Sir?'

'Go on then!'

Aye hurried. As far as he knew, this villa and Government House were the only places in the world where bathrooms were indoors. He ran down the hall with the chequered floor, past the study, and up the stairway, two steps at a time. To Aye, the sunlight that fell upon the wooden banister was in the shape of the fingers of the Burmese convicts who had carved the wood.

The bathroom was through Mr Howard's bedroom. Inside was a white table with slender legs, and towels neatly folded on top. He took two. On the top shelf also rested a box set of Yardley lavender soaps and a canister of Yardley talcum powder, both of which were delivered to the house on days when a ship arrived. Mr Howard always had a slightly tart scent, like old milk, even after using these items. There was also a jar of shaving cream (Aye was allowed to keep the empty jars), a shaving brush with a red handle, and a blade that snapped flat into a matching red handle. The razor had once belonged to Mr Howard's father, and Mr Howard never had to sharpen it.

On the bottom shelf was a stack of newspapers that Aye read when no one was looking. He liked the advertisements, especially for Yardley soap. In one, a woman in a gown held a bouquet of flowers and wore a crown. The caption said, *One powder only for her beautiful English skin.* In another was a taller woman, in trousers that did not look English, hands on hips. The caption said, *Preserve that radiant English beauty.* He preferred the woman in the crown, who looked a little like White Paula. But today there was no time to go through the papers, so he took the shaving tools and ran downstairs.

He paused in the doorway of Mr Howard's study, the best room in the house. On the desk were a collection of strange, scientific things, as well as a model of the *Darya-e-Noor*, the ship that had mysteriously vanished after bringing his great-grandfather to these shores. There were photographs on the walls, including of Jack the Sailor, the Andamanese boy who was captured and dressed in a sailor suit before being taken to Calcutta, for a governor-general's wife. Like the *Darya-e-Noor*, Jack the

Sailor had also vanished, and Aye rolled the mystery around in his head like a brush in shaving cream. In the photograph, Jack sat in a wicker chair with both legs pulled up onto the seat, his head tilted to the right and one shoulder hunched. His face was old.

It was Loka's face. But it could not be. Jack had never come back to the island, and had to be dead by now. But it was Loka's face.

He wanted to step into the study, but there was no time. It was already possible that Mr Howard had changed his mind. He entered the kitchen, to ask Khan Baz for hot water. Then he draped both towels over his arm and lifted the bowl of steaming water in one hand and the jar of shaving cream in the other. Remembering that he also needed a cup, he asked the cook to put one in the bowl. The cook dropped it in, recklessly, splashing Aye's hand. The shaving brush and blade rested on top of the jar, but even when they rattled, Aye walked with speed. Mr Howard was waiting.

He had forgotten the coconut oil. He turned back and begged the cook to lodge the bottle between his hunched shoulder and his ear. The cook took his time. Aye hurried to the lawn.

'Ah, there you are.' Mr Howard had not changed his mind.

The nests had been taken away.

Aye got to work. He tucked one towel into the V of the superintendent's dressing gown. He rolled the second towel and placed it behind his head, where the skull bulged slightly over the neck, so that Mr Howard could lean back comfortably into his seat. Next, he scooped out water with the cup, and, with his fingers, patted Mr Howard's cheeks till they were wet but not dripping. He repeated this motion three times. He rolled the brush inside the jar of shaving cream. He lathered the face. He liked this part. The froth was as smooth and creamy as the sea on certain days, except thicker. He painted two layers on, all the way down the neck and along the ear lobes and up, to the arch of the cheekbones, easy to miss because Mr Howard's bones were unlike his and did not protrude. But he could feel them beneath the brush and feel too that the texture of this skin was different from his grandfather's.

As Aye worked, Mr Howard shut his eyes. It was to be a busy

week, he said. There were licenses to issue Japanese fishermen. The aborigines were keeping guard, but who could trust them? Then there was the business with the skull. At the last minute, the Scottish anthropologist had not taken it, and now Mr Howard was stuck with the blasted bones. He was glad the family had been spirited away, but they persisted, as was their way. 'As if the hunger strikers were not tiresome enough.'

Aye scraped the lather off gently. Not too slow, not too fast. After wiping the blade clean on the towel, he came back to the exact spot as before, missing nothing. Instead of the straight blade in his hands, Aye began to picture the kris of his great-grandfather, whom the British had called a Trusty, a trustworthy convict. The kris had come with an asymmetrical handle and a wavy blade and these days Aye's grandfather was whittling a bamboo replica of it. Aye liked to think of this while working on Mr Howard.

The superintendent opened his eyes. A brilliant gold had pierced the clouds, the sea dazzled. There was no darkness *or light* to match the one that fell in the tropics, he said. He was still, after years on these rocks, attuned to oscillations of light and shadow, though not as keenly as when he first arrived, when every high wind was cause for reflection. There was too much to do, the facility had left him.

'Your upper lip, sir,' said Aye.

Mr Howard rolled the lip over his teeth as Aye began to scrape.

Lunch at the chief commissioner's. The conversation menu would doubtless be the same: continue deporting prisoners, or shut down the prison. Around the same pothole they went.

'I heard a poem once, at the club,' he told Aye, who was smoothening away any last remnants of shaving cream with the flip side of the towel. 'By an American chap. Americans do write poetry, of a sort at least. "I hate to be a kicker, I always long for peace, but the wheel that does the squeaking, is the one that gets the grease."'

Aye tilted his head. The cheek was spotless.

Mr Howard indicated a frangipani flower fallen on the grass. All the servants in the chief commissioner's house wore a blossom. Aye ought to do the same.

Aye picked it up. He slipped the flower behind one ear, then gently removed the towel behind Mr Howard's head.

'Two drops, remember.'

'I remember, sir.'

The coconut oil had warmed in the sun. In the tropics, the salt could strip the hair; Aye hoped the burst of hydration on Mr Howard's scalp would be as dazzling as the light.

'Is the prison too costly to maintain, or is it a deterrent?' said Mr Howard. 'What about women prisoners, should they be spared transportation, even the terrorists?'

'Sir, I do not know what it means.'

'Of course not. Let me tell you something. You will sooner surrender your state of absolute nature than we will surrender our settlement.'

'Yes, sir.'

'Your fingers are fine. You have the right touch.' Mr Howard shut his eyes again, wondering aloud what the greedy Chinese would pay for the nests.

When the massage was over, Aye folded the towels into small squares and replaced the tops on the jar of shaving cream and bottle of coconut oil. The blade and brush he dropped in the bowl, where the water had turned milky and tepid.

As Mr Howard still did not show any sign of wanting to leave, Aye decided to return the items to the house.

'One more thing,' said Mr Howard, his eyes still closed.

'Yes, sir.' Aye paused, mid-stride.

'After my lunch at the commissioner's, I want you to accompany me to the jail.'

Aye waited.

'Do you remember the last time we had to feed one of them?'

Aye froze.

'I asked you a question.'

'Yes, sir. No . . . sir.'

'Which?' The voice was sharp.

'Yes, sir.' How could he forget the tube they had shoved down the man's throat?

'You were too soft, and not told to help. But I know you have the right touch and there is power in those hands. You will feel it too.'

Aye was right. Mr Howard had not forgiven him for the nests.

Half an hour later, he was in Mr Howard's study, helping him to gather the papers he was to take to the chief commissioner's villa. It was not so much help as tidying up, as Mr Howard could seldom find things. Papers littered the floor. The two wide cane chairs, as well as the leather sofa, sagged with files. There was a large elephant statue between the chairs, and on the elephant's back, in place of the seat, lay a large ashtray, a piece of crumpled paper inside. Lately, Mr Howard had been crumpling a lot of paper. Afterwards, he told Aye to help him find it again. Aye salvaged this one, just in case. The wooden floor creaked as he looked beneath the woven reed mats for more discarded pages.

Mr Howard seemed overwhelmed by the mess and stepped outside for air.

Above his enormous teak desk was the photograph of Andamanese Jack, dressed in a sailor suit. He sat in a wicker chair identical to the ones in the study, looking directly at the camera, his head tilted. The way he hunched that one shoulder, Aye realised, was what he himself did when thinking hard, when carrying a load. Right at this moment, in fact. He straightened his shoulders. It was still Loka's face.

There were other photographs on the wall, including Mr Howard's favourite, *A Chain of Three Athletes*, featuring three young men with no paint or tattoos, naked but for crowns of shells and necklaces of bones. Like Jack, they gazed at the camera. The first athlete's left leg brushed the right leg of the second athlete, whose hand lay on the first's shoulder. The hand of the third lingered somewhere at the second's buttocks. Whenever Mr Howard stood before the picture, he said the beauty of native men was in stark contrast to the ugliness of their women, and the third athlete looked 'almost Greek.'

Reminding himself to keep neatening up, Aye uncreased the page in his hand, retrieved from the ashtray. It was from a year ago and looked important.

Reference Paper.   Record Department
                                  (Parliamentary Branch)
Transferred to   Secretary P & J Dept. 6 Jan 1936

EXTRACT FROM OFFICIAL REPORT OF THE LEGISLATIVE ASSEMBLY DEBATES. DEPORTATION OF WOMEN POLITICAL PRISONERS TO THE ANDAMANS 511.

Mr S.C.: a) Are Government aware of the recommendation of the Indian Jails Committee, 1919–1920, to exclude all female convicts from being sent to the island of Andamans on account of absence of all reformatory influences and the resulting demoralisation of prisoners?

b) Will Government please state what special arrangements have been made for women proposed to be sent to the Andamans as regards their location and guard for their safety while in the Andamans?

c) What special arrangement has been made for the protection of their female virtues in the midst of a large number of old convicts and low-class guards?

d) Will Government be pleased to state what arrangements they have made to prevent cases of criminal assault on political women prisoners of high education and of good and respectable families while they will be kept in the Andamans?

The Honourable Mr H.G.: a) The Government of India are aware that the Jails Committee in paragraph 572 of their report recommended that female prisoners then in the Andamans should be brought back to India and that no further female prisoners should be deported there. This recommendation should be read with their recommendations regarding the Andamans as a whole. The Committee suggested first, the gradual closing down of the Settlement as accommodation became available in Indian jails by repatriating convicts to India and by deporting no more prisoners from India and, secondly, the maintenance of a jail at Port Blair for a limited number of prisoners whose removal from British India is considered to be in the public interest. There was also the fact that the conditions described in paragraph 551 of the Jail Committee's Report made it at that time undesirable that women prisoners should be retained in the Andamans, but these conditions no longer exist and the features of the Settlement have profoundly changed since the Jail Committee wrote their report.

(b), (c) and (d). The women prisoners sent to the Andamans will be confined in a wing of the Cellular Jail, Port Blair, set apart for female prisoners and will be entirely separate from other prisoners in the jail and from the settlement. The apprehension expressed by the Honourable Member in part (c) is unfounded, since a female staff is in charge, and male convict warders are not allowed within the wing set aside for female prisoners.

Mr S.C.: Is it a fact that the removal of the prisoner currently undergoing sentence in Lahore is considered to be in the public interest?

The Honourable Mr H.G.: I have no information about any such proposal.

Mr S.C.: I am talking about the woman convicted under section 124-A for a terrorist crime.

The Honourable Mr H.G.: I am quite prepared to ascertain the facts.

Aye slipped the page into one of the ledgers. He could hear Mr Howard outside the study, talking to the cook. He glanced quickly around the room—more ledgers, envelopes, pots of ink, a beautiful pen with the top screwed off, the nib glistening gold, a round and heavy piece of glass that would make the lines of his palm leap forward. But there was no more time. Mr Howard was calling out to him. The file in hand, he followed the superintendent to the chief commissioner's house.

2

After lunch, Mr Howard and Mr Martin, the deputy commissioner, took the *Jarawa* from Ross Island to South Andaman Island, to inspect the jail. The bodyguard Balaraj escorted them. Aye was there too, and the young Burmese boy who steered the ferry.

'The wheel that does the squeaking, Martin,' said Mr Howard.

'I am aware, but—'

'You are soft, dear chap.'

The superintendent pulled off his pith helmet and wiped his brow with a handkerchief. As he stuffed the cloth back into his shirt pocket, his hand brushed a letter, but he had more immediate concerns. There were many, like the deputy commissioner, who thought deportation should cease. He glanced at Martin, whose head was so small the helmet fell over his eyes. Martin would be far better off picnicking up on the mountain with the dim-witted nurse.

'I rather think,' Martin gulped. 'As I was saying—'

'Let me guess. Transport only the especially dangerous ones?'

'Something along those lines, yes.' His smile was a grimace.

'And who might those be?'

'A fine question. As I was—'

'Perhaps you do not favour transporting women?'

'Certainly not! And I hear there is one—'

'And if we shut down the colony—'

'Oh, I don't propose—'

'Then what is one to do with the Local Borns, like these Burmese boys?' Mr Howard turned his chin slightly. 'They know no other life.'

'Certainly, yes, but I don't—'

'Or with the self-supporting lifers who have served out their terms? Do you know the intricacies of the many categories, dear chap? You are new to the islands.'

'I do wonder, what *is* one to do with them?'

'Precisely. The wives come to the settlement of their own volition, enjoying more freedom here than on the mainland. Men and women alike are permitted a vocation, and do you know what the most popular one is?'

'I can't imagine, really.'

'Supervising other convicts. How they embrace the reversal of roles! Are we to deny them these privileges by shipping them back to overcrowded Indian jails, to again stand at the back of the queue?'

Martin finally lifted the helmet off his eyes, speaking in a lukewarm voice.

'What's that?' said Mr Howard.

Martin closed his mouth. Mosquitoes surrounded him in alarming number.

It did mean they bit Mr Howard less. The last thing he needed now was malaria.

'After the last hunger strike,' said Mr Howard, 'in 1933—you have heard of it?'

'Yes. Quite.'

'A few,' he paused, 'well-meaning men like yourself began asking questions. They were,' he paused again, 'misled by the press.'

'Three men died,' said Martin.

Mr Howard took a deep breath. 'We have made too many concessions. Now they are even allowed letters. Remember that when the Home Secretary came to us, he called it a prisoner paradise.'

'It cannot be denied. On star-blazing nights, these islands appear enchanted.'

'Is this to be only your second time up at the jail?'

'It is.'

Mr Howard nodded. 'Even after the Home Secretary's favourable report, the government sent a member of the Muslim League. Yamin Khan was his name. He too found conditions to be entirely contrary to what the press claimed. The cells were not the least bit dingy or small or malarial.'

Martin blinked into the swarm of mosquitoes. 'Why! That is absurd!'

'Do you not see? We have Indian ministers on our side.'

The ferry pulled into the jetty with unexpected force, causing Martin to nearly tumble over the prow. Mr Howard shook his head, stepping onto the wooden landing.

The buggy was late. He cursed and took out the damp kerchief from his shirt pocket. Also in the pocket was the letter. It bothered him. Like the other inmates, the woman prisoner who had arrived last year was allowed letters. She had committed a heinous act. How could he allow a change in the regulations for her?

The letters were given to him by an officer cadet who claimed the orders came from higher up.

Higher up? Mr Howard *was* the higher up. *He* lived on these rocks, so the Empire could sleep at night. Without a doubt, what the superintendent did with each letter was up to him.

As he heard the wheels of the buggy approach, he made a decision. After checking on the strikers, he would wait outside the cell of Prisoner 218 D, till her eyes were raised in anticipation. He would watch as she crawled to the iron door. Slowly, he would show her the letter. Slowly, he would tear it to pieces. He would tell her there were others. They would also be torn, if it pleased him. He knew everything there was to know about her already. She was a murderer. All the Martins in the world could not convince him that women were less dangerous than men. If anything, they were far worse.

'Sir,' said Aye, as Mr Howard got into the buggy.

'What is it?' he snapped.

'You dropped this, sir.' Aye was flapping the kerchief in the breeze, trying to remove the sand.

The buggy was a large rickshaw with plush red seats, pulled by a former convict. Martin, quiet at last, settled next to Mr Howard. Aye jogged behind them. The broad-shouldered Balaraj, who had escorted the superintendent up to the jail on every visit and dwarfed even the Irish jailor, Cillian, kicked the buggy driver when he slowed.

At the jail, Mr Howard found even the prisoners not on hunger strike refusing to work and refusing to line up. The rule was that every week they were to stand in single file, so he could inspect them. Today, they had put their tools down.

'With your permission, sir,' said Cillian.

Cillian scarcely needed Mr Howard's permission. Many prisoners were already being flogged with the help of two other warders. The prisoners cast Mr Howard a defiant stare. They did this. They let him know they were not afraid. He was no fool. He knew what got them, every time.

'Carry on,' Mr Howard said.

Cillian did not carry a whip. He carried a bamboo truncheon tipped with metal in one hand, a lit cigar in the other hand. He pressed the cigar to the neck of Prisoner 691 D, who had been chanting incendiary poems since his recent arrival. The truncheon came down on his shoulder but he did not stop chanting. He had twice tried to enter the yard with an older batch of prisoners, though the groups were to be kept separate. He had twice before been broken. When the truncheon came down again, his collar bone snapped. His chants turned to screams.

Mr Howard nodded.

The backs of the prisoner's knees were also dislodged. Then the lower spine.

Mr Howard had his orders. When it came to security prisoners who engaged in the strike, the incidents could not be reported. Manual methods of restraint were best, then mechanical when prisoners resisted. But the prisoners had to be kept alive.

When he nodded again, the man was dragged away on his back, still screaming.

The remaining strikers still stared ahead insolently. The superintendent knew this could not be a repeat of the strike of 1933, when three men had died. He cocked a finger from one man to the next. 'Return to the mill, or all amenities are nullified.' They were put in bar fetters, without food or water.

It was almost three o'clock, and these were just the tools-down strikers. He had yet to endure the hunger strikers. The superintendent turned to the deputy commissioner, who sweated so profusely that Mr Howard wondered if he would die before any of the inmates did.

'I rather think I will stay here,' muttered Martin.

'Suit yourself,' Mr Howard answered. As he headed towards the cells and the bell in the Central Tower struck three times, he told one warder, 'Don't let Martin perish.'

A Sky of Paper
1937

THERE WAS NO ONE IN the cell next to hers. Twice a day, she heard the heavy doors two cells away open and shut, the same three-step latch, and two male warders making jokes while pulling outside an inmate with a voice that was not a woman's. It happened every day, twice. She had been told there would be a separate wing for women, guarded by women.

Then there were other doors. It seemed every cell on Levels Two and Three was occupied. She heard crossbar fetters and leg-iron chains. They were different sounds. A prisoner in crossbar fetters became immobile and screamed sooner than the one in leg-iron chains, for whom there was a period of dragging the weight around, as though to comprehend it. She also heard manacles rapping on bars, followed by chants of '*Inquilab Zindabad!*' Sounds she could mouth. *Long Live the Revolution!* Then the English horse doctor pronouncing someone 'fit enough to flog!' The sound of twenty stripes tearing flesh.

She had seen neck ring shackles, once, on her way to the Female Factory, which was where she learned that he was a horse doctor. And she had seen the peg on the wall of the empty cell next to hers. The prisoner two cells away could be dangling by his wrists. She was not sure, though.

Other sounds. Boots bearing down, liquid down a throat. She had come to dread these most.

And others. The rain on the railing along the corridor. The rain leaking into her pisspot. The smell coming alive. The wind whistling through the grates of the single tiny window above. Mice. Cockroaches. A live worm in the breakfast bowl of boiled rice.

There was an obsession with tracking her weight. She was measured and weighed daily. Once, she was taken to the hospital. A nurse gave her glucose. 'Have you joined the strike?'

Though she wanted to, the memory of steaming tea and chicken biryani overtook her, so when they returned her to the cell, she did eat, though the worm swaying its head made her weep.

A bird.

A leaf.

It fell through the grate. Plump and rubbery. Sour inside.

She was being watched closely since the hospital, so she would keep eating. At breakfast, there was the scrape of the bowl coming through the trap door, followed by the Pathan warder's boots. The snap of the thick, hard roti her fingers broke into pieces lingered in the air between them. Once, he offered her a cup of fresh water to dip the roti in, looking over his shoulder to make sure he was not seen. The water was sweet. He wore dark blue kohl around his eyes. She did not see him again.

The strange brown roots and stems in her bowl were ground by the women in the Female Factory. They were mixed with stones and mice droppings. She had a toothache since the last time she bit into them, but the warder who watched her now, a woman, at last, would not leave till she finished.

When the bowl was empty, she was taken to the saltwater tank outside to bathe. Three prisoners at a time dipped a cup into the tank twice: first for their armpits, then their hair. The saltwater left white shadows on her skin. The women laughed when she tried to cover herself. The head was shorn every other week.

It would be worse, she was told, were she a man. A man had to clear the swamps. A man had to turn the mill from dawn till after dusk. She stayed indoors, protected from the male prisoners glimpsed only on her way to the tank and factory. The creak of the mill grew familiar. The raw tracks down their backs did not. The warders spoke of Prisoner 691 D, who had suffered the floggings for many days before finally being dragged to the hospital, but who would still not break his strike, and whose voice when he chanted was as sweet as fresh water. As she bathed, she felt the salt on his wounds.

If the men failed to grind their quota of oil, they worked through the night, and through the corridors of the jail she could hear the truncheon-twirling Cillian calling down to the Indian sweeper in the yard. *'Punish them now, Jamadar! Do not reserve for the morrow what can be dealt with today! Cane them within an inch of their lives!'* He stopped right outside her cell, smoking his cigar. The next morning, as she bathed, she still felt the smoke on her.

She was only separate from the men she did not wish to be separate from. Her isolation was turning her into a strange creature, empty of vigour, like the stones she had to eat. The opposite of peace is not war, someone close to her had once said. The opposite of peace is inertia.

The male inmates had each other. Together they planned the hunger strike, together they recited poetry. There were those among them who were shown deference for their role in the freedom movement. Educated men. Men with names. Women warders in the factory said these men had a delicate constitution, and uneducated men offered to turn the wheel for them. 'I will do twenty rounds if he only does five!' they offered, even if it got them caned, or cost them their ration of water.

She was the only woman political prisoner here, and no one, except the Pathan warder who was never seen again, had offered her an extra cup of water. No one had offered to take on her quota of factory work. She was unnatural. She was the same as a thief, dacoit, or prostitute. They all had an equal worth. An equal unworth.

Her days were spent sewing the uniforms of Indian guards and the napkins of British administrators. Her evenings were spent sitting under the window, staring up at that small, small sky. It was smaller even than the delicate squares of linen with pink trim that she spent her days sizing and folding, re-sizing and re-folding. She had come all this way only to be forced into domestic servitude.

Something told her it was not cold, yet she was always shivering.

One word. Just the one, from someone she loved, who loved her. So that she might find the freedom to die on her own terms.

Sometimes, a young boy passed her cell. He was slender and brown and he hurt. He had enormous eyes that tapered at the ends, where the hurt was. He had a square jaw and his cheek was growing into a man's. Perhaps he did not know how to shave. Sometimes, he stood outside her cell till one of the warders started to approach and then he would dart away. Without a sound. He had the feet of a cat. She had seen him before, but could not recall when.

Perhaps he would come today.

She started to hear it, the sound she hated most. They were holding someone down. Soon would come the rush of liquid and the horse doctor's voice. She covered her ears with her hands. She rocked herself back and forth.

From the women warders in the factory she had learned what the hunger strikers wanted. Their demands were hers, too, if they only knew. Newspapers. Light in the cell. Better food. Proper medical aid. No more rationing of water. Warm baths. Bedsheets. No more rough handling. The warders laughed at this.

That other sound. The sound of laughter.

The strikers also asked for the freedom to answer the letters they were now allowed to receive. Why did no one write to her?

One word.

She rocked herself back and forth.

The Bengalis had asked for fish. She did not like fish. She wanted the taste of her mother's love as she fed her cubes of mutton.

How many daughters see their mothers for the last time in court?

She pressed her hands to her ears more tightly, but the screaming did not stop.

He was here! He was here! The boy was here!

Though she had never smiled at him before—he might be another horse doctor! He might be with Cillian!—today Prisoner 218 D looked up and her mouth moved in a way it had not moved in so long, she had to force her muscles to show that she was happy to see him, which she did, because she was.

He did not return the smile. He looked afraid, and was not alone. A very large policeman stood behind him. Then a third man appeared. The superintendent. Like the male prisoners, the women had to stand before the superintendent in single file each week, but today was not the day for it, or she would have been out in the yard. He looked at her through the bars of the door with a greater intensity of emotion than was usual even for him. She had seen hate. Before she saw it in the superintendent, or Cillian, or the men who arrested her, she saw it all over India. She saw it too in herself, every day.

The superintendent gave something to the boy and walked away, his shadow crossing her cell.

'Come forward,' said the boy.

She was confused.

'Look!'

He put something up against the bars.

Something she wanted. It was as much as she registered before her body was crawling on all fours and flinging itself at the door.

The toe of the enormous policeman's boot found a gap between the bars that her slender wrist could never find and expertly kicked her chin.

She crouched lower on the floor of her cell.

The object came back. A square of paper, greater than the sky!

She was back on her knees, moving forward again.

This time, the policeman got her lip, and there was the taste of warm salt inside. She tried a third time but hurled herself less hopefully now and jerked her head back before she was hit. Yet he found her somehow, above the ear.

Something was happening on the other side of the bars. Her vision was no longer clear, and the boy . . . where was he? She could hear the superintendent, but his voice was garbled. Even with her hands to the ground she could not steady herself, the floor began to give, she was back on the ship.

She lay down.

Outside the door, a sky of paper was being torn into a thousand little pieces and the boy was there, sweeping it all up.

The Words You Give Us
1937

WHEN AYE ARRIVED AT THE villa each day, the superintendent was still in bed. From the mess found in his bedroom, it was clear that he stayed up late. Scraps of paper littered the floor, all covered in scribbles. The handwriting was tiny and hard to discern, as though scratched with the fever of ants.

Today, as Aye tidied up, Mr Howard sat up in bed. 'I had a more or less sort of night,' he said.

The cook arrived with the breakfast tray. As the superintendent ate, Aye ran the bath. He made it foamy with lavender scents, the way Mr Howard liked. He timed it so the water was the right temperature when Mr Howard finished his toast. When the superintendent entered the bathroom, Aye slipped off his dressing gown and pulled down his pyjamas. His thighs were lean. The sides of his stomach sagged. When relaxing in the tub, his penis drifted to the top, as though to inspect this warm bed of froth. And Mr Howard's eyes closed halfway.

Aye shaved him. Mr Howard had started preferring it in the bath. The shaving cream, brush, and blade were all there on the smooth white table, with the newspaper advertisements of women with beautiful skin. It was different when Mr Howard had no clothes on. Aye did not have to worry about dirtying his dressing gown with the lather.

He rubbed his scalp. He helped him dress.

Afterwards, Mr Howard puttered about, gathering notes, staring sullenly at the veranda windows. They were closed, because of the eternal rain. He was again scheduled to have lunch at the chief commissioner's. 'All these dreary formalities, when it is clear deportation

119

must not cease.' He would go alone, he announced, and Aye should keep tidying up. 'You do a much better job of it than that half-witted sweeper.'

Aye looked around. Mr Howard would be gone at least two hours, enough time to go through the papers for more Yardley soap women. But the study was also a mess. He decided to work first and then come back for the advertisements.

The bell jar lantern was still on when Aye entered the study. Mr Howard had forgotten to switch it off last night. The ashtray on the elephant's back had more crumpled notes. Paper was shoved beneath the reed mats on the floor. And the desk! The ledgers were tearing at the seams, the once glistening fountain pen was crusted in India ink, the pot of ink had spilled, and the round, heavy glass that Aye had enjoyed experimenting with was lost. Worse, the drawers, lined in smooth green felt and with dainty brass handles, would not shut.

Inside one drawer rested a curious instrument with a needle that moved, but Aye decided to worry about the top of the desk first. He tried to shut the drawer by putting one leg back and leaning with all of his weight. His back foot accidentally kicked the small wooden cabinet behind the desk. When the drawer at last shut, he examined the cabinet. It had the same delicate brass handles as the desk. He opened it. He jumped back.

Inside lay a skull. The teeth were all intact, the eye sockets large, and all of it was small enough to hold in his palm. He knew what it was. The skull of Loka's brother-in-law, promised to one of Mr Howard's visitors nearly two years ago. The visitor had not returned and the skull was still here.

Aye shut the cabinet door. He wanted to leave. He looked out the tall, rounded window. The Indian gardener was there, along with Robinson Crusoe. It was the boy's family who kept coming here, to beg Mr Howard to return the skull, but Mr Howard always sent them away.

He could hear the cook in the kitchen and the sweeper upstairs. Like them, he had work to do. He began to put all the papers in a pile. But this did not assuage his misgivings because he could not forget the way Prisoner 218 D looked up at him from the floor of her cell. She had looked at him on her first day on the island too. Something had stirred in him, as it did each time he stood on the other side of that door, tearing up her letters. With each one he destroyed, he took a piece of her.

A silverfish scuttled across a page on the desk. There was no other prisoner whose letters he was asked to tear, and the letters were always first presented by an officer cadet to Mr Howard in a separate bundle, tied with twine, her name on each envelope crossed out. Aye had an idea, but shook it away, quickly retrieving another page that had fallen to the floor. Something stuck to his skin, perhaps the leg of a centipede. After flicking it somewhere near the two cane chairs, he cleared a space on the desk, and tried to breathe.

His panic resurfaced. He knew, the way he knew how to see in the swiftlet caves, the way he knew that his neighbour Thiri was too good for him, the way he knew that his father was never coming back from wherever he went to when he sat on that rock, muttering to himself— Aye knew that there was a connection between the skull he had just found and the letters staring at him from upon the desk. He did not know what the connection was, but hadn't he seen Loka and the prisoner for the first time on the same day? Andamanese Jack knew it too, as he sat in his sailor suit in the photograph on the wall, growing old.

Aye cleared up the remaining mess without wasting more time and without returning upstairs. He pocketed two letters. He took the ferry back to South Andaman Island.

On the way to his village, he opened the letters.

> Wednesday, 9th June —
>
> My dear sister,
>   I do not feel well. How can I when they have removed you from us, as though you never existed?
>   But you do exist, and I will commit the truth to these pages as I take your name, day after day, to bring you close to me again.
>   Oh, how many times before I have tried to

write, but it is not easy! There is much I wonder if you even <u>know</u>. For instance, did they tell you
that we sent appeals to have your sentence changed,
so like Bina and Kalpana you would also be kept in
India? But the ███████████████████████████
███
███
███████████████████████████

The air smells crisp today. The canal is serene.
It is rain that softens our differences, don't you
think? You used to like rain. Rimjhim. Remember
Baba would tap his fingers to the sound? But I have
heard it rains all the time there, so maybe you have
come to like it less.

I have been staring at this page. There is
much I do not know how to say.

Later —
I should say I am grateful letters are now
allowed. But your actions have cost us, and there
are times when I cannot help myself. I feel angry.
You stole our mother's jewellery. You lied to us.
Because of you, others avoid me. They think I am
unnatural like you. Our mother suffers. Her health
worries me. Nadia's fiancé broke off their engagement. Of course his family did not give a reason.
I know you do not care about marriage prospects
but you did not have to spoil ours. There is wisdom
in holding onto what we have been given, and in
thanking the Almighty for it, even if it does not seem
just. He has His ways, how I wish you had understood. Women are meant to be accepting and pious.
Leave the revolution to men.

How I wish that girl Kaajal had never come
into our lives.

How I wish you to know it has been hard for all of us, not only you.
      Everloving,
      Umbreen

Friday, 27ᵗʰ August–
Dear child,
I blame myself, and I should. I had a terrible dream the night your ship left. I wanted to speak of it in my last letter but did not want to frighten you. Then the dream returned last night, so here it is. I saw your island as pyramid-shaped and snowy white, with a crumbly texture, like cake, and a rounded edge that floated forward and backward in the water, like your favourite gharara. Someone was slowly approaching in a boat of a strange shape, and this man had a peculiar name, the wind seemed to be calling it, Aoi! Aoi!

In his pointy vessel, he slid into an inlet beneath the island's highest point, which was a mistake, for the wind was sharper than an eagle's claw and cut his face. It was bloodthirsty, this wind, screeching his name as it tossed his long hair, forcing him into the treacherous rock. Even so, Aoi tried to resist, to find his bearings. And I resisted with him, as did you, caught between the odd piece of rock with the cakey texture and the vast wind-whipped sea. The skirt-like edge bordering the rock had a greenish tinge and the boy gazed upon it for a long time. He decided to let the wind carry him forward. In my dream I knew the choice was wrong, but though it was my dream, I could not stop him from making it.

The dream is so vivid, even now!

Do you remember the day your father was killed? Of course you do, all the time, and do not need me to recall it in my words, as I began to do last time, before putting down my pen. But it is worth recalling, because how beautiful you

*looked, before we got the news. You were riding your bicycle—
you were always riding that bicycle!—till you saw me standing outside my house and stopped pedalling. I thought to
myself, here is a child born of light! I thought of you as my
daughter, and how proud I would be to have one like you.*

*You caught your breath and so did Faris, who
was running beside you. I often think of that moment, dear
one. Do you remember it was your idea to help me onto the
bicycle? Though I had no idea what to do, the two of you tried
to spin me around! What a happy moment, just before the
terrible news! Let me stop here. Let the memory of that day
end with you and Faris spinning me around on your bicycle
made in Japan, shipped from Singapore, and delighting an
aunty from Calcutta who rode it in Lahore!*

*Oh, but it does not end there, does it? How I
have been shaken! It is hard to go anywhere anymore. I
seldom speak. The pressure to say just the perfect thing in
the perfect way keeps me away. Yet, something urges me, a
sense that if I don't complete what I have started, a part of
me will come undone. It is like the dream I keep having. If
that strange long-haired boy in the pointy boat keeps heading for the island, it is the wrong choice; but retreating is not
the right one either.*

Speaking of not retreating, ▇▇▇▇▇▇▇▇▇▇▇▇
▇▇▇▇▇▇▇▇▇▇▇▇▇▇▇▇▇▇▇▇▇▇▇▇▇▇▇▇
▇▇▇▇▇ *A favourite venue is the railway station, as it is
today, as if to remind us Who Brought Technology. The roads
are blocked. A senior officer is arriving. I can hear the band
play. But there is a change, a droopiness to the pomp, and
people say* ▇▇▇▇▇▇▇▇▇▇▇▇▇▇▇▇▇▇▇▇▇▇▇▇
▇▇▇▇▇▇▇▇▇▇▇▇▇▇▇▇▇▇▇▇▇▇▇▇▇▇▇▇
▇▇▇▇▇▇▇▇▇▇▇▇▇▇▇▇▇▇▇▇▇▇
▇▇▇▇▇▇▇▇▇▇▇▇

Again I meander. Forgive me! I believe the real

reason for all these twists and turns is that I cannot forgive myself, even if I know we must go on. Your father would be proud. Yet, if there is one thing I am grateful for, it is that he did not see you being taken away.
Always in my thoughts, all my love to you.
Aunty Hanan

Weeks passed. Another letter torn. More hunger strikers force-fed. Aye took Nomi and Zee to the pond on the mountain, but did not tell them what he did up at the jail. Nor could he forget what Nomi called him. Liar. She was right. He was a liar, and a thief, but if she and Zee only knew. They stole a lady's gown, but Aye—Aye stole letters, *from* Mr Howard.

One evening, he was walking back from Mr Howard's villa, a third letter in his pocket. He did not know why he did it, nor what to do with them. He thought he dreamed Aunty Hanan's dream, the one of the long-haired boy in a boat. Who was this Aoi, approaching a strange island in a strange boat? *And this man had a peculiar name, the wind seemed to be calling it, Aoi! Aoi!* Could those who had never met dream the same dream? Could they speak to each other, the way Aunty Hanan was trying to speak to the prisoner, perhaps through him? *If that strange long-haired boy in the pointy boat keeps heading for the island, it is the wrong choice; but retreating is not the right one either.*

Why did he remember her words?

What was he meant to do?

Who could he ask?

He paused at the intersection to White Paula's farm. It was close to dinner time, and her mother was an amazing cook. The last time he was there, Shakuntala had prepared a shukto of neem leaves, bitter gourd, eggplant and green bananas, along with a pointed gourd stuffed with cottage cheese, keeping the spices mild in both. She said it was a habit developed for her husband, and after his death, she saw no reason to change. The main course was a fish bhapa, steamed to perfection. What was it like, Aye had wanted to ask her, loving a white man? But he had not found the courage.

If he went there now, Shakuntala would offer him a meal, because she was kind. Kindness was rare, and he could use some.

If Shakuntala was not there, he could lie with White Paula on the cushions on the pretty floor rugs. Her two cats, who were afraid of the fowl outside, would purr as he kissed the spatter of brown freckles on her toffee-coloured skin.

Today, Aye decided, he did not want White Paula. Nor did he want food. He had barely eaten since he was sick on the hospital floor yesterday and even the thought of Shakuntala's cooking could not assuage his nausea. He still wanted kindness, though.

To his left lay the forest. If it rained he could shelter in the arms of the padauk trees, and if he grew thirsty, there was a small creek with sweet water that flowed down to the beach where he first met Loka.

He had not seen him since and wanted to know if he saw him at all. The creek it was.

As he walked, he studied the vines. They usually swayed from the trees, but not today. Even the long, limber petals of orchids appeared stiff with dread. Sepals, not petals, Mr Howard had once told him, but Aye could never tell the difference.

Those rigid sepal-petals, they reminded him of something.

When a hunger striker was fed, two warders held his legs while a third bore down on the chest. After Aye prised the jaws open with a metal instrument that screwed tight against the gums, he snaked a rubber pipe into the mouth, all the way to the stomach. As he stared at those sepal-petals, Aye remembered this. Not because he ever forgot, but because the storm that was coming was causing even these flowers to lament his role in it.

Inside the pipe was a mix of milk, brandy and maybe an egg. It was enough to keep the prisoners alive for the day, provided they were fed right. Mr Howard had faith in him more than in the Indian jailors. He said Aye had steady fingers, because 'while Indians are born old, the Burman hardly grows old at all.'

When Aye took the pipe and looked down into the cavern of a mouth, it was not unlike looking down into the cave of demons. He had to find the right speed while descending. When the prisoner's eyes became the eyes of a bird lying forked tail to sleek head in his palm, Aye drove the tube inside.

He had learned that if the clamp prising open the jaws was not screwed tight, the prisoner could catch the tube with his teeth, preventing it from penetrating his throat. He had also been told to avoid the lungs. *Aim for the stomach.* With the first prisoner he had force-fed this year, the tube had gone in all the way.

'He has beginner's luck,' one of the warders had said.

There were others, and he had not been lucky with them all. There was the one from just yesterday. His screams had been unlike any wind. Aye had to leave the cell, laying down right outside in the corridor, where other prisoners pleaded with him *let us die with honour* till a warder kicked Aye's stomach and forced him to return. The milk went into the prisoner's lungs and he almost drowned, but the horse doctor came inside and sat on the man's bucking torso and fed the prisoner through the rectum.

The hunger strike still did not end, and Aye waited to learn if he was to blame.

The sepal-petals lining his path began to shudder. He hurried to the creek.

The tall mangrove tree was there, the canoe was not, Loka was not. There were signs of a camp: four bamboo posts with a thatch of reeds and a circle of ashes. As he looked around, there was movement in the aquamarine water, and a bony olive-coloured spine cut through it. Aye slowly backed away. The saltwater crocodile drifted, seeming to break the clouds.

He heard the whistle.

Loka came forward, still dressed in oversized clothes, with three arrows instead of one, and a woven basket on his shoulder. Though he again wore no clay markings, he was covered in grey-coloured earth.

They stared at each other a long time.

'Recognise me,' said Loka.

'I do,' Aye replied, before adding, 'recognise me.'

'I do not.'

Aye blinked, wondering what he ought to have said.

Loka broke into a laugh, and started walking towards the creek.

The canoe was tied to the tree. Aye wondered if the movement in the water was a crocodile or a piece of bark, perhaps even a paddle. Either that, or he was losing his mind.

'Why afraid of crocodile.'

So he had been watching.

They sat not in the canoe but under the thatched reeds in the makeshift camp. Loka built a fire. Inside his basket were shellfish, cuttlefish and a wooden box. Inside the box was a honeycomb. Aye began to salivate, but instead of inviting Aye to eat with him, Loka started to burn the honeycomb.

'Grey earth is for mourning.' Loka pointed to his head. 'When we eat no pork and burn sugar.'

Aye was about to ask what Loka was mourning, but then asked himself if he really wanted to know. Already the letters had involved him in Prisoner 218 D's life. Already he was too involved in *all* the prisoners' lives—the ones he had forced into submission, the ones he had nearly killed. And what was this new emotion he had started to feel around Mr Howard, each time the superintendent talked to him without talking to *him*? Aye was the one who shaved and bathed him. Who knew when he was tired and needed a massage, or when he was hot and needed the palm fan—which Aye waved with the vigour of both his hands—or when he was tense about another lunch with the chief commissioner. Who knew Mr Howard's scent better than that of his own father's. Who ran after him when he dropped his kerchief. Who tidied up his desk. There was nothing he had not done for him. And yet . . . now there was something else.

Loka did not wait to be asked. 'I mourn sister's death,' he said. 'She died separate from bones.'

Should he tell Loka that he had found the skull? *No*, he reminded himself, *do not get involved*. Yet another voice said, *then why here*, and it was not a question.

The honey dripped into the fire with green fury.

He had told no one, till now. 'Mr Howard tells me to tear up letters. He also tells me to feed the hunger strikers.'

Loka did not look up from the honey he was burning.

'Also,' said Aye, 'Mr Howard was not happy with the last two harvests. The caves no longer have good nests, the ones you showed me.'

Loka spat. 'Mr Howard does not help. We spy for him. Small man keeps coming. You do not help.'

Aye did not know what to say, because what Loka said was true.

'Return skull and I give anything,' said Loka. 'One thing only. Then I leave.'

'Where will you go?' asked Aye.

Loka threw an arrow at Aye and Aye ducked. 'Pick up,' said Loka.

Aye noticed that Loka's voice was not as calm as the first time they met. And he had not called him 'friend.'

As the last of the honeycomb sizzled, Aye inspected the arrowhead. It was S-shaped and tied to the wooden shaft by a cord with green feathers.

Aye took a deep breath. 'I cannot bring you the skull.'

Loka plucked something else out from the basket. Not cuttlefish or shellfish but a pile of green leaves and a spattering of what might have been insects.

Then he told Aye a most astonishing story. When his sister had been alive and her husband, too, Loka would go with them to hunt cicada grubs in the forest. Tombowagey, they were called, and roasted on a low fire in a wrapping of leaves. They would tell stories about their ancestors, who fought the outsiders and were free. The wars would not have happened if two entities that should not have come together had stayed apart. Ever since, there were evil winds and spirits that fragmented the world, and more coming.

He folded the leaves around the larvae to make a pouch, pushed a stick through it, and roasted each one. 'We keep smells that bind us.' He handed a stick to Aye, who pulled a smoking bundle off with his teeth. The tombowagey were crunchy and delicious.

Loka said that in Andamanese, there was no word for suicide.

When his sister took her own life, there were no prayers his family could offer the gods, no concept through which to ask for their mercy.

Aye stopped chewing. His appetite had once again vanished.

'The words you give us, evil winds,' continued Loka, folding more tombowagey. 'Guns. Suicide. Rape. Chandu Bhai. Jail. Not in Andamanese.'

'I did not give you these words,' said Aye.

Loka ignored him. 'We become like dugong. Not from water or land. Half turtle, half pig.'

'I did not give you these words,' Aye repeated, loudly.

Loka told Aye to prove it by shooting the arrow he had thrown him, there, at the rat. Aye had not noticed the rat. It was running in and out of the canoe. Aye stood up, bounced the arrow in his palm, turned it around, balanced it on his shoulder. Then he pushed the point through the air. The arrow fell flat in the sand, several feet before the canoe.

'Anything,' said Loka, still without looking up from the fire. 'One thing only.'

Monday, October—

I miss you Api. <u>Did you write to me?</u> They are saying letters are allowed except I do not know. If they were allowed you would write to me. Are you well? Api Umbreen is not well except she keeps saying it. I do not say it except I do not feel well either. I watch films. You remember I enjoy them?

I saw Hunterwali. You remember we were not allowed to watch? They were showing it again so Aunty Hanan took me. She said she wished she had taken you to films instead of other places. She would not explain. Hunterwali has Fearless Nadia. You remember the girl from Australia with my name? I liked Hunterwali a lot especially her mask and cloak! Aunty Hanan said it is only in films that women become popular when they fight back. Also now there are colour films! They are saying Fearless Nadia's blue eyes will show. They used to colour it! They are also saying what will they do now Indian women do not look white but natural.

Api Umbreen told me she told you my engagement is off. Please I do not blame you. I prefer to stay home with Ama. Did you get her letter? When she finally wrote Api Umbreen kept telling her what to say except Ama said 'I'm talking to her with <u>my</u> heart!' I was so happy! I am not telling Api Umbreen I am writing to you except she keeps trying to read over my shoulder.

Maybe I should stop watching so many films except I am not like you. But I am your sister forever. Please write to me.

I love you
Nadia (who is not fearless like you)

The Three Cillians
1937

TODAY, PRISONER 218 D HAD to learn to use a sewing machine. The factory supervisor told her how to thread the reel. 'Round and then up! No, *no*, from right to left! No! Take it *down*! What woman cannot use a sewing machine?'

The supervisor had a young daughter. Between the child's fingers was a piece of thread that also went round and up, right to left.

The prisoner had been sewing with her hands for nearly two years. There were not many machines and she had tried once before. When she failed, her ration of water had been taken away.

'That hook, not this hook!' The supervisor spanked the prisoner's hand before turning her attention to a warder at the far end of the factory.

The prisoner tried to look for landmarks. They appeared on the face of the woman across from her, who smiled when the supervisor's back was turned. Checking quickly to make sure the supervisor was still distracted, the woman illustrated how to thread the reel.

The prisoner smiled back. She would give up her quota of fresh water in return for the woman's kindness. She would say thank you with that cup.

But she still could not thread the reel.

The sewing machine had a hand wheel. It also had lots of little metal plates and secret pockets with small round metal parts that fit here and there.

The supervisor was walking away and her daughter gawked at the woman still trying to help the prisoner, who was to embroider flowers on a stack of hankies. She had been given two spools of thread: yellow and blue. She handed the yellow spool to the child, but the girl ran away.

The prisoner turned the wheel. It was always there, at the back of her mind, the rush of bicycle wheels.

The woman across the table was trying to get her attention, to warn her that the supervisor was coming back. The prisoner unwound the yellow spool of thread. She wrapped it several times around a pin that stuck up from the top of the machine and turned the hand wheel, rapidly, till the needle shot up and down, then she began to flick the thread under the needle as it rose and fell, as if to catch it, this was the way to sew, she decided, and the thread got caught and tangled and there was no other sound in the factory, everyone was watching her, and now her sewing was done so she wrapped the remaining thread entirely around the sewing machine and threw her arms up in victory, the way she had done on her bicycle.

The pain in her shin was severe.

While being dragged back to her cell, she was told she had not sewn a single hanky, had wasted a spool of thread, and nearly damaged a machine. The cost of the thread would have to come from the supervisor's pocket. The prisoner would not be given fresh water for the next forty-eight hours. The woman who had tried to help her would forfeit the same. If the prisoner failed again tomorrow, both of them would be put in bar fetters. It was up to Prisoner 218 D to save them all.

Through the grate and into the dark sky she goes.

It rains all the time now, without cease. The ceiling leaks and she moves her bed between the drops but still they fall on her. If the rain slows to a patter, the word for it is rimjhim, one of her father's favourite words. He would listen to the gentle rhythm of raindrops outside his bedroom window, tapping his right forefinger on his left knee, and ask how a single word could mirror the cadence of a single occasion so precisely.

She does not know if these are memories or dreams, but how alive she feels when they visit her! Rimjhim. She has dug deep into the pit of her hollow stomach to find it, the word she would give, if brought paper and pencil again. Rimjhim. A word that means exactly what it is and nothing more, or less.

In her dream-memory, other words returned. She was riding a bicycle (*the* bicycle), dressed in a moss-green top with a silver pattern in the weave. As she pedalled past the neem trees outside her house, the sun cast a mottled mosaic on her cheek. When she saw a girl ride towards her, she dropped one foot down and came to a stop. The filigree shadow of leaves no longer kissed her face, Kaajal did, and when the flush left her cheek, an immense tranquillity filled its place.

'Peace,' said Kaajal, 'I am learning through observing you, is a jewel buried deep in the earth. It is best reflected when left alone.'

Both their bicycles were black and rusted, with hard, narrow seats, so they usually rode standing up. The bicycles looked no different from any others, so as not to draw attention. The prisoner had not yet been enlisted. They were on their way to the picket line, so Kaajal could show her why it was important to enlist.

As they pedalled, the prisoner recalled the first day she had noticed Kaajal. An Englishwoman, the wife of an official, was to visit their school. The girls were told to prepare a plan of welcome. There was a greeting they each had to recite, carrying a basket of marigolds and roses, and as the visitor strolled down the school grounds, the girls were to kneel in unison and scatter flowers at her feet.

On the day of the visit, three girls refused to kneel. It was the first time it occurred to the prisoner who was not yet a prisoner that she, too, did not have to kneel, or scatter flowers, but she had done both.

When the visit was over, the three girls were caned at the front of the class by their teacher, Miss Flora Sparks, who was well liked. She had a Cadbury's poster in the teacher's room with two vertical rows of five chocolate bars. She would often eat Dairy Milk. However, for the prisoner who was not yet a prisoner, it was the red wrapper at the bottom of the second row that was most enticing. Miss Flora seemed to know this. For her birthday one year, Miss Flora gave her a whole bar of Cadbury's Plain.

Miss Flora was done caning the first two girls and began on the third. She wore a long skirt and was sweating across her back. Till today, she was perfect Miss Flora Sparks, the one with Bournville chocolate and slender hips.

The first two girls who were caned were examining their burns and crying. The third one, who started it all, she did not cry, not today and not on her last day either. Miss Flora struck her with zeal, but the girl looked around the room to let everyone know that she considered herself worthy of being a match. Her name was Kaajal.

Cillian was here, the prisoner could smell the smoke. She had started dreaming that at night, he came into her cell.

Cillian was here, and it was daytime. Watching from outside the cell. His stomach spilled over his belt. He took off the belt and held it in the same hand that held the truncheon. The other hand held the cigar and unbolted the door.

As it was morning, doors were slamming.

She was to call him 'Bara Baba.' She was to say, 'Good morning, Bara Baba.'

But she did not.

'What made you do it?'

Still she did not speak.

He cracked the belt against the floor. She was a harridan imprisoned for life and would die a crone, he said. A paunch made of words.

The sweeper crouched beside Cillian, sweeping his dirty rag over her legs. The rag was not unlike the one she used each month. She had to rinse it with saltwater in the morning, when bathing. The women were given only two rags, one for the day, one for the night, both made of a coarse, thick fibre that cut the skin. When the sweeper swept his dirty rag between her legs she was wearing a dirty rag and now he knew it and so did Cillian. She tried to cover herself with her uniform as the men grimaced in disgust.

•

Cillian was here, with new shoes. Brown and soft looking. There had been specks of wet vomit on the hard, black toes of the others. She rocked herself under the grate. Thunder outside. No rimjhim, not now. The first poem she recited by heart had been during a thunderstorm. It would come, this dream-memory, when Cillian was gone.

'What made you do it?' He smacked the truncheon against the wall.

Today she understood the worthlessness of the question. *What made you do it?* She had been asked it also after her arrest. Like Cillian, they were looking for one day, one event, one insult, one man, one woman. She knew only that the answer was made up of as many parts as the rain, and older than her by too many years.

When Cillian used her pisspot, she tried not to look.

Cillian was here, and had a pink penis. Shook it over the pisspot, still holding the cigar. Today she did not look away from the first penis she had ever seen. Small and mouse-like. A truncheon, a cigar, a penis. The Three Cillians.

There were rules at the jail. She could not use the pisspot at night because then it would overflow and the sweeper would not empty it till after breakfast the next day. She had heard that men would go down on their knees to beg the sweeper to let them piss outside. Cillian forbade it, but the sweeper had his favourites. She did not dare become a favourite.

When Cillian used her little pisspot, he was using the last space she had been saving, and now it overflowed.

When it was not piss but sickness that made her need to go at night, she used the floor. 'What the devil have you done?' Cillian would say in the morning. *'Punish her now, Jamadar! Do not reserve for the morrow what can be dealt with today!'* His favourite words, over and over again. She would hold out her hand but the sweeper did not use the cane. He slapped her cheek, first one, then the other.

Today she had not been sick on the floor. And she dreaded the factory less. She had been using the sewing machine with some success.

She had found a tiny bit of soap, and when the time was right, she would give this gift to the woman who had tried to help her thread the reel. It would be better than a cup of water, or even Bournville chocolate.

Her food sat untouched. As Cillian zipped up, the sweeper said, 'Eat!' She did not know where the woman warder had gone. It was now Cillian who walked her to the saltwater tank, the sweeper cowering behind him.

'Whore!' said Cillian.

'Whore!' said the sweeper.

'Murderer!' said both.

They watched the women bathe.

At night, she had stopped covering her ears. Underneath the sound of doors being opened at an hour when they were not meant to be was a different sound. Bicycle wheels. If she could hold onto this, for a few seconds at least, the other sounds would recede. A dream-memory would come.

It was the same day Kaajal took her to the picket line for the first time. When a factory lorry transporting strikebreakers was blocked, they were both part of the blockade. The lorry kept going, crushing everyone in its path. A man pushed Kaajal and the prisoner who was not yet a prisoner aside. Girls should not put their bodies at risk, he said.

The lorry severed a boy as it trudged ahead. One foot bent all the way back to his leg, while the other snapped sideways. Somehow, his slippers stayed on his feet. A crowd gathered around to pull the slippers off, or straighten his feet, or do something to make him less grotesque. But they could not. On the foot warped sideways, the bones of his big toe and second toe had fastened around the rubber strap like jaws, while the foot that bowed backwards stuck to the slipper like an iron to a burned shirt.

The boy looked her age, fifteen or so. Four other people were crushed to death. Those who stayed to pull them from the debris, to give them a proper burial, were arrested. 'They will be tortured for information,' said Kaajal.

As they walked their bicycles up a hill, Kaajal said nothing more
for a while. Then, slowly, she began to speak of Mahatma Gandhi. Ten
years ago, when he had called off the non-cooperation movement, she
said, it was because some of its members had turned violent. But there
was only one privilege the conquered had over those who conquered
them. The privilege of outrage. By calling the movement off, Gandhi
had denied Indians their only advantage, forcing them to claim it
any way they could. 'Did you see the lorry driver's face? Why was *he*
angry? He thinks he has the right to be, but he does not. Did you see
the poor boy's feet? They were angry. They had every right to be.'

The prisoner who was not yet a prisoner knew she would never
forget the feet.

'My father says he senses anger in me,' Kaajal was saying, 'but I
am no different from him. He tells me, "Anger isn't ladylike." But like
which lady? I don't know any ladies who aren't angry.' When the prisoner who was not yet a prisoner looked up, Kaajal whispered, 'Except
you.'

After a while, Kaajal added, 'Do you know that in Bengal, there
are fitness clubs run by Japanese who teach Indian boys jujitsu? The
boys also learn to drive cars, ride horses and use weapons. They say
change will come through the body.'

'Weapons?'

'Yes. According to Gandhi, *the female sex is not the weaker sex, it is
the nobler of the two, for it is the embodiment of sacrifice and silent suffering.*' The words so disgusted her that she began to stomp up the hill.
'Silent suffering is the only change to come through a girl's body. But
what happens to her then? Her anger turns to sorrow. Sorrow sinks
to the bottom, but anger rises to the top. I like anger,' she decided. 'It
wakes me up, as a friend should.'

Cillian was here, in the factory. Pouring her second cup of water
onto the floor. She was allowed only two cups, and could not sew hankies after all. Once again, they had terrible trim. It went across the
square of linen and the linen bunched up. The flowers she embroi-
dered looked like rats had eaten them, Cillian said. She had wasted

thread. She had wasted linen. Because of her, Cillian came to the factory, to taunt the prisoners as well as the women who supervised them.

The prisoner was put at the loom. When she failed at this too, she was put at the grinding stone. The stone was out in the courtyard, close to where the clothes were washed. The sunlight burned the prisoner's shorn head as she put all her weight into dragging that mighty pestle across the stone. Back in her cell, she barely used the pisspot, and when she did, the colour was tangerine.

If her memories once rooted her, they no longer did. She was forging someone's signature on a check. She was stealing her mother's ruby necklace, the one that had belonged to her grandmother. She was raising funds. She was at the Lahore train station, with her father. It was years before his death, and he held her close. A crowd was hitting a man for bumping into an English woman. The platform was full. It seemed impossible to avoid jostling one another. Yet, a cushion of space opened around the woman as the men walked over each other to avoid brushing against her. Her father was too afraid to look up. Her proud father, afraid! Then Cillian arrived. '*Punish him, Jamadar! Do not reserve for the morrow what can be dealt with today!*' The man being beaten was her father. When they were done with him, they came for her.

In the morning, her body hung from all sides, as though it belonged to someone else. And she burned, inside.

Maybe it was not Cillian who came at night but one of the other guards.

Or the sweeper.

No, the nurse.

The horse doctor.

The supervisor at the Female Factory.

The superintendent.

The boy who passed her cell like a cat.

No, it was Cillian, all three of them! All!

They took her to the hospital.

She would not stop kicking.

She would not go to the Female Factory.

She would not lick her torn fingers to twirl the thread to push it through the eye of the needle.

She would not sew or pound grains.

She would not bathe.

She would not use the pisspot.

She would not eat.

When more prisoners joined the hunger strike, she was already with them.

It was the one thing, the last thing, she would do with her body.

Hers.

Muhammad's Web 2
1937

IT WAS NOMI'S FAULT THE prisoner had been put at the grinding stone. Four days ago, Nomi's mother had tried to teach the prisoner how to use a sewing machine. 'Round and then up!' she said, before walking away. The prisoner would not listen. She wasted thread. A whole spool of it, bright yellow in colour, like the eyes of a startled owl. Nomi did not want her mother to pay for it. Besides, hiding the truth was also lying, and she had already lied about going up Mount Top, stealing the lady's gown, and saying the Lord's Prayer. So when the prisoner tried to give her the yellow thread, she ran to tell her mother.

The prisoner was taken away, and now she was back and out in the courtyard, looking very ill.

Nomi could count her ribs. They showed through the uniform, a torn white shirt with blue stripes and torn pyjamas with brown stains. When the prisoner put her weight to the stone, her back curved like Nomi's father's. The other women were also thin, but not this thin. Nomi's mother and Aunty Madhu talked about it, the number of days a prisoner could go without being force-fed, while still being forced to work. When the prisoner leaned into the stone, sweat from her shorn head dripped onto the grain she ground.

Nomi came back inside. She curled on the floor, beneath the table with the sewing machines. Everything in the factory looked different from this angle. The flicker of pink on the spider web across one window looked a little green, like the colour bouncing off her mother's keys, as they dangled from her belt. Nomi shut her eyes. She pictured the painting of Christ at school, the one with beautiful feet. His stomach was pulled in. She could count the ribs.

At first, she thought it was rain drumming on the table with the sewing machines above her head. Then she heard her mother's voice, and quickening footsteps. The prisoners were making no effort to speak in whispers. 'Enough!' they said. 'Have mercy!'

There were male guards, and the nurse Miss Mattie was here, too, with the man at the lake. They were carrying away the prisoner, whose forehead was bleeding.

Through the commotion she could hear the man with Miss Mattie tell her mother to come with them to the hospital. 'We need women guards with women inmates!' the man insisted. 'Bring your child if necessary.' So Nomi followed her mother out of the factory and into the starfish jail.

She had never been inside before. When she passed the courtyard where men were turning the mill, she knew why her father's back was bent. The flogging frame stood at the centre, like a giant bird-sling. They entered a corridor where manacles knocked on the bars of cells and the prisoners began to chant, 'Long Live the Revolution!' She started running through the noise, and all the time the nurse and her mother were carrying the prisoner. When they climbed some steps, there was Cillian, at the top of the landing, with the sweeper. And now they were all going down another staircase.

At the hospital ward, Aye and the superintendent, Mr Howard, were waiting. 'You shouldn't be here,' said Aye to Nomi. She was told to wait outside, with two male guards, while her mother went inside.

The guards frightened her.

After a while, she began to notice things. In the left corner, just above the door, sprawled a spider with long legs. For knuckles it had small yellow points and tinier dots were sprinkled all across a body so blue it was almost black. The face looked grumpy.

She poked her head inside. Prisoner 218 D lay in bed as the nurse explained what was happening to her starving body. The superintendent looked grumpy.

She came back outside, to watch the spider spin a home that was circular and kept growing.

Her mother spent more time at the hospital than the factory. At night, her parents argued about where to leave Nomi.

'It is bad enough that you must work because of my health,' whispered her father. 'The factory I will accept. Not the jail.'

Her mother was unusually quiet.

'Tell me again. Why?'

'I already told you,' she said. 'There are not enough women guards.'

'What happened to the last one?'

'She got sick.'

'And so will you. It isn't safe.'

'Do you think I *want* this? Who will feed us?'

'Leave her here,' her father insisted, 'with her brother.'

'He must study.'

'She is not even eating properly.'

'Why don't you stop going to the store? Why don't you keep her?'

They fought because of her, and Nomi was sorry.

At the hospital, Miss Mattie said, 'This is no place for you.'

Nomi again walked down the corridor outside the ward. There were spiders all along the iron railing. They sometimes lost one or two limbs, perhaps in a fight. Spiders could live without all their legs. She wondered what kind of spider had saved the Prophet Muhammad when he travelled to Medina. She had not yet seen a web big enough to cover the entrance to the jail, but a single spider had been making a web all the way from a branch of a tree to the railing. In that space between the branch and the railing hovered the zigzag design the spider scratched, always with legs in pairs, so it looked like there were only four legs, in the pattern of an X. When she came near, the spider hid behind a hole in the centre of the X. When her mother came near, the sun reflecting off the web also reflected off the keys jangling from the belt around her waist.

It was happening now. Her mother was standing by the door and the light was bouncing across the corridor. Miss Mattie was inside with her boyfriend. Her mother started to pace. She was nervous.

Mr Howard rushed past them, Aye in tow. 'This is no place for you,' Aye said, before going inside.

When the prisoner started screaming, Nomi's mother covered her ears.

She did not go to school the next day, or the next, and her father stayed with her and did not go to the store. What were they doing to the prisoner to make her sound like that? Inside the cradle of his arms, inside the X, she wondered if they had done the same to him.

On the fifth night after Nomi stopped going to school, Aye came to their hut. He wanted her to come outside. Their mother raised one eyebrow. Zee was to go with Nomi, she said. 'It is just outside,' said Zee, irritated. He was sprawled on the floor with a book, a pencil and a ruler. He had stood first in all the trigonometry tests meant for older boys, and Mr Campbell said that, to keep advancing, Zee ought to create his own tests. Zee was drawing triangles and asking questions of himself.

'I will take Priya,' Nomi said.

'Keep the door open,' said their mother.

Aye had a gift for Nomi. A bird. It was green and very light, because it was made of bamboo. He had been whittling for some time, he said. The tail was paper-thin and curled at the top. He hoped she liked it, even if Priya's tail was different. He stroked the hen gently and she clucked.

The bamboo figure was less like Priya and more like the little bird that ran on the ground, the one whose nests were too exposed. Though, that bird had no tail at all.

'You should stay away from the hospital,' said Aye. 'It isn't right.'

In later years, on a day when her brother was not there, not only for the moment when she stepped out the door and not only for the hours he spent testing himself, but was not there for all the life she had still to live, on that day, she would look back at this moment and though it would not be enough and nothing ever would be, she would think, *thank you.*

But on this night, her thoughts were elsewhere. As though aware, even then, that the children too were entangled and implicated in the many Criminal Lines they could scarcely understand, she whispered, 'It's my fault.'

'What is?'

She pulled him to herself, and they stayed this way for a time— Aye, Priya (placid) and Nomi. Then, she did not know why the idea came to her, but it did. She remembered the sun flickering pink and green on the web, on the silver jangling from a belt. She said, 'Mama has the keys.'

The Clay of the Physical Body
1937–38

TELEGRAMS TO MR HOWARD CONTINUED to litter his bedroom floor, warning him that, on the mainland, protests on behalf of the political prisoners were escalating. The public was no longer interested in hearing that conditions in the Andaman jail were 'satisfactory' and 'mosquito-free'. If this were so, why were three-fourths of the political prisoners on a hunger strike? Why had prisoners in India joined them? And if the island was indeed a paradise, why not shift the capital from Delhi to the Andamans?

When Aye arrived in his bedroom one morning, Mr Howard, twisting his pyjama top to locate an itch, was thinking of a Sunday at home with his father.

The year was 1913 and his father was reading a newspaper. Suffragettes were on a hunger strike. There was one who had been force-fed two hundred and thirty-two times. *'They had got me on the bed, holding me by the ankles, knees, and shoulders . . . I set my teeth like a vice and my breath came so quickly I felt I should suffocate.'* His father read the words aloud, doubted they were true, and concluded, 'If they think they are men, let them be treated as such.'

Nearly twenty-five years had passed yet wiser words were never spoken.

Mr Howard was ready to tackle Prisoner 218 D himself. Today, he told Aye, he would forego the bath and the shave.

When he arrived at the hospital, Mattie, the nurse, stood at the head of the prisoner's bed, reluctant to make way for the superintendent. The deputy commissioner, Mr Martin, now engaged to the nurse, hovered close by. Mr Howard told Aye to shut the door, and Aye did as he was told.

'Sir, the prisoner is unwell,' the nurse pleaded.

'Nonsense,' said Mr Howard. 'I hope you do not find yourself attached. They are dangerous, and have a hatred of us.'

Mr Martin tried too. 'I am confident the prisoner can be persuaded through,' he hesitated, 'other means.'

Mr Howard looked from the nurse to the deputy commissioner. He thought it a pity that Martin's time on the island had not changed him, yet it was the same gullibility that allowed a superintendent to speak with a deputy commissioner this way.

'You are aware of the furore on the mainland?' asked Mr Howard.

Mr Martin nodded very slightly.

'The public and the press, both. They have found out about the strike.'

'Prisoners on the mainland too,' muttered Mr Martin. 'Upwards of two hundred.'

'As I am aware. If you ask me, we brought this on ourselves. These are terrorists to whom we gift books and letters.'

Mr Martin looked down at Prisoner 218 D.

'She ought to have been flogged,' said Mr Howard, 'not given a bed.'

'We are far more respectable than this,' said Mr Martin. 'We cannot afford to lose face now, not with the whole country campaigning against us. It is our superior principles that make us who we are.'

'Listen to me. When this is all over, no one will even remember her. They make a lot of noise about "our women" and "our honour," but have you seen how they treat them? Wife-burning and child marriages and slavish dowries and off-with-her-head if a girl so much as looks at a man. For all intents and purposes, your prisoner was already tainted when she was born. If the public is foolish enough to think of her, they will make believe she died in a jail on the mainland, with all the other girls who should have come here.'

Mr Howard summoned the guards. He moved to the head of the hospital bed.

His fingers pried open the mouth of Prisoner 218 D. He had never stuck his hand inside a woman's mouth before. It was hot and slimy and her tongue started to move. As the guards held her, she snapped her jaws like a dog. The guards held her more forcibly. He quickly fastened the steel vice against her gums. His fingers were coated in saliva. He heard a crack. She started kicking. He told Aye to help the guards hold her. He turned the screw. It forced her jaws further apart. He could insert the tube. He did not have Aye's touch, this he knew. As he pushed deeper inside, he could feel the muscles of her throat contract. Her tongue flapped. Somehow this creature who weighed scarcely seventy-five pounds fought with the will of two wrestlers. She started to choke. Blood covered his fist. He tossed aside the tooth he had broken. When it came, her breath was short and rapid and again that heat.

When he pulled out, she was sick all over the bed.

'The same time tomorrow,' said Mr Howard, also breathing fast, 'and every day it takes.'

After mopping his brow, he hurled his kerchief to Aye, doubled up on the floor.

New Year's Eve. The sea glittered.

On Ross Island, at the chief commissioner's house, the settlers were gathered, together with their relatives and friends from across the globe. The hollow walls and peculiar echoes of the old, two-storied mansion were tonight filled with laughter, champagne and a feast never before served in the tropics. Or so the guests said.

It began with calf tail soup, chestnut balls and curried turtle eggs (prized by the Andamanese), followed by stewed eels, stewed Chittagong fowl (from a local farm), pickled pork (ditto), Turbot a la Reine and a saddle of mutton with Breton sauce. For dessert, there were speciality chocolates and bombe glacée. Brandied mangoes and coconut pudding. Banana fritters and baked custard.

Waiters cooled and served the drinks. In addition to champagne and gimlets, there were cocktails with fanciful names.

Commander-in-Chief. East India Punch. Jarawa Joy. The waiters—
Local Born children and settled convicts—were dressed in a white
jacket, a length of dark red cloth coiled tight about the hip and a turban of salmon pink. Tucked behind the ear or in the folds of the turban was a white frangipani flower. 'A murderer makes a first-class table
servant,' observed one guest.

The mansion was still ablaze with Christmas celebrations. Red,
white and blue lights draped the mango and casuarina trees, and the
hibiscus bushes were crowned with threads of tinsel. Beneath the
bushes were strewn gaily coloured Christmas crackers.

When the meal ended and the visitors dispersed, Aye and Mr
Howard watched from the balcony as, down on the lawn, the giddiest
guests started to pull apart the crackers. Mr Martin and the nurse were
among them. Her hair was loose and her dress was a moonbeam. Mr
Martin's shadow bent towards hers in a kiss.

Though Japan had swept across China, Mr Howard told Aye,
the war was far away. The chief commissioner had seen no reason to
dampen festivities on the island, and he tended to agree. He asked Aye
for his third Jarawa Joy. Aye disappeared through the half-door leading
to the kitchen, and when he returned, Mr Howard was examining the
chief commissioner's wife and her considerably younger American
suitors. She was dressed in a tight red dress lined in black-and-white
marabou.

'She matches the waiters,' Mr Howard chuckled, elbowing Aye.
'She matches you. Why so glum?'

'I am not glum, sir.' Aye adjusted his turban to make sure the frangipani was still secure.

'With her long neck and large feet, she could pass for a stork, eh?
Someone ought to tell her it's New Year's, not Halloween.' He chuckled again.

There was music inside; couples began to dance.

Mr Howard headed for the swimming pool, Aye behind him.

'Do you remember, I taught you to swim here?'

'I do, sir.'

'How old were you then?'

'Nine or ten, sir.'

'You were scared. Kicking like a girl, and pissing like one, too. I did not watch from the sidelines. I jumped in. Who else would have done that?'

As their reflection painted the water, Aye was silent.

'I do the same every day, don't I?'

'Yes, sir.'

'Are you my Trusty?'

'Yes, sir.'

'Good. Let's have a drink.'

'I'll get it, sir.'

'No, not you.' Mr Howard snapped his fingers at another boy. 'Two Commanders-in-Chief!'

'Right away, sir.'

'Why are you shivering, boy, it isn't cold.' When Aye's teeth kept chattering, Mr Howard patted his back. 'Chin up. Higher.'

Aye raised his head.

Ahead, the trees drew spells in their sleep. When he first came here, said Mr Howard, on nights such as this, he believed himself to have washed up on a chain of dreaming islands, all glassy bays and whispering surf. Our lovely lost world, he had called it. 'As though there was something here that caused the clay of the physical body to glow.' Though there was much still to be done, one had to remember that a lot had been accomplished already. 'After all, it is men like me who make dreaming islands real.'

Experiments with a Ghost
1937–38

MR HOWARD CAME TO THE hospital daily to feed her, while Aye stood by the door, wondering which was worse: watching, or doing it himself. Sooner or later, it was possible that Mr Howard would toss her to him, like a kerchief.

Then what?

The way she looked at him. The way she had looked at him the day she got off the ship.

And this man had a peculiar name, the wind seemed to be calling it, Aoi! Aoi!

Aunty Hanan's words to the prisoner had become the incantation Aye repeated each night, after another day at the hospital, as he tried in vain to fall asleep.

If that strange long-haired boy in the pointy boat keeps heading for the island, it is the wrong choice; but retreating is not the right one either.

What was he meant to do?

He lay in his cot, listening to the cicadas outside, wondering if Loka was hunting them. Tombowagey. How delicious they were, roasted on a low flame.

At the hospital, before Mr Howard arrived, the nurse tried to explain to the prisoner what happened to a starving body. If in good health, it could survive six or seven weeks. 'But your health was poor to begin with, and Mr Howard is not to let a single hunger striker die.' Mattie looked nervously at Aye, who stood by the door, waiting nervously for Mr Howard. 'Have the hunger pangs ceased?' the nurse kept on. 'It means your body is feeding on muscle, even the muscles of your heart. It means your vital organs are under attack. You can stop that. Here, smell this.' She brought to the prisoner's nose a plate of chicken and gravy.

The prisoner tried to speak.

'Stop whispering. Do you know where they send the insane?'

Mostly, the prisoner slept. She felt very cold. Her lips bled. Aye had seen it before, with the other protesters. The blood and saliva that stained Mr Howard's fist each time he pushed into her were her last protest. They came from somewhere beyond her small and broken body, these fluids that spoke of life, and soon, even they would stop speaking.

Inside the hut, Aye could hear his mother and grandfather asleep beside him. His father had not come inside. He was probably stationed on his usual rock, muttering to himself.

Aye stepped outside. There was a steady drizzle, and his father was looking up at the clouds that folded and unfolded like supplicant monks.

Though Aye had not tried to speak with his father in some years, now he sat beside the man on the rock who continued inspecting the sky. His father's body seemed unable to distinguish between rain and shine. Perhaps, thought Aye, when you were already this sick, there was no getting any sicker.

'How are you?' asked Aye, before adding, 'Ah-pay?'

Of course, there was no reply.

Aye looked at the cheeks he had never shaved. The hair he had never washed. There was a stench coming off him that was not lavender. He wondered what the flesh looked like, underneath the shirt that had not been changed in many weeks. When his mother tried to take it off, sometimes his father capitulated, other times he rolled in the dirt. She was the only one who still touched him. Sometimes, she even succeeded in cutting his nails, though, lately, not the fingernails. They were an inch long. The feet were surprisingly fine, long and with high arches, like Aye's. No doubt he too could have been taught to descend into the heart of the island, to hunt nests. Instead, he had not been taught very much. And perhaps it was just as well, for what had his son been taught, and what had any of the Local Borns been taught, except to obey. In a sense, his father's madness was a kind of protest, saving him from having to do anything at all.

Though his mother and grandfather avoided speaking of the pharmaceutical trials, Aye was certain that for them, too, the act of memory must have fused with breathing.

They were meant to involve one thousand convicts, and to cease afterwards. So the prisoners had been told. But the experiments continued, in secret. The colony's administrators had called the new drug cinchona alkaloid and, finding it advantageous in the fight against malaria, began to include in their experiments even the children and grandchildren of convicts. In the case of Aye's family, only grandchildren. By some peculiar stroke of luck construed from papers that might have resembled the pattern of untold accidents and disappearances scattered across Mr Howard's desk and floor, the experiments were not conducted on Aye's great-grandfather, nor even on his grandfather, but on Aye's father and other second-generation Local Borns. And this group was given increasingly higher doses of the drug that was also called quinine.

First came the chills, accompanied by vomiting. Soon after, the urine turned black. Others in the group suffered identical symptoms and died. Aye's father alone survived, though doctors could not understand how. Nor could they call it a recovery. He was mumbling to himself even at his wedding. When Aye the miracle baby was born, it might have been the only time his parents came together.

Aye's mother had taught him about spirits called nats. There were good and bad nats. When younger, he had believed his father to be possessed by a bad nat, his mother, a good one. He still had no other explanation for her kindness, the way she tended to a husband who never returned her love or offered a single word of thanks. Equally, Aye did not understand his own feelings. When he thought of the experiments, he had no words for what happened to his own body. A fury consumed him, but not only that. A hunger consumed him too, the hunger to know why—why was his father's body satiated with pain, returned yet not returned? What had he been like before—did he laugh? Did he love? Did he know what he had lost?

Aye had spent many nights picturing his great-grandfather on the first prison ship. As the oldest prisoner to survive these rocks, he had become a legend, and Aye's father was the legend's grandson. But how their bodies had been broken! A tattoo had been inked on his great-grandfather's forehead, made by an illiterate woman who had known neither his crime, nor the place from where he had been shipped. It had read:

Tiff

A P

His great-grandfather used to say that he could still smell the woman's breath as she bent over him on the ship, carving his raw flesh with a hot copper needle and blue ink. The godna, or penal identity, was meant to read *thief*. He had not wanted to die in its shadow and had tried to remove it with island roots, but the potions had brought blisters and high fevers. In the proper light, when the fevers passed, there remained the scars of a tell-tale error, a trace of shame.

Aye sat beside his father tonight, picturing two different needles pierce the flesh of two different men, each of his own blood, each affixed with a character that was not his. Though, when he looked again at his father—you are not *crazy*, he wanted to say—the needle was shaped like a rubber tube.

He tried to chase the image away. Though he did not know what he felt about all he had lost, there were things he did know that he could keep.

He did know that Mr Howard had held him when he taught him how to swim, and his own father had never held him. He did know that Mr Howard occasionally talked to him. For instance, when Aye finally began to kick in the pool, the superintendent had said, 'The Burman has splendid legs and feet but his chest and arms are pitiable.' He did know what Mr Howard ate, and where. He did know when

Mr Howard was distressed, and why. He did know who wrote to Mr Howard, and to whom he did not write back. He did know who liked Mr Howard, and who did not. The deputy commissioner did not. The nurse did not. Perhaps even the trusted guard did not. But Aye did.

He knew Mr Howard better than his own family.

Aye walked to the tree at the foot of which his grandfather stored bamboo sticks and two carving knives. Nearby was a muddy cane basket. He gathered these things, then returned to his father.

The clouds were beginning to disperse and the raindrops slowed. Soon, the sun would rise and boys would come out to play before heading for school. ('The Burman is a gentleman till he goes to school and sometimes even afterwards,' he could hear Mr Howard say.) If it was 'kick the basket,' Aye occasionally joined them. While they stood in a circle, one boy balanced the cane basket on his knee, instep, or toe-tops, before kicking it. There were no sides or points, no winning or losing. There was only one rule: hands could be used only to pick the basket off the ground, but not to catch or pass it. The game did not exercise the arms, and the best part was the kick. (Mr Howard had supposed it was why Burman arms were pitiable, and their legs splendid.)

'Have you ever played, Ah-pay?' asked Aye.

The man on the rock was looking down at the longyi covering his knees. The cloth was torn.

Aye picked up the basket. He dropped to one knee and spread his arms. He angled the basket into the air with his free foot. It was a beautiful kick, because it was soft. Only pitiable players kicked hard. His father did not look up. Aye picked up the basket again and dropped to the other knee. He spread his arms wider, embracing the air between them. This time, he tipped the basket with his chin. Still his father did not look up. He picked up the basket a third time, held the whole world in his arms, tipped it with his forehead. And on, till he had used every part of the body that was his to use.

When he was done, he lay down in the dirt. '*Nay kaung lar?*' he asked. 'Are you well?' When there was no answer, he added, 'What should I do?'

The next day, when Mr Howard was again at the chief commissioner's, Aye opened the cabinet in the study. He took out the skull. He held it in his palm. He was surprised to discover that it did not frighten or even repel him. How many bones had he already touched when he walked on the sea bed of broken coral, or stole nests with shattered shells? These bones were dry to the touch and rough like sand. The teeth were large. It was only when running his finger across their edges that a slight shiver coursed up his spine. He wanted to look through the huge eye sockets but this, he decided, was a risk. A bad nat might look back at him. He folded both palms over the round cranium. The feeling was close and warm, like holding a child to himself, like wanting to be held.

When Aye's great-grandfather first came to these shores on the *Darya-e-Noor* in 1858, he had been told it was to a place where men and women would forever be separated from every possession held dear. But what was left of the living with the death of the past? The ship had been the bridge between the living and the dead. She was both a bad and a good nat, tearing him from one world and guiding him to the next. Afterwards, she had disappeared, to herself become a ghost.

The longer Aye cupped the cranium in his hands, the more he understood why he had been saving the prisoner's letters. It was as though through them he had found a few scraps of a disappeared world, even a disappeared father. This man whose bones he held— his life, his spirit, it had to rebone itself. The letters and bones were a link to a lost world for a people who were lost. In his hands, the people were somehow linked.

Yet, he reminded himself, as he put the skull back in the cabinet. He was Mr Howard's Trusty.

What should he do?

The next evening, it was Nomi who gave him an answer, though Loka might say he gave one first.

Aye came to her hut with the gift he had been whittling. The bird with the curly, paper-thin tail. The one with his grandfather's flourish. He had never seen a hen like it, but hoped she would find that this did not make it wrong.

'You should stay away from the hospital,' he said, when Nomi came outside.

She held the bamboo bird in one hand, the real bird in the other. She held Aye.

Then she told him about the thread, about the prisoner being kicked and punished and put at the grinding stone and dragged away to the hospital. What were they doing to her? she wanted to know, and before he knew how to answer, she blurted, 'Mama has the keys.'

How could it occur to her, when it had never occurred to him? Though, hadn't it? Hadn't he known for some time now that he could do something? He could be a bad nat who became a good nat.

Soon, the prisoner would leave the hospital for her cell. She would continue being fed by Mr Howard, the horse doctor and, eventually, by Aye. In the cell, she would not have the nurse's care or watch. At night, she would be left to Cillian and the sweeper. She would either die or be sent to Haddo, this prisoner who once had a name, who once had a family. He knew. He read her letters.

There was someone he could ask. Someone who knew this island better than anyone else. Someone he had already told. Someone who had already told him: anything, any one thing, in return for a loved one's bones.

'Go back inside,' he told Nomi, and she did, not knowing that in return for the rude shape of a bamboo figurine in her hands, she had left him with an answer bearing a whole new set of questions, including the one she would ask him herself.

Aye turned away from her hut and started walking back home. Behind him, and ahead, moaned a wind he could not name.

New Year's Eve. The sea glittered. At the chief commissioner's party, Mr Howard had collapsed on a sofa on the balcony in a deep and drunken sleep. His guard, Balaraj, pursued the daughter of one of the waiters, and had also been drinking. Aye left the party without being seen, to enter the superintendent's villa through the study window. After taking the skull, he hid it behind a tree. He then returned to the chief commissioner's house, helped Mr Howard back to his home, up the stairs to his bedroom, removed his shoes, slipped off his shirt and trousers, slipped on his pyjamas, switched off the light.

An hour later, he and Loka stood outside the jail.

Aye had never entered it without being told to. What he was about to do could lock him inside forever. The stars illuminated the metal decorating the exterior wall. There were iron manacles and arm bands of every size, including his own. The heavy shackles for the feet—*his* feet—seemed to sidle up the wall like monitor lizards. The bayonets swivelled in his direction. If the guard in the watchtower was looking his way, it would be his last free night.

Never before had he thought of himself as free.

He glanced up at the three levels of the jail. The prisoner would not be in her cell; she was still in the hospital. Though Miss Mattie watched over her, tonight she was still at the party, as was the horse doctor. Aye would have to climb up to the second floor, hoping it was not during Cillian's shift, then creep to the corridor's end before sliding down to the mezzanine level, in order to get to the hospital.

He was a climber, though. Perhaps this was why he had been scaling cliffs in search of nests. He was about to steal something bigger now, but the ascent would be easier. His feet would comfortably sink between bricks, finding only the inclines that supported his weight. The guards would be nothing compared to the demons that circled him in those caves.

Gathering his strength, he waited for the sign. Loka had said he would climb first. As he waited, Aye was thankful that he did not have to involve Nomi. Loka had been confident that he would not need her mother's keys, though had not explained why. Aye wondered what was taking Loka so long. He thought he could hear voices. Laughter, even. No, it was only Loka, giving him the sign. He was singing like a cicada.

Aye walked through the gate.

Goodbye, Friend
1942

AYE LOOKED AT ZEE, asleep beside him after his first swimming lesson. The two friends had split between them the half-green sari that smelled of old newspapers. Each wore their quarter piece as a skirt. Their bodies had still not dried completely and it was cold in the forest behind Haddo's sugarcane field, where Japanese troops were headquartered. Zee was hiding from a world he had to know could not be hidden from. His teeth chattered as he dreamed. Aye put an arm around him.

Should he tell Zee that he had once been given a gift, expansive and beautiful, of being able to show kindness? He had seen too much else, up at the jail. He could not watch more prisoners die. Nor could he force them to live, not through a feeding tube. So he used the gift he had been given to help Prisoner 218 D escape, but this, it turned out, was also wrong. Had he saved the gift for tonight, Zee would live.

Nomi would ask him one day, 'Whose life is worth more—a friend or a prisoner whose name you did not even know?'

And he would say that had he known, four years ago, where he would be tonight, of course he would never have done as he did. Of course he would have kept Loka's *anything* for Zee. Yet, in his heart he knew and so did she: given the chance to reverse his choice, he might still have misgivings. It seemed to be the way of the island that whenever there were only two sides, neither was right.

Moisture dripped from Zee's hair onto Aye's bare shoulders. Frogs called. Sugarcane rustled. What would the Japanese do to Zee? To them both? Should he risk leaving Zee alone to look for Loka? If there was one person who could navigate the troops on land and sea, it was Loka.

But Aye remembered his promise to him.

Any one thing, Loka had said, for the skull of his sister's husband. When Aye told him what he wanted, Loka said it would not be the first time an aborigine helped a prisoner escape. He would do it, but the condition was the same: return the bones.

They each kept their word.

Afterwards, Loka swore to leave Aye alone, and said Aye must do the same. For though Aye was not British, he was still an outsider. The wars would not have happened had their worlds stayed apart, he reminded him. They shook hands, and roasted tombowagey to seal this second promise too.

'What will you do now?' Aye asked as they ate.

Loka said he would move with his remaining family to North Andaman Island.

Four years had passed and Aye had not seen him since. North Andaman Island was far; it might as well be India. Besides, they had shaken hands. They had shared food. They were never to look for each other again.

He gently pulled away from Zee, positioning him against the trunk of a tree. He took off his sari-skirt, securing it under Zee's head, like a pillow. Then Aye slinked back into the pond. He ducked his head underwater, and once the night sounds were obliterated, he could hear the noise up at the jail, on that New Year's Eve.

Loka was singing like a cicada as Aye walked through the jail's gate. The laughter Aye had heard was coming from the third level. When he climbed up to the second, Loka was waiting for him. In the distance were two guards enjoying a feast. Food from the party at the chief commissioner's villa. Aye knew, because he had served it. There were plates of mutton and Chittagong fowl all over the floor, and the guards were taunting the hunger strikers by holding the food out to them through the bars.

Aye understood now why Loka chose this night for the escape. The guards were drinking Jarawa Joy and Commander-in-Chief and did not notice anyone slipping down to the mezzanine floor. The warder stationed outside the hospital ward had passed out. The kerosene lamp beside him was flickering in the breeze; shadows fanned across a cheek coated in brandied mangoes.

Aye waited by the door of the ward, peering through it as Loka stepped inside.

Aside from Prisoner 218 D, there was an Indian woman with a wrinkled new-born baby. Loka had drugged both mother and child with the plant he said was not deadly like Chandu Bhai, though Aye was not so sure about this. As he waited, he remembered Mr Howard once say, inside the ward, 'Good lord. All babies are best to somebody, aren't they? Even the ugly ones.'

The laughter up on the third level showed no sign of ceasing, Cillian's voice rising above it. '*Punish them jamadar, do not reserve for the morrow!*'

The prisoner was barely conscious. Loka tossed her over his shoulder and the three left the jail.

As they headed for the canoe, Loka said the lightning in the sky was a pearl sent by Biliku, the north wind, to help them move swiftly. And they did, reaching the creek where the canoe was tied and setting off without being caught. The moon was not red, Loka assured Aye, also a good sign. It meant the moon had seen no enemy tonight.

As the canoe cut the sea and the stars cast a silver sheen on his skin, Loka kept whispering stories. The moon grew red with rage if he saw another light. A torch. A fire. Biliku brought deadly storms if provoked. If, for instance, she heard her children—spiders and cicadas—in distress. Spiders could not be killed and cicadas liked to sing. Chopping down trees silenced their happiness. Tonight, Biliku was pleased. Tonight, she helped them. And on, the skull glistening around Loka's neck.

The prisoner was quiet, but for a sob uttered just once. It happened when Aye unfurled her fist and dropped her letters inside. He had not forgotten the one from Aunty Hanan. He was going forward in this canoe, on this night, towards a pyramid-shaped island ahead. Her words haunted him: *If that strange long-haired boy in the pointy boat keeps heading for the island, it is the wrong choice; but retreating is not the right one either.*

He looked for ships, rocks, torches and, most of all, for what he could not yet know. The starfish jail lay behind them, yet followed, still. But Loka said there was no need for Aye to keep turning his head. There were no Lau, the pale hairy water spirits that caused men to drown. The moon stayed white. The moon's wife, the sun, was painting him lovingly with clay.

'One day, your wife will do the same,' Loka said. 'Tonight, we arrive. And then, goodbye, friend.'

THREE

Directions for Watching the Sun
Set in the Andaman Sea
1942

ON THE NIGHT ZEE WAS taken away, Nomi stayed behind in the hut with their mother and Priya. One half of the green sari still lay on the floor. She did not fold it away, and neither did their mother. She could still smell Zee's half when she ran to him. The nothingness in the space between their two halves stretched wider than the sea.

Nomi asked herself what else she could have packed for him besides *She* and the cream for his skin. Seeing his pencils, she began to cry. Priya, who had been hiding under their parents' cot, rushed forward, but now Nomi hated her.

Their mother was on the prayer mat, keening. Aunty Madhu and Aunty Pooja were with her.

Aunty Madhu said, 'Everything will be all right.'

'I have only one son!' said their mother.

Aunty Pooja said, 'God will be kind.'

'Why must I keep suffering?'

Nomi remembered all the promises she had broken, all the lies she had told. She remembered and she knew: Priya was not the only one to blame.

She did not hear the aunties leave. She did hear their father return. His back was bent so low he was almost Nomi's height. His face looked as though it had been swept away in a storm and had not returned.

'Where is he?' their mother asked.

'Safe,' he answered, but would say no more.

No one burned a candle. They waited. They did not have to wait long.

The Japanese thought Zee was Aunty Madhu's son. They banged on her door that same night, one of them shouting in English the same question their mother had asked and the same question Nomi kept asking herself. 'Where is he?'

Aunty Madhu's hut was next to theirs and they could hear the flourish of things being thrown. There was a slap, a scream, and then came another sound. Nomi leaped off the floor, into their father's arms. There was a popping noise, higher pitched than a bullet. At first, she thought it was their father's heart. When it happened again, it sounded like rain, yet it could not be, because instead of becoming cooler, it was growing very hot.

Aunty Madhu's hut was on fire.

Outside, other families had already gathered, and Uncle Bimal was helping Aunty Madhu and her daughter to safety. More troops surrounded them than Nomi could remember seeing two days ago on Mount Top, when she went up there with Zee. She recognised the soldier with the round glasses and caterpillar moustache. The one who had said 'Wait!' as they fled back down the mountain. It was this soldier who now did the talking.

'If you do not tell us where he is, we will burn all your homes.' He marched beside them, as they threw water and sand onto Aunty Madhu's hut. 'There will be no one left to save you.'

The huts were made of timber. A second caught fire, and then a third. The wind was carrying the fire north, away from Nomi's hut.

'Your houses are burning. Tell us where he is and we will help you save them!'

No one said anything. No one gave their family away.

Their father leaned into her, coughing from somewhere so deep within that she feared his lungs would rupture. She thought about hell and all their mother's warnings. Hell was a pit of fire in which she would end up if she did not tell the truth. In the past, whenever their mother said this, Nomi imagined the pit as a giant cup. Now she could see that hell had no shape. It moved. It spread. Whatever it brushed became it. Hell was not a pit of fire, but a rash, a mighty one, mightier even than the kind Zee would get. Sometimes, Zee would surrender to the rash by scratching it. He would scrape and scrape, and his relief would be so great that Nomi could see heaven on his face! Then his expression would change. He was bracing for the moment when the pain would come tearing back, much worse than before, and consume him.

Their village was doing the same. They were only scratching the pain. They could put out the fire, but it was lying in wait, an ember here, a crackle there, ready to pounce, ready to swell.

How long could they postpone it?

'Very well,' Caterpillar said, sounding suddenly like Mr Campbell at school. 'You may return to your homes. We will give you till tomorrow, at dusk. If we do not have him by the time the sun touches the sea, you have seen nothing yet.'

Their parents argued all night, and all of the next morning. Though Nomi did not want the sun to set, not ever, it meant their parents would never stop arguing, and hell would only spread. Their mother wanted to postpone it. Their father said they could not. 'Look what happened to those huts. We cannot make more families suffer.'

'But we put out the fire!'

'What was left behind? And what about the fires tomorrow?'

'Do you still think they are here to help?'

Nomi hated the sound coming from his chest.

'We should go, right now,' their mother insisted. 'We should join him.'

'This is an island, Fehmida. There is nowhere to hide.'

'We can try. Where is he? You said he was safe.'

'If we do as they say tomorrow, they will show mercy. If we all run, they will spare no one, including her.' He tried to lower his voice but of course Nomi could hear.

'You always do as they say.'

'Me?' His voice was angry now.

'We could be leaving the island, yet there you sit!'

'What happened when I tried?' Nomi could see his outline in the dark, pulling the collar of his shirt away from his neck, baring the scar.

What she had heard was true.

Now their mother was quiet.

'Think!' he wheezed.

'I don't think!' their mother screamed. 'I only know!' She started sobbing. 'He is your son.' When he said nothing, she fell to her knees. 'Please. *Please.*'

And their father sobbed the way he had never sobbed, not even when their mother would put mustard oil on the wounds on his back. 'He is my only son.'

When morning came, they did not notice Nomi leaving the hut.

The Japanese said to return Zee before the sun touched the sea. Which sea? Into how many bodies of water did the sun fall?

Families were still gathered outside, where the fires were still smouldering. The soldiers kept watch. White Paula and her mother, Shakuntala, had come all the way down from the farm. Shakuntala was telling Aunty Madhu and Aunty Madhu's daughter that they could stay with her for a while, if they needed to.

Nomi looked for Aye. She thought he might be at the jetty. She started walking towards it, but Shakuntala came after her, saying it was not safe, everyone must stay together. Then Aunty Pooja's daughter Leela said, 'Come into our hut.' She took Nomi's hand, and Nomi did not know she was tired till she was inside Aunty Pooja's hut and given milk and Leela was saying, 'Do you remember Priya's first egg?' while planting a kiss on her cheek.

Yes, she remembered, and it was a good day, announced with a soft cluck. She tried to put herself back there, the way she had stroked the hen on the mat where she slept while Zee snored beside her. When Priya began to fidget, Nomi combed through questions in her head. Where did an egg come from? Why was it pointed at one end? Priya was nearly twenty weeks old when the pink comb down her face had turned bright and she began fluffing up her feathers and walking around in a daze. Their father said she would lay soon, it would happen with sunlight. This would be Priya's 'cue'. He was right. As the first rays of the sun turned her golden feathers the colour of fire, Priya's shifting grew more agitated, and then Nomi heard the cluck. 'Good girl,' she whispered, still stroking the glossy feathers. There was a second cluck when she slid a hand under her, and found the egg. She told Zee, who was waking up beside her, 'Look what Priya did.' He said the egg would be dirty because it came from *there*, the same place as poop. Yet, in the light streaming through the window of their hut, she could see that it was smooth, spotless, and the same colour as the tuft of feathers around Priya's ear holes. Most of all, the egg was warm.

The hut was becoming crowded. There was no warm egg in her hands and no Zee snoring beside her. There was only chatter. She could not see the sun rotate in the sky, she could not tell it to stay.

'Has Zee come back?' she asked. The chatter stopped for a moment before Leela planted another kiss on Nomi's cheek. The women went back to talking. She tried to remember who they were. She examined Leela. She was Aunty Pooja's daughter, this much was clear. Older and prettier than Nomi, with long lashes. When Zee was around, Leela looked at him sideways. Now Zee was not around and Leela was not looking sideways.

The women around Nomi seemed to be saying that Zee should be brought back, before more damage was done to their homes. They were also discussing the last time there was a disappearance. Then, it was the British who came into their huts and threw things. They were looking for the prisoner, the one who got away. It was the first time Nomi had ever heard a siren, long before the air raids began and then stopped. As the sun appeared in the sky and the siren blew, their father was rushing out the front door. 'A prisoner has escaped!' he said. Never before had she seen him so excited. Even Zee was out of bed without fuss, to join the congregation around the shop. Someone said the prisoner would be eaten by sharks, while another said he would be eaten by Jarawa. '*She*,' someone else interrupted. 'A woman has escaped.' But no one believed it. There had been a few successful attempts made by men, but a woman could never escape. As they argued, their father asked, 'Are we ready for when they come into our homes, to search for her?'

In the evening, they came. Nomi was helping their mother slice tomatoes that were pointed at one end, like eggs. As she dropped them in the sizzling oil, she let Nomi add the spices, and Nomi was trying not to let the turmeric stain her fingers. Zee was outside with the other boys. The door was shut so Priya could not run outside. There were shouts. Their father opened the door. Nomi grabbed Priya.

Six policemen, all Indian, came into their hut. They spilled the tomatoes, kicked Priya's nest box, tore one of Zee's notebooks. They even shook out the cloth tucked in a cup on the windowsill, inside which she had saved Priya's first egg. The egg cracked on the floor. They smashed some of the little bamboo figurines Aye had given her. That same night, after the policemen had left, people began to say that the runaway's ghost was lurking around their huts.

Now the light inside Aunty Pooja's hut was growing dim. The Japanese soldiers had given them till dusk today. Nomi rushed outside, wondering, again, into how many bodies of water the sun set.

She recited the names, as she had done at school, when catching raindrops from the ceiling with Zee. The Arabian Sea. The Andaman Sea. The Bay of Bengal, which was not a sea but part of a sea. The Indian Ocean. The Pacific Ocean. Black Water, the name for exile.

In all this time, no one had told her where the sun would set first. No one had told her where the sun would set last. Which sea did the Japanese mean?

From Andaman sky to Andaman Sea, the sun was now no longer a sphere. It was moving, spreading, till whatever it brushed, became it.

The Totality of Exclusion
1941

FOUR MONTHS BEFORE ZEE WAS taken away, the dentist, Susumu San, was expecting his own arrest. As he hopped onto his bicycle, he was nearly run over by a car. There had been more cars since the war in Europe began and more European visitors flocked to this rock. They drove recklessly, believing themselves to be the only ones here, yet he knew it was the humble bicycle that would forever change the face of the war.

He wondered whether to go right or go left. Right was Browning Club, left, his lonely cottage. The sign at the club's door read *No Women or Indians*. Though neither, he was never invited inside. How he wished to conquer the totality of his exclusion!

He turned left. 'Goodbye, Susumu San!' the children giggled, following his bicycle out of Aberdeen. He rang his bell.

There were no fishermen due at the creek today, but he could go there anyway; it was relatively cool and mosquito-free.

On his way, he passed the pretty nurse—the one betrothed to the deputy commissioner—and a few of her friends. They did not see him.

The taxidermist and his wife had left the island. He would never know if they were caught. Before fleeing, they had given him their collection of stuffed birds and mammals, as well as a living frog that Hatsu had grown especially fond of. He had them all in his cottage, but somehow it only made his living arrangements lonelier. He had still not been to Marriagetown to find himself a woman and now it was probably too late.

At the creek, he breathed deeply. He had found this the best place to improve his jujitsu skills, better than his own house, despite still having no one to practice his throws with. He stretched his limbs, focusing on the mangrove tree immediately ahead, where the Andamanese who spied on him frequently anchored his canoe. He had not seen the man in some time, and with reason. Susumu San's work was done, and he was soon to be arrested.

Content with his breathing technique, he started landing punches and kicks an inch before the tree. His mind was strong. His movements were fluid and economical. He did not take his eyes off the tree. If he looked away, at the bird or the leaf, he would lose sight of the entirety of his assailant.

This was not a sport but an art, and art alone could overcome the questions he could not answer.

In the five years since his arrival on the island, he had continued to familiarise himself with its geography and with British military installations as much as possible. There were barracks on Ross Island for the occupying troops, who still only numbered a few, and for the visiting officers that came to escape India, swim in the enchanted seas, and cavort with the society-starved women who lived here. The parties at the chief commissioner's mansion, the only brightly lit building in the entire bay, were but proof of this. The glimmering villa could be a target, but the British still carried on as normal, as they had done even during the Blitz.

The only major harbour, Port Blair, was in the village of Aberdeen. A small fleet of ships was permanently anchored there, but he knew the sailors spent their days at Browning Club, drinking gimlets and playing cards, or raiding Marriagetown for convict brides and their daughters, or sons.

There was an abundant and quite beautiful tangle of creeks and rivulets, quite like this one, leading to different points of the island, where there were no harbours and no sentries.

True, there was the central tower of the panopticon prison up on Atlanta Point. But those hundred eyes up there in the tower—did they even exist? He knew there was only one guard and it was the fear of what the guard saw that caused convicts to keep imagining him, even after leaving the jail. Yet, he had never been able to confirm the might of the hundred eyes. After all, even during his short time here, a prisoner had been able to escape. A woman, no less!

There were other places he had not been able to fathom. Caution, first. He had never entered the barracks without invitation, though the invitations—if he could call them this—had been plenty, as the troops had dismal teeth. (Their fat-soaked diet and sugar intake he would never understand.) He had not stolen classified information. He had not disclosed any findings on the telephone, assuming all lines to have been tapped, though he had reason to believe that they had, in fact, never been tapped. He had never been caught on camera, not even when American photographers went everywhere unencumbered, taking whatever they pleased.

However, he had not escaped the aborigines, the true security guards of the islands. Their hundred eyes did exist, which was why he would soon be arrested, still without understanding *why*. Why did they cooperate with the English, but not with him?

He was covered in sweat and breathing wildly as he rolled on the sand and lifted himself up with minimal steps and maximum timing.

He was puzzled by something else. He and his childhood rival, Goro, had both graduated from the Imperial Naval College not eight years past, both with honours. Yet it was Goro, not he, who had been sent to the American territory of Hawaii, to be greeted by a high-ranking official of the Japanese Consulate, garlanded with leis, and housed in a lavish chalet in the consular compound. From what he had heard, Goro spent his days in a teahouse, lovingly tended by geishas. He even had a title. Chancellor Goro.

In contrast, Susumu Adachi had no title (other than 'dentist'), wore no lei, had no geishas, had met no Consular General, and lived in a remote and dingy cottage. This was a far-flung outpost, at best. There was no glamour to his station.

Still, he had done his job. Though he might disapprove of Goro, come what may, he knew that neither would ever give the other away.

And it was a curious thing. All the places that consumed him most—Japan, Britain, the Andamans, even Hawaii—all were islands. What was it about islands?

A week passed and he was still not arrested.

The fishermen gave him more news, including of Chancellor Goro. Their destinies were intricately linked not only because they had graduated, with honours, from the same college. Equally, they were both sons of policemen and both served briefly aboard the same submarine, till repeated bouts of stomach upsets forced them both to forego a lustrous career in the Navy. They were both given a second chance—one by becoming Japan's only military spy in Hawaii, the other Japan's only military spy in the Andamans. They were the same weight, height and age (twenty-eight), and their birthdays were but two weeks apart. If the fishermen were to be believed, Goro had even started wearing his glossy black hair in the same style as Susumu San—just below the jaw, and combed back—and was praised for his elegance, even if history would forget who pioneered the look.

And to think that this man spent his days in the two-storey Japanese Consulate on Nuuanu Avenue and his evenings in a mountainside teahouse, where he could have geishas *and* a view of Pearl Harbour! The teahouse even had telescopes; Goro could work and be worked on, at the same time. Afterwards, he was driven back to his chalet by a chauffeur.

Susumu San sighed. The only harbour worth watching on South Andaman Island was still Port Blair, about which he had gathered and transferred everything there was to know. He had no telescope. He had no car. And there was no teahouse up on Mount Harriet, the only place from which he could get a proper view of the port.

That evening, he wondered again if the arrest would be tomorrow. He had made the necessary preparations, but something told him to wait.

The next day, a fisherman dropped into his hands a pamphlet

called, 'Read this alone—and the war can be won,' written by Masanobu Tsuji. It promised the liberation of the conquered peoples of Asia, and detailed how to survive war in the everlasting summer of the tropics, down to the food, jungle terrain and hygiene.

The jungle terrain was different in Malaya than in the Andamans. Susumu San believed himself capable of writing a better pamphlet. But he decided not to, because he was expecting his own arrest.

By the end of the year, the fishermen were telling him that their troops had invaded Malaya, on bicycles. It happened on the same day Pearl Harbour was bombed.

Even then, the British could not accept that war was coming to these islands. Even then, Susumu Adachi was free. The British High Commissioner of the Malay States said, 'I suppose we'll shove the little men off.' Field Marshal Archibald Percival Wavell said, 'They are but an army of gangsters.' The parties at Browning Club and the chief commissioner's house continued.

At noon on 23 December, when they finally realised their mistake, Susumu San was having lunch on the veranda of his hut. The meal was a plate of eight giant mantis shrimp. He examined them closely. Each had five pairs of legs, including an enormous one shaped like a scythe, with which it hunted creatures twice its size. They were aggressive, friendless animals who burrowed in the sea bed and would not hesitate to slice a human thumb. On the island of Kyushu, where Susumu San's mother was born, they were a delicacy. Shappa, they were called. When he was a boy, a gift of shappa from the cold Ariake Sea had been occasion for much celebration. He had noticed that in the Andaman Sea, mantis shrimp were more common and came in many varieties. Those from the Ariake Sea had an orange hue, with lilac streaks that darkened when the shrimp were boiled. But on the plate before him were what the British called peacock mantis shrimp. The head was blue, the body green, and the front claws red, with white leopard-like spots. He had boiled water in a pot but was not yet ready to drop the animals inside.

Two hours earlier, Japanese aircraft began bombing Rangoon. Once Japan had Burma, thought Susumu San, it had India. He looked up at the sky that was as clear over these rocks as it must have been over the city hundreds of miles away, before it was hit. As a gentle breeze blew in from the south, he pictured the flames, he smelled the flesh. Rangoon stood on marshy ground upon which no air-raid shelters could have been built.

He dropped the shrimp into the pot.

Since he had been expecting his arrest, he had already destroyed his documents, from the maps to his notes on the geography, topography, fresh water sources and native tribes. He had left only his observations of the British settlers, including the chief commissioner's wife and her many lovers. There was nothing else to find, but his body.

He scooped the shrimp out of the pot and ate each one with tenderness. The flesh was so sweet it dissolved on his tongue before he was done chewing. His mouth was full with saliva but he resolved to go slow. He knew he would be arrested today, and this time he was right. Within the hour, Indian police would arrive, preventing him from watching his troops dismount at Port Blair, Corbyn's Cove, and Rangachang in March of next year, many on bicycles. It was thanks to him that they would know where to land, though all evidence of this—with one exception—had also been destroyed. He was, at present, in the process of eliminating this one exception.

Though he regretted being unable to create a pamphlet on the jungle terrain, he was proud of all he had done here, almost every day, for almost six years. He was left with only one doubt, which he tried in vain to push aside. If the rumours he had heard were true, then in the weeks leading up to the bombing of Pearl Harbour, Chancellor Goro had found himself more involved with geishas than with telescopes, and was removed from his post. When, after the bombing, policemen entered the Consulate, arresting Japanese officials and transporting them to San Diego, Goro was not among them.

Susumu San had eaten all eight shrimp. He stepped inside the hut to retrieve the frog Hatsu Takora had left him in a small glass case before fleeing the island with her husband. The frog was tinier than his thumb and hunted by the Andamanese, who used the toxins from its glands to tip their arrows. It was a translucent orange, not too different from the shappa variety found in Kyushu. He looked at the frog and the frog looked at him. Yes, he wanted to say, though perhaps the frog already knew.

There was no point in waiting. He would complete the most sumptuous flavours he could find with the most vile. He lifted the top of the glass case and, before the frog could escape, slid it, whole, down his throat.

Immediately, he started to gag. The stench was of old, putrid leaves and discarded fish guts rolled in layers of forest slime that he tried not to bite but only to swallow, yet the frog would not go down and already the poison was erupting like a furnace in his mouth.

If the rumours he had heard were true, he thought, while pushing down the frog with his finger—how it expanded in his mouth!—then Goro had changed his name, cut his hair and been fitted with a new set of teeth. Their destinies were to intersect once again. Eager to make up for his disgrace in Hawaii, Goro had set out on an intelligence mission to Malaya and Singapore, and had helped to create a Japanese special operations unit committed to aiding independence movements all over the British Empire. The nationalism of the Indian soldiers in the British-Indian Army who had been captured in the Southeast campaign had found a friend in Goro. They had been recruited into an alliance with the Imperial Japanese Army and a new force was emerging, it even had a name, the Indian National Army, and the army was headed for these very islands. India would be free of British rule, while Japan would extend its rule from Malaya to India from these very rocks that Susumu San had helped to secure. Goro, whose name had changed, would find his name in history books. His story would go on. Susumu San's would end here.

His final thought as he gazed for the last time upon these shores was this. If Goro was indeed on his way, then these good people and their children would suffer worse than the fire tearing him apart.

The Closeness of Exile
1942

TWO AND A HALF WEEKS before Zee was taken away, when Rangoon fell and British women were evacuated from South Andaman Island, there was a wedding in Marriagetown.

The bride, Aditi, worked at Shakuntala's farm. She had arrived six years ago, shackled to the prisoner who got away. Aditi's prison term was complete. As promised, she would become a bride.

Her groom had been married twice before. During his second marriage he had served the settlement so industriously that he had been declared a Trusty and made the headman of the village of Ferrargunj. Soon afterwards, his second wife had died of tuberculosis, leaving behind their five children. He was now sixty years old. Aditi was twenty-seven. As Japanese planes crisscrossed the sky and the British departed, Aditi was to get a second chance at society.

Shakuntala walked to the wedding in a magenta sari, a pair of intricate gold-and-pearl jhumkay at her ears. She had no idea what was coming, but who would have thought, even during a war, there could be a celebration. Before his death, her husband Thomas had told her how the headman had lost his first wife. It happened in 1911, the year of the Delhi Durbar, when King George V and Queen Mary declared themselves Emperor and Empress of India. To memorialise the event, the Emperor had set free one thousand prisoners from South Andaman Island. The headman's first wife was chosen. He was not. Before leaving him, she confessed to being married already, and to having children back in India.

When Shakuntala arrived, the headman was waiting outside the office, his five children and five grandchildren hovering nearby. Nineteen forty-two was the confluence of different events than 1911, but perhaps he too was wondering what lay in store for him and his new bride.

Aditi's face had been painted by the young make-up artist Rani, who named herself after Devika Rani, the heartthrob of Bollywood. Rani's make-up always came from one of her many suitors, this time, possibly the very officer overseeing the wedding. Rani had styled Aditi's hair in finger waves and made her eyebrows pencil thin. She gave her a lipstick so deep it was almost black and there was a thick line of kohl along the lower lids, deliberately smudged to create a smouldering haze. Yet Aditi's skin still bore the scars of the boils that marked her face on the day she landed on these shores, and two sores were fresh. She held a red dupatta with gold trim across her cheek to hide them.

The officer asked the headman if he agreed to the marriage. The man nodded. The officer asked Aditi. 'Ha Khudawand!' she answered, head bowed. There was no document and no clergyman of any faith. The officer pronounced them man and wife.

Rani started to dance and another woman played a tambourine made of deer skin stretched between a bamboo frame. Metal brace-lets, discarded keys and other materials that had washed ashore now dangled from the tambourine's frame. The woman passed it around so every child could have a turn. Afterwards, Shakuntala escorted Aditi to her new home in Ferrargunj under a pink cloth with silver sequins. Aditi hummed softly under her breath, '*Na ro puttar, sajna.*' Don't cry child, beloved one.

A week later, on the dawn of the fourteenth of March, there was a knock on Shakuntala's door. White Paula was still asleep. Throwing a shawl over the shirt she slept in—Thomas's shirt—Shakuntala peered through a window. The light was hazy. Seeing no one, she tiptoed to a different window. Andrew Gallagher, Jr, senior officer of the Indian police, was staring back at her.

She quickly pulled away. Andrew had many times tried to be her suitor, without success. He could not possibly have come here for entertainment now, she thought, at this hour! Besides, he should have left the island days ago.

There was another knock and now her daughter shifted. Shakuntala cautiously opened the door.

'What has happened?' she whispered.

'I must speak with you.'

His hair was dishevelled. It was unlike him. She stepped outside, shutting the door gently behind her.

He looked around. 'Inside would be better.'

'My daughter is sleeping.'

'Very well.' He moved to the kitchen step, from where he had a better view of the approach to the house. It was where she normally perched every morning, as the animals were fed. 'Sit beside me, Shakuntala. I will attempt nothing.'

He was normally familiar, but not so direct. She sat beside him.

'As it turns out, the last evacuation was yesterday.' His voice was low. So low that she was not sure what she had heard.

'The *last* evacuation?'

'Precisely.'

'Then why are you still here?'

'Precisely.'

She waited.

'The ship was meant to return. It was sunk by a Japanese submarine.'

'Oh.'

A rooster began to crow. Hens scattered.

'Further evacuation is expected to be suspended.'

'How many of you are left?'

He hesitated. 'Very few. I will be leaving shortly on a motorboat, along with Mr Howard, and three others. It is dangerous, but I see no other way.'

'And the rest?'

'They will follow when possible. That is not why I have come.'

She waited.

'It seems likely now that they will take these islands. Given what we are hearing of their activities elsewhere—' He did not complete the sentence.

She had never seen him unshaven. If he were Indian, she would guess it had been two days. But his hair was as fine as Thomas's. At least four, she decided.

'I am here to ask a favour of you.'

'Me?'

Standing up abruptly, he walked to the troughs where the pigs were starting to grunt. The workers would not arrive for another hour and usually the animals waited but Andrew had stirred them. The troughs were along the southern edge of the pen, about a foot off the ground. They were empty, save for an inch or two of water. Andrew stepped into one.

'What are you doing?'

'I want to show you something.' He held out his hand to her.

'They drink from it.'

'I am leaving, Shakuntala. Humour me.'

She gave him her hand and stepped with her rubber slippers into the dirty water.

'Can you see?'

She saw only the row of trees lining the edge.

'The ocean is there. So are their submarines, and so is the *HMIS Abdiel*, laying our mines.'

'Well, I cannot see any of it.'

He put his arms around her waist and hoisted her like a child. Her shirt rode high up her thighs but his arms were tight and the shirt was caught in them. 'Look,' he said.

'Put me down.'

'Look, just once.'

She glanced at the ocean. 'Put me down.'

He put her down.

She headed for the kitchen.

He followed her. 'I want you to understand why I am here.'

'Then get to it, Andrew. You have already caused enough disturbance. Paula is probably awake. The animals are restless. I am tired.'

'I don't expect you've read *Paradise Lost*? From where the ship gets her name?'

'I don't expect you're here to test my knowledge of books.'

'*So spake the seraph Abdiel, faithful found among the faithless, faithful only he.*'

'What?'

'It seems fitting, no? As we leave our paradise, an Abdiel must keep watch.'

'An Abdiel? Do you mean me?'

'Of course not, my darling. You are the widow of a former deputy commissioner and will likely be suspected right away. We need someone invisible, someone you can help us reach. The headman of Ferrargunj has a new bride. She has taken a liking to you.'

'A liking—to me?'

'Do you realise you are repeating everything I say?' Before she could answer, he continued, 'Pay his new bride a visit, and speak to the headman. Tell him we will not abandon these shores. I will personally return, but it will take planning. They must cooperate.'

'How?'

'They must allow me access to their village, without informing the Japanese, at any cost.'

She looked at her feet. They were wet from standing in the trough and mosquitoes were circling her ankles.

He took her hand and whispered, 'Are we in agreement?'

'You want our help, yet the Gurkha battalion is gone. If the Japanese turn on us, what then?'

He dropped her hand and walked away. 'As I said, we will protect you.'

After that day, Shakuntala began slipping out of bed while Paula slept, to stand in the dirty water of the troughs, glimpsing what she could of the sea. She was there on the day the saw mill on nearby Chatham Island was bombed. For as long as she could remember, timber from the mill had been sent to London and New York, and there were still men inside, working the machinery, when the bombs fell. She could not hear the men, though, not over the cries of the burning elephants.

She was there on the morning that Rani, the make-up artist, arrived on the farm to say that Andrew Gallagher, Jr did leave in a motorboat with the superintendent and other men, including the jailor Cillian. The boat had not returned. Of the few Englishmen who remained, one was the officer who oversaw Aditi's marriage to the headman. He was indeed Rani's lover, and also the harbour master. He had told Rani that there were no more merchant vessels for Japanese gunships to sink. The *HMIS Ramdas* was lost. The *HMIS Sophie Marie* had struck a mine in the Macpherson Strait, between South Andaman Island and Rutland Island. Andrew's motorboat may have suffered the same fate.

But what if Andrew was alive, and planned on returning? Shakuntala wondered. Should she help him and speak to the headman? She wondered too what Andrew meant when he said *from what we are hearing of their activities elsewhere*. What activities?

Shakuntala was also at the troughs on midnight of the twenty-second of March, when she heard a gunshot. Though she did not know it then, a Japanese battalion and a naval constituent of two detachments from special Base Forces had sailed from Penang with the intention of landing on South Andaman Island at dawn. Aware that the British had left behind no army, the Japanese fired the shot to ensure that the only answer would be silence.

At first, it was the only answer they got. Then there was an explosion. The wireless officer in charge, who had also stayed behind on the island, had been given instructions to destroy all the wireless installations before Japanese troops disembarked. When he heard the shot, he blew up the station.

Then, silence again.

Shakuntala continued gazing at the sea, wondering how far she had come. If she could measure it in miles—how far? Long ago, when Thomas first asked if she would accompany him to these shores, she had measured the distance on a map with her forefinger and thumb. The width of her wrist—that close. But what had the closeness of exile come to mean? To say that she lived on the crossroads of two great oceans and two great empires would mean as little to her as the knowledge that she lived nearer to Penang than to Chittagong. To say that she lived on a penal settlement that also served as a footstool to India and Burma would mean even less. She knew only that, on most nights, she could feel the world closing in on this little rock. Like the children in Marriagetown that Shakuntala once tried to help, she and Paula could be suffocated in their sleep. And the world would never know. Their deaths, like their lives, would be witnessed only by the clouds passing overhead. Only they could carry the truth to somewhere else, if someone but cared to look up.

And then yesterday, on the twenty-fifth of March, another shot was fired, this time by Zee. Though Shakuntala did not hear it, later that night, she again slipped out of bed. As she stood in the trough, it seemed to her that in the direction of Aberdeen, there were sparks in the sky. When the course of the wind changed, smoke billowed towards the farm. Was the island on fire?

The next day, she and Paula hurried down to Aberdeen.

The Last Colour of the Day
1942

'DON'T STARE DIRECTLY AT the sun,' said Shakuntala. 'It will damage your eyes.'

She stood on one side of Nomi, White Paula on the other. Other women had come outside. They were still saying that no one had given away Zee. The Japanese wanted to know who had fired the shot, but the village had not answered. The Japanese wanted to know where the boy had gone, but the village had not answered. Yet, how long could they keep quiet? The Japanese had dropped no bombs since their arrival, had they? If Haider Ali cooperated, everything would be all right. The Japanese might even take them all back to India.

Now Dr Singh was here, telling the women that Haider Ali was going to hand over Zee. They cheered, and hugged each other. Dr Singh asked that the women go back inside to comfort Zee's mother. When he saw Nomi, he picked her up. 'Santri,' he whispered, 'God be with you.'

When the sun touched the sea, her arms were open, ready to seize it.

The sky turned scarlet. It was the colour of Zee's rash.

She had watched him up on the mountain, gazing at the sea, always at the sea, with a tuft of thick hair pointing to the sky, like the comb of a rooster. A mosquito had landed on the dark bristles of his cheek and after he slapped it, when she flicked it away for him, her finger was smeared with blood. His cheek would have more bristles by this evening. She had not packed his razor because he would not have used it anyway, because of the rash.

There was a commotion behind her, and now she noticed Aye and her father approaching, accompanied by several Japanese soldiers. Zee was being handed over.

People were coming out of their huts, filling Aberdeen Square. They were saying the Japanese would keep Zee in the starfish jail. After a few days, they would show mercy and set him free. So they said. Why, then, did the soldiers keep Nomi from going to him when she ran ahead? Why did they keep her mother from doing the same? They were marching Zee back to the spot where he had fired the shot. She could hear boots, hundreds of them. Caterpillar Moustache was here, shouting for everyone to come out and see. Everyone did.

Zee was pushed to the lawns of Browning Club, at the far edge of the square. It was the club to which he had many times accompanied Mr Campbell, tilting sideways while carrying the teacher's briefcase. Once, Nomi had walked behind them, with Georgina on a leash. Now it was as though Zee was on a leash, and she could feel the warmth of him, feel how wildly his heart skipped.

His handcuffs were taken off. She had not noticed them before. She thought it strange, the way the soldiers seized his arms, because Zee was so scrawny, so scared, he could not have hurt even a mosquito then. His eyes were barely open. She could not see bruises on his face but she could see that his skin was on fire, his petticoat was torn, and his half of their mother's green sari covered him in shreds, like feathers. His hair was flat against his head. There was no rooster comb.

The soldiers told the crowd to move back. '*Back!*' yelled Caterpillar when their father and Dr Singh began to argue and their mother started to scream. '*Back!*'

Shakuntala picked Nomi up but she kicked her, hard, and called out to him. 'Zee! Zee!'

The soldiers still had his arms.

One shoulder per soldier.

There was something about that hold, even before the rest began, something calculated and precise.

They started to twist each arm. Zee did not speak—had not said a single word, nor looked in her direction—but now he tilted back his head and threw open his mouth as though he would like to say something. They were breaking him. She could hear it, a sound like a great bird warring with a twig; snapping it off, failing, snapping it off again.

Then one soldier slapped him to the ground like flat dough on a pan and the other forced him up and slapped him to the ground and it happened so many times and so quickly that she did not know when or if it ever stopped.

One throw per soldier.

The sound of each landing came later, louder than a gunshot.

Once, he said, 'Ouch!' That was all. It was so tender he could have been saying, 'Sorry!'

Then Zee began to yell. His beautiful warm voice, the one that had stopped cracking at fifteen, the one that made Nomi follow him all the way up Mount Top, that voice was all tangled up.

Through the green blur of sari feathers she could see that his hips had dislodged, his shoulders were hideous wings.

Caterpillar was circling the square, explaining that his men were trained in jujitsu, a submission art, and no one could defeat the mastery of their grip. He also explained that they had entered Aberdeen unarmed because they were here for them, and had trusted them, but that local boy there—he signalled behind him with his thumb—he had fired the first shot. Did they understand that from now on they could show only respect?

The crowd murmured.

'Understand?' he repeated.

The crowd shouted, 'Yes!'

He turned back to Zee, raised an arm, and a firing squad executed him.

The family were told they could keep the body.

She wanted to ask Zee how it could have been only two days ago on the mountain and yesterday when the shot was fired and maybe not even an hour ago when she tried to seize the sun. Why was time moving so strangely? Though she was twelve years old, a day had become a year, so that tomorrow she would be thirteen and by Monday she would turn sixteen and long before the start of the summer monsoons she would be lying beside Zee in the grave that their father and other men were digging for him. She even looked forward to it. The earth would be cool and dark and time would stop moving this way.

She wanted to ask where he had spent the night. Had he slept, or had he, too, been afraid? What had he thought of, to pass the time? Was it also the toddy cat, the one they saw together up on the mountain, as they sat on the bench? 'Instead of teaching us to read,' Zee had said, 'don't you wish they'd taught us to swim?' And then the cat had arched its back. When it hissed, was it at the soldiers pissing behind them? Was it trying to warn them? Was it also why Priya had behaved so badly? When she attacked the soldier, had she only been trying to help?

She wanted to ask Zee why she still thought there were those who wanted to help, when no one *could* help, not even a cat, who ran only for its own life, not even a chicken, who was only stupid and confused.

So when their father and the other men were done digging his grave, and Aunty Madhu and the other women surrounded their mother inside the hut, nobody noticed that the strangely moving time that had become Nomi's sole companion was doing something odd to her body. It took her in a grip from which she could not escape. She began to separate. One half of her stood still, watching the other half become everything she had ever seen. She was a shrew spiralling backward into the sea. A parachute dropping mines. A spool of yellow thread. Green feathers on grisly wings. And on, till this strangely moving time came to Priya, running outside the hut. As one half kept watching, the other half grabbed her by the neck. She marched her down to the jetty, where the battleships were still big and close, where soldiers still smoked and yawned. She swung her once, twice, and slapped her down into the sea. 'Swim!' she cried after her. 'Swim!'

Then she returned to the first half and together they stood still.

Baishunfu
1942

TWO DAYS AFTER ZEE WAS buried, the Japanese took more prisoners. They divided them into two groups: Europeans and the Indians who had worked for them. Among the former were Rani's lover, the harbour master, and Mr Martin, the deputy commissioner. Among the latter were the teacher Haji Sahib and the kind Dr Singh. Caterpillar—who was to be called Major Ito—again assembled a crowd in Aberdeen Square, promising an Asia for Asians and freedom from the enemy. To prove it, Japan would do what Britain had never done: the local populace would be represented in a civil administration and allowed Home Rule.

The first step to Home Rule was freeing the Indians who had worked for the British, to allow them a second chance. And so Haji Sahib and Dr Singh were released in the same square where they were arrested and the same square where Zee was executed.

The second step was the creation of a Peace Committee. Among the Peace Committee's many tasks was the re-arrest of convicts who had been freed from the starfish jail by the Japanese soon after they arrived. The convicts had been stealing from villages and frightening women. 'It is not we who do this,' said Major Ito. 'It is the convicts we set free. They do not want to be free.'

The Peace Committee had ten local members, including Haji Sahib, Dr Singh and Mr Rana, the new superintendent and new owner of the Aberdeen shop. All ten members were told to address the public, to explain why the Japanese were here.

Dr Singh was pushed forward first. 'We never succeeded against the British because they divided us. The Japanese will help us attain freedom and keep us together. They deserve our cooperation . . .'

After all the ten members had spoken, Major Ito named himself Governor of the Administration. He scanned the crowd and selected twenty more men and asked that they, along with the Peace Committee, join him tomorrow morning at Navy Headquarters at Browning Club, to discuss the responsibilities of the Administration.

Then the crowd was allowed to disperse. Among them was Shakuntala.

It was two weeks since Andrew Gallagher, Jr had told her to speak with the headman of Ferrargunj, and left her to weigh her options. She had carried the weight to Zee's torture. Afterwards, the weight shifted. The image of his elbows extruding from their sockets still haunted her today, as she left the crowd.

Shakuntala decided to visit the headman.

As she walked, she tried to remember a different time, when she, Thomas and Michael Ferrar—after whom the village was named— had hiked here together. Michael had been the chief commissioner at the time she and Thomas arrived, and while on the island, he had studied Persian, Urdu, Punjabi and Pashto. He had also collected four thousand Lepidoptera, many along these hills. When they were all together, Michael spoke to her in Urdu, she answered in Bengali and Thomas interrupted in English. Once, around this very turn, Michael had chirped, 'See the auric titly! There, the pellucid chipkali!' while Shakuntala insisted, 'Butterfly is prajapati, not titly. Lizard is tiktiki,' and Thomas conceded, 'You have to like friends with vocabulary.'

She also remembered English words Michael had tossed at her. *Deracination. Dislocation. Dissociation.* She could not remember the context—it could be that he spent too much time perusing the letter D in the dictionary—nor whether the words had been aimed at her (for marrying Thomas?), or at Thomas (for marrying her?), or at them all (for landing up here?). But she was carrying them now, between images of Zee's monstrous execution, while making her way to a former Indian convict on behalf of a possibly former English officer.

She carried, too, the knowledge that after Thomas's death, Michael had wanted her moved to Marriagetown, to remarry and have more children for the settlement. He let her be in the end, but only because of the quality of meat from her farm, which she gifted to him, generously. She had thought they were friends. Even when he pressured her to move, it had been through his servants.

Now she kept her eyes on the grass for snakes.

Should she trust Andrew Gallagher, Jr? If he had managed to escape the island on that motorboat, would he use Ferrargunj to help those left behind?

As she approached the village, Shakuntala passed soldiers on bicycles. They had mostly been stationed around Aberdeen and other points east, but the occasional guard still drifted across her path when she moved further inland. Her workers reported that they were frequently groped on the way to the farm, or at the very least, the soldiers made rude gestures. She kept her head down as she walked.

There was a different smell on the island.

Mr Rana, the new superintendent and new owner of the Aberdeen shop, was paying less for her goods. The Japanese ate more vegetables and fruit than the British, he told her, and cared little for chicken and ham. Once a week, a ship arrived with wheat, rice, ghee and onions. Unlike the British, the Japanese paid local men to unload the cargo, destroying British currency and liberally distributing their own. People were also given free saplings and seeds of tapioca, sweet potato, legumes, okra and other crops as part of Major and Governor Ito's 'grow more' campaign. He said to never waste excrement, and so people collected their own. The island was beginning to smell of it.

Along with the soldiers, Shakuntala passed local men and women clearing new grounds to cultivate more fields. She also passed the site where an airstrip was being built. Half the re-arrested convicts had been put to work here, the other half on building a new road through the jungle. They were not paid.

She reached Ferrargunj and climbed the hill. Aditi, still dressed as a bride, welcomed her into the main hut. When the headman arrived, Shakuntala told him of her conversation with Andrew Gallagher, Jr. The headman listened. He wore a white turban and his youngest granddaughter sat on his lap. The child Aditi bore him would be younger than the girl, thought Shakuntala, sipping tea. The headman had spent forty-one years on the island. He could recite the name of every chief commissioner and deputy commissioner and superintendent and senior and junior officer who had ever come to these shores, he said, but the best was Ferrar Sahibji, who had called him Trusty, and made him headman. With his own hands, he had captured butterflies of every hue for Ferrar Sahibji's enormous collection. When he said 'enormous,' the headman's eyebrows shot upward and his eyes, which were slightly grey, brightened. Then he realised what he had said and offered, 'Your husband, Best Sahibji, was a good man.'

Shakuntala smiled.

There was a pause, after which the headman said, 'If I had been there, I would never have let the snake bite him.'

Shakuntala smiled again before trying to bring the conversation back to Andrew. 'He said he would return. Obviously, it is a dangerous and secret mission.'

The headman listened. Were it not for Ferrar Sahibji, he told her, he would have had to wait longer than three years for his second wife and for the granddaughter in his lap. Shakuntala looked at Aditi, who had not spoken. There was still a thick line of kohl along her lower eyelids, but her lips were a lighter shade of red than on her wedding day. She was not humming today. Shakuntala wondered if it meant she was happy or if it meant she was not.

'He was a good man, like your husband,' the headman concluded. 'Gallagher Sahibji will come to you, but I do not know when.'

'I understand.'

'Please be careful.'

'I understand.'

Shakuntala too understood. The headman would not betray his memory of Michael Ferrar.

On the first of May, Shakuntala's workers reported that at sunset, everyone was again to assemble in Aberdeen Square. She could tell what they were all fearing: there was to be another execution.

At the square that evening, she found Mr Martin, the former deputy commissioner, handcuffed and standing beside Major and Governor Ito. Mr Martin had been under house arrest since last month. The other European prisoners of war—the harbour master and the wireless officer in charge—had been sent away.

There was an announcement that Mr Martin had been found assembling a wireless set. The charge was read aloud by none other than Balaraj, who had once been the superintendent Mr Howard's faithful security guard. Treason, Balaraj said, was the most serious crime. A witness, Mir Mohammad, came forward. He was none other than the sweeper who had once been at the jailor Cillian's feet. Mir Mohammad confessed to being Mr Martin's accomplice. Mr Martin, he said, had asked him for the wireless pieces to transmit secret messages to the enemy. Mr Martin denied the charges.

Major and Governor Ito declared Mr Martin guilty of conspiracy against the Emperor of Japan. The punishment was death.

At first, what happened to Zee happened again. Mr Martin's arms and legs were twisted backward and his spine was smashed. But then, as he lay curled on the ground, a few men from the crowd came forward. More approached. Soon, his body was no longer visible and he was no longer screaming. Major and Governor Ito declared that though Mir Mohammad was a co-conspirator, he had showed courage by confessing to his crime, and would be pardoned. A few people cheered while the rest dissolved in silence, one woman whispering, 'Poor Miss Mattie will never see him again.'

At the end of the month, Shakuntala learned that soldiers had come into one of the huts in Marriagetown, to take away two girls.

The girls were being kept at Army Headquarters in Haddo. They were fourteen and fifteen years old. According to Shakuntala's workers, a group of local men had found the courage to assemble outside Major and Governor Ito's office in Browning Club to beg for their release.

Shakuntala looked towards the house, where Paula was eating lunch. She would not leave her daughter alone anymore. She took her by the hand, and soon all of the women were making their way down to Aberdeen, to join the men outside the club.

A representative of the Peace Committee had been sent by Major and Governor Ito to reason with the crowd. 'They were play women,' the man said. 'Do not forget it.' He looked around, and a smile crossed his lips. 'Baishunfu. Do not forget it.'

For many that day, the word for prostitute was the first word learned in Japanese.

When the crowd continued to argue, the representative asked, 'What about the times Englishmen came to your tents? Did you insult the men? These soldiers, they are our brothers. They build an airfield for us. They grow crops for us. They free us. But they are far from home. It is your duty to welcome them.'

A week later, a crowd again assembled outside Browning Club. Two more girls had been taken away. This time, they were recruited by a village headman. Shakuntala searched for Aditi in the crowd. The nod Aditi returned was like an icy finger creeping up Shakuntala's spine. The headman of Ferrargunj was protecting his own grandchildren from the soldiers and, equally, diverting attention away from his alliance with Andrew Gallagher, Jr. The headman had lived on the island for forty-one years, had recently married for a third time and was not ready to die.

The same representative of the Peace Committee who had addressed them last week stepped out of the club. 'Do you not see,' he shouted, 'if not these girls, whose? We are maintaining order and keeping your daughters safe.'

Then Dr Singh stepped outside the club. 'Go home to your families,' he pleaded. He assured them that soon, other arrangements would be made. When the crowd refused to disperse, he pushed through it, walked down the square, and knocked at his friend Haider Ali's door.

The Many Mistakes of Haider Ali 2
1942

HAIDER ALI WAS DREAMING OF the glass at his father's shop. His father had been a hakeem with herbal remedies for everything from arthritis to hair loss, and it was Haider Ali, the third son, who was meant to take over the shop after learning his father's cures. His older brothers had proven themselves unworthy for reasons that mostly involved drink, as well as their own peculiar natures. In contrast, Haider Ali dutifully put in time at prayer and then at the shop, where he would refill all those glittering blue and pink bottles with the precious herbs he helped to collect, pound and label. His only vice was sometimes spending excessive time playing with the cork. How he loved to pop the stopper of each bottle before twisting it back down again!

Haider Ali shifted in his sleep, hearing the squeak of cork against glass. The tonic he had prepared was ready for his father to sell. There was a fragrance that mingled with his pleasure, and it came from one of the most beloved ingredients in the shop, Multani mitti, a mineral so rich it could remove the body's impurities without compromising its natural oils. Haider Ali's mother would sometimes feed it to him in powder form to strengthen his gums, or apply the mud directly to his hair. 'Living is a graceful task,' she would say, as he inhaled the rich scent. 'Remember, it is easier to hate those who wrong us than to love those we wrong.' Then she would quote a favourite verse from the Quran. 'Believers, be witnesses for justice. Never allow the hatred of people to prevent you from being just.'

She was a gentle woman who never raised her voice or spoke ill of others, and who, it felt to Haider Ali as he slept, had been considerably concerned with love and hate.

He shifted again. There was now the smell of the coconut oil his father massaged into his own scalp each day with long unbending fingers and, occasionally, a rasping voice.

This was his family. His children's lineage. The plants he collected for their grandfather, the joy of winning the old man's approval, the soil that fed the plants, the rafters where the pigeons roosted, watching him as he worked: all of it belonged to his children. Only through ritual could continuity be maintained, and so could tenderness.

Haider Ali rolled onto his back and for a time his sleep was dreamless. Then the vision of glass bottles lining his father's cabinet returned, except it had changed. A small egg was caught inside one of the pink bottles, lit by fragments of early morning light. The light fell on Haider Ali, and he awakened.

He shut his eyes, willing himself back to sleep the way he had done each night and each morning when up at the jail. The only difference now was that his dreams were sweeter, and waking was worse.

Once awake, his thoughts were always the same.

His wife had been pregnant with Zee when they arrived on the island. He had never spent time with Zee as a baby. He had never heard the baby cry, or asked what his first words might have been. Zee had never slept on rooftops on summer nights. He had never felt the crisp coolness of a cup of water from a clay matka. He had never memorised the Quran. He had never known a favourite aunt. He had never tasted real sweets—khoya burfi, pista burfi, gur. He had never learned that fennel and saffron could make a nose sing. He had never picked a goat for the ritual slaughter at Eid. And Haider Ali had never described any of it for him. He had been too busy distancing himself from the knowledge that it was not in Jalandhar but in Aberdeen that Zee was growing up, and that, by the time they first met, his son already liked his English teacher more.

Haider Ali could not even remember the first time he held Zee.

Sometimes, when Zee was here, Haider Ali would move from the cot to the floor mat where both his children slept and whisper the Ayat Al-Kursi, the Quranic verse his own father had taught him, while stroking their hair. But Haider Ali had not taught Zee the Ayat Al-Kursi. The night he sent Zee away, he could at least have given him this, for the poor boy to recite when afraid on his last night.

That egg in his dream, it was always there. He could not get to it, but it was there, as though to offer a parallel truth, one in which things could start all over again. He had only to smash the bottle without hurting the egg.

They made me cut down my own son.

In his English school, had Zee been taught the tale of Ibrahim and Ismail? Or was it Abraham and Isaac? Did it matter, when the father, by any name, was a murderer?

In that last hour, when the Japanese marched Zee to the square and Haider Ali could feel himself dying inside—because he had not died yet, not in all the years when he thought he was dead—he had prayed. It was his first prayer since his arrival on these shores, with the exception of that night on the site of the gurdwara. *Dear God, let this be a test. It must be. Your hand will intervene.* When they broke his son's right arm, he kept praying. *I will never doubt You again. All my suffering at the jail was no suffering at all.* When they broke the left arm. *Let me be Your sacrifice, not my boy. Let me serve You.* When they slapped him to the ground. *I submit my will to Yours.* And slapped him again, faster. *Ask anything else of me. I will give You another son. I will change my ways.*

Then they executed him.

Haider Ali was not very drunk when he heard the knock on the door. His drink had almost finished, and he was saving what he could till he found a way to get to the store.

When the knocking did not cease, he finally looked outside.

'Hello, my friend.' It was Dr Singh.

He had been here, several times, since Zee's assassination. Haider Ali tried to shut the door, but Dr Singh held out his arm.

'I must speak with you,' said the doctor. 'Where is Nomi?'

Haider Ali looked inside. The child was with Zee's books, and did not look up.

'Good,' said Dr Singh. 'Keep her here. You and I must speak somewhere else.'

'Another time,' said Haider Ali. Realising that the doctor would need more convincing, he added, 'My wife is sleeping.'

'We can speak outside,' said Dr Singh.

Haider Ali decided it was easier to give in for a short while than to continue with his protests. He followed Dr Singh around to the back, to the small plot of land where the crops were drooping. Dr Singh looked around. There were no soldiers here. He sat in the dirt, which was unlike a man of his grooming. Haider Ali sat beside him.

Dr Singh crossed his legs once, twice, then cleared his throat. 'I am lightening my load onto you knowing how much you carry already, because, you see, we need each other. I hope that, in time, you will share your hurt with me. I am your friend.'

Haider Ali coughed.

When the cough subsided, Dr Singh started to talk. He told him that two more girls had been taken to Haddo. 'That makes four. Do you know what they call them?' He leaned towards Haider Ali, who was studying his wilting tomatoes. 'Ni-ku-ichi. It means twenty-nine to one. Do you know what I am saying? And what happens when the girls are replaced? What then?' Dr Singh did not wait long for a response. 'The Japanese command knows it has to develop trust among people, especially—' He leaned forward again, leaving Haider Ali to complete the sentence. *After what they did to your son.*

'They are afraid of diseases,' the doctor continued. 'They want to go about this in an organised way, with medical tests. Because I am a doctor, they want my help.'

Haider Ali realised that his friend was crying. Dr Singh, the most dignified of men. The sobbing was silent, but the shoulders rose and fell. Haider Ali wished it would stop. *Look how my back already bends.* It was not kind, and he had thought the doctor was kind.

'There is more,' said Dr Singh, breathing deeply. 'I am not alone on the Peace Committee in saying that our women cannot become their slaves. And, as I said, they need our trust. So there is another proposal. They will bring women from other territories, and house them, of all places, in our gurdwara.'

'Gurdwara?'

'We cannot suffer this outrage. We cannot let them destroy the sanctuary we built together. What is to be done?'

'What is to be done?' repeated Haider Ali.

'Yes, my friend. That is what I have come to ask.'

The two men were silent for a while. Dr Singh's fingers traced the dirt around them. The dirt was dry, as it had not rained in some days.

'What they do to those girls and will do to others is an insult I already cannot endure. But they also intend to insult our faith. Yours and mine. I cannot assist them.' He picked up the dirt and let it fall.

Haider Ali stood up.

'I must thank you for listening,' said Dr Singh, also standing. 'I do not take the effort lightly. I know you blame yourself. And now, I am also implicated. But you and I, we are not the ones to blame. Do not lose heart, Haider Ali. You must think of the child who still lives. You must protect and love her with every part of you. It is what your son would have wanted. You are still a father.'

Haider Ali did not hear it. He was the man who took his only son to the slaughter. 'I killed two Sikhs,' he said. 'It was an accident. I gave them the wrong bottle, and the wrong dose, from my father's clinic. That is what brought me here, to this island, with a pregnant wife, and now, a dead son.'

In finally sharing this awful secret with his friend, Haider Ali felt no relief. Nor did he find relief in the expression on the doctor's face, which let him know that his only accomplishment was hurting someone else.

'It changes nothing between us, Haider Ali,' said the doctor, his voice low. 'Forgiveness is every god's gift to us.'

But Haider Ali could not hear it. 'Our god is the same,' he said, shuffling back to the hut. 'This doesn't make him good.'

Silence and Song
1942

IT WAS SHAKUNTALA THE doctor approached next. He said there were women on the way, and because there were no Japanese women and only one doctor and two nurses left on the island—and both nurses were overworked—would Shakuntala be willing to help?

His speech was very muddled. It started. It stopped. First Andrew Gallagher, Jr, and now Dr Singh—why did grown men keep coming to her?

'Help how?' she asked the doctor.

Dr Singh was visiting her farm for the first time. As he held a teacup, his hand shook. 'I do not yet know,' he answered. 'I have never done this before.'

'But neither have I,' she said. 'I am not even a doctor. I am not even a nurse.'

'The worst part is, the location is to be the gurdwara. The one our men built.'

'That is the worst part?'

'A house of worship will be turned into a whorehouse. So, yes, I imagine that is the worst part.' He thanked her for the tea—left untouched—and said to let him know if she, or a woman she could recommend, would be willing to assist. Then he took his leave.

By the middle of August, one of the first two girls to be kidnapped was returned to Marriagetown. Her name was Neha and she was fifteen years old. She was pregnant and frequently throwing up, so they had let her go. Her mother would not welcome her back. While two other women took Neha into their tent, most women kept themselves and their children away from her.

Whether they spurned Neha or not, the women were united by the numbers. Ni-ku-ichi. Twenty-nine soldiers to one girl. There were now three left in Haddo, which meant the ratio was further perverted, when it already was, when the first girl was raped by the first man— and there, each woman stopped thinking, her mind had hit its limit. At night, there were sobs coming from more than Neha's tent.

In the morning, silence again.

During the day, the gurdwara was reconstructed into an ianjo, a comfort station. As with the airstrip and the new road, the work was done by re-arrested convicts. The gurdwara, built to be one room for all, was now divided into chambers, partitioned with curtains. At the entrance was a reception desk. At the back was a toilet pit concealed by another curtain, and outside, on a small table, was a bottle of disinfectant. The two outside taps for washing hands and feet before entering the temple remained.

Slowly, the face of the gurdwara transformed from a temple to a jail. It had tiny cells with rush mats for the cold, damp floor. On one day, blankets arrived. On another, three beds were carried across from the deserted British villas on Ross Island, two for naval headquarters in Browning Club. Furniture was also looted from the villas—teak desks, wicker chairs, lamps—all built by Indian and Burmese hands, all brought on the ferry that had to navigate the mines.

A wire fence was constructed around the property, and though the soldiers did not allow loitering, people paused and looked, the way they had looked when prisoners arrived on the *S.S. Noor*. They continued to look through the heavy monsoon rains when the roads grew muddy and the insects grew thick.

Next, the women appeared, two with young children. The same night, the ianjo opened, and the three girls still in Haddo were released.

The day after the ianjo's opening, Dr Singh again arrived at Shakuntala's farm. He said the medical tests would take place every Saturday morning, so she could continue to manage her farm. He seemed to have stopped caring about propriety and used words he had previously been unable to speak. They were tests for, in particular, gonorrhoea and syphilis. All the women had been cleared before their arrival. Mostly, her presence was needed because they were terrified of being examined by men.

He said other things. The majority of women had been tricked into coming here. They had been told they were going to the front, to work for their countries. They had not been told what work, only that it would pay off family debts. There were women who had been bought for bags of salt, women who had been lured by red shoes. Others were taken by force. Each had been registered according to her real name, Japanese name, date of birth, the address and profession of her guardians, and even comments on her behaviour. For instance, if she had a drinking habit. There were Chinese women taken from Singapore, Korean women from Burma, Indonesian women from Penang and a Filipina woman from Davao. Like the prisoners once forcibly shipped here, the women had travelled great distances. The difference was, each had ended up an ianfu.

So this was the fourth Japanese word to reach their shores. Ianfu. Comfort woman.

What could Shakuntala do, now that she had heard this? What could she ask, including of herself? 'How much time off do they get?' she whispered. 'I mean, to rest?' It was not the first or even second question she wanted to ask.

Dr Singh shook his head. 'An hour or two a week. No more, even when they menstruate.'

The detail stunned her, as did his boldness in sharing it. As his beard grew ragged, his conversation grew free.

He was telling her the soldiers had low morale and fought amongst themselves. It was believed that women would uplift them. He added, 'Local women will be safer.'

'My God,' whispered Shakuntala.

'The Japanese are suspicious of anyone in any way associated with the British, especially if fluent in English. This includes you and your daughter. You should be seen as helping them.'

Shakuntala looked outside, at Paula on the kitchen step. She shut her eyes.

Today, Dr Singh drank his tea. 'Eight o'clock on Saturday, if you agree.' He thanked her, and added, 'You will also be helping me. That is no reason, I understand, but—' He sighed. 'They are already so frightened. And I am not like these men.'

On Friday, after Paula had fallen asleep and Shakuntala secured the door with latches, even barricading it with the kitchen table and Thomas's desk, as had become her habit, she lay in bed, remembering Thomas, remembering their wedding night.

It was the second night of her periods. 'At least there will be ample evidence of your virginity,' said Thomas, and Shakuntala's womb tightened in anticipation of the pain. 'We can wait, Shakuntala.'

She had not told him how afraid she was, and not only because these were the heaviest hours of her cycle. What if they did not ever have sex? Would that be all right?

She did not ask.

On the fourth night, they had sex for the first time. Afterwards, they showered together. He lathered her very tenderly, and a part of her liked it but a part of her did not. She was used to washing alone, even as a child. The bathroom in her father's house had been outside, and she never liked how public it was. When she could shut the door and throw the latch, even to her mother, the smoothness of soap and slow scooping of water from a pail with her small palm grew patient and peaceful, and all of it became hers.

When Thomas bathed her, there were places he overlooked, and places he over looked. She was still bleeding, and the water running down the drain was not a peaceful colour. Most of all, she hurt. Had she been alone, as the water hit her, she might have contemplated the hurt. She might have spoken to it, or waited till it spoke to her. With Thomas so close, there was no time for the exchange, and this confused her.

When they were done, he wrapped one towel around them both and this part was sweet. Her cheek inclined on his cool breast—she was that much shorter—and the blood trickled down her thigh. They held each other for a long time.

When she woke up on Saturday morning, she was sobbing. This became her habit for the next seven Saturdays.

She learned that there were rules. The men were given a ticket a day, submitted to the paymaster at the reception desk inside the ianjo. Each ticket represented a percentage paid to the women and fixed by the army. If a woman became ill, or needed supplies, she bore the entire cost herself. If she had no deductions, she had to put her portion towards national defence. No ianfu Shakuntala met would ever receive payment.

At first, only military personnel could use the ianjo. But in the coming weeks, once the women were no longer new, civilian employees of the army were also allowed inside, though at different hours. Balaraj and Mohammad Mir were seen there, daily.

By the beginning of October, if accompanied by Balaraj or Mohammad Mir, a few select members of the local populace were also permitted inside.

By the middle of October, Shakuntala decided to tell the doctor that she could not come to the clinic on Saturdays any more. She could not stand that the women had stopped feeling embarrassed as they pulled down their pants and allowed him to do the pelvic test and take a fluid sample. They used to scratch his hands. No more. She could not stand the stains on their clothes. She could not stand how they looked at her when she put a hand on their shoulder, or spoke to them in a language they could not understand. She could not stand that there was a security guard even inside the room, while the interpreter had vanished. She could not stand that they were starving and she was not allowed to bring them food. She could not stand that women from Korea, China, Malaya and the Philippines were to the Japanese even more downhill than black Portuguese to the British. She could not stand that Asia for Asians was as much a lie as Asia for Europeans, though she had never concerned herself with either. She could not stand that when a woman got sick or pregnant, or another local man paid off Balaraj or Mohammad Mir, the terrible ratio of women to men worsened, and Paula woke her up in the middle of the night because she was screaming. She could not stand that after leaving the clinic, the women were allowed their only 'free' hour, during which the ones who could walk walked, escorted by four guards, in a small circle. She could not stand that she was a witness to their suffering in the vile clinic because she was a woman. She could not stand that she gave no comfort to anyone except the doctor, who was a man.

And so she had to stop.

On Saturday, 17 October, she arrived early, relieved to find the doctor already there. Then she noticed the bruise on his left temple and the cuts on his knuckles. The guard had not yet come inside, and as they arranged the tray, ignoring the doctor's condition, she told him she could not stay. He started again to tell her things she wished he would not. Two weeks ago, he said, after Shakuntala left the clinic, one woman, whose Korean name was Song and Japanese name Momoko, came back inside to tell him to see how it was for her. 'Just come into the second room on the right, doctor!' she said through an interpreter who was surprisingly willing to let her speak.

'Is that why there is no longer an interpreter?' Shakuntala interrupted.

'Undoubtedly he has been punished,' replied Dr Singh.

This past Wednesday, he continued, he got into the ianjo somehow, pushing past everyone in line, saying a woman was sick. When he pulled aside the curtain, Song was eating rice balls with a man between her legs. She begged for morphine. She had learned the English word. It was 8 p.m. After 8.30, the men would not have access to her. Only their officers would. They were yelling at each other to hurry up.

'Please stop,' pleaded Shakuntala.

Dr Singh, who was having trouble moving his right arm, said he had been dragged outside, and had spent the last two nights in jail.

The security guard came inside. The women arrived. The doctor was gruff, dismissing each one without using a single cotton swab. The sentry appeared not to notice. After the ninth exam—though Shakuntala doubted it could be called this—as the sentry stepped outside, Dr Singh hurried to a small cabinet by the wall and grabbed a syringe and a bottle. Waving these at Shakuntala, he told her to prepare the injection.

She was horrified.

'Hurry up.'

'No!'

Dr Singh pocketed the syringe and the bottle.

The sentry returned.

Shakuntala tried to leave but the sentry snapped, 'Two more hour!'

'I need air.'

He stood in her way and she was forced to return.

When an hour later the sentry again stepped outside, Dr Singh prepared the injection, secreted it away, and told Shakuntala, 'You must distract him when I say.'

Song came into the clinic. She was not walking so much as forcing her body forward, a hand pressed to her side. Shakuntala was trying not to see, she had been trying not to see, Song was not the only one to come to the clinic hoping to die.

'Now,' Dr Singh whispered to Shakuntala.

Shakuntala walked over to the sentry. She repeated that she needed a break. When he grabbed her arm, she dragged herself out, pulling him with her. 'I must use the toilet!' she screamed. 'I am sick!' Two more men arrived. They carried her back inside and tossed her on the dirt floor.

Song was rolling off the table, her eyes misty. She was walking straighter.

'Next!' said Dr Singh, and another woman came inside.

By the middle of November, Dr Singh was again arrested. It was anticipated that he would be killed in much the same way as Zee and Mr Martin.

By the end of the month there were rumours that Dr Singh was being kept alive. He enjoyed a status with the local populace that threatened to make him a hero if assassinated. When Major and Governor Ito next called an assembly, he said the doctor was a thief. He had stolen morphine from army supplies. He was not a man, or he would understand the natural desires of men.

The following Saturday, Shakuntala was called back to work. There was another doctor, a Japanese one, whom she regarded with the same indifference that she regarded herself for no longer sobbing. She returned to the clinic every week till the Allies started bombing the island in December.

The Other Side of Love
1942–43

'At last I see the real girl. When you appear with wild hair and angry eyes
. . . you are not your normal self, but are unbalanced, unnatural.'

—Rabindranath Tagore, *Char Adhyay*

MILES AWAY, PRISONER 218 D studied green streaks in the sky, try-ing to determine if they were parachutes or parakeets.

She could not see across the abyss, and knew nothing of the death of Zee or other horrors on South Andaman Island. A delicate mist hung over her own rock, which she did not call by any name. She had lived here, in silence, for four years. What she knew was that she no longer had to be Prisoner 218 D. She was the prisoner who got away. The prisoner who no longer existed.

There had been ships in the water and planes in the sky. There had been sirens followed by bombings, bombings followed by sirens, and all of it followed by stillness. Lately, the bombings had started up again. She did not understand any of it. The boy who brought her here had vanished. Even the Andamanese man who had accompanied the boy and sometimes returned to sing with the islanders, who were not Andamanese, had not been seen in many moons.

Today, the islanders left their huts, and lingered along the shore-line with their arrows, also looking up at the sky. She knew them well enough by now to know that they were tense. The green streaks—par-akeets, she decided—had melted in the mist. The islanders spoke to each other in low tones and eventually returned to their huts, though two men were left to keep watch. The prisoner who was no longer a prisoner sat with them, saying nothing. If they smiled at her, this too she accepted.

They had not always smiled and she had not always accepted. A tight ball of poison, like a seed of arsenic, was buried deep in her bones. How deep, her mind still could not grasp. Had it begun on the night of her escape, the day of her arrest, or earlier? The question did not interest her, yet. For now, most mornings, she would wake up sensing that something had changed.

When first brought here from the jail, it had seemed to her that even this small rock presented a vastness impossible to fathom. She dug herself a nest in the sand, something to cup her hips and warm her shoulders and never allow so much as a hand to pass.

Other days, she lunged out of the nest, hit by something unnameable. 'Where were you? *Where?*' The same mangled conversation played out incessantly, with whom, it was unclear, causing her to grow ever smaller and more grotesque to herself. At such times, there was such malice in her eyes that those who watched hung back.

Each time her fury passed, she collapsed back into her nest. Then commenced the slow, dark process of restoring herself. The sand was cooling. She scooped the grains around her, encasing herself in a death shroud, and the pressure was good. Yet no space seemed to fit her anymore, which could again cause her to fly out of her burial nest.

Adult islanders called her Ineny-lau, foreigner. Children called her Kwalakangne, the southwest wind whose temper brought the monsoons.

It could last a few minutes. It could last several weeks. The interval might be marked by a memory. For instance, the sharp *chink!* of the nurse at the hospital, trimming her nails to keep her from tearing her flesh. As for the beginning of the storm, here too there was no pattern. It might be the sun shining down on her like a furious flower, or the sound of chain links on the prison ship. Then she was back in the factory, being flogged. Back in the hospital, being force-fed.

•

The memory of liquid rushing down her throat still overpowered her today, as she lingered along the shoreline with the two men with arrows who were tense because the bombings had started again.

She left them, to crawl back to her nest.

The shape of the nest kept shifting, as though her body wished to shed its shroud, or find a looser one. Strange relics caught on her fingernails—how the nails grew, with no nurse to cut them!—from pretty shells to rusting metal to leaf wreaths once tied to a tree, marking the death of a child. She also found a scrap of cloth, the colours bleached away. She twisted it around her wrist, and then her hair (long, salt-stripped), and when evening came and the moon began to wax and a once-familiar spasm snatched her stomach (she could not say when the pain had last visited), she pushed the cloth between her legs.

After a while, one of the two watchmen went inland to hunt. Food and coconut water were left for her at the opening to her nest, as always, with the soft call of her name. *Ineny-lau.*

She could not remember when she had first begun to taste the food, but there were never any mice droppings, of this she was sure. Beneath the cool moonlight, the offering was crispy and warm. She washed it down with the fragrant liquid. There were flecks of fruit on her tongue. She pressed them between her teeth the way she had once pressed the meat of almonds, after they had been soaked overnight. This taste was sweeter.

When she believed no one was watching (though they were), she dug out another scrap of cloth and hurried to a far cluster of trees behind which she could empty her bowels. A lizard followed. It was four feet long, with massive claws. When she screamed, it was chased away by the man called Lala Ram. He gestured to her that he would keep watching for lizards. She moved behind the tree trunk, to squat.

Unknown to the prisoner who was no longer a prisoner, the fragment she wiped herself with was of a Union Jack that once flew from the

Earl Kellie, in 1825. The ship had been on her way to Rangoon from Madras when the crew realised it wanted fresh water. Eight soldiers of His Majesty's 13th Light Dragoons set out for this island in a boat. As they searched for streams, aborigines watched from behind trees. Unable to find a source, the crew spread out, and found a camp with a fire still burning and mussels partly cooked. The aborigines who abandoned the camp had left behind bows and arrows.

The soldiers shot the arrows around the camp and entered the huts, helping themselves to whatever they found. Nets, pottery, skulls. When the aborigines returned, they were killed with bayonets. Those who survived did not leave a single one of their dead or wounded behind when they retreated back into the jungle.

Eventually, the crew found a freshwater pool, the only water hole on this side of the island. After raising the Union Jack, they returned to their boat, taking with them barrels overflowing with sweet water and as many bows, arrows and souvenirs as they could carry, and leaving hundreds of dead aborigines.

Their descendants, unlike the Andamanese of South Andaman Island, had never been enlisted to track or kill Indian and Burmese fugitives. When Loka had arrived with the girl, though he was from a distant tribe, the islanders knew why he asked this favour of them. Once before, they had sheltered a runaway. The man had eventually married a native woman. Their only offspring, Lala Ram, still lived here, chasing monitor lizards for the prisoner who was no longer a prisoner.

She dug her nests as the bombs hit the sea and the aborigines slept inside conical huts on sticks. Twice before—when the rains had been heavy, and when the fires out in the water had been too close—they gestured for her to come inside. Both times she had screamed. They had stopped inviting her. She wondered if, were they to ask now, she would finally agree. When they lit a fire and roasted mussels and cicadas, she had stopped running away. Even when digging, she did not go far from their huts. On a few occasions, she had dipped her toes into a creek and regarded, from behind a tree, Lala Ram and the woman called Lulu, who was perhaps his mother, collecting crabs and fish. She grew so mesmerised by the way they tossed their nets that once, when a wild boar rushed past her, she forgot her fear.

Another time, there was a rainbow. She watched it come and go.

One day, she saw four men return from a canoe carrying a large turtle. They flipped the turtle onto its back before hacking it to pieces. She did not know how she knew it was a turtle. There were no turtles in Lahore, as far as she could remember. As she watched the hunters, she did not flinch. Hunger overcame her.

The meat was shared with her that night. One piece was tender, the other, inflexible. There was also a bowl of deeply replenishing soup. After eating, she settled back into her sand nest—somewhat larger than the last one—rubbed her stomach, burped.

Her sleep was without dreams.

In the morning, the rain fell in her mother's voice. *Stay soft. Those knots in your body, it is you they will destroy in the end.*

It fell, too, in the hushed tones emanating from the conical huts. The huts kept moving further away from the coast and she kept moving with them. She realised that for some time now, whenever the islanders built a fire, it was small and put out quickly. The men were often sent to the shore for news. She still did not understand the information they brought back, but the planes more frequently hit the ships that carried flags with a bright red sun, and one of these flags was now burning in the sea, beneath the rain.

When it stopped raining, though the sky was sour with fumes, the aborigines brought their beds outside. They no longer danced or made music, but the women still painted the men. This activity had always arrested her, and she was glad it had not ceased. The fingers of women brushed the skin of men with as much serenity as her mother's had once brushed the skin of women when applying henna. The women here used clay, and decorated the entire body. She liked the smell.

A woman devoted more care to the application of clay when a

man returned from a big hunt. She had noticed this before. The pattern used to be that, after eating, the hunters reclined, the fire still burning—it burned brighter in those days—while women adorned them in different colours in very many designs. When the men started using their canoes less and even fish became scarce, the women either stopped painting them or did it in the slipshod way her mother prepared henna after quarrelling with her father.

Then, last night, the hunters had killed the turtle. The women waited till this morning to start painting, and the fire was put out. They worked slowly, lovingly, before stepping back to examine their work. One man wore red on half his face and torso, olive on the other half. Another had a sequence of white dots running all the way from shoulders to feet, and up again, repeatedly, till he was a curtain of silver pearls. When his muscles flexed, the pearls danced.

After the hunters had been decorated, though there was no dance, the celebration did not end. Their habits were growing familiar but their nakedness was not. The prisoner who was no longer a prisoner never had brothers, and her love for Aunty Hanan's nephew, Faris, was entirely chaste. She had kissed him only once on the mouth—how slimy and disappointing it was!—and never sat on his lap, even when he asked. With the islanders, it was the man who sat on the woman's lap, and she held him almost as she would a baby. They caressed. There were noises. The men would have to be painted again.

Days passed. She noticed a man and a woman from Lala Ram's hut sitting with their backs to each other, at a distance, with arms crossed. They remained this way for hours, it seemed to her, though she could not measure time any more than she could distance. It had happened before, and she loved these moments. When two people had been apart their reunion was fraught with tension, until something magical happened.

When the sun was visible above the treeline surrounding their encampment, the magic began. The man stood up, went to the woman and cautiously sat on her lap. Gradually, she extended her arms. Together, they cried. During the long embrace—which today promised to be longer than the partition—the prisoner who was no longer a prisoner gathered the letters given to her by the boy who had brought her here. Once the couple were no longer crying but simply swaying, she went for a walk, letters in hand.

She recalled the night of her escape, her body dead in the boat, but for the frail fist into which the boy had dropped the three letters. The fist had curled with life, foetus to placenta, and the boat became a womb. Now, as she walked, the fist tightened again. She had read the letters many times. None were from her mother. These, she had decided, were among those torn in front of her, in jail. Words she could be holding in her hands. The storm inside her began to roil.

She headed for the shallow creek. Small crabs scurried around, leaving their underground tunnels in nervous haste. If she extended a toe, down the crabs went, back into their holes. If she stood still, eventually, one extended a claw and started scooping mud into its mouth, till others appeared.

Kaajal had once told her: it only takes one to draw them all out.

After her mother, the person she most wanted a letter from was Kaajal, but Kaajal was dead.

She followed a path down to a pebbly patch of shore, and paused, picturing India somewhere beyond the smoky horizon. As the waves swirled around the coral and the stones, she listened to the beach-bumping music of it. Then she unfolded Aunty Hanan's letter and skipped to the parts that haunted her most.

> *Friday, 27th August–*
> *Dear child,*
> *I blame myself, and I should . . .*
>
>   *Do you remember the day your father was killed? How beautiful you looked, before we got the news. You were riding the bicycle, dressed in a moss green top with a silvery pattern in the weave. As you pedalled, the sun fell through the neem trees and cast a mottled mosaic*

on your cheek. Then you saw me standing outside my house and stopped pedalling, dropping one foot down for balance. I thought to myself, here is a child born of light! I thought of you as my daughter, and how proud I would be to have one like you . . .

Do you remember it was your idea to help me onto the bicycle? Though I had no idea what to do, the two of you tried to spin me around! What a happy moment, just before the terrible news! Let me stop here. Let the memory of that day end with you and Faris spinning me around on your bicycle made in Japan, shipped from Singapore, and delighting an aunt from Calcutta who rode it in Lahore . . .

Your father would be proud. Yet, if there is one thing I am grateful for, it is that he did not see you being taken away.

Before the ships with the bright sun arrived, there had been a woman who tossed nets far into the sea in a single movement that was an extension of her breath. Now, as the prisoner who was no longer a prisoner put the letter aside and started pouring sand over her head, the woman came to her. Lulu. Her body was compact and her skin glistened. The berth of her neck was more generous than that of the woman the prisoner when still a prisoner had been shackled to on the prison ship. Her singing, as beautiful.

Slowly, she climbed onto Lulu's lap.

As she wept, she saw herself as Aunty Hanan had done, riding her bicycle in a place where she was beautiful and loved. She started to envision every woman she loved. Her mother, Nimra. Aunty Hanan. Her grandmother, Firoza. Her sisters, Umbreen and Nadia. Her dearest friend, Kaajal. The woman who had held her on the ship, whose name she did not know. The woman in whose lap she now sat, whose name was Lulu. She chanted the litany many times, and in this way, it was a long embrace.

On the day her father was killed, her parents had an argument. Her mother was a sensitive woman and her father could be frightening in his silence. So after that day, she tried to tell herself that though it was not their first quarrel, at least it was their last. The cause was this. Her father was to travel with his friend Mr Mehta in a secret caravan to a protest. He was a civil servant and had never before joined the freedom movement. Her mother insisted it would put the whole family at risk. He would not listen. Worse, he wanted to take his daughter. Not Umbreen, who was too afraid, and not Nadia, who was too young, but the middle child.

She could hear them argue in the next room. She was nine years old, and recently forbidden from wearing a frock unless accompanied with a pyjama, to cover her legs. The pyjama never looked good with dresses. When her father began raising his voice, it was worse than his silence. So she went out into the veranda, only then realising that she was clutching a frock, a blue one she did not even like, and no pyjama.

Even on the veranda, she could hear her father say, 'We have become slaves.'

Though her mother answered, the voice was lost.

'All we do is watch!' he said. 'Are you going to teach our daughters the same?'

'What else can they do?' She could hear her mother now. 'They are *girls*. You want her to be like you, but in a year or two, you will want her to be like me. And when she isn't, you will blame me!'

The next sound was of the door slamming, and when she peered over the railing, her father was leaving. She ran after him. Her mother ran after her. When she caught up with him and turned around, her mother was standing by the gate, calling her name.

He had a distinct scent, her father. She always believed it to be lotus-oil balm, as his skin was so very smooth, but years after his death, when she finally got hold of a bottle, it smelled nothing like him. It saddened her still that she never learned the name of his favourite perfume, which still wafted over her when she least expected.

That day, as they met up with a large crowd, her father explained that she must stick to him. She did not remember this till later because, at the time, she worried that her mother might still be at the gate, calling her name. When her fingers came unstuck from his, she was pushed into a side gully, in a part of Lahore with a transient name, such as Sort-of Chowk, or Type Town, as though made from a jigsaw puzzle. There were people behind but not ahead, and they were moving forward, the way an estuary moves out to sea. She passed tall trees just like her own and could hear children play. The people who moments ago had been pushing her now scattered into their own islands.

She turned into another street and her mother was still there. Mr Mehta's house could not have been far, though it seemed she had gone to the very ends of the world.

She ran to her mother. Faris had also come outside, standing with the bicycle he had taught her to ride. Her mother did not scold her too much so she hopped onto the bicycle, and after Aunty Hanan came outside, her mother returned to the house.

Faris was slight and fair. 'Crisp' was her father's word for him, and for his family, who owned lands in Bengal and degrees from Cambridge. 'Faris has "will pursue studies in England" written all over him,' her father always said. That one time Faris kissed her, she learned that the pearl-like beads of his perspiration, which resembled his spectacular buttons, had absolutely no odour. All of Faris was like the smooth inside of a shell. Now he was bragging that the bicycle was made in Japan.

'Why don't you ride it?' she asked Aunty Hanan.

'I don't know how,' said Aunty Hanan, 'I am too old to learn!'

'You are not too old,' she said. 'I'll hold while you sit.' She got off the bicycle.

Aunty Hanan hopped on, accidentally scraping the bell, which made them laugh.

They were still laughing when her mother ran out to say she had heard it on the radio: the Viceroy's men had intercepted the march. Protesters had been shot. Two were dead.

Later, they learned the names of the two men. One was her father.

The other was not Mr Mehta, who had noticed that his friend's daughter was missing. He told the police, who came to the house believing they were reporting two tragedies.

For her, it would always be two tragedies. If her fingers had not come unstuck from her father's, she might have died with him, or something might have happened instead, something to make the bullet fly somewhere else.

She left the lap of the woman who tossed nets far into the sea. *There*, she thought. *I have recalled the day.* She walked along the creek, the mud caking her ankles. Butterflies sipped moisture from her feet. It started again to rain. A curious calm enshrined her. She wanted to say, a symmetry. It rested in part on accepting a simple truth. She wished for someone to share it with. The truth was this. Her father died in the midst of making her. He left this task incomplete. It falls on children who lose a parent early in life to keep making the parent. So she did, hoping to succeed at least as well as he would have, if things were right, if he had lived to watch her grow.

Aunty Hanan was wise. At least he had not seen her being taken away.

Days passed. She learned to accept other things. For instance, the boar that ran wild were related to pigs. She was not allowed to eat the meat. Yet, she had been eating it. Her sister Umbreen would warn of hellfire. Kaajal would laugh.

She filed her nails with a crab claw. Her flesh had darkened to the colour of bark. Her clothes had long since rotted and mostly fallen off her back. She ate pig meat and did not cover her hairy legs.

The next time the man called Lala Ram sat beside her, she let him. As he talked, she gazed at his body, not with any emotion she was aware of, but in the same unfastened way she watched children play, or chewed insects. He was taller than the others of his tribe, though still shorter than she. His chest was smooth, his stomach round. When she touched her own chest, her ribs protruded. What did she look like? She had seen no mirrors here and did not recognise the person whose reflection greeted her in the creek.

Lala Ram had fashioned a tool with which to comb his shiny hair. It was made of the bones of some creature who once flew in the trees, or came up from the sea. She had noticed many colourful birds and the people who looked after her had different ones painted on their bodies. Lala Ram had offered her the comb before. Today, she took it. Her hair was tightly knotted and she could not pull away the tangles. He returned with a liquid that he poured gently over her skull. It was pungent and when he began to massage her scalp with his long fingers, she pointed up at the sky, at the planes. 'What is happening?' She could not remember the last time she had spoken aloud, and was astonished that the man who massaged her scalp answered both in a language she could not understand and in a language she could.

'Kugebe. War.'

She still did not know if her past raided her as dreams, visions, memories—or cleverly blurred all three. What she knew was that there were moments of wakefulness.

It was 1932, three years before her arrest. She was with Aunty Hanan, who was dressed in white cotton, as usual. Aunty Hanan was usually private about what she did in the mornings, after offering prayers and playing her beloved tambura to her beloved koel, but today, she asked, 'Do you want to come with me, to the study circle?'

'Yes.'

'We will hear women speak, things not spoken of at your house.'

Of course Aunty Hanan had only made it more enticing.

At the study circle, there was a girl she knew. Kaajal, the one who had not cried when their schoolteacher caned her for not kneeling before an Englishwoman. She and Kaajal had just started college, and they looked at each other now, as a woman began to read from the pages in her hand.

'The most painful thing in life is to wake up from a dream and have nowhere to go. So unless you see a way out for these dreamers, it is important not to wake them . . .'

'It is dangerous to wake women up,' someone interrupted.

There was applause. There was laughter.

The speaker continued. *'Nora was living contentedly but was eventually to wake up to the fact that she was a mere puppet manipulated by her husband, and her children were puppets manipulated by her. And so she walked out.'* The speaker adjusted her sari. 'But you know this already. The question is, what would stop Nora from leaving?'

'To stay in the dream, of course,' answered another woman. 'The better question is, who was manipulating Nora's husband?'

'Exactly. At least Nora's country was free of the British.'

The last comment was Aunty Hanan's. 'Our struggle is two-fold. To free ourselves from imperialism as much as domestic slavery.' She cocked a finger across the room. 'Nehru himself has asked that differences between men and women be erased *in times of war*. What about at other times?'

The women started arguing, with the majority favouring comradely cooperation between men and women.

'But can't you see?' insisted Aunty Hanan. 'When they dangle this carrot—permission to leave the house—it is only if we follow them.'

'What has come over you? You followed him, and did the right thing.'

By *him* the woman meant Ghaffar Khan, a disciple of Mahatma Gandhi. Two years ago, during the Salt March, Aunty Hanan had taken part in a procession led by Ghaffar Khan, and nearly been arrested. Since then, she had grown private about her movements, though neighbours pointed to her white khadi and said she remained a supporter of satyagraha, non-violent resistance to colonial rule.

'I would do it again. But remember, at first, Gandhi told women not to take part.'

'It no longer matters.'

'But it does,' argued Aunty Hanan.

'I agree with Aunty,' said Kaajal, 'and I have another question. Will civil disobedience be enough?'

'Such talk is not permitted here,' snapped the oldest woman there. 'Show your elders respect.'

The speaker waved the pages in her hand. 'As I was saying. Nora left, but what kind of life did she have? Ibsen did not say, and now he is dead—'

Aunty Hanan snorted.

The speaker began reading again. '*Once, at a banquet, women showed their appreciation for* A Doll's House *and its insights into the emancipation of women. To everybody's surprise, Ibsen said, "That isn't what I meant—I was simply composing poetry."*'

Aunty Hanan and Kaajal were the only ones laughing.

By the end of the year, Aunty Hanan had left the group, saying Lahore's middle class was 'too European.' She still wore white khadi, and now the whole neighbourhood knew that she regularly picketed foreign cloth and liquor stores. For continuing to question the men in the movement, she found herself quite alone, including among women, and spent more hours playing her tambura.

When one day Kaajal asked her if she would ever consider armed resistance, Aunty Hanan answered, 'Never.'

Kaajal and the prisoner who was not yet a prisoner did not tell Aunty Hanan when they joined a different group and became couriers, distributing anti-government literature on their bicycles. Arrangements at these group meetings were spare. There was a mat on the floor. There was tea, water, biscuits. There were still separate cups for Hindus and Muslims. This was commented upon with derision by some, and expected by others. The conversation often veered to social reform, specifically, female education and an end to purdah. Muslim women also wanted an end to polygamy and Hindu women pressed for the right to widow remarriage, divorce and a share of parental property.

At the gathering one day, Kaajal argued that since they all agreed on the need for social progress, why did they not focus instead on direct action?

On that last day, one woman, whose hair was lined with silver and whose feet were lined with dust, answered Kaajal. 'I will picket their shops. I will brave their lathis. This is direct action. I will risk death, but I will never risk exile.'

There were nods. Paper fans swished.

'Why not?' said Kaajal. 'It is better than sitting all day.'

'We do not sit all day. We recruit. We collect funds. We carry letters. We organise strikes. We put up posters. We—'

'We know what we do,' said a woman with a clipboard. 'Who will volunteer for delivery? For the factory?'

'She means the chemical factory.'

The room erupted in protest, with a few women threatening to leave.

'Do you want to get sent to the Andamans?' said the woman with silver-lined hair. 'You know that as women we must look for quieter ways. They send us, too. The government, the media, even the men who fight—none will speak of what happens to women who cross black water.'

A fearful silence descended upon the room.

Then came a whisper: 'The women who go there are polluted.'

Again, silence.

Eventually, someone ventured, 'What about the woman who helped Bhagat Singh? Do we even know her name?'

'She was Bengali.'

'Naturally. She was a brave woman. She could not have been Punjabi.'

'We do not do what we do to be remembered,' interrupted Kaajal, but no one was listening, because the woman who had made the comment before hers was vehemently reminded that it was on the banks of the river Ravi, 'in our beloved Lahore,' that the Indian flag was first hoisted, *by a Punjabi woman*, and now there was no bringing the conversation back.

Kaajal left, and the prisoner who was not yet a prisoner followed.

They were among the first girls to cycle in public in Lahore, and rode partway home together, as had become their habit. When there was a descent, they took their feet off the pedals, and when there was an ascent, they pedalled standing up.

'They do not want enough,' said Kaajal. 'Do you understand?'

'I am trying.'

'Have you noticed that when men want freedom, the conversation is about the nature of action, violence or non-violence? But when women want freedom, the conversation is about the nature of women, natural or unnatural?'

They were cycling past Lahore jail, where, in March of last year, the freedom fighter Bhagat Singh had been hanged. When he was arrested, every woman at college except Kaajal condemned what he had done: dropped two bombs in the Legislative Assembly. While in jail, Bhagat Singh was also found guilty of manufacturing bombs and killing an English policeman. Kaajal alone said not to forget that, back when Gandhi wanted only dominion status, it was Bhagat Singh who called for complete independence, arguing that force, when used for a rightful cause, had moral justification.

The two girls now spun around each other, sometimes pedalling backwards. The prisoner who was not yet a prisoner wondered what happened to the woman who helped Bhagat Singh after he shot the English policeman. She had posed as his wife on a train out of Lahore, taking with her the baby she had with a man she married at the age of eleven. Singh had cut his hair. The baby and the woman helped his disguise. But the following year, he and the woman were both arrested. She might still be in jail, she might be dead, and the prisoner who was not yet a prisoner did not know her name.

'Did you see the book in everyone's hands?' Kaajal asked, pedalling forward again. 'It was the same as at the other meetings, the ones with your Aunty Hanan.'

In fact, she had noticed. It was again *A Doll's House*. For middle-class Indian women who wanted change, Nora, when she slammed the door behind her, became the surest symbol of defiance. But not for Kaajal, who felt Nora was too much of a fairy tale. The story she had grown attached to was not a thunderous statement of revolt but an actual fairy tale, 'The Little Mermaid'. That day, Kaajal explained that the little mermaid's tale was truer to what was happening in India, and possibly all over the world, where most women were not slamming doors but choosing between identities.

'Do you know the story? The mermaid wanted what she could

not have. Most people think the object of her love was a human being, but that was not all. The object of her love was another world.' Kaajal paused, looking far into the distance with her deep-set eyes. 'She was given legs to enter the other world, but at what cost? She lost her community. She became neither mermaid nor human. It is the saddest story I know, and sometimes I feel we're in it, girls who fall in love with freedom.'

Kaajal's curls fell in a jumble at her shoulders, for she seldom bothered to tie them up. Her eyebrows were as wild as crow feathers. Her mouth was sublime. It was the softest part of her, a pink ribbon sloping gently to a smile so sensuous and private, it was a privilege to behold. No matter how solemn the eyes, there was always a sweetness to her lips. It was upon them that the eye of the prisoner who was not yet a prisoner now fell.

Kaajal leaned forward and kissed her once on the cheek for a very long time. There was the scent of sandalwood, khas and something else. The prisoner who was not yet a prisoner inhaled deeply. When she found it—cardamom—Kaajal was saying, 'You should not follow me.' The pink ribbon of her mouth twirled like a top, and she was gone.

The prisoner who was not yet a prisoner wanted badly to follow her. But it was getting late, and she already lied to her family about where she went after college. It was the lies she hated. She told them she sought Kaajal's help in maths, and they believed her. She hid how far she took her bicycle, though Faris had more than once told her to ride only on their street, with him. She touched her cheek. Kaajal had left a warm glow upon it, something Faris had never done.

She did not see Kaajal at the meeting the next day. There were no letters or pamphlets to deliver, and the printing machine was broken. And so, after looking for her friend, she came home.

The next morning, at breakfast, the cook told her family that a girl dressed as a man had tried to detonate a bomb and been shot dead. She knew, even then, but pushed the thought away. To avoid arousing her family's suspicion, she waited before racing on her bicycle to the meeting house. When she arrived, a man she had never seen before was waiting for her. He said Kaajal had been at the home where the printing machine was being repaired, where a large stock of weapons was concealed. Someone must have tipped off the police, who came inside just as Kaajal hid a grenade under her shirt. She was shot before the grenade could go off. 'She has died a martyr,' the man concluded.

As her world tipped, the prisoner who was not yet a prisoner thought she could hear the man's voice somewhere in the great distance, telling her that the printing machine and all the weapons had been seized. They would need help replacing them. He dropped into her hand a piece of paper with an address.

The death of her friend affected her more deeply than even her father's, nine years earlier. She had a buoyancy as a child that had saved her from the scars of adults. Now she was eighteen. Kaajal's age. Now she did not seem younger than Kaajal.

The night became her only comfort. It was always in mourning, and so was she.

When day finally returned, she hauled herself back to the meeting house, only to find that she had changed. All the talk of 'disparity' and 'injustice' sickened her. What did they know of it, this thing—this gap—of being different, of not being understood, of being a girl, of being expected to *be*? Be good for her mother, be chaste like Umbreen, be pretty like Nadia, be polite, be patriotic, be silent, be useful, be a wife, be a mother, be behind the brave men who fought for what she wanted, equally, and could fight for, equally, if she did not have to *be*. Kaajal alone would understand this mania that now possessed her, in which her sole desire was to destroy the gap, even by plunging through it. A mania with no beginning and no end, as unbroken as breath itself.

She had woken from a dream, but where was she to go?

By the end of the year, she had located the man who had delivered the news about Kaajal.

January 1943. It was soon after she pointed to the fires in the sky and sea, and Lala Ram told her there was a kugebe, a war. Though Lala Ram was never far, it was his mother she wanted. Yet the woman who had captured her in a net was nowhere to be found. She tried not to worry, telling herself that all the islanders liked to roam. Lulu would be back. She tried to deny that when she walked alone by the creek, it was partly to look for Lulu.

To distract herself, she re-read her sister Umbreen's letter. *They think I am unnatural like you. Ama suffers. Leave the revolution to men.* Not long ago, the words would have enraged her. Not today. If anything, she wished she could be more like Umbreen, and like sweet Nadia, too. The one content to spend her days in prayer, the other, in movies. Quiet lives, sanctioned by men and women alike. She was sorry her actions had hurt them. Sorrier still that her mother suffered. It was this that saddened her most. She did not know how much time had passed since the dates on the letters, but her mother might no longer be alive. Had she been more like her sisters, she would know. She would say goodbye the way every daughter ought to say goodbye to a parent. She would grieve with a family that had no cause to call her unnatural.

She kept walking, besieged by the question she had heard more than any other. *Why did you do it?* And she wondered, as always, why they kept asking for one answer, when they knew as well as she did that freedom was made of many parts.

Someone outside a door she had delivered a parcel to once put it best. 'Wear and tear, that is their weapon. Wear and tear.'

A million answers lay buried in the deep pockets of wear and tear.

But if they insisted on only one answer, it was this. She did not do what she did to avenge her father's murder, or to avenge Kaajal's. The people who explained her actions thus wished to confuse justice with revenge, to avoid turning the question on themselves. She did what she did to turn the question on them. Why did *they* do it—steal a land and its people, rape and torture them, ship them to alien shores and confine them within their own? The bullet that killed her father was but one. The bullet that killed Kaajal but another. She was not merely carrying one or two. She was carrying them all. The greatest violence was the silence that accompanied each one. All they had to do was stop trying so hard to forget.

Were they to try, even a little, she might speak to them, because it had been a long, long time since she spoke, and she was waking. Those words she ought to have written in Calcutta, when paper and pencil were given to her for the last time, they were surfacing. Somewhere in the great sky beyond this sky of planes was a star made entirely of words. And on the star lived as many different kinds of words as birds in all the skies, fish in all the seas, and clay patterns in all the hands of adoring women. Some words were cautious as the crabs nesting on the beach. Others, bold as the giant hornbills prattling in the trees. Then there were those that made no sound, but were equally fearless, folding their arms and waiting for her to sit on their lap. The prisoner who was no longer a prisoner was gathering all these many words to herself and would speak them, if there were but someone to listen, even a little.

As there was no one, she was left to contemplate the last word she had been given. *War.* The one happening in the sky was not the sort she had seen before, and these bombs were like nothing from a Lahore factory. How the sea raged, beneath the sparest of words. *War.* In every other language known to her, the word was given more letters, or at least more syllables. *Jang. Yuddha. Hrb.* And now, *kugebe.* Yet in English, there was no tongue or teeth to it. *War* could be whispered with lips closed. Like *go.* Like *home.*

Lulu was not to be found at the creek. She pushed on, towards a part of the island normally avoided. The trees here were so dense that they looped around each other and came out the other side of love, with arms raised, as if they had been caught. Hardly any sunlight slinked through their tight knots, and as she moved forward, day turned to night. Her last time here, she had witnessed a sight that must have astonished even God. A man was hacking at one of the trees, forcing a path through its roots. He hopped aside just in time to escape the thorn-spread vine that came swinging in his direction from someone's idea of heaven. Each thorn was the size of a small knife. She had wanted to ask, Revenge or justice?

Now she paused by the knots that obliterated the sky. She did not know why she went this way. Something compelled her. A baby boar came out of the darkness, skipping daintily aside when it saw her. The grass was high and leeches covered her bare legs. She started to hear the river and moved towards its source. Red and yellow parakeets swooped along the roof of the forest, worrying a crow-like bird with a yellow bill and a very long tail. At the tail's tip was a knob the shape of a badminton racket, and she wondered how it flew, dragging that weight around. She used to play badminton with Faris, and, when he was alive, with her father, who told her that the rules of badminton were determined in Karachi by the British. It was the sort of thing he would know. They played without a net, and so the shuttlecock, like the bird with the racket-tail, flew low to the ground.

As the rush of the river grew louder, she cut right. There was an incline with four boulders arranged like steps. They were polished with moss and, as she slipped, sunlight glanced her cheek. She cut right again, towards the light. She stopped abruptly.

Four men, two English and two Indian, were pulling two small boats out of the river. 'Is this the place?' one of them asked, and an Indian replied, 'Yes, Mr Andrew.'

The men hauled their boats ashore and started to unload their packs. They wore dark green shirts and carried fish nets and Sten guns. Andrew alone carried a gun and a rifle. After concealing the boats, still without noticing her, they trekked deeper into the forest.

'We should wait till after dark,' said one of the Indian men.

'There are no yellow bastards here, Haroon.'

She followed them. The man closest to her, who made up the rear, was the one called Haroon. From the way he tilted his head to the side, she suspected that he sensed something. But her footsteps were light. It was the four men in boots who snapped twigs and rustled palms and caused a flock of birds with badminton racket-tails to caw-caw-caw. A murder of crows, her teacher in Lahore had once told the class. Miss Flora Sparks, who taught the girls to speak with mouths closed and caned the ones who would not kneel. Caw-caw-caw.

The men advanced slowly. It grew darker and they carried no torches. They were slow outlines between swinging vines. Even their whispers had ceased. Her arms and legs were badly scratched but it did not occur to her to stop, or to wonder how she would find her way back to her nest.

At last, one man said, 'Here.' They dropped their packs. She sat on her haunches, aware that the last time she saw a white man was in jail. When a ration of food was distributed, she sniffed. She had eaten only meat, fruit and insects for years. Now she smelled ghee and rice. Real rice, not the kind they had fed her in jail. There was also a vegetable, though she could not say which, followed by a sweet smell. Chocolate! Yes, she was sure of it. Chocolate!

She shut her eyes and listened to the wrappers. That crisp, clean sound. Her mouth filled with saliva. Her heart hammered. When one year Miss Flora gifted her a whole bar of Cadbury's Plain for her birthday, she had pulled the silver wrapper down and licked the dark sweetness slowly. She had tucked the moist wrapper back into the smooth red sleeve with the name Bournville written in swirling script. The next day, she had done the same, preserving the bar for two full weeks. But in the hands of these men, the chocolate was disappearing. Her heartbeat did not slow.

'We are far from Port Blair,' the other Indian said, and it sounded as though his mouth was full.

'Tomorrow, the real test begins.'

'Reach Middle Strait by nightfall, we're golden.'

'We travel against the current. Lucky to get ten miles past Homfrey.'

And so they talked, and she lost track of who said what. All she could understand was that they planned on leaving tomorrow, which was one tomorrow too late.

A twig cracked. She was certain it was not her.

'What was that?' a man whispered.

There was no reply. In the darkness, she could make out the shadow of an arm.

'A dwarf with a medieval helmet,' a man finally answered, followed by chuckles.

'Goodnight, sleep well.'

She was still poised on her haunches when she heard them snore. She had to pee and in her position it would be easy, but the scent might carry. She wanted the chocolate. There had to be more. When the pain in her bladder was severe, she forced herself upright. Her legs hurt. They had never entirely ceased aching since her transportation across the Indian Ocean, shackled to the woman with the foul smell and sad song.

And memories far worse.

She swished around in her mouth the star made only of words. What she wanted was to unwrap it. While all who slept awakened, slowly, slowly, she would speak, and they would come to know:

All the times she was hit. From the day she joined the picket line, to the day of her arrest, to the day when *he* hung her from a hook. Cillian. Even now she did not want to speak his name.

All the times he and the sweeper came into her cell. Three consecutive nights. But this she would never speak of, ever, for then even the birds and rainbows would disappear, even Lulu and Lala Ram. So she would speak of the fourth day, the start of her hunger strike, and the fifth, the day of the hook, and the sixth, when they dragged her from the factory to the hospital.

All the times Mr Howard came with the feeding tube. First he tore her letters, then her torn body. When her gums were too swollen, he took that tube and forced it through her nose.

Most of all, she wanted them to know it was the helplessness. She was abandoned, utterly. Miss Mattie stroked her hair as if she knew, all of it, but could do nothing. If she tried, the world would forsake her too, and she could not have withstood the pain. Because once a body is in pain, it is always in pain.

Only the devil had taken care of her, in his way. The devil fed her a tight ball of poison. The devil made the rain fall in her mother's voice, sat her down in Lulu's lap, built her nests of sand, accompanied her on long walks along the creek. The devil told her to follow the fierce and twisted trees of the forest, to these four men.

She stretched in the darkness, inches from where they slept.

When she had worked in the Female Factory, she knew. The same was being done to the other women. They looked at each other and then at the sewing machines and grinding stones and with that looking away they let each other know that every moment on the island brought each one closer to the complete confiscation of her worth.

She moved towards the sleeping men swiftly. If twigs cracked, she did not care.

As she bent down to pick up the rifle, an arm shot up and grabbed her own. Before she could free herself, all the men were pointing Sten guns to her temple.

'Wait!' said the man holding her arm. 'We can't get into a mess with them.'

'Then what do we do with her?'

'Speak English?'

They thought she was an islander.

'We are your friends.' The man loosened his grip on her arm. 'We are going to save the islands.'

'All we need is your cooperation. Yes? We need your help.'

They wanted *her* help? *Her* cooperation? She threw her head back and laughed.

The men were too stunned to say anything, at first. But when her laughter turned to grunts that turned to some other sound, one of them said, 'By Jove, she's a nutter.' He lowered his gun and the others did the same.

'Well, she seems quite harmless.'

'Are you hungry?'

'Here.'

Food was thrown at her. She sniffed. Not chocolate.

'She's not half bad-looking. Tall too. I thought they were all midgets.'

'That grinning mouth, it's evil.'

'I tell you, she's not half bad. Who'd know?'

There was a scuffle as he reached for her, and she was told by another man, 'Get on with you.' The rifle was unguarded. She lunged, but it was kicked away by two men with arrows. One was Lala Ram. The other was the man who often kept watch at night.

One of them had snapped the twig, she thought.

The rifle was somewhere in the tall grass, and no one was looking for it.

'We come in peace,' said the man called Andrew, raising his Sten gun. His men did the same.

Lala Ram faced the Englishman with an arrow.

'We'll be gone by tomorrow. We come to save you, from the Japs.'

As the guns faced the arrows the seconds began to stretch.

Behind her eyes appeared two images.

The first, from her past. She was in Lahore, gun in hand. She had only fired it once before, at a pile of rocks, her only training as she arrived at the residence of the man whose life was to be taken.

The second, from her future. If she pulled the trigger of the rifle she had spotted, it would only be her third shot. She might again hit the wrong person. It might be Lala Ram, who was ready to defend her. It might be the man with him, whose name she had never learned. She would lose everyone who kept her alive. And today, she had felt alive. That star in her mouth, it had not faded.

She took Lala Ram's arm and started walking backward into the forest. 'We go.'

'She speaks English,' said the one called Haroon. 'I think she's Indian.'

'Hey, how do you know English?' asked the man who had tried to grab her.

'Let them go,' said Andrew.

'What if she's with the Nips?'

'Let them go.'

Slowly, the distance between the arrows and guns began to increase.

Later that night, the whispers in the conical huts grew louder. She guessed that, like her, they wanted to know what those men were doing here, how many more there were, and most of all, what would have happened had she killed one or all of them. Perhaps they also wanted to know who she was, and whether they should still feed her.

As Lala Ram walked by her nest, she said, 'I know why you kicked away the rifle.'

He considered her calmly but did not want to stay, did not want to oil her hair.

She pointed to the sky. 'We have war already.'

He went inside his hut, then came out again, an arrow pointed at her face. She flinched. No one here had ever aimed an arrow at her.

'Lohaye,' said Lala Ram, touching first the arrowhead and then her hand.

Was this her new name?

After he left, she repeated the word. *Lohaye.* She had seen the islanders diving for iron, for their arrows. The Urdu word for iron was *loha.* Could it, by some coincidence, be similar in their tongue? *Lohaye.* She liked it better than *Ineny-lau.* She would rather be iron than a foreigner.

The murmurs in the huts had ceased, but she could not sleep. She dug into her nest for the letters she had learned to tell apart even in the dark, their tattered edges becoming new letters.

She fingered them, again recalling Aunty Hanan's answer to Kaajal about taking up arms. 'Never.' The expression of distaste around Aunty Hanan's mouth had deepened as Kaajal began reciting names. Pritilata Waddedar and Kalpana Datta, who helped raid the armouries in Chittagong. Bina Das, who fired five shots at a governor. Shanti Ghose and Suneeti Chaudhury, the fourteen-year-olds who shot dead a district magistrate, in his bungalow and in his face.

'Were they brave or were they wrong?' asked Kaajal.

Aunty Hanan had looked away before answering, 'They were both.'

Yet, in her letter, Aunty Hanan did not pass any judgement. She had written, *I thought of you as my daughter, and how proud I would be to have one like you.*

The prisoner who was no longer a prisoner had been wrong about one thing, though. She had misfired. The man whose idea it was, the one who had told her about Kaajal's death, had been trained. She was only his backup, in case he was caught. Which he would not be, he assured her, when she contemplated the gun he placed in her hand. She did not know how to hold it, when they went outside to practice, once, on a pile of rocks. She held it again before a mirror, the night before. In place of her own reflection, she pictured the Inspector General of Prisons, stepping outside his residence. All those men and women in captivity—all across the country and all the way to the Andamans—and the Inspector General had done nothing with their protests and petitions. While she pointed that gun in the mirror, the inspector was sleeping soundly.

The next day, the man she was to meet was not there. He had been caught, she decided. When the Inspector General of Prisons came outside, it was what she had already pictured, yet her hand began to shake. He was with two women and two children. (Did the hand shake before or after she realised that he was not alone, she often wondered, but could never still her hand, never find an answer.)

The first bullet grazed his thigh. The second struck one of the girls. It also killed the bull terrier in her arms. The man who was supposed to meet her was never seen or heard from again.

Now, outside her nest of sand, in the great sea, beneath the great sky, a bomb exploded. How bright the stars, despite man's fury!

She wondered what the man called Andrew had meant, when he said he was here to save them. In Lahore, there had been talk of Japan saving Indians from the British. Now the British were going to save Indians from the Japanese? Was the flag with the red sun theirs? Would they come to this rock, to take her home?

When lightning cracked the sky and a violent rain began to fall, she crawled back into her nest. She remembered that Andrew and his men still had the chocolate. She hoped the devil would wash it all away.

And in fact, it did. Andrew Gallagher, Jr, senior officer of Indian Police and Commandant of Military Police, woke up his three companions early the next morning to find not only the Bournville chocolate run into the mud, but cans of dehydrated potatoes and pumpkin pierced by razor teeth and all the bananas molested by equally malicious things. Feathers of every colour embellished their sacks, including a skinny blue one with an odd lump at the end, and a glossy scarlet, pocketed for a child. Clusters of tiny bejewelled fuzz coated their weapons. The rice crawled with ants. The ghee had footprints.

Between the footprints darted a fat pig, which the other Englishman, Sergeant Stock, a wireless and telegraph operator, told the Indians to hurry up and shoot. 'Don't forget the silencer,' Andrew reminded them, 'or you'll wake up the midgets.' Haroon hesitated, but the other Indian, Peter, pulled out his weapon. They were both forest workers who knew the islands well, but not well enough to see that the sow was disorientated, because of the war, and already breeding. Nor did they hear the winds.

The northeast wind, Mayakangne, woke up her quick-tempered sister, the southwest wind, Kwalakangne. Together, they woke up their mother, Dare, and now all three stood between Peter and the pig. The gun recoiled. As the blood gushed from Peter's cheek, Andrew Gallagher, Jr began thinking quickly.

Since his departure from South Andaman Island in March of last year, he and the men who accompanied him had been busy. They had seen many strange things in the months spent training in Colombo, from where they had travelled in a Dutch submarine to conduct this secret mission of communicating to the Headquarters of Military Organisations conditions of the islands under the Japanese. Yet, possibly, that column of wind now swirling ahead was the strangest thing he had seen.

Before coming onto shore yesterday, they had spent three days submerged in the Dutch submarine. It was earlier in the day than they planned to return to the submarine, but Peter's condition could be dire. They should, ideally, get him to the headman on South Andaman Island whose trust, Andrew assumed, Shakuntala had helped to secure.

He made a decision. He and the sergeant put up the two white canvas squares that they and the submarine crew had agreed would be the signal for the submarine to surface. The squares would only be seen if the periscope was elevated, and the signal was going up earlier than planned. It would take a miracle for the crew to spot the squares. He waited.

The three winds, Mayakangne, Kwalakangne and Dare, waited too. When the pregnant pig safely returned to her family, the winds glided to the top of a tree with a generous supply of honey. Once sated, they decided to get rid of the men.

Out in the water, the periscope suddenly surfaced. Andrew rejoiced and took down the canvas. As his men dragged their small boats to the sea, leaving chocolate wrappers behind, the three winds watched.

Later, the crew would tell Andrew and his men that the canvas squares had not been seen by them at all. The periscope and even part of the conning tower had come up involuntarily after the submarine scraped a coral reef, damaging the asdic apparatus. 'It was purely an accident,' the Dutch captain would say. To which Andrew would reply, 'The best stories always are.'

FOUR

A Missing Letter
1943

ANDREW GALLAGHER, JR AND his men travelled against the current and did not get far. Two nights later, they were only about ten miles from where they had encountered the column of wind. They camped in an abandoned Jarawa hut. Nobody slept. On the third night, they entered Andaman Strait, which carried them east to South Andaman Island. After hiding their boats in the forest undergrowth, they trekked the remaining miles to Ferrargunj, reaching the village the next night.

It was Aditi, the headman's bride, who communicated these details to Shakuntala, on her farm. 'Gallagher Sahibji has come to us,' she whispered. 'He has our trust. He has seen extraordinary things. Winds that fight bullets. Tall aborigines. Magic submarines.'

Shakuntala did not ask to know more, but in the coming days, Aditi told her that a few Andamanese, along with residents of a nearby village, had also been brought into the network of spies. With everyone's help, information was left for Gallagher Sahibji in a box in a hole under a tree about—

'Do not tell me where it is!' hissed Shakuntala.

'Sorry, miss. Miss?'

'What is it?'

'I do not understand how signals are sent.'

'I do not either. I do not want to.'

'I want to,' said Aditi.

It was the most vibrant Shakuntala had seen her, as though Aditi could not believe the role she played in the lives of big men from big worlds.

Leave them to it, thought Shakuntala.

Though she tried to keep to herself the information Aditi relayed, her daughter found out soon enough. And Paula told Aye.

That January, in return for what Paula revealed, Aye told her everything about the prisoner who got away. How he and Loka had helped her. How Loka had vanished with the skull. How Aye wished that he had saved Loka's favour to him for Zee.

Because Aye told Paula, Paula told Shakuntala.

It was a small island where secrets became too heavy not to share.

One day, the three were having lunch together, sharing a comfortable silence. They had become a family of sorts. Aye spent every Saturday at the farm, to ensure that Paula was not alone when Shakuntala was at the clinic. Shakuntala had come to accept him, in her way. It was a small island where suspicion could grow as heavy as secrets, and there was a war. If a mother could not trust the man her daughter wanted, whom could she trust?

Because the Japanese did not care for her pigs and poultry, lunch was spare compared to the lavish meals she once prepared. There was no fish bhapa, and the chicken had been marinated in yogurt whose quality had diminished, as the farm, Cha Bagicha, was now run by those who did not understand the natural pairing of spices and dairy.

'It isn't spare,' said Paula, glancing at Aye for corroboration. As usual, he did not look up from his plate, where the pan-fried eggplant with tangy tomato chutney was swiftly disappearing. Shakuntala had once tried to tell her daughter: if he's the one, forget about having conversation during meals.

After putting more rice on his plate, Shakuntala bit into the chicken curry. It was succulent, she had to admit. There was an explosion, but she had grown accustomed to this since the bombings restarted last year. Two of her windows were cracked. She had covered them with cardboard.

'You are an excellent cook,' said Aye, looking up. 'Thank you.'

Paula leaned over to kiss his cheek.

His blood was melancholy, thought Shakuntala, and her daughter wanted to nurse it. 'When I am able to buy prawns again,' she said, 'I will feed you delicacies. A daab chingri marinated in a paste to make you salivate.'

'That is her speciality,' said Paula. 'You don't know how lucky you'll be.'

'Once,' said Shakuntala, 'back in Chittagong, I presented a chingri to Thomas's mother. She wrinkled her nose, and so did her Indian cook, who was to only make dishes from her bible, *Little Dinners, How to Serve Them with Elegance and Economy*. But after we went to bed, when I came downstairs for water, the cook was eating the rest.'

The children were laughing as Shakuntala cleared the plates and Paula saw Aye to the door. But Aye did not leave yet. He wanted to give something back, and all he had to give was news they would already know. So he told them instead of another time, another place: a letter he had not given to Prisoner 218 D, upon her escape. It had been found afterwards, just before Mr Howard left the island.

When he asked Paula if she would like to see it, Shakuntala answered, 'Of course!' She added, 'What happened to her? And didn't your Mr Howard get into trouble when they failed to find her?'

Aye reminded her that soon after the prisoner's escape, the hunger strike had come to an end. It had only ended because of a telegram from Mahatma Gandhi, asking the strikers to call it off. Though the telegram arrived independently of the jail break, it was good luck for Mr Howard. The prisoners had listened to Gandhi, India had celebrated, and the papers had carried only news of this, with no mention of an escaped prisoner. Her name was easily removed from the prison records.

On the floor cushions, as a cat walked over them (the other had died), they read the letter.

Cambridge

18th—IX—1937

My Love,

The public continues being swayed by Gandhi. They think of

him as **the** leader of independence. They do not see there is
more than one. Even the British call him **the** leader. I have
come to believe that all our differences could be summed up
in a single article, with Hindus saying 'the' and Muslims saying 'a'.

Behind whom should we march? Congress is dominated
by Hindus. The Muslim League cares nothing for political
prisoners. So I am not with them, either. It made my blood
boil when that Muslim Leaguer Yamin Khan came back from
the Andamans saying conditions in the jail were 'not so hard'.
How many days did **he** spend in lock-up? I am equally fed up
with the public's protests. The loudest are always for Hindu
prisoners. The press is no better. What can you expect when
most of the journalists are Hindu? Is it any surprise, dear girl,
that no one has done a story on you?

As for me, well, I will admit I have had some good days
here in England. Of course the weather is miserable and so is
the food, but I have met people who are courteous, surprisingly so, and when I come into London and walk the streets
(though I seldom find the time), plenty of them turn their
noses up but have not yet been more offensive. So though I
was angry with Aba for sending me (to **his** college, he insists),
there are days, I will admit, when my heart races with the
thought that I am just starting out, and anything is possible.

I am sorry, that was a thoughtless thing to say, but I
have always been completely honest with you. Dear girl, you
were the one who could always take it. My life at St John's
has a quiet focus, and people value this. As you can probably imagine, my favourite place to be is the library. Shall
I describe it for you? It is the oak bookcases that arrest me
most. I am told there are forty-two in sum, and each is so
beautifully carved that when no one is looking, I rub the
wood to trap its fragrance on my skin. Shall we call it, Zaib's
fragrance? There are also smaller cases, with a kind of desk
on which to rest the books we read. The windows are high

and pointed, with delicate tracery at the top, in a style called Gothic. Outside flows the River Cam. On pretty days (it does happen), the river shimmers and a light flows through the library and do you know what I think of most? I think that it is a mystery to me. If only the British could live as lovingly as they collect. There is **every** book imaginable to be found here. Several thousand are extremely rare and on every subject: philosophy, theology, history, mathematics, medicine. **Everything**. The binding is almost perfectly preserved and the reverence each of us feels in their presence is shared and, I want to say, holy.

I know I speak only of myself. I cannot imagine where you are or how you are. I can only say I feel the distance between us each day and I know you began feeling it earlier. Do I think you unnatural? No, because I knew you differently. But when you changed you changed me. You are the reason my only peace is in the hushed corners of these enormous walls. It is as though, when I am here, I become one with the stone. Like you, I did not choose this. Like you, I am not free to leave. If I were religious, I would pray that, like me, you have found something to give you hope. Is this too much to wish? If we could be together, you could answer me.

With a heavy heart,

Faris

'What a horrible man!' said Shakuntala, when she was done reading.

'*Shall we call it, Zaib's fragrance,*' said Aye. 'Is that her name—Zaib?'

'Zaib could be anybody,' said Paula.

'It is just as well she did not get this one,' said Shakuntala.

'Why? He seems to miss her,' said Paula.

'Oh, my love!' said Shakuntala. 'He's *gloating*.'

'You're too critical! It makes you gloomy! He calls her *my love*.'

'He also calls her unnatural.'

'No, he doesn't. He says he thinks of her differently.'

Half an hour later, as Aye left, though they were still arguing, Shakuntala insisted on keeping the letter from the man called Faris. His details of the bookcases and books reminded her of Thomas's library, in the house in Chittagong that she was glad to escape.

Some Misunderstandings Have Arisen
1943

UNTIL THE START OF THE Allied air assault, two shipments of cargo had arrived every week. They delivered guns, ammunition and medical supplies, as well as grains, ghee, vegetables and seeds of crops not previously grown in quantity: shakarkand, tapioca, lobia, bhindi. Though Major and Governor Ito's 'Grow More' campaign hurt local farmers like Shakuntala, it kept the island fed.

Now the cargo ships arrived less frequently, but when they did, Aye helped to unload them. Afterwards, like all the labourers, he was paid in Japanese rupees. The notes had a pretty design: a tier of pointed pagodas, in the style of a Burmese temple, bordered by palm trees and coconuts. The payment was issued by the agriculture officer, Sir Osaka, a slender man with inky hair who lived in the villa once occupied by the dentist Susumu Adachi. After the payment, Sir Osaka distributed free seeds and reminded everyone to never waste a single day of excrement.

He was one of seven Japanese officers to have, since Dr Singh's arrest, dissolved the Peace Committee. The task of upholding law and order now fell directly on their own group, the miniseibu, or civil administration. All seven miniseibu officers wore white military uniforms. In only a few months, they had overseen the building of two roads and several footpaths through the jungle, an increase in food production, and the completion of the Lambaline airstrip, from where, before the air assault, regular flights to Rangoon and Singapore had operated. These had ceased, yet the miniseibu now decided to build another airstrip, between Mithakhari and Hathi Tapu. The men who were given free seeds were to construct the new airport, for the re-arrested convicts who had built the first one were either dead or grown too frail. The task of cultivating the fields was now left entirely to women, who were not paid.

The miniseibu also ran a two-page news bulletin in English, the *Andaman Shimbun*, distributed to every household for free. It had opened a school on Ross Island, which, since the start of the air assault, had to be shut.

When the school was open, on his way back to South Andaman Island, Aye would walk past the villa that he still thought of as the chief commissioner's, the one with the swimming pool. It now belonged to Admiral Ishikawa, head of the Japanese Administration of the islands. The Japanese had their own cooks, and the smells coming from the kitchens carried shorter distances. There were no croquet tournaments, no parties. Officers of the miniseibu had their own comfort women, and Admiral Ishikawa kept two with him in the mansion. Aye never saw them, nor did he hear splashes from the pool. Unlike the British, the Japanese preferred to swim in open water, and seemed happiest when at the beach, where they would also play board games and cards.

Today, Aye had unloaded the last crate, a heap of pretty paper in his pocket. Mr Howard used to say that Burmese boys had strong legs but weak arms. Now Aye's arms would impress Mr Howard. His chest and stomach too had filled. His hair had grown.

Before the men dispersed, Sir Osaka reminded them of what the special edition of the *Andaman Shimbun* had announced this morning. School was to reopen tomorrow, at seven o'clock. The location had shifted from Ross Island to a 'new' one, on this island: the school building abandoned by the British. Communication between the Japanese and local population had thus far depended on interpreters, but now all Local Borns under the age of thirty-five would learn Japanese. This morning's paper included a complimentary copy of a language guide, *Nippon—Go-Annai*. Extra copies were left at the port.

Aye had not read the guide this morning. He picked it up now, as he left the port.

Ever since the arrival of the Japanese Government, we have longed to learn Japani. Despite our English habits, the Japani have been friendly and assist us in attaining freedom. Some mis-understandings have arisen, the reason being that we do not speak Japani. To remove this difficulty, this small book has been printed. It can fit in our pockets . . .

He slipped it into his pocket. This morning's paper also issued a warning that had become common since the start of the aerial attack: all spies would be eliminated, slowly.

Aye headed not for home but for Aberdeen. He was going there to look for Nomi.

Nearly a year had passed since Zee's death, but Aye had not been able to reach her. He whittled grasshoppers and butterflies and crea-tures with no names. He waited outside the hut so she would come and take them from him, but she did not take them. He sent White Paula, thinking an older girl better suited, though in his heart he knew Nomi did not like her, and possibly this had to do with him. She turned away from White Paula. She also ignored Shakuntala, who often invited her to the farm.

It seemed that she only left the hut to walk across Aberdeen Square to the shop, because her parents seemed to have forgotten the world, and possibly forgotten her too. She had taken it upon herself to buy the food, though since her mother was no longer working at the jail, he wondered how they ate. Any money saved would be in British currency, which was no longer accepted. Whenever he waved to her, she retraced her steps back to the hut from the shop, or if he tried to intercept, she walked past him, often with nothing in her hands, and with an expres-sion so stony it frightened him. She had just turned thirteen but looked like her mother used to look before any of this happened.

He had not yet found a way to tell her that he was with Zee on the last night. How heavy her brother was, as he held him in the water, under the sky that called him to herself. Why had the sky wanted Zee, and not another boy—not Aye? He did not know, nor did he wish to burden Nomi with questions. He wanted only to offer answers. *Here is this gift I have whittled. I am sorry I can do no more.* But she rejected his gifts. It was as though every time he came to Aberdeen to find her, it was with the hope of another day, but every time she pushed him away, it never quite worked out that way.

He wanted her to know that he knew what it was, in part. He had a father who sat on a rock. How often he would think of this in the deep chasm down which he had hurled himself, to collect nests for Mr Howard. Those demon birds—they could never hurt him enough to drive away the hurt.

On the other hand, Aye had a grandfather, tying him to something alive. Who did Nomi have?

What if the days were like raindrops falling from a ceiling into a bowl? Then he could gather them the way Nomi would, when she stood with Zee after school, moving the bowls here and there as it rained. They could let a few days fall away like raindrops, catch only the ones they liked.

There were times when he passed her and her expression was not stony but contorted, which worried him no less. She put a hand to her back or to her hips as though the effort to move the twenty or so feet from the hut to the shop was too great.

On the day she would finally let him near, she would say that her child's body changed after what they did to Zee. Her bones began to creak. At night, a terrible pain shot through her elbows, keeping her from straightening them in the morning. Her kneecaps slid. She could not turn her head. She did not know whose body she was in. And she would try to explain that what contributed to all the clicking and clacking was that her parents carried the loss as though it was only theirs. Her father in drink, her mother in prayers, and neither noticing the daughter that was still alive, or trying to be.

But she would not let him near yet. For now, with his hands in his pockets and without Nomi to admire his beautiful feet, Aye went about the island, trying to understand the many changes around him, and trying to understand his love for Nomi.

When Aye reached the square today, she was there. 'Hello Nomi,' he said.

She walked past him.

He followed her into the shop. He had not done this yet because he did not want to embarrass her in case she had no money, but today, he had to know.

There were three aisles. Nomi walked down the aisle furthest from the door, her head to the side. With her left hand extended very slightly, she brushed the food on the shelves. She reached the end and came up the middle aisle, right hand extended. When she went down the first aisle, it was the left hand again. There were others from the village in the store and they greeted her, but she looked past them too. Kind Uncle Bimal was there, asking after her lobia plant—did she need help tying it up on the trellis?—and when she did not answer, he offered to buy her milk and bananas. The cashier, who was the son of the store owner, complained to Uncle Bimal that Nomi came in every evening to wander around like a ghost. Uncle Bimal told the boy to hold his tongue.

Aye caught up with her as she again began going down the aisles. She was wearing a muddy white frock and muddy white pyjamas. The top button at the back of her dress was undone. He could see this only because her hair was crooked across the neck, as though she had trimmed it from behind herself. The hair was still thick, and in profile, her large nose commanded attention. Zee had compared it to the beak of hornbills, and it occurred to Aye now that the hornbills had left. It also occurred to him that she looked nothing like Zee, whose eyes had been large and light brown and who might have grown into a good-looking boy once the rash on his face cleared. Nomi's dark eyes were small and close-set, and she did not have any extraordinary feature except, perhaps, those long eel-like arms. Yet, taken all together, that girl walking down the aisles without slippers or shoes and without her beloved hen had a presence he had never seen before in a girl.

He wondered if the hen was even alive. He once knew a chicken that lived to be fifteen. Older than Nomi. He decided to ask. 'How old is Priya now, Nomi?'

She left the store.

'Nomi, look.' He pulled out a wad of Japanese rupees. 'Are you hungry? Let's go back inside.'

She kept walking.

'Will you come to school tomorrow? It's opening again, at the old school. Will your father bring you?'

At that word, *father*, she seemed to wince.

'I can walk with you.'

She entered the hut, shut the door behind her.

'Nomi.'

He Made Her Mother
1943

THEIR MOTHER WAS BEAUTIFUL when she slept. Her stomach rose and fell because she was alive. *Alive.* The breath that left her was quick to return, flowing down to the pit of a once-full belly where Nomi could see the pulled skin with delicate ripples from where she first carried Zee and then her. They were of their mother and every breath reminded Nomi of the closeness of *us*. But their mother had forgotten this. Zee was the first piece of her. He made her Mother. By the time Nomi arrived, the woman who was beautiful when she slept was Already Mother. Without him, she was No Longer Mother.

As Nomi watched her sleep, she decided this was Zee's mother, not theirs. She was learning to separate from her the way few Indian girls learn to separate from their mothers. Those stomach ripples she loved, they were like ocean waves telling her, *you have been very together and very apart.*

The lines on Zee's mother's face were also plentiful, especially around the mouth. It was as though the breath leaving her lips called out to the part of her that would not come back. *I am empty*, it said. Nomi wished to fill the emptiness, if Zee's mother would let her. *Let me love you*, she thought, but not in so many words, not yet. The day she found the words, she would understand that Zee's mother would never hear them, and that too much of her own life had been spent knocking her aching body into that emptiness.

For now, she was learning only that Zee's mother was a very difficult woman to love.

There was still a place at the table for Zee, where Nomi kept his books, pencils, the sweet-smelling eraser, the green plastic sharpener. During the day, when she arranged his things and sat down to read and write, only two thoughts came to her. Already Mother. No Longer Mother. She spent the day waiting for the night and the night waiting for the day. She noticed that this way, she was more awake. *Awake.* For instance, during the day, as she held a pencil in her hands, his notebook open, she thought that were it night, she could watch Zee's mother sleep, spread her palm over her head, and ask, 'Are you my family?' Or, during the night, when she watched their father sleep and he did not look all that beautiful, she imagined that were the sun coming up, he might call her Daughter.

She wanted other things too, regardless of the time of day: to hold Zee's mother's hand and walk with her, even to the factory; to be given a piece of thread; to have her sleeves rolled up so they would not become wet when she washed her hands before eating. Somehow, when she did it herself, the sleeves rolled down.

At least she had stopped wanting Priya to die. She did not pet her, but she had decided not to kick her away, or toss her into the sea. She accepted that she could not have done this, on *that* day, she had only imagined it, because Priya continued to run around beside her, stupid and confused, and she did not mind as much.

But she had not stopped dividing into two, even three. Not only did she imagine herself at night when it was day, or the other way around, but she still watched herself do different things in the same moment. For instance, while sharpening a pencil, she was transported behind Zee, who tilted to the side as he carried Mr Campbell's briefcase. When she came back to sharpening the pencil, she was tilting too. The leather straps of the briefcase had left marks across her own palms, and as she continued sharpening, she examined them the way she examined the lines around Zee's mother's mouth.

Another time, the noise of the bombs suddenly stopped, though she could see, standing outside the hut, that there were still fires in the sky. Zee was running ahead. Slippers coasted over the huts like bamboo birds. When he chased after them, so did she. As the silent fires continued, she and Zee passed out to everyone in Aberdeen one shiny red slipper with flowers and another muddy white slipper with holes. Afterwards, he wheeled away in a pygmy parachute. All the while, she watched from the door. When she went back inside, she was also wearing mismatched slippers.

Earlier today, when Aye followed her into the store, calling her name, half of her ran to him, yes it did. Yet, at the word *father*, the other half rose into the air and went toppling backward into the sea. There it drifted, without fear, beneath a sky of Japanese rupees. When Aye called again, she stopped counting coconut palms and pointed pagodas and returned to the hut where no one noticed the door open and shut.

Now tonight, she did not watch Zee's mother sleep. She sat at the table, as was her habit during the day. Her stomach rumbled. She had done what she could with the seeds distributed for free. After she saw that the ladies' fingers wanted full sun, and a lot of space, they sprouted in less than two weeks. When they bloomed, she picked the soft pods, and the spines dug into her flesh. Then she became their father, picking oakum up at the jail. The black-eyed peas also loved full sunlight, but needed less water. It was Uncle Bimal who told her this when he saw her giving too much. He also said to feed the plants tea leaves before they flowered, and to train the vines better. Till the aerial attacks began, she would sometimes sit patiently in the dirt, arranging the vines. It helped her to forget that her body was aching.

She had exhausted her supply of beans and was saving the ladies' fingers.

Outside, the sky was hungry too. She could hear it growl. It was still growling the next morning when the newspaper boy dropped the *Andaman Shimbun* at the doorstep and shouted, 'School!' It was still growling when their father reluctantly left the bed to ask Uncle Bimal to escort her.

Uncle Bimal's son, Aqeel, sat next to her at school. Aye and White Paula were in another batch, because they were older. The classroom was the same one she had lessons in when Haji Sahib was her teacher. Now the teacher's name was Sir Saha. The first thing Sir Saha did was tell each child to take turns standing up and giving his or her name. Then he assigned a Japanese name, which was written in a ledger. Next he asked, in Japanese, 'How are you?' He taught them how to say they were fine, thank you, and to ask Sir Saha the same question.

The first two children managed after the question and answer were repeated by Sir Saha a number of times, with great patience. Aqeel was next. He could not stop laughing. He made all the children laugh.

On Sir Saha's desk was a black rectangular vase in which floated the flowering stem of a palash tree. Nomi counted sixteen flowers, each outstretched like a bright orange claw. On the yellow wall behind the vase was a grey rectangle, where the portrait of Jesus Christ and his feet used to hang. Near this empty space hung two portraits. One was of a man the children were told to bow to as they entered the classroom, while saying, '*Banzai!* Long Live the Emperor!' The other was a portrait that used to hang in Susumu San's clinic. It was of a travelling dentist carrying a large box of tools. He had a white beard and wore a crumpled purple coat. On his feet were heavy blockish shoes. She could not understand how the shoes worked. She stared at them almost as intently as she had stared at Christ's feet.

The children had stopped laughing and so had Aqeel, who still could not say the two simple sentences. Sir Saha told him that his name was Akio, which did not sound too different from Aqeel. He said it meant 'bright boy' and all the children laughed again.

When it was Nomi's turn, her name stayed the same because it was already Japanese. 'It means beauty. It was my grandmother's name.' Sir Saha smiled at her. What was expected of her was not difficult. She said, '*Genki desu. Ogenki desu ka?*'

She was the first to get it right the first time. Sir Saha pulled out from under the desk a box of toys, like the ones the dentist used to have. She was told to come forward.

She had been with Zee, the time he went to the dentist. Now, as she walked to the front, Zee walked beside her again. His lips

THE MIRACULOUS TRUE HISTORY OF NOMI ALI

and tongue were numb, because he had been given medicine with a syringe. To prove it, he had stuck a pin through his lower lip. She rummaged in the box for the toy he had won that day. A submarine. She found instead lollipop-shaped rattle toys painted in vibrant colours with swirling patterns. There was also a blackface doll in a suit and tie playing the trumpet. Across its chest was written Tik Tok Noise Maker. When Sir Saha wound the doll with a key at its back, there was a jingle and the doll's mouth opened and shut as it said Tik Tok. There were also trucks, planes, a Cadillac—'Very expensive,' Sir Saha said in a mix of Hindi and English, 'I pick it'— tricycles, trains, flying saucers and a horse. But there was no submarine.

She took the horse. It was very light. 'Thank you,' she said.

'Arigato,' said Sir Saha.

'Arigato.' She did not know if it meant thank you or welcome, and added, 'Banzai!'

'Good child. Ii ko. Take two, for your name and your cleverness.'

She did not know if it meant good child or take two, but she chose a rattle toy. It was red and yellow and when she moved it sideways, there was a sound like leaves in the wind. 'Arigato,' she repeated.

'Ii ko.'

When she returned to her seat, Zee was already there. She sat between him and Aqeel and Akio. Sir Saha was telling the class to be as clever as Nomi.

After a while, Aqeel and Akio began to cry. The sound was soft, but his breathing had changed. Zee said, his mouth not moving too well, because of the pin, 'He was always a cry baby,' and then Zee was gone.

Nomi could no longer feel the teeth on the right side of her mouth. She tapped the floor of her mouth with the tongue. Nothing. She sat still, toys in lap, listening to the boy beside her cry.

Once, long ago, when she sat in this same classroom, the teacher Haji Sahib told them that Germany had invaded France. She was young, and struggling with her lessons. She seldom had time to go to Zee afterwards, to help with Mr Campbell's chores, and saw Georgina less. She was so slow at writing out the times table or a paragraph

from a book that Zee would come to her instead. He got impatient
if she lingered, but she could not help it. After the teacher told them
what Germany did, he also said that Germany had invaded the Low
Countries. Aqeel who was only Aqeel raised his hand to ask if this
meant the countries were under the sea. A girl said no, it meant
there were no hills, no Mount Harriet and no Atlanta Point. There
was laughter and even Haji Sahib was amused. Then Aqeel who was
only Aqeel again raised his hand. He said if there were no hills, where
did they put their jails? The teacher told him to recite the three times
table. When class was over, she and Aqeel, who had asked the stupid question, were left behind to finish their work. Tears splashed his
notebook and there was snot trickling to his lips. He kept licking it.
Though she felt sorry for him, she wished he would not do this.

He was doing it again now. As Sir Saha talked to a small girl in the
back row who struggled with *Ogenki desu ka?*, the boy next to her was
swallowing his snot. She put a horse in his lap. Then she put the rattle too.

The introductions complete, Sir Saha sang the national anthem,
Kimigayo, which he said meant His Imperial Majesty's Reign. He
pointed to the portrait of the man behind his desk, not the travelling
dentist but the other one. He sang in Japanese, translating each line
into Hindi that was also Urdu and Urdu that was also Hindi, telling
the children to repeat after him. Nomi should go first, he said. She
thought she could memorise the anthem as easily as she once memorised the Lord's Prayer. Yet, when she opened her mouth, it was still
numb, she mixed up all the languages.

Kimigayo khusa badshahat,
in earth as it is in heaven.
Chiyo ni,
hamesha hamesha.
Amen.

Sir Saha told her to sit down. Aqeel and Akio gave her a big smile.
After half an hour, when no child had sung the anthem to his sat-
isfaction in any language, Sir Saha swayed his finger like a conductor

as they made sounds without words but they did it together so no one felt ashamed.

The last lesson for the day was writing numbers. Sir Saha told the small girl at the back to hand out notebooks and pencils. The children were to write their new names on the notebook covers and then, on the first page, write the anthem in Roman letters. They were to leave a page blank because tomorrow they would write in Japanese, after they had memorised the Kimigayo at home tonight. Now, on the third page, they were to write to ten in Arabic numerals and in Sino-Japanese Go-on. He held up a cardboard sheet on which both sets of numerals had been written.

Nobody knew what to do.

'Nomi?' he said.

She played with her lip, and the horse came back to her lap. Sir Saha sighed. 'These are Arabic numerals,' he said, pointing to the numbers they had been writing in English their whole lives. 'Write them down, please.'

The children picked up their pencils. They finished this task quickly, and were pleased.

'Good. Now repeat after me . . .'

Once, when she was stuck on her times table and Zee told her to hurry up and she put her pencil to the page, concentrating so each loop was even, *three times six*, the nib broke. Zee had two more pencils in his pocket, one sharp and one dull. He gave her the dull one before sharpening hers with the sharpener that was green and plastic and new. When Haji Sahib went to the toilet, Zee sat on the teacher's desk, though this was not allowed, looking upon her with annoyance. Haji Sahib returned, saying he had to go home and could not keep her after class any longer. She did not know if this meant she could leave.

'What is three times seven?' he asked.

'Twelve, Haji Sahib.'

'Wrong. What is three times four?'

She did not want to cry.

'Hurry up, child!'

She started to cry.

'Sir. Excuse me, sir.' It was Zee, who had hopped off the desk before Haji Sahib returned. 'She has an appointment with the dentist. I will help her finish her tables later today.' Only one was a lie. Haji Sahib let her go.

Sir Saha was saying time was up and asked the small girl at the back to collect the pencils. The children were dismissed from having to write the numbers today, but they had to do their homework and learn the anthem written in their notebooks for tomorrow.

They ran outside shouting, '*Chichi, nai, shan, shor, go, ruko, ruko, ruko!*'

She had not written anything in her notebook. Aqeel and Akio took her hand but it probably had snot on it so she pulled away. Then Aye was there, with White Paula, who tried to kiss her. 'What a pretty toy!' she said, meaning the horse. Aqeel and Akio presented the rattle toy. White Paula kissed him. 'What a pretty toy!' Then Aye pinched her cheek as though he had suddenly become an uncle. Half of her wanted to run to him, yes it did. Uncle Bimal was coming towards them with a bunch of bananas. The sky was hungry, and the growl was in her stomach. But she would not eat, not in front of them, and was glad when Uncle Bimal started to walk her quickly back to the square.

Before reaching the hut, when no one was looking, she ate two bananas.

Inside, their father was lying in bed and Zee's mother was on the prayer mat. Neither looked up. Priya clucked softly in her box, growing thin. She had not laid an egg in some time.

When Zee's mother was done praying, she asked, 'Did you see Zee?'

'Yes.'

'How was his rash?'

'Better.'

'Does he need more cream?'

'No.'

'I will make him some anyway.' She stood up and folded the prayer mat into four small squares and tucked them behind the curtain where, on a rod drilled from one wall to the next, her factory uniform still hung. From somewhere inside its pocket she pulled out a set of keys, then took these keys to a drawer that was not locked, unlocked it, and pulled out a sheaf of leaves that were not medicinal and started to pound them with a wooden pestle that had not been used for spices in almost a year.

'You're making a racket,' said their father from the bed.

Zee's mother did not hear it. The expression on her face was intent, as though she might still be praying, but then her brow grew furrowed and her full lips puckered. She had forgotten the recipe. 'What am I missing?' she asked.

'Milk,' said Nomi. 'Zee likes milk.'

'We have no milk.' Her lower lip started to tremble. 'Why do we have no milk?'

'You could use ghee. Maybe we have ghee.'

Nomi knew they had no ghee either.

'Where is the ghee?'

'You're making a racket,' their father repeated.

Zee's mother seemed to forget what she was doing, and raised one eyebrow. Nomi had not seen her do this in as long as Priya had not laid an egg. Did it mean more of her might return?

Nomi sat on a peerhi, picking the straw strung around its sides. There were three other peerhis, including Zee's. He had plucked the straw from one end of the seat and scratched one of the wooden legs with his sharpener. They had all sat together for dinner, but she was the only one in her chair now. 'Let's eat,' she said. The legs were about three inches high and she began to rock on them.

'If only you knew how I feel!' said Zee's mother.

'I'm hungry.'

'You're making a racket,' said their father.

Nomi stood up and walked towards the stove. There was a little wood, a little wheat flour, four ladies' fingers, one tomato and two cloves of garlic. But there was no ghee. She lit the stove, blowing into the narrow pipe the way their father had done, knowing that she did not have his steady movements. When she waved the hand-held fan, she was not trying to coax a child to sleep. She was trying to coax two parents to awaken. She made four chapattis, ate two, and gave them one each. There was a cucumber, which she also ate. The only reason she had been able to buy the food she could not grow was because Aunty Madhu or Uncle Bimal or who-knows-who-else had been sliding Japanese rupees under their door about once a week, at night, before the curfew hours. There was not very much but it was enough to buy milk, ghee and flour. If Priya laid an egg, she would eat it now. She would not save it.

When she was angry with them it was partly because they lived like this. Zee had hated that their father had lived off their mother. What would he say now that they all lived off who-knows-who-else?

His death had killed their honour.

While Nomi was eating, Zee's mother had fallen asleep. Her breath came in three jagged steps. First, the breath that entered the nose. Next, the one that caught in her throat. After this, the stomach lurched once, stopped and lurched higher. Then she exhaled.

For a long time, Nomi watched that stomach rise and fall. Occasionally, in place of the second half of the third movement, a prolonged sound emanated from the throat, as though her body fought for air.

Nomi tiptoed outside. It was raining and her body did not split. Only one Nomi walked down a muddy lane, leaving behind no one else. For three hundred and sixty-one days, her time had been spent going to the store and back to the hut. To the toilet, back to the hut. To their father's tomatoes and her beans and bhindi and back to the hut. It was Zee who had led her further afield. It was one of many things she missed. He had made her world less small. Today, she had gone back to school. Today, she had gone further on her own, with some help from Uncle Bimal and Aqeel and Akio.

She kept walking down the lane. Before reaching the end, Nomi turned around once to make sure she knew her way back. Already she was unsure which lane, which door. She retraced her steps. And paused. The rain sped down her dress and began to wash away all the life she had held for this world. She stood there, arms extended, the rain coursing down to her fingers and into the dirt. She raised her arms, dropped them, raised them higher. The speed of the course stayed more or less the same. There seemed to be a reason for it to go the way it went, to take the life from her and put it where it would. The same reason seemed to lead her forward, towards the jetty. She knew that if she jumped into the lullaby of waves, one half of her would not watch, would not be standing at the door of their hut, to bring her back. All of her would go.

There was thunder. Behind her, near the gates of Browning Club where Zee's body had been broken, a lightning bolt shaped like a branch with thorns tore the sky in two. Beneath the bolt, a toddy cat was moving swiftly.

The life that had been washing away from her seemed mildly unsure about leaving. The thunder clapped closer and the air was grown cool but the feeling on her skin was warm. The civet skipped down the lane towards Nomi, sniffing and spraying this hut and that. Two feet away, it rolled onto its back, sliding from right side to left, deep in mud. There go the spots, thought Nomi. The cat repeated the movement before continuing down the lane.

It circled her, long tail high in the air. 'Zee,' said Nomi. When she reached for the tail, the cat sprung sideways, looking at her. 'Zee,' she repeated. The tail swished and the white band across the forehead was like a single curious eyebrow. *Go inside,* the eyes said. She shook her head. The single brow furrowed. *Curfew. It isn't safe.* She could hear voices now, and footsteps. The soldiers were coming near. The curious brow became a worried mask, and a shudder ran up the arched back. *We'll play again.* 'Zee. I miss you.' The voices grew louder. 'She misses you too.' *Please.*

Only when Nomi ran back to the hut did the toddy cat bound forward, melting easily into the night.

The Flower that Bows to Her Guests
1943

NO ONE BOTHERED ABOUT sanitation anymore. The water drains dripped an iridescent cobalt colour never before seen on the island. Blue flies, everywhere. Shakuntala shooed them away one Saturday, on her way to the clinic.

Since Dr Singh's arrest, two different men had taken charge of the medical tests. The present one, Dr Mori, was thorough. In a medical journal, he kept a record of every woman's blood test, urine test, unusual discharge and treatment, consulting the file on her family name and background, writing both in Japanese and English. If relocated, he explained to Shakuntala, his replacement might be an Indian not fluent in Japanese.

While Dr Mori worked, she considered the ordinariness of men who committed extraordinary wrongs. How easily she stood beside him, growing accustomed to his un-evil face, his elegant hands. He spoke to her in a steady voice, frequently using *please* and *thank you*. There was even a hint of concern when he recorded the test results. She knew it was not for the women but for his men, yet he appeared so impartial that this was easy to forget. Equally, it was easy to forget her familiarity with even-tempered men who looked away when they had to. She was being trained to do the same, yet her training had already begun.

When Thomas was alive, she had rarely concerned herself with the fate of the prisoners up at the jail. Nor with Cillian, the Irish jailor and torture specialist, nor the Englishman Mr Howard and his reign of terror over the hunger strikers. Her focus was the farm. How, then, was she any different now?

The same doctor who was polite with her was rough when probing his patients. The boundaries between her body and theirs: how she tried to reconstruct them, while watching him insert the swab, take the blood, pull the needle away—*away*. The women knew this. In the months since she began working at the clinic, their eyes had stopped asking hers for help. Aware that she would not help, their eyes had filled with hate. The women did not aspire to the doctor's power, but *she* could be their equal, if not for her good luck. It was she who betrayed them.

Today, after the women left, Dr Mori asked after her while tossing her his fluid-soaked gloves. (They will end up in the drains, thought Shakuntala, for blue flies to feast upon.) 'Thank you, doctor,' she answered, 'I am well.' He asked after Paula, which made her cringe, but she quickly arranged herself to look unvexed. Next, he asked after her farm, whether her business was surviving. In this way, he held her back. She noticed that every Saturday, she was a little later coming out of the clinic.

One day, after the usual round of farewell questions, he asked if he might walk her partway home. Taken aback, she turned her face away from his. Did he suspect her involvement in sending the Ferrargunj signals, or was he interested in a different way? Which would be worse? She could not avoid him entirely without further arousing his suspicion. And she had not forgotten Dr Singh's warning that her marriage to an Englishman, fluency in English, autonomy on the island and half-English child were already four strikes against her. She could not afford a fifth.

By the time she faced him, she had once again arranged herself agreeably.

They walked together. His stride was nimble, even when navigating the muck of the streets. The main storm-water drain running into Aberdeen had been blocked, and Indian men were digging trenches in the flooded grounds, their faces covered in slime. The doctor himself was very clean. Every Saturday, she could smell soap on him, and his flourishing salt-and-pepper hair had a not-unpleasant, slightly floral aroma. She was reminded of an incident from years ago, soon after her marriage. In the drawing room of their Chittagong house, as Shakuntala offered tea, Thomas's mother examined her hands, to gauge whether they had been scrubbed with Dettol. Shakuntala had wished for the courage to say that the English had barely washed their hair till finding shampoo in India! 'If not for us,' said his mother to him, 'their streets would be filthy!'

'You are somewhere else,' said the doctor, after they passed the first checkpoint.

She tried to smile. Where the overflow from the gutters had evaporated, mud steamed in the afternoon heat.

'Do you like tea?' he asked.

She was again taken aback. Could he read her mind? Did he know that she held, but moments ago, a teacup in her hands from a different time, a different place?

'You must,' he said. 'You are Indian. And your husband's family were planters.'

'I do like tea, yes,' she said softly. What else did he know about her?

'May I make you some?' When she hesitated, he smiled. 'At your place, if you prefer. I have brought the tea.' She noticed then that he carried a small bag in his hands. 'I am certain you have never tasted anything like it before.'

Her stomach contracted. She did not want him in her home.

They passed the second checkpoint. The soldiers bowed before the doctor with great deference, and she wondered who he was, how he got here.

'You have not answered,' he said. 'We will part here then.' He tipped his head cordially, and walked back in the direction from whence they came.

The next Saturday, he treated her no differently. She was jittery, dropped things (to avoid even grazing his hands), muttered apologies under her breath (while looking for his bag). He was calm and economical in his movements, as always, waiting for her to pick up what had fallen or hand him the right tool and speaking only when necessary. Even then, she did not hear most of what he said, so consumed was she by all the rumours of alleged spies being taken away and shot.

Afterwards, he again asked if he could walk her partway to her farm. He had the bag. She was certain he had been hiding it. Then she was certain she was overly suspicious. Then she was certain she had every reason to be. *What of those who are taken away, but not killed?*

As they walked, she wiped her brow with the back of her hand. He handed her a hanky. It had the same not unpleasant floral scent as his hair. He was a thick-set man who looked as though he could do those moves the soldiers here all seemed to know, the ones used on Zee and Mr Martin. The ones probably being used on the men and women up in jail.

She put her hand to her chest, inhaled.

'The tea I would like to make you,' said the doctor, 'has many health benefits.' When she looked at him, he was smiling. His teeth, slightly bared, were dazzling. His English, perfect. 'It helps with circulation and is good for the skin.'

'You are welcome at my home, doctor,' she said.

He tilted his head in the way he had done last week when taking his leave. She noticed that he had a slight cut on his jaw, where he must have shaved this morning. The jaw was square and the cheek smooth and slightly grey beneath his prominent cheekbones. Again she found that his face was not unkind. It was the sort of face that, if encountered elsewhere, she would gladly have tea with.

But he was a medical officer of an occupying army. How did he have time for her? The only answer had to be that he was still at work. Either that, or she was to be his comfort. She felt faint.

They had passed the third and final checkpoint to her farm when he said, 'Others who are here were forced into exile. You have chosen yours. Why?'

She steadied herself, beginning to wonder if she was going about this in completely the wrong way. What if she were to talk openly to him about herself? About the unbearable alienation of her childhood in Chittagong, with a mother who considered herself Portuguese, and a father emasculated by the Portuguese and the British? About creeping up the hillside, from Das to Vaz to Best? About hating the top of that hill, that white and splendid mansion? She had never shared her story with anyone but her daughter. He would approve, would he not? At the very least, it might divert him.

She was still considering the option, when he asked, 'What do you know of Japan's history?'

'Nothing, I'm ashamed to admit.'

He tilted his head and she came to understand the gesture as one of acceptance. He accepted that he was not invited to her home last week. He accepted that today he was. And he accepted that she was ignorant.

He started to tell her that for a time, more than two hundred years, in fact, Japan had lived under the laws of Tokugawa Ieyasu, a shogun, or supreme military commander, who imposed sakoku. 'It means, "seal the country." No foreigner could enter and no Japanese could leave. We became an island within an island, poor but peaceful.'

Before they turned into a lane that would take them to her farm, he pointed out another lane, where his villa was. The area was thickly guarded and now she knew why.

He continued. 'Sakoku was enforced in part to resist the colonial powers of Spain and Portugal. There are many Catholics in southern Japan,' he added, and again she wondered what he knew of her past. 'Our seclusion weakened us economically, but fortified us aesthetically. Theatre, painting, woodblock prints—I am very partial to these, ukiyo-e, they are called, pictures of the floating world—they thrived. Tell me, how do you spend your time in seclusion? Do you paint? Do you dance?'

She shook her head. 'I have very little talent.'

'I doubt that is true.' He stepped aside, ushering her into her own driveway. 'Here we are.'

How did he know?

As they walked up the path that had not been driven on since Thomas's death, she asked, 'How did Japan's seclusion end?'

'The way it always does,' he said, eyes glittering, 'with a foreign power.'

They entered her house. This morning, before leaving for the clinic, she had tidied up, fearing she might not return alone. The cushions were piled into one heap. The curtain separating the sitting room from the bed was drawn. The dishes were clean. Paula and Aye now spent Saturdays in his village, for her daughter was safer there, with his family. (Paula grumbled, but eventually agreed.) Shakuntala wondered if she should have asked Aye to stay this time, but decided he would be no match for Dr Mori.

When Shakuntala offered him tea, the doctor laughed, reminding her why he was here. He asked to be shown to the brazier, then took out from his bag a tea whisk and tea scoop of bamboo. He apologised, a little wistfully, for not having all the utensils. His preferred way of heating water, he said, was in a cast-iron kettle suspended over an open flame. 'That is how you taste water.'

His movements were as measured and unruffled as at the clinic. She hovered nearby, also as though still at work. 'Good tea,' he said, whisking the powder in a bowl that was also his, 'comes from the first leaves of spring, such as these.' He took out two cups. They were small and translucent blue, shot through with gold seams, with a smooth rise where her finger was naturally inclined to rest. She found them quite beautiful. He poured the tea and sat back, to watch her drink.

The colour was pale and the flavour too floral. When he asked what she thought and she smiled, he sensed her dissatisfaction and did not tilt his head. It struck her that the taste resembled the scent of his hair. This made her want it less. It also struck her that he was a man who had just served her tea. Surely in Japan, as in India, this rarely if ever occurred.

Once again he read her mind. 'I have always enjoyed making my own tea. My mother disapproved of the habit, but grew to enjoy it, provided no one else knew.'

Shakuntala's remaining cat, white, with a black-tipped tail, slinked out of the bedroom through the curtain. The tail brushed the doctor's trousers.

Shakuntala's fingers shifted on the teacup. The ceramic intrigued her, more than the tea. There was something about how it rested in her palm, something that brought her, unaccountably, peace. The next time she took a sip of the too-floral beverage, she let her lips brush the cup's gold seam. It was rough around the edges, and this too was a kind of relief.

The doctor was smiling. 'What you are experiencing is mono no aware, when something outside oneself evokes a pathos. Not everyone is capable of being moved in this way. It requires a special sensitivity.'

Shakuntala looked down at the cup. 'It is broken.'

'No. It is impermanent.'

The doctor spoke of the art of repair, kintsugi, the mending of pottery with a lacquer of silver or gold. As a philosophy, he said, kintsugi honoured the full worth of an object, visibly featuring the repair, instead of concealing it. 'The result is more precious than the original. Damage is illuminated as a necessary event in life, instead of a reason to reject life. It is a reminder that all life is transient.'

'That,' said Shakuntala, unable to withhold herself, 'that is the most beautiful thing I have heard in too long.' She put the cup to her chest and breathed.

The doctor tipped his head.

'Chittagong,' he said, 'the home you chose to leave, it is also home to the English tea trade.'

'One of its homes, yes.'

'When we win the war, do you see Indians drinking our tea, or will you stick to the English variety?'

'I see us doing both,' she said. 'My father always preferred green tea to black.'

He leaned forward to fill her cup, but she did it instead. He tilted his head. Not for the first time since the arrival of the Japanese did she wonder how far into mainland India they had reached. Chittagong was a port city. Were its waters also teeming with battleships and mines? Were its skies filled with smoke? Was her family alive?

She heard something outside, the sound of an engine, perhaps. As the blackened windows were kept shut, the air inside the house was humid and the light dim. The cups and the cat were the brightest beams in the room.

He asked again, 'You have chosen seclusion. Why? After your husband's death, you could have returned to India with your daughter. You could have remarried.'

Again she did not know how much to say. Something in her felt she *could* talk to him. Then again, she was not quite ready. 'I was happy here,' she said simply. 'I had my farm. And this is the only world my daughter knows.'

'You can be happier. Freedom is coming for India.'

The tea was gone. If he left now, she doubted she had given him any reason to be suspicious.

'Next time,' he said, standing up, 'I will bring a different tea. You will like it better. If you come to my villa, I can show you examples of the floating world.'

'You mean the woodblock prints?'

'I have two. After the end of sakoku, when the Americans forced us to open our doors, the West began to mimic our artists. They have done the same in India. They consider you effeminate, crude, while profiting from your beauty, your grace. What I cannot understand is why Indian women prefer them.'

She was sitting on the rattan chair while he stood over her. For a moment, his smooth skin was crumpled, a porcelain cup turned to cloth. But he collected himself as well as she did, and neither was ready to take off the mask. She stood up, and began washing and drying the cups, her fingers shaking.

'Every tea has a name,' he said, while packing his bag, 'to capture its true essence.'

'What is this one called?'

'The Flower that Bows to Her Guests.'

Outside, a car was waiting for him. It was why she had heard the engine earlier. A chauffeur opened the door and he stepped inside.

When he was gone, his aroma lingered. Why had she chosen not to return to India after Thomas's death? The simple answer was not incorrect. Her farm was here. But even before the war, she had begun to question her decision, not for herself but for Paula. Her daughter had devoured all of Thomas's books. The school once run by the

British, she had long ago outgrown. About the Japanese one, Paula refused to speak. If she had sent her daughter to Chittagong, neither her own family nor her husband's would have done right by her. This was her home. But what awaited Paula now?

Shakuntala set out for Aye's village, to bring Paula safely back home. Only then did she notice that the doctor had left behind a single teacup, the golden lacquer glinting in the light of the open door.

The Five Spy Cases of a Dentist's Rival
and One Free India
1943-44

IN EARLY MARCH, A MISSILE EXPLODED near the ianjo, injuring a woman who belonged to a miniseibu officer. The officer kept a typewriter and a bed for himself in her cell. The typewriter broke.

The next day, a bomb nearly struck Army Headquarters in Haddo. It killed an inmate of the asylum, a man locked inside decades prior for reasons no one remembered. He bled to death believing that the view of the sugarcane plantation opening before him through the blasted wall was of paradise.

The attacks grew in intensity, especially when a shipment of cargo was to arrive, causing huts to shatter, animals to flee and children to take turns comparing their black snot to each other's.

One day in April, a submarine surfaced along Rangachang Beach and opened fire, killing one hundred and twenty-one Japanese men who were bathing in the sea, and changing forever the force of the occupation. As the island turned red not with the blood of comfort women and mad men, but of soldiers, the local population awaited Major and Governor Ito's wrath.

The next day, he held an assembly in Aberdeen Square. Even Haider Ali, Fehmida and Nomi were seen there, for the first time as a family since Zee's death last March. They were looked upon with sorrow by those who knew that someone would have to pay, and, as ever, it could not be their son.

But no one was expecting what happened next.

'Who among you assists them?' Major and Governor Ito shouted.

Nomi's father coughed, leaning into her. He wore nothing besides a shalwar.

'You will be caught,' the major said, 'always.' When he stepped in front of Haider Ali, poking his bare stomach with the end of a bayonet, the crowd gasped. 'From where are the messages sent? Speak.' Haider Ali coughed harder, and the point of the spear dug just below his navel, an area sparsely protected by white hair. A thin red line trickled down. Nomi looked directly into the eyes of *that face*. Noticing her, he moved the bayonet away. It now rested between Nomi's eyes.

'His sister,' he said, lips curling. 'It is one year, yes?' He tapped the spear between her eyes. 'Your teacher says you are clever.'

Nomi said nothing. She kept staring.

'The one to watch.' Tap tap tap.

From somewhere in the crowd a wail was heard and Major and Governor Ito's attention shifted. It was Uncle Bimal's son, Aqeel and Akio, carrying a pretty rattle toy in his hands. He shook the toy and the sound of whispering leaves accompanied his cry.

The smile on Major and Governor Ito's face widened as he moved towards the boy. Above the round rims of his spectacles, two triangular eyebrows appeared. 'You will help me pick.'

Two soldiers pulled two villagers from the crowd.

'Which one?' asked Major and Governor Ito.

Uncle Bimal said, 'Please. He is very young.'

Major and Governor Ito laughed. The soldiers also laughed.

'Either you pick one,' he said to the boy, 'or I take your father.'

Other children started to cry. Parents, too.

Major and Governor Ito stooped till his face was so close to Aqeel and Akio that their noses touched. 'Pick one!' he yelled, and the boy leaped back with a shriek.

'Please!' said Uncle Bimal. 'Please!'

A soldier hit Uncle Bimal, hard, on the side of his head.

Aqeel and Akio screamed, 'Him!'

He was pointing to one of the two men before him, a man who might have been his father's age. The soldiers shoved the other man back into the crowd. Two more were brought forward. Aqeel and Akio was again told to pick. The boy had stopped crying. He shook his head. The soldier again hit Uncle Bimal. 'Him!' said Aqeel and Akio.

And so it continued till one hundred and twenty-one men—the same number of soldiers killed—were selected by the boy who would never again cry.

Midway through the proceedings, a few men tried to volunteer themselves, Aye among them. They were told to be quiet, or they would be shot.

Afterwards, as the men were marched up to the jail, Nomi ran to Aye, who held her as though he had been waiting. 'Everything will be all right,' he said. From between his arms, she watched Aqeel and Akio being carried away by Uncle Bimal. Why had the boy cried, why had he shaken the rattle toy she had given him? Though she would never have the chance to ask him, she knew even then that had he not, it could just as easily have been her instead, sending those poor men up to the jail.

A new senior officer of Japanese Intelligence arrived on the island. He was none other than Goro, who had once been the dentist Susumu Adachi's rival. His name was now Akira.

Within a week of his arrival, Akira launched a series of spy cases.

The first took place on 30 March 1943, soon after one hundred and twenty-one men were rounded up with the evidence of Uncle Bimal's son. While they were kept in jail, seven more men accused of spying were taken to the beach and shot.

No one could say when the second spy case began, but by October of the same year, several hundred men and women were confirmed missing. Prison guards reported that the prisoners were, like Dr Singh, subjected to Electric Shocks, Piercing of the Nails, and especially the Water Method, in which hands and legs were bound and water poured on the face. The guards compared it to force-feeding, though the intent was not to keep prisoners alive against their will. It was to kill them against their will.

As the local population waited for the third spy case, Akira unfolded a different plan.

Unknown to them, but known at one time to Susumu San (whom the island had mostly forgotten), soon after leaving Hawaii in 1941, Akira (then Goro) had been busy. While travelling in Southeast Asia, he had encountered Indian nationalists living in exile, as well as Indian troops in the British-Indian Army captured in the Southeast campaign. Akira was able to recruit these men into an alliance with the Imperial Japanese Army, called the Indian National Army.

By the middle of 1943, Subhas Chandra Bose, a prominent leader of the Indian independence movement, had become the INA's leader.

After the second spy case, Akira set up an Andaman branch of the INA. The *Andaman Shimbun* ran articles reminding people that the INA was under the leadership of Bose, popularly known as Netaji. If *he* could trust the Japanese, why couldn't they? The paper routinely restated Japan's commitment to bringing independence to India, and asked that people join the INA.

Men and women enlisted in impressive numbers. Reports of their fundraisers and drills were carried on the front page of the *Andaman Shimbun*. However, no guns were provided at the drills, and when one local INA member began to question the purpose of the meetings, he disappeared. The rest were assured that there was now an Azad Hind or Free India Government, launched in Singapore. Pacified, the members continued generating publicity for their fundraisers and weaponless drills.

Then one day Major and Governor Ito held an assembly in Aberdeen Square to announce that the Imperial Government of Japan was now ready to place the islands under the rule of the Free India Government! 'Is this not further evidence of our willingness to help your struggle?' he asked. There was cheering and weeping and, despite the shortage of food, sweets were distributed.

The following week, even better news. Netaji had written to express his delight at the handing over of the islands to the Free India Government. His letter was read aloud. '*These islands stood as a symbolic hell of British tyranny, where our freedom fighters were treated with inhuman tortures. The return to the Government of Free India of the Andaman Islands, the first part of India to be liberated by the Japanese*

Army from British rule, has infused a new hope in our fight for freedom.'

As people cheered, Major and Governor Ito held up his hand. 'There is more. Netaji himself will be visiting these islands.'

And now the applause drowned out what Major and Governor Ito had next to say, but the smile on his face indicated that he did not mind. Above him, on the balcony of Browning Club, Akira.

Netaji arrived on South Andaman Island on 29 December 1943. The crowd that gathered to hear him speak was larger than anyone could ever remember seeing. Even Aye's father left his rock to come down to Aberdeen Square. As more people kept assembling, old men climbed onto the shoulders of young men, and a few old women did the same.

'*Like the Bastille in Paris,*' said Netaji, '*the Andamans where our patriots suffered are the first to be liberated in India's fight for independence and it is always the first that has the most significance . . .*'

The broad-shouldered leader wore round spectacles and stood very erect. He was dressed in the INA uniform of khaki pants, a bush shirt, cap and riding boots. Before his arrival, there was a rumour that he had formed a women's infantry regiment, named after the Rani of Jhansi, who had fought against the British in 1857. The women wore the same uniform, so everyone said, including the boots.

After his address, he was taken to Ross Island, to the residence of Admiral Ishikawa, Head of the Japanese Administration of the Andamans.

Back in Aberdeen, Haider Ali spoke openly of how Netaji would come to know all that had been happening here. He would come to know what they did to Zee. 'You will make sure of it?' he said, to anyone who passed by.

'Be careful,' a passer-by warned him, '*you* cannot be the reason he comes to know.'

'But I am the reason! He was my son!'

The next day, one of the five interpreters who escorted Netaji around the islands was told to take him to the jail to see those being

kept there. The interpreter agreed, but reported back that Netaji's itin-
erary had been meticulously planned. There was no opportunity for
any Indian to speak directly to him, not even the interpreters, who
were themselves vigilantly watched.

Later that same day, on 30 December, Netaji unfurled the Indian
flag. It was the first time the flag was raised on free Indian territory.

He was scheduled to leave the islands on New Year's Eve, but
there was an Allied air attack, and his departure was delayed. He continued to be watched like a hawk, even when visiting the jail, and if he
suspected something, no one would ever come to know.

Netaji left for the Headquarters of the Free India Government in
Singapore on New Year's Day.

After the departure of Netaji, the spy cases started up again. What
would come to be known as the third spy case was in fact a combina-
tion of two separate spy cases, both in January 1944, not two weeks
after the hoisting of India's flag on free Indian territory.

It happened like this. Though the waters had become unsafe for
fishing, one day the Japanese decided to send out four Bengali fishermen in a boat, along with a Japanese guard. When an Allied submarine surfaced, only the guard was shot dead. Upon their return, the
four fishermen were thrown in jail, and by the end of the month, they
were hanged.

The same month, forty-four prisoners were taken in trucks to a
village called Homfreygunj. Among them was the barely recognisable
Dr Singh, emerging from jail after fifteen months. He had no hair or
beard and his fingernails were missing or mangled. After the war, those
fingernails would be seen also on those who survived. Their children
would come to learn that a large iron pin or gramophone needle had
been pushed beneath the nail and brought to a flame till the pin was
burning hot. Each finger, in slow succession, repeatedly. The children
would say that the occupation had left its permanent imprint on their
own thoughts, through this continuous vision of a parent's touch.

That January, the kind Dr Singh was accompanied by other prisoners, including members of the local INA and police. They were told to dig an L-shaped trench, and when they were done, they were all shot. The crowd was told to bury them in the trench.

For the fourth spy case, in June 1944, twelve men were arrested before being released on the same day. No one understood why, least of all the freed prisoners.

The fifth spy case was in September, after yet another cargo of food, medicine and armaments was bombed. The exact number of men and women killed was unknown.

Food shortages became dire. The Japanese now openly raided villages, stealing the crops they encouraged everyone to grow. Cows and buffaloes were slaughtered. Chickens disappeared. Shakuntala's Chittagong fowl and even her pigs were taken away. The school was now closed.

Nomi Stores the Seas. Thunderbolt.
1944–45

ON THE DAY THEY CAME for Priya, Zee's mother said, 'We should have killed her first.'

She was looking hungry now, and Nomi wished to help her, but could think only that Zee died for this, for the hen that was stolen anyhow.

More than Priya's soft clucking, Nomi missed salt on the burnt edges of an omelette, on the thin skin of a plump tomato. She also craved fish. There had been none since the four fishermen were killed. The price of sugar was now a hundred rupees per pound. Last week, a child had been caught stealing it from the shop, and had disappeared.

At night, when Zee's mother slept, her stomach did not rise and fall as much because it too was disappearing.

When their father slept, the scar around his neck began to bulge like a muscle. He was ill. He had been ill Nomi's entire life, but she only realised it now, as she pressed that ropy scar, counted his ribs, considered his feet. They were not beautiful. The toenails were grey and hard and the skin around them was severely cracked. His eyes were milky. He had been drinking less since Japanese rupees were no longer left under their door. She began lying beside him, and he began telling her about himself.

'Nomi, when the war is over and they ask what happened on the island, remember the beginning.'

'What is the beginning?' She was resting her head on his bony shoulder and they both looked up, at the wooden beams of the hut.

He took a long time to answer. It had become like this.

'The beginning should be the chicken, not me. It is better they not learn about me, at first.' He was wheezing and a handful of white hairs poked through his torn vest. The price of clothes too had tripled. A new shirt was four hundred rupees. A used sari, two hundred.

'What do you mean "at first"?' She knew he wanted her to ask. She knew there were things she had to help him say.

'They will have to learn how I got here, of course. Why I got here.'

'How? Why?'

He chuckled. 'You are as clever as Zee. I made two clever children.'

She enjoyed this.

'How old are you now?'

'Baba, you know I am fifteen.'

She held a dirty cloth for him to cough into. After using it, he pointed to his wife on the prayer mat. 'She wants you to marry soon.'

She knew.

Before long, she could hear their father snore.

Another time, she helped him walk to the back of the hut, where his crops used to be. The earth was wet because it had rained. He wished to lie upon it. She lay beside him. Together, they looked up at the sky, wondering when the flying fortresses would come. They flew over the island almost daily now, and most people stayed indoors. But not Aye, who trekked down from his village to offer her what food he could, and bring a bamboo gift. She wondered when he would come next. The windows of all the huts and the main store were black. Even stray dogs stayed away, or were eaten.

'If your mother was well,' said their father, 'she would never let us out here.'

'I think she's getting better,' Nomi lied.

'The last time I was here, it was with the kind Dr Singh. He asked for my help but I could not give it. I abandoned my good friend. I abandoned my good son. And you—I did not abandon you?'

He was not asking so much as pleading. 'No, Baba,' she lied again. 'You did not.'

Nomi looked down at her wrist, recalling the silver bangle upon the doctor's wider, darker wrist. She had played with it whenever he visited. Nomi had told no one that, just before their father gave Zee to the Japanese, the doctor had come to her. He called her santri and blessed her, and she would never forget that he was there when her own father and Zee's mother were not. This memory, it filled her with love for the doctor and with love for Zee and with love for their father, who had not known what he was about to do. The man beside her would not forgive himself, but she had to forgive him. She wanted to tell him that she already had, but could not decide if this was true.

Forgiveness was what consumed him, too. He said, 'I told Dr Singh what brought me here and his last words to me were, "Forgiveness is every god's gift to us." Now I will tell you.'

Though she had been waiting for it, she was not ready. Waiting for her father's story was like waiting for his death. She could not explain why. She had seen a lot of death and heard a lot of stories but *this* one was different. She did not want to know. She wanted him to live.

He started not with his arrest but with the night he tried to escape the island. 'You have to understand,' he pleaded, 'I had been living in Cell # 84 as a C-class prisoner for one year. I had been turning the mill and picking oakum. Look at my hands. *Look.*'

She had seen them, many times, the scars from the coconut tines. She leaned forward, to again witness his pain. Then, slowly, she folded his hands over his chest, keeping hers with his for a time.

He inhaled. The breath was drawn with deliberation, to discourage it from turning into a cough. When his lungs expanded as far as they could with no cough, the simple victory brought him peace.

'I lay in the dirt, just like this, on that night,' he continued. 'Then, too, there was nothing to eat. But I was happy. And you know what else? At first I was not thinking of your mother or Zee. I was only thinking of my escape.' He sighed; again, no cough. 'If I had escaped, I don't know that I would have come back for them. You would not have been born. You would not be here, listening to your father speak.'

'Okay,' is all she could think to say.

'The sun that rose the next morning, my first and only morning as a free man on this rock, it was the most beautiful thing I have ever seen. If only I could describe for you the colours and flavours of apricots and loquats. That is how the sun looked. Delicious. I never described it for Zee, but I want you to know. One day, who knows, maybe you will taste them for yourself. When the war is over. Who knows?'

She wished he would not talk about food.

'I did think of her later, Nomi, I want you to know. I wanted to build a raft, for them both. It is what I was thinking, when the hunters found me.'

There was a single bird in the sky. Round and round it went.

'I couldn't leave them, you see, though I had my chance. And on the day you were born, the sun looked beautiful again. It was the same oranges and yellows. I was glad I had not escaped, for then you would not have been born.'

He rolled onto his side, trying to hoist himself up. When he coughed, the dirt was flecked with blood. His legs were like a chicken's, but his scar was a succulent fruit.

She leaned into him and he held her with whatever life he had left.

'We should go inside,' she said. 'The sun is not good for you.'

'Ah, but the sun is you! The most beautiful thing I have ever seen!'

'Did it hurt, when they tied the rope?'

He shook his head. 'They were quick and the knot was tight. The only pain I felt was knowing I had probably made the rope myself. I was to blame for missing my chance. That is how they get you.' He paused. 'With your own sweat. Remember. That is how they get you.'

As she helped him back into the hut, he said, 'I never told you how I got here.'

Behind them, the grey ocean roiled. She could not escape this story. She would have to know how he crossed the seas, all of them. The seas were the stories she would store in her breast, to keep him alive.

They had run out of wheat and vegetables. There was only one cup of milk left. Their father would not have it. She offered it to Zee's mother, who took one sip before pushing the cup away, so Nomi drank it down in one gulp. Her stomach was bloated. She had not passed stool in five days, and that was not all. Leela, Aunty Pooja's daughter, had told her that underweight girls stopped menstruating. It was Leela she had gone to, when they began, and Leela who said that girls, like chickens, made eggs. But Nomi had not had hers in three months, which meant she had only had them twice, ever. Now they had stopped and Nomi was more uncomfortable, not less.

She saw children digging for roots. She saw them throw stones at grasshoppers and pigeons. She slept a lot. So did her parents. Aye had not come to her with food in some time.

The last time she saw him, Aye had told her that he was with Zee, on that last night. Zee had swum, at last. He had become a fish. She did not cry even then.

Now she lay on the floor mat with Zee's books to her left, where he used to sleep, and her notebook from the Japanese school to her right, by Priya's empty nest box. School was closed, though a part of her wished it was not. She was good at learning new words, even if she could not easily speak them. Besides, it had given her somewhere to go.

As she twirled Zee's pencil in her fingers, too listless to write, their father left the bed to shuffle out of the hut and return, somehow, with half a pumpkin. He would not let her eat it raw. He lit the stove himself with one of two wood pieces left, at first blowing into the pipe, the way she loved, and then, after searching for it, waving the hand-held fan that had fallen behind the stove the last time she had reason to ignite it. When the pumpkin was roasted, he fed it to her with his hands. Then he fed two bites to his wife.

He settled on the mat, beside her. He stroked the top of her head, recited the Ayat Al-Kursi. She did not know from where he got his energy today. It worried her. *Don't leave me,* she wanted to say.

After blowing the prayer over her, he whispered, 'Do not wake up your mother!'

She said nothing.

'You should not blame Priya for what happened to Zee.'

'I don't. Not anymore.'

'Your mother was right. You should have eaten her first.'

Nomi hoped the soldiers who had eaten her got sick. She hoped Priya made sure of this.

'Now I will tell you how I got here.'

And so he told her about his father, the hakeem. About the beautiful bottles, and his mother, who he said she had taken after, and how she had made the best gajrela, kheer and gajar ka halwa.

'Don't talk about food, Baba,' Nomi snapped. 'What was in the bottles?'

'Remedies. For everything.'

'For hunger?'

'That I do not know.'

His father had wanted him to take over the shop, he said, but instead of learning the remedies, he enjoyed the lovely fragrances, the pretty coloured glass, and most of all, the sound of cork as he popped each one. One day, while his father was away, he mixed the wrong concoction for a couple who came into the shop. What he ended up prescribing, purely by accident, was a very strong emetic.

'What's that?'

'A medicine that makes you vomit. In case you have taken poison.'

'A poison for poison?'

'Yes. That's it.'

It might not have killed them, he said, had he cautioned them to take very little. Of course, had he known what it was, he would not have given it at all. They overdosed. They were Sikhs. The husband was a senior officer in the army, not unlike Dr Singh. The British would not believe the deaths were accidental. They shipped Haider Ali off with a pregnant wife.

'Does Ama know?'

'Of course.'

'Did Zee?'

'No.'

'Did they have children?'

'A boy and a girl. They wanted a second son, which is why they came to me.'

After a time, he concluded, 'I have made terrible mistakes.'

He did not speak after that, and fell asleep beside her, on the floor mat.

Now that she had heard it, she felt surprisingly calm. She would hold this story, too, with sorrow both for the children whose parents had mistakenly been killed, and for her father, who was caught.

The next morning, she brought the *Andaman Shimbun* inside, repeating the date to herself. *8 June 1945.* Their father was still alive. *Alive.*

She headed for the toilet outside. Leela was already there. Earlier this morning, Leela said, thirty people had been caught trying to flee the island. She also said that Uncle Bimal's son, Aqeel and Akio, had become an informer.

Nomi crouched in the dark cabin infested with flies while Leela kept watch. Her urine burned, and she had to push. She thought about those thirty people. They must have done it out of hunger. Aqeel and Akio must have had the same reason. Other children too pointed out false spies for a cube of sugar, or a corner of a stale roti. Her urine was a tangerine trickle that she saw because of a gap in the wooden slats. She decided to finish, and now she stood watch while Leela went inside.

'What will happen to them?' she asked Leela, through the wooden planks.

'What do you think?'

She asked no more questions. The last time Nomi saw Aye, he had told her to be careful, to show no kindness for those who were caught. You never know who's listening, he had said. The man they feared most, Akira, was now like the man in the watchtower, when the British were here. His were the hundred eyes in the puddles on the streets, in the blue flies swarming the drains, in the children giving them away. So Nomi did not tell Leela that she felt sorry both for those who were caught, and for those who gave them away.

When Leela stepped outside the toilet, she said, 'See you.'

'See you,' Nomi replied.

Aye came to Aberdeen that evening, to be with Nomi. There were not many spaces left for friends to watch the night sky together, so she took him to the back plot. When he told her again to be careful, she said, 'I know.' He had a bamboo crab. It looked like half a spider. She balanced it on one knee, as she sat with her back against the wall of the hut.

He also had a bamboo bowl and a cloth with dried leaves. He sat beside her.

'Roasted cicadas,' he said. 'Delicious.' He dropped one onto his tongue.

She did not hesitate long before doing the same. After five, she thought she might vomit.

The earth was wet and the sky overcast. Two pale stars slipped through the migrant clouds. He pushed his slippers aside and though it was dark, she could see the curve of his feet. They had an hour till curfew, which meant he would have to leave soon, as he needed at least forty-five minutes to make it back to his village. Zee would have been proud of her new improved skills in maths. But he might not have been happy with her reminding herself daily that she was now as old as he would ever be.

She wondered where those thirty people who had been caught earlier today would be buried, if they were killed. Zee's burial site was not far, but the ground was full. Also, some of them would need to be cremated, but cremations were a signal to the enemy. Most likely, they would be tossed in the sea.

'I miss him,' she said.

Aye held out his arm and she moved in closer. 'I miss him too.'

And now they had maybe ten minutes left.

She wanted to tell him that she still dreamed of it, what they did to his body. She dreamed of it every night. When she woke up, instead of Nomi, there was only the clicking of knees, the popping of shoulders, the splitting when she tried to stretch. She wanted to tell him that she saw wriggly lines everywhere. The walls were not straight. Her hair was not straight. Everything was Zee's limbs becoming wriggly lines. She wanted to ask how long he had lived like that before he was shot. She wanted to ask how long she would live like this, in the relentless images, in the grip of Major and Governor Ito. She wanted to say that she hoped the people today would only be shot, but something told her this was not a good thought. When she tried to push the thought away, the wriggly lines returned.

Aye began to talk. 'Nomi, in Burma there's a ritual between brothers called thunderbolt. They mix their blood in a bowl and drink it. I've never done it. I have no brother.' He took a knife out of his pocket, the same one he whittled with. 'Thunderbolt, from an old prophecy that foreign rule in Burma would end with a bolt of lightning.'

She looked up at the sky. Thicker clouds. The two stars had vanished.

'If you do this, you have to finish the cicadas. They're good for you.'

'Okay.'

He cleared his throat. 'Nomi, no matter what happens, how hungry I am, how hurt and how frightened, I will never betray you, I will help you the way I should have helped Zee.' He made a small cut on his arm and the blood dripped into the bowl.

She was squeamish about blood, even her own, when her periods had come. But she wanted to always be friends with Aye. It was among the things she wanted most.

She held out her arm and squeezed her eyes shut. 'You do it.'

The cut was quick. Only when he told her to open her eyes did she feel the pain.

'Aye, no matter what happens, how hungry I am, how hurt and how frightened, I will never betray you, I will help you the way I should have helped Zee.'

He was holding the bowl to her lips but now he put it on his lap. 'How could you have helped him?'

'I could have kept Priya inside. I could have told Baba about the gun. I could have gone with him.' By the third sentence she was crying so loudly that Aye, afraid people would think this was not a ritual of allegiance between friends, but a ritual of treason between spies, had to cover her mouth with his hand. In his haste, he forgot where the bowl was balanced. It toppled off his lap. The blood spilled.

'I'm sorry!' Nomi cried, louder, the way she had cried only when Zee was alive.

As Aye held her, she breathed his scent of—how could it be?—cinnamon. Aware that he would never make it back to his village before the curfew, she gripped him tighter. He stilled her. What she felt with him was the opposite of the feeling she had the night she left her hut alone in the rain and the rain washed away all the life she had held for the world. Aye was the rain washing life back into her.

'We could make the cuts again,' she said to his shirt.

'There is no need. You have my promise.'

'You have mine.'

It began to rain, but this was not the only crackling in the sky. A flying fortress hovered over them. As they watched, a great globe of fire came hurtling through the sky, and as the downpour quickened, the fire spit and the rain flared. The ball disintegrated into smaller pieces, a portion of the plane's wing landing below the balcony of Browning Club, and the shadow of Akira. The rest hit the fuming waves.

The men of Aberdeen were told to put out the fire. Curfew was delayed and Aye returned safely to his village.

In the morning, the front page of the *Andaman Shimbun* said the plane was not brought down by a lightning bolt. It was brought down by the Nippon Army. They were winning the war and India would soon be free.

She checked the date. *9 June 1945. Alive.* Then she noticed on her dress a streak of blood, hers and Aye's. Remembering her promise to him, she finished the cicadas.

The Five Spy Cases of a Suitor
and One Reoccupation (Part 1)
1945

FIVE TIMES ANDREW GALLAGHER, Jr organised a mission to Ferrargunj to meet the headman. Once, when a Japanese official and an Indian interpreter knocked on the door to ask the headman for a census of the village, Andrew hid in a secret passage of the hut, concealed by bhoosa and other farming materials. The hill from where Andrew sent signals back to the Headquarters of Military Organisations came to be called Signal Hill, and Andrew came to be called Andaman Bond.

He spent the rest of the war in central India, recovering from two bouts of dysentery in an airy villa on the banks of the Narmada River, with his Indian wife (who reminded him of Shakuntala) and their newborn son. He liked to think that his son would grow up in Nagpur, in the tiger capital of India, and that his work in the Andamans was done. His next assignment would, he hoped, involve post-war reconstruction. When the phone rang one morning, soon after Victory in Europe Day, he expected to be told something along these lines. It was the Chief Secretary of Post-War Reconstruction and Development telling him instead to get to the Home Department in Delhi 'in a hurry.'

He arrived in Delhi the next day to meet Sir Richard Tottenham, who told him that Sir John Colville, the acting Viceroy in Lord Wavell's absence, wanted to see him 'in a hurry.'

He left Sir Richard and met Sir John, who told him that he had been chosen for a 'somewhat unusual task,' which turned out to be the reoccupation of the Andaman Islands. Sir John added that Lord Wavell would soon return from London and would want to see him 'in a hurry.'

THE MIRACULOUS TRUE HISTORY OF NOMI ALI   289

Andrew did not know how to respond. Despite what he had told Shakuntala when they last met—*I will be back*—he never imagined he would be the one to retake the islands. It seemed the sort of task for someone else, the former deputy commissioner of the islands, Martin, perhaps, had he not been killed. Then again, Andrew had likely been selected because of his success with the five Ferrargunj missions, thanks to which, enemy targets had been struck with outstanding precision. He had proven himself better than any deputy commissioner.

He asked who his staff would be.

'At present,' said Sir John, 'you are the staff.' When Andrew began to sweat, Sir John suggested two other men with knowledge of the islands 'to help things along.' Andrew met the other men. Like him, neither had experience with reoccupying an island. One man recommended power shovels, the other, fish hooks.

When Lord Wavell returned, Andrew went to meet him. At first, the viceroy regarded Andrew in silence. When he finally spoke, it was to say that he would give him a letter to take to Lord Mountbatten, Supreme Allied Commander South East Asia Command, and that he better get to him 'in a hurry.' He added that he hoped Andrew would succeed in the only part of India to be occupied by the Japanese for a significant length of time. 'We don't want a mess on our hands.'

Before meeting Lord Mountbatten, Andrew told his two-person staff to search for men with experience on the island. 'In particular,' he said, 'locate the jailors. They did a marvellous job securing the penal settlement.'

The next day, he flew to Colombo, but before being taken to Mountbatten's headquarters in Kandy, Andrew was told to consult two officers on Mountbatten's staff. The officers mostly ignored him, speaking amongst themselves not about the reoccupation of the Andamans, but of Burma. 'That is where the world looks,' said one of them, an Air Vice-Marshal, finally noticing him.

He met Mountbatten and gave him the letter. Mountbatten mulled it over before declaring, 'You *have* got a nice picnic ahead of you.'

South East Asia Command, according to Mountbatten, already had its hands full. However, he added, the Japanese also had their hands full, thanks to the American Navy. And so, for the past twelve months, Mountbatten had successfully placed a complete blockade on the islands.

Andrew pondered this. When he had left the islands last summer, people were suffering from food shortages, but there was no blockade, as such. 'It is quite possible then,' he said, 'that the local population is starving. It is quite possible they are dying.'

'It is quite possible,' Mountbatten agreed. The best option, he suggested, would be to wait for an overall surrender of the Japanese, while, at the same time, preparing to move in when it happened. However, at present, he was planning a major action in Malaya, for which supplies were already set aside. And so Andrew would not get very much, particularly with regard to shipping and medical personnel. As an afterthought, Mountbatten added, 'How can I help?'

Andrew asked for two things. First, to be put in touch with the Air Force in Delhi. Second, to be put in touch with any Japanese prisoners of war from the islands.

Mountbatten assured him of the first, but was less certain of the second. 'Their most successful spy—your counterpart, in fact—committed suicide. Swallowed a venomous frog, I'm told, to keep us from learning his secrets.'

'They will eat anything.'

'Yes,' said Mountbatten, 'they will.'

The Winds of Aye 2
1945

THE NIGHT OF THE THUNDERBOLT was the last Aye would spend in his village for some time. He already knew this as he and Nomi parted in Aberdeen, but did not speak of it. There was a lot he still had not told her, and this weighed on him. She knew that he had spent Zee's last night with him. She did not yet know how often he wished he had been able to do more—by helping Zee escape, by keeping Loka's *any one thing* for Zee.

Now it was morning and he had to leave his village. He had to walk into another future he could not know. At least he had been able to promise Nomi his love. Even if he called it *a ritual between brothers*.

His father was on the rock. He looked up, as though sensing something. His grandfather came towards them from the direction of the Temple of the Buddha. Unlike the gurdwara, the Japanese did not house comfort women there—'Asia for Buddhists,' they still said—but nor did they take off their shoes before going inside. His grandfather had taken to sweeping the temple himself.

His mother was carrying a small bundle with a clean shirt, his whittling knife and two mangoes. Aye looked from her to his grandfather, wondering who had hidden the food. He kissed them goodbye, and kissed his father too. Only when leaving the village with five other men did he realise that he no longer noticed his father's smell.

With no more cargo to unload, all local men between the ages of fifteen and sixty were forced to do other work. They had already been digging trenches and fortifying bunkers. Now they were to build a new landing strip between Mithakhari and Elephant Point. They were no longer paid in rupees. When Mr Howard had fled the island, the large quantities of opium he left behind in his cabinet had not only become the new currency, but also the only anaesthetic. Aye hoped that whatever else his work entailed, it would not involve surgery or amputation.

When he arrived at the construction site, he found four crude huts with dirt floors and roofs. There was no other shelter from the monsoons, already heavy this year. Only that first night, when their work was done, did the men find coconut palms to pad the roofs, but the rain still leaked through. There was no kitchen. They had only dry rations. They had to find a way to cook these themselves.

The overseer was the Chief of Police, a man named Mitsubashi, who had served in Nanking. Without knowing more, the men understood that something terrible had happened there. Mitsubashi would become the shadow of Akira's shadow, brought to them daily by sub-overseers who were Indian. However, he stood before them in flesh today, as the men arrived.

The translator who paced beside Mitsubashi reminded the men that a plane had been shot down last night. It was a sign. They were winning the war.

And yet, thought Aye, while examining the site, the jungle was waging a different war. He might as well have been his great-grandfather, the man with the 'tiff' tattoo on his forehead, pushing back a ruthless tangle of roots upon his arrival on the rock, not one hundred years ago. Aye was living the stories of his past. He was seeing for himself how swiftly the clearing melted back into the jungle.

For three weeks, the men worked eighteen-hour shifts, covered in mud and leeches, shivering with malaria. There was no quinine, even were Aye to agree to take the drug that had destroyed his father. There was only opium, which the men smoked each night after cooking what they could and foraging for roots and fruit, or stoning a bird.

On the twenty-second day, the skies opened and dumped ten inches of rain. Aye had been collecting sand and coral from the nearest beach, for levelling the runway's surface. He had walked the mile from the beach to the site and back five times, the sacks growing heavy in the rain. Each time, he passed the six-inch coastal guns that were everywhere, sticking out of the bushes that lined the beaches, erect and rusted over. If they opened up, where could he run? He was covered in cuts and sores and some were infected. He was too tired to forage for food. He had not seen his family in three weeks. He had not said goodbye to White Paula. He had not checked on Nomi. So tonight, as he crawled into a hut with mosquitoes and men who reeked like the grave, he smoked.

Ten years ago, the Andamanese who led him to the swiftlet caves, Loka among them, had been smoking Chandu Bhai when they met. Imagining himself that long ago startled Aye. He was a man now, and how different it had been then. How sweet the smell, and how happy he had felt as golden orioles circled him like a wind! The yellow angel, he had called it. The winds that were his companions once had long ago left. His former enemies, the swiftlets, kept their distance. Perhaps they alone were glad for what the island had become, for now their nests were no longer harvested.

The chandu tonight was not particularly sweet. Around him, men peeled away each other's leeches, leaving the earthen floor carpeted with fat, blood-filled bodies. The oldest worker was an irritable Indian with the worst leech bites Aye had ever seen. He also had an angry ankle. With the help of three other men, during the day, the old man constructed a mat from scrap steel, to strengthen the landing strip. After dumping sand from their sacks over the mat, when an overseer blew a whistle, these men ran back and forth to soften the sand. This morning, the old Indian had tripped while running, and when he complained of pain, he had been whipped. Tonight, the ankle ballooned.

As on most nights, they could hear the planes coming. It was only a matter of time before the clearing became a target. They preferred not to speak of this.

'These overseers,' said one man, 'they get the girls. The ones in the gurdwara.'

'They say it smells worse than a toilet.'

'They say they won't touch the girls. Not even if paid.'

'They lie,' said the old man. 'They go every night. So would you.' He pulled his vest off his back, tying it around his ankle.

Aye was certain that the culverts he helped to lay were overflowing. The chandu did not keep him, or the other men, from knowing that by morning, the runway would have washed away in the rain.

What they did not know was why they died for this.

One day in early July, as the men set to work, Aye noticed only one guard. Normally, there were at least two. Unlike the others, this overseer had never flogged a man, and today, he had even brought a plank of wood for the old Indian, to use as a splint for his damaged ankle.

Aye had taken over the old Indian's job. The steel matting, some three hundred feet long now, was perforated with holes to facilitate with drainage. It would have been easy to trip over the sharp ridges as he ran over them with sacks of coral and sand, but after years of descending onto slim ledges in dark caves, his footing was unfaltering. The guard paced nearby, randomly blowing his whistle. Now that he was alone, thought Aye, perhaps the guard would talk.

'Your friends okay?' he asked.

The guard spat. 'They are not my friends.'

When Aye slowed, he could feel the cuts on his feet.

'No rain today,' he said.

The guard looked up. 'Not yet.'

The sky sagged, threatening to dump another ten inches. The men had a ration of two cups of water per day, which they had to retrieve from the runoff of a nearby drain infested with flies. Aye had already drunk one cup of water this morning. Like everyone here, his morning cup had been followed by a stinging stream of diarrhoea. His vision was blurry and his mouth was a forest of blisters. The smell of old vomit lingered in his nostrils, and the smell was from him.

'It is quiet today.' Though his breathing did not come easy, Aye kept moving, kept talking.

The guard brought the whistle to his mouth, then let it drop back to his neck, where it dangled on a black thread. He shrugged. 'They are busy with the round-up.'

What round-up? The question seemed too direct. How could he ask?

'What round-up?'

The guard looked around. Two workers were dispersed on different parts of the runway, and one had gone for more sand. The others, including the old man with the splint, were further away, each with a shovel in his hand, though to what purpose, it was not clear. For a moment, the guard looked at them, as if wondering whether to do his job. Instead, he told Aye that this morning, seven hundred men, women and children had been rounded up and taken to the jail. 'It is not an arrest,' he added, but his brow furrowed, as if to ask himself, what is it then?

'Why?'

The guard frowned again. Then he blew his whistle. 'Forward, march!'

Aye ran over the sand he poured on the perforated mat.

That night, the workers were smoking chandu in the huts and did not seem to notice that no guard watched over them. Of course there was no point in trying to escape. They would only be brought back, perhaps flogged to death first. Still, they were alone.

Aye's body was hunger. It was a skeleton in dirty rags, it was torn and bloody feet, it was a bitter and daily death. But tonight, even as hunger overcame him, someone else slipped into the hut, someone without flesh. The men did not seem to notice this either.

It was a cold, familiar wind, from deep within the bowels of a cave. Something was happening tonight, the wind said. The round-ups. Whatever they were, they had only just begun. Hunger wanted him to drift into a slow end without memory, but the wind wanted him awake. The two forces waged a war inside him.

During the war in his body, Aye remembered that the cold wind would come to him at that point in the cave when he had only so much time to jump to a different ledge, or he would fall. He had called it the father wind. It had never before given him strength, but tonight it was attempting to do just this. The wind began to take shape, the shape of his father before the pharmaceutical experiments, when he had been able to distinguish between rain and shine, between soiled clothes and fresh. When he had laughed and loved. This wind that was taking shape, it was standing up, with feet that were very fine. Aye, too, must stand up. He must not surrender to the chill in his body and resign himself to sitting on a rock each day. For if he stayed in this hut, working on that runway, he would end up just like his father. Like the men around Aye in this hut tonight, Aye's father had been given more than he knew what to do with. But Aye could not surrender. He had a power his father did not have. He had taken after his great-grand-father, who had lived here longer than anyone else. The old man had never been a Trusty, and neither was Aye. Neither could be affixed with a character that was not his. Aye had his own character: he was a healer. There were people who needed him, the way the prisoner had needed him to salvage her letters, the way Loka had needed him to salvage the skull. He had been right that day he took the skull: his hands were able to link people, and they still held this power. Aye had done right by Loka and the prisoner, he would soon see. He would do right again. *Stand up!* said the father wind, rising now to its full height, dwarfing the rock on which it had once sat. *Stand up and receive this world again!*

One by one, the men in the hut lay down on the cushion of leeches. One by one, they fell sleep. When the last man was snoring, the hunger that had been weakening Aye moved to the side.

He left the hut, crossing the runway to enter the jungle. For the first time since the war began, the island had spoken to him again. It had shown him his father as he had never seen him before. It had shown him, too, that it was not only towards his father that he now ran.

The Other Side of India
1945

I

IF NOMI COULD OPEN HER mouth wide enough to swallow the sea, two things would happen. First, she would never be hungry again. Second, she would reach the other side of India. Not this middle-of-nowhere India, but the real one, with big cities she had only heard of. Delhi. Calcutta. Lahore.

She tried to picture it, the day their father had come here with a young wife who held Zee in her stomach on the *S.S. Noor*.

But Nomi had never seen the inside of a ship. Though she and Zee would flock to the harbour when the *S.S. Noor* arrived, she had never even tried to imagine the inside of a ship. Their family must have made the same journey, yet she did not have a single photograph of them, not even a painting. The British had images of men they wanted remembered, and so did the Japanese. She did not have any of Zee. When she tried to imagine him inside his mother inside the ship, she saw a baby's body with the face of the boy who took her up Mount Top. She could see him, but she could no longer hear his voice, even as she knew it was a beautiful one, even as she remembered his words. 'You're on nobody's side, okay? Because nobody's on our side.' If she knew the *feeling* in those deep, rich tones, how, then, could she not *hear* them?

She was arranging his belongings on the floor mat on the morning the round-ups began. His sharpener, pencils, books. She touched them, smelled them, and it was in doing this that she realised she had lost his voice but not the words, and then she kept remembering more of his words. One day, when they had gone to the dock to watch new prisoners arrive, he had told her about the *Darya-e-Noor*, the Sea of Light. It was a story within a story and if she opened her mouth wide enough, she could store it, her hunger would subside, she would find herself on the other side of India. The *Darya-e-Noor*, he had said, was named after a diamond. To keep it for himself, King George V had swallowed it.

How long could a body live without a meal after swallowing a diamond?

There was a knock on the door.

She looked up from the floor to Zee's mother, asleep on the cot. Their father lay on his side, facing her. He nodded to indicate that Nomi could open the door.

It was the newspaper boy. Normally, he dropped the *Andaman Shimbun* outside the door without knocking. Today, there was no paper. 'Akira is coming,' the boy said, before running away.

She looked to her left and to her right. Aberdeen Square was empty.

Their father held out his arms to her. She was afraid, and went to him.

Sometimes, in her sleep, she could feel it, the ship's undulations on the wild sea, the terror of all the families, including hers, as they huddled in the hold in chains. How did she know this? Perhaps the same way she knew of sharks and crocodiles, which people said had grown ravenous since the Japanese began feeding them corpses.

There was another knock on the door. Zee's mother shifted and rolled onto her back, but did not open her eyes. Every person Nomi lost was a light extinguished within herself. She was coming to understand this. His mother was meant to be the boldest light. Nomi could not give up on her, not if she hoped to stay alive. And she was learning that she wanted very much to stay alive.

She placed a hand on Zee's mother's hollow stomach, to feel it rise and fall. Her father left the bed to open the door.

It was a Japanese census-taker and his Indian translator. 'Good news!' said the translator, who was not really translating, since the officer had not spoken. 'You are among the chosen families!'

'What are we chosen for?' asked their father. 'Will we get food?'
'You will! You will be shifted to a virgin land with plenty of food!'
'A virgin land? Where?'
'On a nearby island.'

Their father stepped back. He tried to shut the door. The translator pushed it open. 'Do not be alarmed! Please collect a small bundle of things—one bundle per family—and follow me!'

All the families in Aberdeen were told the same, and a crowd was assembling in the square. When they saw each other, they were less afraid. Perhaps the translator was telling the truth. Perhaps they were the chosen ones. They were assured repeatedly that this was not an arrest, but when told to follow a guard up to the jail, some families turned back. The translator remained calm, promising that the island to which they would be taken was paradise. Its soil was rich. They would never again go hungry.

Nomi had packed a bundle for the family. It contained one clean change of clothes per person, which for Zee's mother was the prison uniform. It also included one of Zee's pencils, and the sweet-smelling eraser. She wanted to pack all the bamboo gifts Aye had given, but there were now too many to choose from. In the end, she took two: a fish, a bird. She also took one of Priya's golden feathers. Zee's books would not fit. She had to leave them behind, and the crowd was already moving fast.

They were taken in trucks to the jail. Once there, they were housed in an empty wing, and given clean water and surprisingly fresh roti. There were hundreds of people, all famished. As they ate, she looked for Aye, but did not see him. She did not see Shakuntala or White Paula either. After a few hours they were again given roti and now a few men said it would be okay, they would be better off.

But their father was uneasy. He was again inside a prison cell. The doors were not locked but they were the same doors that *could* lock. As he sat on the cold floor, he rocked back and forth. Zee's mother leaned into him. They held each other. Nomi had never seen their parents this way before. Zee's mother even stroked their father's cheek, looking at him with an expression of love. Did she forgive him, at last, for bringing her here? Did she forgive him even for what happened to Zee? It seemed a strange time to forgive. Then again, perhaps it was the best. The two seemed to have reversed roles. Now he was the one lost somewhere in a terrible darkness that she tried to shield him from, wrapping her body tightly around his.

There was only one small window, high above, protected with thick iron grills. When the cell began to grow dark, Nomi guessed it was about 5.30. Aside from lightning bolts and bombs, the only thing that fell swiftly on this island was the night.

Before the light entirely left that cell, she saw, scratched in the wall close to where they sat, under the small window, a single word, just one. Rimjhim.

They were again put into trucks. The boats were waiting, armed guards inside. People hesitated to step off the jetty, but the translator—a different one, less patient—said to hurry. The rain grew heavy and children began to cry. Fathers reminded them that they were promised paradise, and this was calming for a while. Then, through the ink-blackness, someone uttered the dreaded word. 'We are again being transported.' Like a nightmare, the word hung in the air. As the boats pulled away, Nomi wondered if the dreams she had been having of their father's transportation had in fact been visions of their future.

With a few differences. The boats, eight in sum, could have lined up on the *S.S. Noor*, so small were they. There was no hold. On the deck, passengers pressed into each other, looking for their kin. Zee's mother was still petting their father, yet still absent somehow. Both, dreamwalkers in the night.

Nomi guessed there were a hundred people on each boat. And how different the sea had become, now that she was upon it—for the first time! The sea that once sealed her on a rock, aloof yet perpetual, was now flesh and foam, rising higher than a prison wall before hurling itself onto the boat. She was swallowing the sea, just as she had wanted, except it did not bring her to the other side of India. It brought her further away from everything she had known. The sea that had been one hill ahead and one echo behind now permeated those who screamed and those who slept, equally, so that, by the end of this journey, they would have nothing of their own private selves left, if ever they had one on land. And Nomi began to understand the unfathomable sorrow of their father, who was once a convict and a convict again. Before being made by a rope of his own making, that scar around his neck was made by the sea.

A wave that was slate-grey and solid as a fist was sliced by a fin. Through the clamour of the surf and the rain came the planes. The second nightmare began.

II

Aye was glad for the night. It had helped him flee the campsite by the runway, helped him slide waist-deep through narrow streams with beds of slippery algae, helped him sneak unnoticed through the crowd at Aberdeen jetty, onto one of the boats. But the night his ally was also a rival. Where were his family? What if they had not been rounded up, and were still at his village? Where had the father wind gone? He had taken a chance and did not know why. He knew only that the winds did not lie. He was here not only to escape the camp. He was not only running away but running towards—what? As he pushed past the wet and terrified bodies—surely the leech-littered floor back at the runway was more spacious—he felt very alone. His family could be on another boat, but each time he thought he saw the man who had stood up from the rock, the night swung around without a face.

He was one of very few Local Borns to have crossed these waters beyond Ross Island, to the island where the prisoner lived. Or had lived. Perhaps the Japanese had taken that rock too. In the dark he could make out no land mass at all, not even the outline of Ross, which they had to have passed by now. There was nothing ahead except white-caps, fingers of mist and the slant of other boats. Once, just once, as the mist scattered and the horizon extended, a moon lit the sea. He remembered that on the night he and Loka had helped the prisoner escape, Loka had told him that when the moon was white, he was happy. It meant his wife, the sun, was painting him. As Aye remembered this, a girl, two boats away, was caught in the moon's rays. Her hands grasped the side of the boat as she looked down into the water. Nomi. He knew it was her. He called her name, but she did not hear him.

And now he again pushed past the crowd. When next he looked up, the moon was turning red.

He heard the planes, even as the engines were muted by the raging sea. There was panic in the boat. He still had his eye in the general direction of where he had glimpsed Nomi. Beside him, a huddle of men and women was prodded with bayonets. Two guards, one Indian and one Japanese, told them to jump.

'What?' shouted one of the prodded men.

'Jump in the water! The land is not far!'

When nobody jumped, they were kicked. When still nobody jumped, they were pushed overboard.

Now Aye heard the cries. Hundreds of bodies thrashed in the water. He watched as a woman was dragged backward with her long hair towards the boat's propeller, her mouth open to the sky. Why did the night not hide this too? He did not yet understand that there was fire on the water, that they were being attacked from the sky, that children drowned each other to save themselves.

He could be the only one who knew how to swim. When he accepted this, he jumped.

III

The year of the terrible storm, when Zee had chased after books but let slippers fall where they would, and people walked around with mismatched pairs, Nomi alone had worn correct slippers. They were her own, and she had found them in the bathhouse, next to the drain where she and Zee used to watch leaves, roaches and even small centipedes spin. Round and round they would go, before Zee shoved them with a gush of water down to the bottom of the world. Her blue rubber slippers had been there, side by side by the drain, as if waiting patiently for her to arrive. How had they fallen through the wooden planks of the bathhouse? How were they right side up? She had slipped them on. They fit exactly as before. She left the bathhouse wanting to tell their mother of the strange occurrence, but their mother was upset. 'We are in the middle of nowhere!' she was saying. 'We will blow away!' And Nomi saw many strange things, including herself rising into the air, still wearing the slippers.

And now, as she was pushed off the boat, she was still wearing them. A voice told her that keeping them on was the way to stay afloat. She did not know that she was fighting to stay calm. She did not know that her body, the same that creaked and clicked and had only just discovered how very much it wanted to live, was telling her to focus. If she could tip her head back very slightly and lift each foot while keeping each slipper on, she was, in effect, kicking. But not splashing. Subtle and centred, that's how each movement had to be. First the right foot then the left. Repeat. For now, she did not look for her parents. She had seen something else. She had seen it from the boat, circling her. A fin. If she could see her slippers then she could see her feet and her feet were not in its mouth. There were bodies coming closer, crying, and there was more than one fin and one tipped back and she could see the mouth open. She kicked a little faster now and turned to keep an eye on the second fin but could not find it. Her right big toe caught the top corner of the rubber flap of her slipper just in time to keep it from slipping away, like a fish. She had to not lose that slipper and she had to not scream.

What if the fish was Zee?

He came to her as a toddy cat, once. What if he had come to her now as a shark? Her body was losing the fight to stay calm. The right leg kicked sideways. The right slipper was gone. She fumbled with the left foot, but it was fast dropping away from the rest of her. When she squeezed the first two toes together to seize the left slipper, it had a different texture, like sandpaper not smooth rubber. The sandpaper had a long thick body. She started to thrash. She was swallowing the sea.

Inside a halo of fire, she surfaced. Around her were burning planks. There were fewer missiles breaking the water. There were bodies everywhere, and some appeared to be alive. She rolled onto her back and started to kick towards what might have been a cracked boat seat. Even when kicking harder, she did not move. She called to her parents. When there was no answer, she screamed, 'I am Nomi!'

The sea alone answered, with a wall of water that curved like a giant claw. Behind its summit rose a series of claws. They seemed to hover, all foam and fire, wondering whether to strike or to find another prey. For now, they did neither. The claws retreated, sizzling mystically into the deep.

She lay on her back. She could no longer see the seat of the boat. Up in the sky, there were no more planes. Wind and sea spray slapped her face. She could not tell them apart from the rain. The black water was tinged with a green hue where the flames were prominent. Half a wooden oar slid by, the broad side still intact. She grabbed it. When again she was grazed by the sandpaper body, she held up the stick.

Someone called her name. 'Nomi!'

Their father's voice! 'Baba!'

'Keep kicking!' said a different voice, after some time. A woman's. 'Land!'

When the next wall of water rose and then curved, a thin blue light illuminated a strange compilation of bodies, small and vast, all suspended in its clasp. She was lifted higher than on Mount Top, and for one magical flickering moment, she could see land. Then she was flung as far below the sea as she had been carried above, and as she struggled to come up again, she started to spin, like a leaf in a bathhouse drain.

IV

Aye could not find his family, but he had found Zee's mother. She was a slip of a thing on land, but hefty in the sea. He treaded water, holding her up the way he had once held Zee. He could not let her go. He owed her this.

He had seen the fins, the blue luminescence gliding through the water like lightning bolts. He had seen that though the bombs stopped falling from the sky, there were explosions from beneath the sea. Mines. Perhaps the boats had set them off, as they departed. There were no boats left, of this he was sure. Around him, body parts nodded and dipped in pious surrender before being pulled under water. There was oil, too, burning green. The stench had twice made him vomit, once on Zee's mother.

He did not hear the familiar voice anymore. 'I am Nomi!' Yes, he had heard it, and had tried to change direction, but the weight in his arms would not let him. 'Keep kicking!' it said.

Something soft and slimy had been nudging him for some time, and he guessed it was not a fish or a corpse but a blanket of seaweed. Land was not far, then. He could even see it, though just barely, when he tilted his head in the firelight. If he began swimming again, while there was still life in him, he would save himself and Zee's mother. But how could he leave Nomi?

There goes the phosphorescence, he thought, and his other thoughts disappeared. This fin was twice the size and sharpness of the pickaxe he had used to clear the jungle. It swished, too, piercingly, as it plunged. Zee's mother started to moan and Aye covered her mouth with one arm while hoisting her up with the other. Sharks could smell, and he did not want to take any chances in case they could also hear. There were others who were screaming. For a brief, terrible second, he prayed, *Let it go to them.* She pushed away his arm from her mouth. 'Keep kicking!' she said once more. 'Land!'

And then he saw an enormous wave lift higher than a mountain top, with the enormous shark coiled inside.

He started to kick.

V

Haider Ali, the father of Nomi and Zee, knew the sea was taking him. He knew that this time, it had not come to break him, not in spirit at least. It had come for his flesh, and he was ready. As his lungs collapsed, they filled with the love Nomi had for him, and the love he had for her. He began to pray. Many years ago, he reminded God, he had asked Him to keep both his children safe. On the night Zee was brought to the Japanese, he had asked again. The prayers had not been answered. Tonight, he could finally accept this, knowing he would soon be reunited with Zee. But his daughter was somewhere in that water wall. To her, his final breath. And so he prayed. 'Please, return her to earth. You have Zee, let the living enjoy the one whose heart has room enough for sky and sea.'

The prayer came to him like the movement of the waves, till it ceased to be a reminder of past injustices, ceased to come from a wound. Someone was cradling him, his wounds were closing, his heart was opening. Was this, finally, faith? Already he could see birds of every colour flock to his one living child, to carry her back to shore. Already he could hear the wingbeats as gifts were brought to her in each bird's beak. Love, laughter, hope, Dr Singh's bracelet, and the bond between her and Zee. It would hold true, this bond, and the one she had with her father would hold equally true.

Haider Ali was drifting towards his home in the Punjab, towards his mother and father, towards Zee. The sea came to him as a friend, and he had nothing to fear. There were no more mistakes to be made. How good it felt, this infinite embrace.

Who Is Your Dead?
1945

THE PRISONER WHO WAS no longer a prisoner was looking up at a tree. It was in bloom for the first time since her escape to this island. The flowers were plentiful and pink, like her mother's tea roses in Lahore. She wanted to know if they smelled like black tea (her mother's seldom did), but they were high up, which perhaps meant they were not tea roses, even if the petals wavered in that same undecided way.

On one flower stalk swung the brightest bird she had ever seen. It had a golden head and a breast with delicate black speckles, as though touched by ink. The wings were also the colour of the blazing sun, with solid black edges that accentuated the gold. She had the skills to reach the top, to smell the flowers. In Lahore, too, she had been good at climbing trees. Her time here had only made her better. But then she would disturb the bird, and, besides, that small yellow flame atop the pink blossoms had already lifted her.

Reluctantly, she pulled away. She had work to do, on a different tree.

If she had learned to count the passing of time correctly, it had been two years since she began collecting honey, one year since a storm raged inside her, and seven months since she went into one of the conical huts to sleep beside Lulu. Two nights ago, she had returned to her sand nest. Lulu understood. The prisoner who was no longer a prisoner had grown too used to her own company to abandon it for very long.

As to how much time had passed since the boy and the Andamanese man left her here, she preferred not to count. It might cause the storm to return, which might disappoint the islanders, who still fed and even talked to her.

She had learned to feed them, too, which was why she stood now beneath a tree that was not in bloom, at the edge of the forest.

She liked honey, very much. But the islanders favoured it more than any food, except meat. They would even fight the gods for honey, though Lulu had explained, through her son Lala Ram, that when honeycombs were visited by spirits, she should avoid the harvest till she had learned to read the signs. Otherwise, there was no knowing what Kwalakangne, the fierce monsoon wind, would do. Lulu had laughed when she said it. No one had forgotten that when the prisoner who was no longer a prisoner first came to this rock, and the storm would seize her, the children had called her Kwalakangne.

She had been Prisoner 218 D, Ineny-lau, Kwalakangne and Lohaye. Yet only those whose letters she still kept close when she slept knew her real name.

She looked up at the tree for signs of the spirits. Lulu was right, she had not quite learned how to read these. Last spring, when the trees with the biggest beehives had been carved with phalluses to mark them as taken, the spirits had imprisoned the winds and the rains. The island had grown hot and dry. But this year, the storms were torrential, starting just after noon and ending with the arrival of the planes at night. The gods had a rhythm, and the war worked around it, though to men it might seem the other way.

Twice, the Japanese had come to this island in small boats. Both times, she had been in the forest with Lulu, and had not met them. Later, she was told they had brought swords, and were sent away with arrows. The second time, she went into a storm. What if they had come for her, to take her home? No, insisted Lala Ram, they had not. He had drawn ships and weapons in the sand, opening and interlocking his arms to indicate the vastness of the sea and its connection to his tribe's history. When he was done, he walked away. Worse, Lulu avoided her for days. Because she needed them to like her, she said nothing further. But ever since, she had taken to climbing tall trees, to see for herself who came here.

It was early morning yet. The sun was strong. The tree she stood before had no carvings; she did not know if this meant it was safe to climb. She was sweating inside the paste of tonjoghe that covered her skin, as protection from the bees. The paste was made of leaves, and she carried the leaves, dried, in a wooden pipe. As she climbed, she lit the pipe. The smoke repelled the bees. A few fell to the forest floor, which pleased the birds, including a bright yellow one like the one seen earlier.

She reached the honeycomb and poked it with her finger, licking the warm, luscious liquid that flowed down her wrist. She began to feel very strong, a knife in one hand, sugar in the other. Slicing away a thick hunk of the honeycomb, she admired the perfectly formed cells, some with eggs still inside. Her tongue tingled with paste and pollen. No memories or visions visited her. She found stillness in this single task.

When her work was complete, she tucked the pipe and knife into a leather belt around her waist, and looked again for signs. Thankfully, no spirits had been disturbed. Then she peered past the branches, towards the sea.

It was pale green, with the flat texture of cream. But that was not all. She blinked several times, to clear the sweat from her eyes, to see correctly. The sea was littered with debris. The sky was swarming with birds.

What had happened there? A group of islanders had assembled on the coast. They were looking out at the wreckage, but also looking to their right, at something outside her field of vision. Still clasping the hunk of honeycomb, she extended a foot onto the next branch. At the point where she could stretch no more, she saw a black waterspout rising from the sea. It was a sign. The mother of Kwalakangne, Dare, was ascending to her home in the sky.

The prisoner who was no longer a prisoner started to descend. As she hastened out of the forest, she could hear a tree crash to the floor. She did not turn around to see if it was the same one.

On her way to the coast, she stopped by Lulu's hut. The only person inside was an old man with a tattoo of a bird on his shin. He was surrounded by dogs that wagged their tails as she approached. She cut off a small piece of the harvest and gave it to him, dropping the rest in Lulu's nautilus shell cup. The dogs followed her as she headed again for the shore.

Before long, she could see the bodies. The sea that had appeared green from the treetop was now red. Two corpses had washed ashore, one with no legs. Lala Ram was trying to keep the dogs away, but one of them was hauling the other corpse, which lay face down, further up the beach. The dog released the sleeve it was tugging and started nudging the face, as if to roll the body over.

The prisoner who was no longer a prisoner was uncertain how to take it all in. She had never seen so many birds, or heard them screech so maniacally. In the distance, the waves were growing in height, blues and greys that rendered sky and sea indecipherable. The birds flocked that far, which meant bodies drifted there too. When she forced herself to confront the shoreline, she met a wasteland of bark and blood, fabric and flesh. The stench of rotting meat stuck to her more stubbornly than her suit of tonjoghe. She wished the paste could shield her from the reek the way it had shielded her from the bees.

Lala Ram said it was not a Japanese ship that had sunk, for the bodies were not Japanese. When she asked how he knew, he said two men had been sent out in canoes to find out more. They had discovered hundreds of bodies. The faces that had been left unpicked by birds and fish were Indian and Burmese.

'If not a warship,' she asked, 'then what was it?'

He glanced to his right, at the water column still spouting there. This was some unknown magic, he seemed to say, and even the gods were taking to the sky.

The dog had managed to push the body onto its side. A girl. Lulu told the men to step back. She said the girl was alive. The prisoner who was no longer a prisoner crouched beside Lulu. The girl looked familiar, but did not look alive.

Two other women arrived, one with a necklace of bones. They chanted, burned leaves, and when it started to rain, they carried the girl inland, towards the huts. They spoke rapidly amongst themselves, telling the prisoner who was no longer a prisoner to leave. She shook her head. When Lulu frowned at her, though she would much rather have stayed, she returned to her nest.

The nest was near their huts and made of harder soil than those burrowed by the shore, in the drier season. It was larger than the others, more a blanket than a death shroud. Inside, she had arranged a mattress of palm leaves and dead grass, materials used for thatching huts. It was early, and she was not ready to retire for the day. She sat at the entrance to her burrow, wondering why the girl looked familiar.

As she waited, more women passed her on their way to Lulu's hut. If the girl had any life left in her, they could revive it. After all, they had done the same for her.

She had learned that women were the doctors on this rock. They knew which trees blossomed, and when, and how to turn the flowers, roots and stems into medicine. They had an herb even for malaria. All that time in jail, while she and other prisoners had been forced to keep working with the fever, there was a plant that could have helped.

But they never wanted her near when preparing their herbs. And, as far as she knew, they had never brought a drowned girl back to life. The woman with the necklace of bones, Minare, was one of many women to have made similar necklaces after a death. Hers were the bones of her drowned child. When the body had been found, Minare shaved her head before shaving the child's too. Then she painted them both. Olive clay for herself, white and red for her boy. He was placed in a foetal position in a shroud of leaves before being buried in a grave in the centre of his hut. Next to the grave Minare had left a nautilus shell full of her own milk, so the child would not go hungry. She had not been lactating. It was one of many mysteries the prisoner who was no longer a prisoner no longer pondered. The trees around the hut had been strung with leaf wreaths, and after many months, the wreaths were taken down and the child's body was exhumed. The bones were washed in a creek. Minare made her necklace.

Afterwards, everyone danced a dance called The Shedding of Tears.

The day after the dance, Lulu, with Lala Ram's help in translation, had spoken to her of Kali, the black Hindu god, a woman too. 'She is not our god but there are things she knows. Skulls and such,' Lulu had said. On that day, the prisoner who was no longer a prisoner had come to learn that she was saved in exchange for a skull. The Andamanese man had been wearing it around his neck the night he left her here.

'You have the same traditions as the Andamanese?' she had asked Lulu.

'Not all. But this one, yes.'

'Whose skull was exchanged for my life? A child's?'

'No,' Lulu had answered, 'a husband's.'

After a while Lulu had asked, still through Lala Ram, 'Who is your dead?'

Women stopped going to Lulu's hut. Whoever was meant to be inside was inside.

When it started to rain, she ducked into her nest, stretching on her stomach while peering out of the hole. When fireflies began to dance, she knew the rain was resting. She could amble to the creek that led through a mangrove swamp back to the coast. She was lonely, and would not mind talking to Lala Ram. Besides, fireflies glittered more brightly in the swamp, and there was less chance of trees falling on her there. Coconuts in particular did not like mangrove mud. She had learned other things, too. How to slash coconuts diagonally with an axe made of scrap metal from the sea. How to relish the gummy fullness that settled over her after eating plantain bananas. How to read in the dark.

She rolled onto her back, fingers searching the dip in the soil where she put the letters. The one from Aunty Hanan, the two from her sisters. Were they alive? She traced the paper's edges. They peeled away, like dead skin.

Who is your dead?

After her father had died, when the police brought back his body from the morgue, her uncles had bathed him. When they took him to the graveyard, the women had to stay behind in the house, even his wife and three daughters. This had never struck her as strange till the day Minare performed the funeral rites for her dead child by herself. Ever since, it had bothered her that she never saw her father returned to the earth. What happened to her father, not only when he died, but even after he died, was done in her absence. She had put flowers on his grave only *after* it was covered. She knew too little about what happened to her dead, and the omission was like an open grave.

She had never been a 'washer' of a woman's body. She wanted to perform the bathing ritual for her mother, when it was time. She wanted to be the one to clean her corpse three times with her own hands, to wrap her in the kafan, to take the time to say goodbye. She wanted also to leave a little honey, still in the comb that was shaped like a womb, beside her mother's grave. A honeywomb. She wanted to somehow keep it pure and ant-free, just for her mother.

She had other dead, too. Kaajal had been cremated, but it had not been safe to attend the funeral. She knew no other girl who had died. With one exception. The daughter of the Inspector General of Prisons, whom she had killed with the second bullet meant for him. The girl had been the taller of the two daughters to come outside that day, with two ponytails the colour of beach sand, wearing a white dress with an orange sash tied on the side of her waist in a bow. She remembered the plump face and the way the girl had squinted. She remembered the flat head of the bull terrier in her hands. The dog had barked, once. She could picture it well.

Other faces she could not picture, including those she had worked beside at the Female Factory. Besides their cropped hair and stained uniforms, there was no single feature that the prisoner who was no longer a prisoner could recall.

But there was someone else from the factory she *could* recall. And now she knew why the girl who had washed up on the beach today looked familiar.

She hurried out of her nest to Lulu's hut. From outside, she called, 'Is she alive?'

'Alive,' Lulu called back. 'Go now. Tomorrow.' She said it in Urdu, kal, the word for tomorrow, and also for yesterday.

Again she turned back. She lay awake, clutching her letters, the bones of her dead. She pictured the face of the girl from the factory, and the face of the girl she had shot. Had the girl she shot been squinting at the sun or at something else? Was it the face of all English girls displeased with the sight of an Indian? The prisoner who was no longer a prisoner curled into a foetal position, placing a palm leaf over herself to mirror Minare folding her son in a shroud of leaves. This sand nest was roomy, but it might one day be her grave, in which case, she wondered what the last image to confront her would be. She wondered, too, if the policeman who shot her father had ever stayed awake at night, remembering his face. Or were all Indian faces so alike to him that he could not find a single feature—not even a squint—to tell them apart? She wondered if the policeman had ever felt that, after pulling the trigger, his life had needed to begin again. She wondered if there would ever be a time when an Englishman would have to face the same consequences. And then again there was the face of the girl from the factory, and the face of the girl she shot.

Her last thought before falling asleep: a dead parent is your conscience.

It was three days before the girl left Lulu's hut, followed by the dog who had turned her over on the beach. She did not go far, just wandered about, looking up at a canopy of leaves, listening to the hammering of rain. She drank coconut water and ate a little yam. She reminded the prisoner who was no longer a prisoner of herself.

'Do you like dogs?' These were the first words they exchanged.

The girl nodded.

'Do you remember me?'

The girl nodded again.

'Do you want to see my home?'

The girl went back inside Lulu's hut.

The next day, when they saw each other, the girl said, 'I want to go home.'

'I know,' said the prisoner who was no longer a prisoner. She offered the girl a few edible roots dug up just that morning.

The girl sniffed, in much the same way that she had once done when Lulu or Lala Ram had held them out for her. The girl ate the roots.

'What is your name?'

'Nomi.'

'What month is it?'

'July.'

'What year is it?'

'1945.'

'I thought so.'

'I want to go home.'

'What happened out there?'

The girl started to cry.

After two more days, she tried again to speak to the girl. She too had survived on this rock with the love of Lulu, Lala Ram and others, she said. She too had come up for air. A boy had helped her escape. He had torn her letters on the orders of the superintendent of the jail. She showed her the remaining letters. She told her more, and Nomi pooled these stories with those she already stored.

One day, Lala Ram came to the prisoner who was no longer a prisoner with news that fishermen had discovered a group of men, women and children stranded on an island some miles away. The fishermen did not usually go that far, but since they saw smoke and the island was uninhabited, they decided to investigate. Most probably, the people were survivors from the wreck.

'Should we tell the girl?' she asked.

'The way is not safe. We do not go back.'

She hesitated, knowing how difficult it had become for fishermen to go out in boats. The mines could be triggered even by a canoe gliding through the water, as though they could sense water being displaced. It had happened once. A fisherman had gone out alone, so tired was he of being without lobster. The boat had blasted into the air and no part of his body was ever found, no necklace made. Some of the fuses seemed to be on a timer, for there were days when no one was out there, yet there was an explosion. The men saw a pattern to these; they went off near where the fisherman had shot into the sky. Then again, they had also seen mines dropped by parachutes that drifted in the wind. The mines could be anywhere, and the fishermen grew frightened even of wading in with their nets, in case they hauled fire along with fish. The sea, their oldest ally, was now an invisible threat.

She could not help herself, though. 'What if the girl has family stranded there?'

'They will not live long.'

'Then we should take them food.'

He shook his head, as if to say, We have helped you, and the girl, but this is not our war.

Reluctantly, she walked away.

She could not shed the feeling that something had to be done. But how? She could not swim. She could not steer a boat. Should she try talking to the man they deferred to, Taleme, the one painted with red clay on half his body, olive on the other? How would he respond if she approached him to ask for a boat? Would Lala Ram translate?

She stood by the shore, where the stench and debris had somewhat cleared, but where birds still squabbled and dogs still snarled. Before doing anything, she had to know what had happened.

She returned to her nest. To her amazement, the girl was curled inside, asleep. The prisoner who was no longer a prisoner walked to the mangrove swamp to her crown of fireflies. Then she was back, two fireflies trailing her. One green, one yellow. The girl was on her stomach, half in the nest, half out. Earlier that day, she had eaten honey from a nautilus cup, and now the honey was gone.

'Hello, Nomi.'

The girl wriggled on her stomach, staying in the nest only from the waist down. To the prisoner who was no longer a prisoner the nest looked like a tail. 'Do you know about mermaids?' she asked.

When Nomi shook her head, she told her about Kaajal, their bicycles and secret work, and the story that Kaajal had told her, the night before her death. 'The mermaid was given legs in exchange for her voice.' Nomi listened, her head resting on the cool earth.

The prisoner who was no longer a prisoner wondered how she could let this sweet child live the story too. How could she leave her stranded?

'Speak,' she told the girl. 'Don't keep it in there.'

She held up the empty nautilus cup being inspected by ants. 'You know what this is?' The girl shook her head. 'It's a letter. And this,' she plucked one of the ants, 'another letter. See how they find each other? See how they make words?' She told her of the many different kinds of words, and the star on which they all lived. 'Some do not even make sounds, but they are there, and they are yours.'

'I know about frogs,' said Nomi, reviving somewhat.

'Frogs?'

'Yes, that one.' She pointed to a small brown frog with steep ridges for eyebrows. It had paused near the hole, as if wondering whether to hop inside.

'It is also a half-land, half-water thing. Like mermaids.'

'And turtles.'

'And manatees.'

'And crocodiles.'

They laughed.

Nomi said, 'I saw you arrive.'

'When?'

'From the ship. I saw you walk up to the jail, the first day.'

'Oh!'

'I saw you in the factory. I saw you in the hospital. You were sick.'

'I remember you in the factory. Now it is you that is sick.'

'I am not sick. I am Nomi.'

The frog skipped away.

'What happened out there, Nomi?'

'I want to go home.'

'I will help you. But you must tell me.'

Nomi again lay her cheek in the dirt. When next she looked up, a wet leaf was stuck to her skin. She started to talk: about being forced onto a boat, about being pushed into the water, about the wave.

'Why did they push you?'

But she could not speak of other things she had seen, and wriggled backward into the nest. She did not come out later to eat. She was not bothered by the rain. She was not bothered by the planes.

The prisoner who was no longer a prisoner slept in Lulu's hut.

The next day, she asked Lala Ram to take her to Taleme.

He shook his head.

'Please,' she insisted. 'We cannot keep her here.'

His large eyes, normally calm, were troubled. He looked at her a long time. She had never asked why he did not wear clay, or how it was for him, being part aborigine, part Indian. The Indian part had faded, she assumed, for he spoke of the tribe he lived with as his own. She had never asked how many generations ago his Indian forefather had come here, or how many languages he spoke, or if he wanted to know another world. Was this one enough for him? Not for the first time did she see in his eyes a longing. She did not think it was for another world. She thought it was for her. He oiled her hair, combed it and waited for a sign. She had no sign to give.

'Why speak to Taleme?' he said at last.

'I want to take the girl to her family.'

'They are not her family.'

'They might be.'

'Lohaye,' he pleaded, 'bad things happening there.'

'I know.'

'You do not know.'

'I can learn.'

He shook his head and walked away.

She went alone to Taleme's hut. From its roof hung a string of pig skulls that twirled around her as she tried to explain to Taleme's wife why she was here. His wife said he had gone deep into the jungle to hunt. There was more she tried in vain to communicate before moving to the cot, to indicate that she was sleepy. The prisoner who was no longer a prisoner understood that she was no more welcome, and left.

When the same thing happened the next night, she returned to Lala Ram.

She found him in the same place where she had stood some two weeks ago, if she counted the days correctly, staring at the pink blossoms that resembled her mother's tea roses in Lahore. The flowers had bleached in the sun. The ground was littered with petals. She wanted to thank him for all he had done. All the times he had chased the big lizards away, massaged her scalp, fed her, or just kept her company. Even the time he kept her from shooting the Englishmen who camped here. She wanted to, but the way he stood, looking up, she decided instead to follow his gaze. It was the bright yellow bird. They did not speak, but when the bird flew away, she embraced him. He held her the way Lulu did. He held her like a mother. When they stepped away, she said, 'I promise, I will ask for nothing more.'

They left the next morning. The canoe was packed with yams, dried boar, dried turtle meat, plantains, star fruit, fresh water and honey. There were also two axes, for slashing coconuts. The prisoner who was no longer a prisoner promised Lulu, 'I will not trouble your son again.' She added, 'I also want to go home.' Lulu hugged Nomi goodbye but walked away from her.

As she watched Lulu's back recede, it struck her that this was to be her third time on the water. The first had been in the prison ship, when she had been chained to the woman who hummed. The second, the night of her escape. She had sat between the boy and the Andamanese man, and in place of chains, there had been letters. Her fist began to curl, as it had on that night, but there was a change. What was this boat, her body wanted to know—a tomb or womb?

She sat in front and Lala Ram at the back, with Nomi between them. Lala Ram said to set the pace, but when she started to paddle, they did not move. 'I can watch for obstacles,' she said, hopefully. He swept the paddle gently, only once, and that was all the effort it took. They began to glide.

For a time, nobody spoke, except when Lala Ram told her to row on the opposite end. She did as he asked but her strokes remained as ineffectual as her words to Lulu that morning. Nor was she having much luck spotting rocks in the water. It was Nomi who sometimes called out, 'There! And there!' as they went, though no one directly mentioned the debris, some of which had to be from the boats on the night Nomi had been tossed into the sea. At least the stench had cleared.

The winds did their job, blowing softly but steadily away from the island. The water spout had not been seen again. The sea swirled in an emerald cloud over coral to which their boat sometimes came so close that Lala Ram had to tell her to lift her oar from the water. As they drifted, she thrust her hand down, to explore which surface would cut like thorns and which was smooth as stone. She and Nomi had been imprisoned by the sea but now the two of them were choosing to be here, and she saw the sea for the first time as something sweetly unleashed—clams with lacy lips, jellyfish with beating hearts! How breathtaking was their captor! She thrust her hand down a second time when they passed a lovely conch, but it rolled away. She was amazed and frightened, but it was Lala Ram whose face was furrowed as he cautiously arced his oar. When the water grew choppy and the boat bumped the reef, they all started to peer through the silt for shells more ungodly.

Most of all, she tried to learn the way, in case she must return with more food, in case this was her way home. If what Lala Ram had told her was true and the British had left South Andaman Island just before the Japanese took over, then what had become of the jail? If she was discovered, would she be re-arrested? Surely, all she had to do was tell the Japanese who she was. A prisoner of their common enemy! Surely, they would find her a passage home. Imagine her mother's joy, when she stepped off the train!

The water was now a dark azure, with occasional splashes that looked like fins. When Nomi cried out, the prisoner who was no longer a prisoner spoke of turtles and manatees but the girl looked unconvinced. The little debris they had passed earlier was clearing, and the occasional driftwood and cloth could have been from another century. The bodies had been picked clean off the bone and the bones had become one with the sea. There was only the full, fresh odour of fish. They stayed clear of the ships with the bright red sun, though she wished they would go to them, she wished Lala Ram would trust her on this. If they were seen, no one rushed forward with handcuffs or chains.

Lala Ram said there were lost ships lying face down on the ocean floor.

'British?' she asked.

'Yes. Over there, a very old prison ship. Maybe the first.'

'The *Darya-e-Noor*!' said Nomi, surprising them with her excitement.

'What is the *Darya-e-Noor*?' she asked.

'Zee said he would find it.'

'Who's Zee?'

'My brother.'

'I hope we meet him.'

Nomi was quiet.

They passed several small islands before Lala Ram at last steered the canoe towards one of them.

Please no, she was thinking. *Not this one.* The sky was a cloud of shifting shadows that raged over strings of carrion. Immediately she knew Lala Ram had been right. She should not have brought the girl here. What if her family had survived the ocean, only to perish on land?

Two men were standing on the shore, waving. When the canoe came closer, the men dashed forward. 'Help us!' they said. When they saw the food in the boat, they grabbed it. One carried away the plantains, the other, the bucket of water. He drank so feverishly the water poured down his throat, which made the other man drop the bananas in the sea and lunge towards him.

Lala Ram fished out the bananas. Now the other man had the water, drinking in the same clumsy way. The men were skeletal and had the crazed look in their eyes that she had seen in jail. It was a look that said they would do anything to save themselves. Around her waist was the belt where she kept her knife. Her hand was on the knife.

The birds scattered but still swooped close enough for her to feel the wind on their wings as Lala Ram hoisted the canoe onto shore and began unloading the remaining food. The girl was looking straight ahead, at two other figures shuffling towards them. 'Ama!' She rushed out of the boat.

The prisoner who was no longer a prisoner had been trying not to hope for this, but here it was: the return to the child of her mother. Though all of the mother was so shrunken she might have been only an apparition, she must have appeared beautiful to Nomi, who buried her face in those bones.

Next to the woman was the boy who helped the prisoner who was no longer a prisoner escape the jail. He had an angry bruise above his right eye that could have been made by a falling coconut, or a fist. He walked with difficulty, and soon she saw why. His feet were covered in sores and there was one the size of a large plum oozing on the inside of his right ankle.

'How many are you?' asked the prisoner who was no longer a prisoner.

'About a hundred,' said the boy, 'including the dead.' He pointed behind him, at the bushes, eyeing the food. The girl's mother was already pawing through it, and Nomi turned her attention to the boy. Lala Ram began slicing the coconuts that littered the shore with one of the axes brought on the boat. The two men who had finished the water now rushed for coconuts. They leaned over Lala Ram, telling him to hurry up. When one of them raised his fist, Lala Ram raised his axe. The man lowered his fist, mumbling curses beneath his breast.

'What happened?' the prisoner who was no longer a prisoner asked the boy called Aye.

As they talked, no one understood how precisely roles had been reversed. Aye would realise it only later, when the war was over, when he told his story to those who asked the same question. *What happened?* He would speak of the night that seven hundred men, women and children were forced onto boats before being pushed into the ocean in a storm, as bombs rained down on them. One hundred and eighteen washed onto this rock, somehow, only to die of starvation, or die at the hands of men who fought each other even for insects. And as he told this to the few reporters who came after the war, only then would he realise that had he helped Zee escape from the Japanese instead of helping the prisoner escape from the British, had he been able to reverse their fates, the way he had wanted, then Aye might not be alive, and neither would Nomi. For then there would be no prisoner to help them.

But for now, as Aye picked up the other axe, slashed a coconut and drank the water that brought him life, he did not appreciate the extent to which fate had connected them, perhaps from the very day that she stepped off the *S.S. Noor*. She had looked at him and, separately, at Nomi on her way up to the jail. One day, he and Nomi would remember this.

As for the prisoner who was no longer a prisoner, it never occurred to her that she and Lala Ram had brought this boy back to life. She was too stunned by what she had just heard. Hundreds of people, all pushed into the water? She had thought this was her way home. Now it turned out she was better off on that other island, which was not her country, with Lulu and Lala Ram, who were not her family.

She left the boy to eat, carrying some of the food deeper into the bushes. She saw a man's body being picked apart by vultures, while a boy lay beside him, moaning softly, looking up at her with ravenous eyes. The two were so emaciated there was hardly any flesh *to* pick, yet the vultures would not stop. She saw bodies that would never be washed or buried. She saw bodies with no name, no story. She began to give each one a funeral, leaving a few leaves here, a few shells there. Her lips moved in a prayer, or a chant. Occasionally, especially if the body was a child's, she would bend down and glance the cheek or hair with her palm. For the living, she left a little dried meat, a morsel of yam, and kept on.

There were twenty people or so still alive. The boy had said there were about a hundred. Where were the others? The island rose steeply past the forest, at the edge of which she hovered.

There was not enough food. What was she to do? The food she had brought was from Lala Ram's supplies, and his people were also running short because they could not fish.

And what about Nomi—was she to leave her here? The girl would not be separated from her mother, nor from the boy, now that she had found them again. Nor could they all fit in the canoe. She had promised Lala Ram she would ask for no more. Even if she could, what about the others? Whose life was worth more?

She made her way back to the canoe. Lala Ram had sliced all the coconuts he could find, and distributed them as widely as he could. He was looking up at the sky. It would not be long before the sun touched the sea. The clouds were not too thick, but they were stirring. He was ready to leave.

She decided that she would go back with him, but would return, alone, to this terrible place. She would bring food she had foraged. She would tell no one. For now, she took the belt off her waist, the one with the knife, and handed it to Nomi, telling her to use it if she must. They both looked at one of the two men who had finished the water. He was throwing up in the bushes.

Before she left, Nomi asked, 'What is your name?'

In the boat, once they had pulled away, Lala Ram said, 'I know what you are thinking.'

'What?'

'You will return.'

'I am thinking you were right. We should not have gone there.'

He was quiet.

She was also thinking this. If somewhere there was a star made entirely of words, then perhaps there was also a star made entirely of pictures. Her memory was selective, this she knew, but who controlled what her memory selected? Why were the images that returned too often of moments she did not wish to keep seeing—at least not alone? That boy who lay beside the body picked apart by vultures, if he lived, who would share the memory with him? And whatever it was that Nomi saw out in the water, on that terrible night, who would come to know? As for herself, who still woke up some mornings next to the three Cillians, why could she not forget? *Why?* If somewhere there was a star made entirely of pictures, then everyone would have to look, together, with fearless, soundless words, and the silence would not be a separation. It would be a dance. A shedding of tears.

Lala Ram was talking to her, rapidly, with his oar in his lap, and with both arms extended. She had been lost in her thoughts and saw this only now, as she turned around, amazed at the risk he took, the man who was normally cautious. The boat was bobbing on an increasingly choppy sea and it was starting to rain. He was upset, because now, all because of her, he had also seen those who needed him and he was also torn.

'Lala Ram. We are drifting.'

He did not hear her, and kept talking. All because of her, he repeated, he was now wondering how to convey what he had seen to his tribe, how to convince them to get involved, when no good had ever come from getting involved in the wars of men who should have stayed apart. There was a pattern to everything. There was an order. Did she not understand?

There was a garish gold halo around the descending sun, and the horizon was a lustrous rose. Yet, beyond that slim, fiery band between sea and sky, the world wore the colours of ash. The rainbow hues she had seen underwater on their way out had vanished. She was not inclined to dip her hand below the surface, to find those lovely conches. There were whitecaps ahead, the rain was a sharp slant, and if she was not mistaken, this was the same place where—no, she could not think it. 'Lala Ram,' she repeated, loudly. 'We are drifting.'

When he looked at her, it was as though he had forgotten where he was. Then he looked as though he had never before forgotten where he was, least of all in a boat. Soon, a third expression crossed his face. She knew already. They were near where a fisherman had blasted into the sky. If the fishermen were right, then this part of the sea, which had been steered clear of on the way over, was teeming with munitions. Then again, there was no clear sense of a design, no map. They could be floating over the same magnificent colours she had seen earlier, and would see again if the sea were not so irregular, so dark!

She wanted to assure Lala Ram of this, but he was out of his skin livid, stirring up the storm inside him as he rowed.

She shut her eyes and the last thing she saw before the explosion was a picture from one yesterday, that yellow flame on her mother's pink tea roses.

The Five Spy Cases of a Suitor
and One Reoccupation (Part 2)
1945

SINCE HIS MEETING WITH Lord Mountbatten in May, Andrew Gallagher, Jr had enjoyed reasonable success with his reoccupation army of three. In addition to securing transport and fuel, he had also acquired food, medical personnel and hospital equipment. The officer best suited to command the operation was a steely-eyed brigadier who decided they could work together provided Andrew looked after only civil affairs. After they shook hands, Andrew busied himself with enlisting the help of jailors with pre-war experience in the Andamans. Among them was a former head jailor by the name of Cillian.

It was now July. A question that troubled Andrew was the future of the penal settlement. He knew that Indians had long argued for its abolishment. Though he disagreed, the war made him wonder if the local population had suffered enough. Was it time to pardon the prisoners and their children, the Local Borns? Should they be awarded the choice of repatriation to the mainland, or continued residence on the islands? This would have the advantage of dampening the furore over the arrest of thousands of protestors on the mainland seeking an end to British rule. He had no plans of returning to the islands after delivering them back to the Crown, nor did he have plans to ever quit India. His wife (who still reminded him of Shakuntala) was pregnant again, and he still had every intention of raising his sons in Nagpur, hunting tigers and other game. Abolishing the penal colony could be just the symbolic gesture needed.

He discussed his scheme with the Viceroy, Lord Wavell. He also asked for the *S.S. Noor* to be relieved from its war efforts, to transport prisoner families back to India or Burma. When Wavell eventually agreed to both proposals, Andrew took a chance and asked for more.

'Something must be done to help the local population. Even if the prisoners are pardoned and eventually repatriated, if India finds out that they have been starving, we would not appear favourably.'

'What do you suggest?' asked the Viceroy.

'What about the Red Cross? Or an airlift to deliver food?'

The Viceroy was sceptical, but drafted a letter to Mountbatten. Once again, Andrew took a plane to Colombo, from where he was driven to Kandy, a letter in his shirt pocket. Mountbatten read the letter in silence. Then he reminded Andrew that the Navy had worked very hard to impose the blockade. 'Undermining it will prove to be markedly unpopular.'

When Andrew argued that doing nothing would prove to be more unpopular, for surely Indian nationalists would capitalise on the suffering of a starving population, Mountbatten conceded that Andrew had a point. He agreed to hold a meeting with the Naval Chief of Staff, Admiral Power, the man who would next month sail to Singapore on the *HMS Cleopatra*, to oversee the final surrender of the Japanese.

The meeting was brief. 'What about rescuing the whole bloody lot?' said Power before storming out of the room.

In the hush that ensued, Mountbatten and Andrew regarded each other. Finally, Mountbatten advised that an airlift would benefit only the Japanese. The best option would be a mercy ship.

After leaving Kandy, Andrew began assembling a medical team to prepare packets of food. He also assigned two officers who had served on the islands and the head jailor Cillian the task of assembling a list of all the convicts sent to the Andamans, along with the dates of their arrival and details of their sentence.

When the three men consulted the records, there was no mention of Prisoner 218 D, who had disappeared one night from the jail. If Cillian remembered her, he kept this to himself, confident that the memory would fade as enduringly as the ink in the pages he compiled.

The mercy ship flew under a white flag, with a team of only civilian personnel. Among them was Cillian, who had impressed Andrew with his fast and fastidious recordkeeping of convicts and their crimes.

The ship set sail on 5 August 1945. After it sent back a signal to Andrew—*All's well*—he left for the islands with a convoy of cargo ships, the troop ship, a flotilla of Indian Navy minesweepers, and three sloops of the Indian Navy.

Before reaching the harbour, they received a signal warning that the acoustic mines dropped by the Royal Air Force were not moored at any particular location. Moreover, they had been laid not only along the shores of South Andaman Island, but also of neighbouring islands, to keep the Japanese from occupying these. In some areas, the mines had drifted and clustered together and appeared to be collecting so much sea debris that they detonated quite by accident. The Indian Navy minesweepers were not equipped to deal with this.

Andrew's reoccupation force had to unload personnel and stores outside the harbour. Aside from this delay, the convoy arrived smoothly, and when they met Cillian from the mercy ship, he assured them that the six-inch coastal guns lining the shore would not fire, the Japanese had been cooperative. Andrew sent a signal to the Viceroy. '*Reoccupation accomplished without incident.*'

He was told there had been two boat campaigns in which the local population had been taken out to sea. The second was but a day before the mercy ship had set sail. According to a guard who had escorted the families, on the first campaign they were 'helped off the boats,' while on the second, they were taken to a nearby island and shot. All three hundred. If survivors of either campaign existed, search parties could not be sent out till the arrival of minesweepers equipped to deal with acoustic mines.

In the meantime, a policeman informed Andrew that all the collaborators had been rounded up and put in jail till an investigation could be held. After he was done speaking, the policeman lingered a while longer than necessary.

'What is it?' asked Andrew, a little impatient.

'One of the collaborators,' said the policeman, 'is a woman you might know.'

'Oh?'

'She owned a pig farm.' As an afterthought, he offered, 'The farm is in shambles.'

'How can that be?' said Andrew, certain he had heard incorrectly. When the policeman nodded, Andrew asked, 'Where is she?'

'Still at the farm. I have not arrested her, as the Indian who made the accusation—a servant of a Japanese medical officer at whose house she was seen—is himself untrustworthy. I thought you might want to speak to her first.'

'Right,' said Andrew. 'You can go.'

In the evening, when he walked to her farm, he noticed that the handsome sports ground where he had often enjoyed a good game of cricket was entirely flooded. He discovered the reason soon enough. The main storm-water drain had been blocked, and the area was a muddle of half-dug holes and trenches. Moreover, the drain was an iridescent blue that scattered each time he blinked. Blue flies, hundreds of them. 'Revolting,' he muttered.

Shakuntala was drinking tea on her kitchen doorstep. She had missed the strong, pungent aroma. She had missed the sweetness.

The cup she held in her hands, white with a black wreath near the rim, was all that remained of her grandmother's wedding gift to her and Thomas. It was not Adams China, as Thomas's mother had pointed out while Shakuntala unwrapped the set. His mother had collected Adams China and spoke often of its 'unique clay formula' and many designs, favouring patterns that were geometric and Eastern in aesthetic. Now, instead of her mother-in-law's voice, Shakuntala could hear Dr Mori say that once Japan had been forced to throw open its doors, 'The West began to mimic our artists. They have done the same in India.'

Her attention shifted to the beautiful blue cup he had served her tea in, and left behind. It rested on Thomas's bookshelf and the gold seam sparkled, as on that day, affirming that it was not damaged, but impermanent. He had watched her face as she admired the translucent shape nestled in her palm, filling her with a feeling for things outside herself.

She had not seen very much of the doctor after that day. Because of the embargo, there were no medicines left on the island, at least none for the comfort women. The clinic had closed to them in April of last year.

Before the clinic shut, the doctor had been cordial, as always, but did not invite her back for tea. Did he decide she had played no part in sending the Ferrargunj signals? Did he decide he had better things to do, after all? Once, as they parted, he seemed ruffled. His soldiers were all 'starving, exhausted and infected,' he said. He looked thin, though she assumed men of his rank would be secreting away food for themselves. Then he surprised her even more by asking if she was well, if she had enough to eat.

The Japanese had been watching her, of this she was sure. Often, when she came to the end of her driveway, a car would drive away. It was the same car that had picked him up from her farm. Till the arrival of the mercy ship, there was hardly any food left on the farm, and with news of the two boat campaigns, she had known even less what to do.

What she had known was where he lived. It was not far.

After the first boat campaign, as vultures circled the island, she knew it would soon be their turn. The morning after the second boat campaign, while Paula wept in bed, the cat moaning plaintively on her pillow, Shakuntala sat beside them, thinking. Aditi and her husband, the headman of Ferrargunj, had been taken away. So had the children and grandchildren from his previous marriage.

Why had she and Paula been spared? Did the doctor have something to do with it?

She could not shake the feeling she got from him, that she *could* talk to him. If.

She could not shake these two lean letters either. If she were not a woman. If he were not a man. If he did not have blood on his hands, and gloves.

If doing nothing did not mean starving to death, or being next on a boat.

'We must do something,' she had said to Paula.

Her daughter had sat up, gazing blankly at the blackened windows. She no longer arranged her light brown curls in the mirror. ('The colour of crème caramel,' Thomas used to say, while playing with those baby curls.) She no longer practiced pouty smiles. She no longer read her father's books. How selfish Shakuntala had been in keeping her here after his death! She could have made peace with her own family, and even Thomas's, if for no other reason but to secure her daughter a future.

'You need to come with me,' Shakuntala had said.

'Where are we going?' Paula had asked, her voice flat.

'To Dr Mori's house.'

'Dr Mori? From the clinic?'

'Yes.'

'You hated the clinic.'

'Yes.'

'So?'

So she told Paula of the day she and the doctor had tea. Of his promise to make her a different one, more to her taste. Of the cup he left behind (which, till then, had been hidden from Paula). Of his asking after her, despite his wilted demeanour. Of her conviction that he had something to do with why she and Paula were still alive. Of needing his continued good will, if they were to keep surviving.

Paula looked horror-struck. 'Do you not see what they are doing?'

'I know it sounds strange. I—' She took a deep breath. 'I cannot help but—'

Paula turned around to face her mother fully, fury in her eyes. If nothing else, thought Shakuntala, she had brought life back to her daughter's cheek by outraging her.

'What?' Paula snapped, raising her voice. 'You cannot help what?'

Shakuntala got out of bed, scooping up the cat that had dropped to the floor in fright, kissing the silken triangle between her eyes. 'I grew up with hate,' she tried again, softly. 'Between my parents.

Between Hindus and Christians. Between Indians and the British. Between myself and my in-laws. Between myself and my mother and then her father, who had nothing good to say about mine. It is hard to explain, but when you grow up between so many worlds, something changes. It is why I came here. To get away from all that hate. And your father and I found on this rock a way to love each other, in peace. Here of all places. An island where so many Indians have suffered because of your father's race, which is now half of yours.'

Paula only looked more aghast.

'What I want to say is, I only saw your father as a human being, as someone I loved. It can happen.'

'Are you saying you *love* the doctor?'

'Goodness! Of course not!'

'Then what are you saying?'

'I am saying I see him as a human being. I am saying I have only just discovered it is the one talent I have.'

Paula stood up, turned away, pulled back her curls. When she faced her mother again she had arranged herself in much the same way that Shakuntala had trained herself to do when attempting to wear a mask.

'Mama. They put seven hundred people in boats. Aye was among them.' Her voice remained impressively even. 'Then they put three hundred more people in boats. They torture people in jail. They have labour camps. They kidnap and rape women. You *see* the women. So does your doctor. They destroyed your beloved farm. He could have stopped that, if he didn't want us to starve. You are willing to seek the help of such a man?'

The cat leaped from Shakuntala's arms as if also to raise an objection.

'I do not disagree with anything you say,' conceded Shakuntala.

'He's like a jailor. They all are. Do not forget what the women in Marriagetown always said about jailors who brought them *gifts*.' Paula looked up, as though expecting her mother to repeat what the women said. When she didn't, Paula did. 'Once she accepts the *gift* of protection, she's his.'

What had her daughter become? At one time, it was Paula who scolded her mother for being 'gloomy.' Since when had they begun reversing roles?

'If what you say is true,' said Shakuntala, 'then we are already his. Do you want to die in the sea, eaten by sharks?'

'Oh!'

Shakuntala realised, too late, that she had just drawn the picture her daughter had been trying not to see. With one stroke, she had caused Paula's remarkable control to crumble. The child fell back into bed, weeping.

That same afternoon, she and Paula arrived at Dr Mori's villa.

On their way, Shakuntala thought: if talent were not indiscriminate, she would rather put it towards being a better mother than towards making officers human beings.

On the kitchen doorstep, Shakuntala was still savouring the tea from the food packets. She twirled the white cup in her hands, thinking again of her mother-in-law's Adams China, and wondered what Paula was, if not clay of the West, design of the East—or *vice versa*.

She could hear her daughter inside, washing dishes after their dinner of rice and lentils, also from the food packets. It was the most extravagant, most magnificent meal the two had ever enjoyed, though Paula cried afterwards, so guilty did she feel about Aye 'starving somewhere.' Like everyone who had rushed to the port yesterday to greet the ship with the white flag, Shakuntala was at first startled to see the hated jailor, Cillian—his stomach rounder, his belt tied lower, and without a baton or cigar—handing out the food. Jailors giving gifts, she had thought. The Japanese were even bowing before him.

What did it all mean? she wondered. Was the war over? The only news of a war beyond the islands had come to her when a villager trained to operate the wireless spread a rumour of the Japanese being defeated in Imphal, north of Chittagong. Thousands of their soldiers were dead. Thousands of Indian soldiers in the British Indian

Army were dead too. The man did not think anyone in Chittagong had been killed.

'You have chosen seclusion,' Dr Mori had said, the time they had tea. 'Why?'

How Shakuntala wished for a peaceful way to end Paula's seclusion now.

She stood up, licked the bottom of the cup so as not to waste a single grain of sugar, and was about to go inside when she saw a shadow glide past her desolate pen. It was Andrew Gallagher, Jr, looking even scruffier than the last time they met.

'Hello, Shakuntala.'

'Hello, Andrew. You're back.'

'As promised,' he said. 'You have our protection again.'

'Will you come inside? Will you have tea?'

'No. I will get right to it.'

But he did not, and looked behind him, at the empty water tank and deserted corral.

'What is it?' she asked.

'They are saying you have become . . . familiar. With the Japanese.'

'Familiar?'

'Yes.'

'How?'

He faced her. 'That is what I have come to find out.'

It was too dark to see his features clearly, particularly as he now wore a proper beard. A halo of mosquitoes hounded him. He seemed as unbothered by this as she was by what he had just said. Perhaps it was the caffeine flowing through her veins after so long but she was ready for this challenge too. She sat back down on the step, tapping the space beside her. When he hesitated, she reminded him that when they last met, he had asked the same of her.

He accepted her invitation with a sigh, one that said he did not believe the rumours.

'Have you heard of the boat campaigns?' she began. 'There may be survivors.'

He told her, brusquely, that it was being taken care of.

'Is the war over?'

He nodded. 'There will be a formal surrender soon.'

She tried to understand what this meant. Would school open again? Would the women in the gurdwara go home? Would their families welcome them back?

'Shakuntala. I have work to do, as you can probably imagine.'

'Actually, I cannot. But I am trying to. Your mission was successful, then?'

'Which one?'

'I mean the Ferrargunj missions. They were successful, yes? Thanks to the headman and his wife, who are now both dead.'

He ignored this. 'They are saying he was a medical officer.'

'I too did what you asked of me.'

'Or was there more than one?'

'How dare you! Do you have any idea what has happened here?'

'Shakuntala. I am giving you a chance to clear your name. If you do not answer me, I cannot take responsibility for what happens next.'

She turned away, arranged herself. 'I will tell you exactly what happened.'

The afternoon she and Paula arrived at Dr Mori's villa, they were brought into a room with sliding doors made of papery material. Were the windows outside the room not blackened, the sun might have seeped through the lattice, illuminating those inside. Instead, the room was lit by a single kerosene lamp. They sat on rattan chairs not unlike her own. She assumed they came from one of the British villas, as did hers. There was a low table between the chairs, padded mats on the floor and two paintings on the wall.

Paula's eyes were swollen from the tears shed earlier that day. She sat opposite Shakuntala, with arms crossed. They did not speak to each other. Both were staring at the low bench at the centre, where a table had been set for one: the other translucent blue cup with gold seams, a matching plate, a napkin with a floral pattern, a pair of chopsticks on a plain wooden holder. Overall, Shakuntala was surprised by the sparseness of the décor.

When the doctor arrived she introduced Paula, but the girl did not stand up. Nor did she uncross her arms. The doctor raised his eyebrows before turning to Shakuntala. 'I am surprised to see you,' he said. He had grown even thinner. His hair was wholly white.

She apologised for the intrusion and tried to explain that she would not have come had there not been cause for concern.

Perhaps it was the word 'concern' that made the doctor laugh, without cheer, before leaving the room.

After he was gone, Paula said, 'I think we are being ignored.'

Shakuntala ignored her.

The doctor returned, followed by an Indian servant carrying a tray with a slender porcelain jug and three thumb-sized porcelain cups.

Paula refused the cup.

Shakuntala sniffed hers. The liquid was warm and smelled strongly of alcohol, but not of gin, Thomas's preferred drink. She took a sip, and immediately began coughing. Paula rolled her eyes and the doctor kept sipping.

'From my last bottle,' he said. 'You do not like our tea or our liquor.'

She apologised again for troubling him. She had come to speak plainly, she said, believing she could. It was just the two of them, her daughter and herself. They were vulnerable and hungry. He once asked if they had enough food. They did not. Her Chittagong fowl and pigs had been slaughtered. Her money was running out, and besides, there was little left to buy. She had come to ask if she could leave with her daughter for Chittagong. Also, he once asked if she would come to his villa to see pictures of the floating world. She was here, and would like to see them.

Laughing again, the doctor stood up, teetering slightly on his way to the prints on the wall.

'Good heavens, Shakuntala!' said Andrew, interrupting her. 'I have not come all this way to hear you speak of art. Next you will say you fell so in love with his fine collection that you became Shakuntala Das Vaz Best *Mori*!'

'I felt I could talk to him. That is all I'm trying to say.'

'Did he ask you to do anything for him?'

'He did not. If anything, after showing me the prints, he tried to get rid of me. I think for this reason. He knew what I could be accused of, just by being seen with him.'

'Assure me you have saved the Best for last.'

'I assure you.'

'Then we're done.'

'But you have told me nothing. Will you not say what has happened elsewhere in the world? What about Chittagong?'

Even in the darkness, when he turned his head, she could see the sweat glisten as it collected across the rim of his lips. Without thinking, she raised the hem of her dress to wipe the moisture away. Her thighs were exposed and a cool breeze caressed her damp flesh. She savoured the feeling, the hem still at Andrew's supple mouth. Through the sheer fabric, his breath was warm on her hands.

She did not know him, not at all, and was certain she had never wanted him. But she had not come this close to a man since Thomas's death. Her belly was full, the war was over, and how right it felt, to touch someone.

She moved her fingers up, still through the netting of the dress, exposing more of her body to the dark. She found the indent below each eye, and circled around, to his eyebrows. They were short and a little bristly. His hands were on her stomach. She released the dress. Beneath it, Andrew's hands moved to her breasts, still full and firm. She ran her bare fingers through his hair, which was fine, almost as fine as Thomas's, then ran her fingers down the back of his neck. His mouth, when it touched hers, was rougher than she had felt it to be through the fibre. She moistened his mouth with her tongue. His taste was acrid, but she did not mind.

'Mama!' said Paula, opening the front door. 'Are you out there?'

Before Paula could make her way to the step, Shakuntala had pulled away.

'What is it, Paula?' she called out, more sharply than intended.

'I just wanted to make sure you're okay.'

'I'm fine.'

'Do you need anything?'

'No!'

'All right, then.' Paula went back inside.

Shakuntala and Andrew both stood up.

'Well,' he said.

What could she say, she wondered. Thank you for stopping by?

She looked towards the tanks that were now empty. A part of her wanted him to lift her up in one, as when he was here last. Tonight, she would welcome the embrace. Instead, she pointed in the general direction of the sea. 'Are the waters safe?'

'We are taking care of it,' he answered.

'Well,' he said again, after a time. 'Goodbye, Shakuntala.'

'Goodbye, Andrew.'

She watched him leave before moving towards one of the tanks. Still too short to see very much, she thought, laughing softly to herself while stepping inside. What did it mean to be forty years old? When she talked to herself, it was in the same voice, the one that had told her to trust Thomas when she was sixteen.

The clouds were shaped like plump pigs. There was a flash of lightning in the distance, near the island of Tarmugli, where three hundred people had been shot.

She would never forget the prints the doctor had showed her, and thought it a pity she never got to that part of the story with Andrew. Perhaps it was just as well Paula had forced them apart, for what kind of man would not want to know?

Both prints were by Utagawa Hiroshige, the doctor had said, during the period of sakoku, when Japan closed its doors to the world. Shakuntala had been transfixed by the first image, in which a full white moon lay inside a brown case, like an egg in a nest. Wisps of grass floated across it. The moon was so corporal and close, she wished to pluck it from the picture, to cup it in her brown hands.

The doctor tilted his head. 'You do not like our tea or liquor but you like our art.'

'I do. Very much.'

'What do you see?'

'At first I saw an egg. But, I do not think so. The moon is an island. A very secluded island. Sleeping peaceably in a forest for hundreds of years.'

The doctor stared at the picture.

'What about this one?' he said, finally moving away. 'I know you like cats.'

It was a larger print. A seated white cat was looking out of a slatted window. In the distance loomed a mountain, and above the mountain flew a flock of birds. The birds were described in delicate strokes, in a deceptively haphazard design that, upon closer inspection, contained all the order of those who know how to navigate the world. It was the birds she liked best. There was something about the cat, though. She could catch only a glimpse of its face, upon which lay a small scowl. There was little in the composition to suggest the serenity of the other picture, the one of the moon-island. There was instead an overwhelming regret.

'You prefer the first one.'

'Yes. Though I like this too, in a way.'

'You will like it less when I tell you what it says.'

Their shoulders were touching. When she turned to her right, to look into his face, she noticed that his eyes were puffy, almost as puffy as Paula's. 'What does it say?'

'In the distance is Mount Fuji, and the sun is setting over the rice paddies. But if you look inside the room, you will see a towel tossed on the ledge, next to the cat, and a bowl for cleansing. You will also see hairpins, popular gifts.'

'Gifts?'

'Do you not see? The scene takes place soon after a client has left, before the tearoom has been cleared. The white cat gazing through the bars at the world beyond her own represents the courtesan, who is not allowed to leave.'

From behind her, Shakuntala could hear her daughter shift on the rattan chair.

'You have taken a great risk by coming here,' said the doctor, still staring ahead, at the print. 'You put us all at risk. I must ask that you not return.'

'But you can help us.'

'You mistake me.'

'Then why do I see your car? Why does it keep a watch on us?'

'Do not push your luck,' he said, his eyes hardening. 'I do not approve of how you raise your daughter but her instincts are better than yours.' Without looking at her, he left the room. The servant began clearing the porcelain jug and cups.

She stepped down from the tank and went inside. Paula was asleep, the cat on her pillow.

In the coming week the Japanese were made into a labour force, to clean the streets and repair the buildings—from the asylum at Haddo to the gurdwara in Aberdeen—damaged by the bombings. She learned that prisoners and their families were to be repatriated, if they so desired, on a 'first come first repatriated' basis. With her it was not a question of repatriation, as such. It would be a while before there was space on the ship to carry her and Paula back. She learned, too, that the search parties had found twelve survivors from the first boat campaign.

Now that it was possible for her to return, even if she had to wait for space on the ship, she wondered if this was what she really wanted. What if she went back to Chittagong only for a short while, to meet her family, and to leave Paula? Could she keep the door to this island open for herself, after bringing back more fowl and pigs? With the prisoners repatriated and the war over, could life here happen again?

When she asked Paula, she was surprised to find her delighted at the prospect of leaving, despite discovering that one of the boat campaign survivors was Aye. Like everyone else, Paula had changed. She did not want, ever again, to know fear of the kind she had faced. She did not want to go hungry. Perhaps she did not want even to love, not yet. She began questioning Shakuntala on Thomas's family, not the way she had done before, for wry anecdotes about his mother, or the cook. Now it seemed she was increasingly identifying them as her own. She would not hear that they would not see her that way. Shakuntala had feared losing her daughter to the Japanese. In a sense, she had. Paula was English now, more than before. And though she talked to her more freely than Shakuntala had spoken to her own mother, like Shakuntala, it seemed Paula would not mind distancing herself from her only parent—perhaps because of the doctor, or some other reason only a daughter could know.

It was through Paula that she learned a date had been fixed for the official surrender, to be held on the renovated sports ground. Paula went. Shakuntala stayed away. Later, her daughter re-enacted the commanders handing over their swords, mocking their shame with her own unconcealed glee.

Two days before the surrender, Shakuntala was walking past a ground being cleared by a Japanese solider. He was wearing a vest, the muscles of his arms flexing as he shovelled. Children jeered at him, while hurling stones. She saw that it was not a soldier, but Dr Mori, thick in dirt. Without looking up, he paused, so as not to flick the earth in her direction. She told the children to stop, but the look in his eye told her that he would rather bear their insults than have her rescue him. That was as much as he would acknowledge being seen by her. In the late afternoon light, against the brown sludge, his white hair seemed to glow. Like a moon-island, she thought, and continued walking.

Whittling
1945

THE STAIRCASE CURVED BEFORE Aye. All the way up to the bed-room he would run, caressing the wooden bannister, to fetch the blade to shave Mr Howard. Always, his sharpest eyes were his feet. Yet, today, each time he tried to sit up in bed, to again climb those steps, something was in his way.

His mother and grandfather stood in the doorway, sturdy as the staircase behind them. A nurse by the name of Anne gave him injec-tions. Afterwards, though no pretty orioles danced before him and no yellow angel tickled his ear, he relaxed, wrapped in a kind of cotton made of smiles. His mother often bent down to kiss his cheek and rearrange the cotton.

If the nurse did not come, he felt a terrible throbbing far below his right knee. He remembered something swollen and warped there, like a clump of waterlogged wood. Then the leg would become the coiling staircase outside the door. Only one leg. The other stayed in bed. This effort to hold the two halves in one body—the grotesque leg, and the normal one—exhausted him more than building a run-way or force-feeding a prisoner; more than scaling a prison wall or saving a drowning body. He did not know which was worse, the memories or the contortion of his leg. There was something about that last memory, though, the one about cradling bodies. At times the body was Zee, on his last night, in the pond behind Japanese Headquarters. Other times, it was Mr Howard, as he shaved and bathed him. Or it was Zee's mother, as she thrashed in the sea. He was always cradling someone, and he longed to stop. He was tired.

Then the nurse and his mother were there, one with a syringe, the other with open arms.

As the drug chased away the memories, he noticed that his mother was dressed in a new blouse. It was green, shot through with red lines, and more fitted than her older ones had been. Either that, or she had put on weight. He looked more closely. Yes, his mother was no longer starving. He shut his eyes. He said a prayer of thanks. When he opened his eyes, his grandfather was also by his bedside. His mother was speaking to him in whispers, believing Aye to be asleep. Was it the drug, or was his father there, too? He was walking around the room, his longyi hitched up high, as though he was about to wade into a river. How had his father left his rock?

Then one day, Aye did not feel the throbbing in his leg anymore. He had a knife in his hands, he believed. The blade caught the sunlight, reminding him that he had work to do. When he hoisted himself up onto his elbows, before him lay a magnificent array of knives. There was the one used to scrape Mr Howard's cheek, with a razor that folded forward into a heavy red handle with a snap. There was the one given to Aye by his grandfather, for whittling. The blade had frequently to be refitted into the bamboo stem, till a tiny dot of foam collected at the stem's surface. Next to it was the knife that had belonged to the prisoner. She had left it behind, after giving everyone food. The handle was long and sanded smooth, and the blade of bone fit inside with slender lashings of rope. There was also an axe for slashing coconuts. It was covered in blood. And, finally, the dagger in his hands, which had an asymmetrical hilt and a wavy blade. His grandfather's replica of his great-grandfather's kris. A pillow was tucked behind his neck, but he was no longer comfortable. The bannister was still before him. He still wanted to run up the steps.

He swung his legs out to the left side of the bed and tried to stand but fell to the floor. Only then did he dare to meet the rest of his body, to see that he was without a right foot. Though he had cradled so many others in distress, Aye had never before known the sound of his own scream.

The nurse arrived, with the needle.

⟨✿⟩

He was told not to put any weight on the 'residual limb,' which started about two-thirds of the way up his leg. There had been an infection. It was spreading, and would have taken the entire leg. He was lucky to have saved the rest, and to have had the surgery with anaesthesia, of which there was still only a limited supply. The nurse gave him a few pills for the pain, warning him not to waste them. The flesh around the wound would stay tender for some time. He was instructed not touch it.

Then he was told to leave the hospital. There were not enough beds.

Sometime after the nurse left, two journalists came to see him. They asked what had happened on the island where hundreds of skeletons had been found. When Aye moaned, his grandfather shooed them away. Next, a policeman arrived, to tell Aye and his family that they could be repatriated. Because Aye's great-grandfather had been among the first to set foot on the island, under the policy of 'first to arrive first to be repatriated,' if his family wished to return to Burma, they could set sail on the *S.S. Noor* at the end of September. The same ship that had transported prisoners would now take them back. The policeman left.

Aye's mother helped him to sit up. His father still paced. His grandfather sat on the floor, whittling. He said he was too old now to return to a country he had never seen. What would they do there? Where would they live? He had no siblings and his son, Aye's father— he pointed to the man who paced—would not know the difference between sitting on a rock on an island or a rock in Rangoon. When he said this, Aye winced. *He can hear you*, he wanted to say. But he could not find it in him to reproach anyone, and besides, Aye's grandfather was making him a cane. It was what the old man had been doing all this time. The cane was of padauk, which, under the British, Local Borns had been forbidden from using. The chief commissioner had kept in his house a dining table made from a single trunk of the tree, and Aye had often admired its interlocked, swirling grain and natural shine. It had still to be there, for who could move it?

He lay in bed, listening to his grandfather whittle while speaking of the futility of leaving. For a time, as Aye drifted in the wood's delicate aroma, he mastered his grief. When his loss resurfaced, he tried to picture all the colours of padauk: rich crimson, brownish red, chocolate brown with black streaks. When again he had to push back his anguish, he recalled other firm facts about the tree. For instance, Mr Howard saying that padauk was superior to teak, white oak, or hard maple. For a time, these names and textures were a comfort to him. Then he called his mother, and she was there, with his pills.

The nurse again reminded him to leave. Aye took the cane in his right hand. Padauk was a hard wood, not easy to shape. He was aware, while leaning into his mother, that his grandfather's skill was more extraordinary than he had realised, but the way the old man watched him hop to the door made Aye want to weep. Those old, magnificent hands were trembling as they moved through the air in Aye's general direction, perhaps to catch him if he fell, but wasn't it Aye's job to support *him*? Aye could not find the strength to look more closely at all the figures etched exquisitely in the walking stick. He could not find the strength to thank him. And when Aye's father glanced in his direction once, aware that something was happening, he could not find the strength to thank him for, at last, standing up from his rock.

The makeshift hospital was in Mr Howard's villa. The operating room was in the study, which was why he had been seeing the staircase to Mr Howard's bedroom. The portrait of Jack the Sailor was still there, above the bed where they had cut off Aye's foot. The one of the Three Athletes had been removed.

Outside the study, he touched the wooden bannister he had dusted more times than he could remember. He looked around, at the doors and window-frames. All made with Burmese hands.

Nomi came to his village. Her stomach was a bloated sphere, but her arms and legs were like twigs.

It was only through observing her that he would slowly come to understand the changes in himself. These changes were not visible to him, so consumed was he by the loss of his foot. But that day she came to him, he could see that the changes in her far surpassed a distended stomach. And he remembered the girl who used to walk down the aisles of the shop in Aberdeen for a whole year after Zee's death, dressed in a muddy white frock and pyjamas. The top button at the back of her dress was always undone, the hair crooked across the neck. That spot of exposed flesh—he wondered if this was the first part of her to capture him. She had taken it upon herself to keep trimming her own hair, when her parents were grieving. This was the Nomi that had kept on surfacing on the island where they were stranded.

Once, before the search party found them, he had watched her bite into a green fruit. Her front tooth caught in it. She licked the blood on the green meat, then pulled out the tooth, stuffed the fruit in one corner of her mouth, and chewed slowly, singularly intent on discovering its taste (and perhaps more falling teeth). This was how they changed, he and Nomi: one mouthful at a time. Through clawing for survival on that island, they grew more resolute, and more self-governing. If they found something to eat, something to drink, afterwards, Nomi would sometimes curl into Aye's arms and sleep, while, at other times, it was as though she barely knew him. From what she told him, he was the same. She said she often awoke to him speaking of Mr Howard, his father, or the labour camp. She never disturbed him. She let him sleep. There was something both loving and feral in the understanding that had developed between them, perhaps even before being trapped on that other island. While the wound on his foot kept oozing and his infection spread, they both understood that Feral Aye and Feral Nomi would never completely depart.

She had not talked very much on the other island. She had mostly foraged for food, or slept. But after one especially difficult night for Aye, she began to speak. Slowly, at first, about her parents, after Zee died. Her father in drink, her mother in prayer. The more she spoke—always punctuating her sentences with 'after Zee died,' with an emphasis on *died* that alarmed him—why did she not say 'passed away'? Or 'left'?—the more the strange intimacy and trust that they bestowed

upon each other seemed to grow. She spoke of hearing her bones at
night, after Zee died, of not being able to turn her head—she demonstrated by turning it now, first left then right, that same intent expression on her face as when chewing green fruit. She frequently paused,
mouth open, the gap from the missing tooth making her look like an
old and batty aunt. She also spoke of her time on the island with the
prisoner, of hearing about mermaids and being told to *speak* because
everything from a twig to a baby was a letter waiting to join another
letter. She folded her spindly arms over her narrow chest as though
uniting two letters. She flashed him an extraordinary smile.

It was when they were both stranded that she finally let him near,
telling him things he had wanted to know all those times he came to
her after Zee's death, and telling him much more, to distract him from
his own pain. He came to see that fifteen years for a girl like her was
at least twenty-five for anyone else. To some extent, she and Aye were
the same age. And she already seemed to understand this.

But there were things he was not certain she would understand.
He had not told her that the night they were all pushed off the boats,
he had heard her in the water. 'I am Nomi.' He had tried. Truly. It was
her mother who gave him permission to stop trying, to instead save
himself, and her. And so he had left Nomi behind. Would she understand this?

Now she came to see him in his village, after his surgery. She
carried the knife of the prisoner who was no longer a prisoner. She
arranged it on a table next to the cot on which he reclined. He had
been talking of nothing but knives, ever since his surgery, she said, so
she wanted him to have this one too.

So he was still talking in his sleep. His mother and grandfather had
not told him this, but Nomi reported all things—small and grand—in
the same nonchalant way she had trimmed her hair or pulled out her
tooth. The gesture was not refined but, to her, it was necessary.

As he touched the knife, she examined his walking stick. The base
was an elephant, the handle a globe, and the shaft a long figure with
the globe in his left hand. 'Who is it?' she asked.

But the ghost of his waterlogged foot appeared before him, so he ignored her question. She met his silence with silence. When he eventually spoke, it was about the sea. Unlike other Local Borns, he told her, he had never grown up resenting the sea. Even before he could swim, he loved how it sighed after unburdening itself on land, over and over again. After learning how to swim, he fell in love too with its warm currents and playful ways. It never frightened him. 'Never,' he repeated. 'But that changed the night they pushed us off the boat.'

She asked if he wanted to go outside, if he wanted to practice walking with the stick. He was too tired, he said. He had no more he wanted to say, and so she left him, and returned the next day.

It continued like this. He said things already shared, on that other island. Things that obsessed him. For instance, what had compelled him to leave the runway for the boats that night? Had he not, would he still have his limb, or would it have rotted in the rain anyway? It had already been cut, numerous times, from the sharp edges of the steel mat, and then the walk through the jungle to get to the boats that night.

'Do you know how old I am?' he asked her once.

'Fifty?' Nomi shrugged.

'Twenty-one. I am an old man. Do you see my hair?' It had been cut too short for his liking, and the hair at his temples was receding.

'Look at my fat stomach,' she said, and they both laughed.

She sat with both feet tucked beneath her, and for a moment he ached with the knowledge that he would never move with such fluidity again, even as she said, 'Did you hear that? My bones still creak.'

She shared with him news of the present, to which he had been indifferent since his surgery. Photographers were swarming Aberdeen, Nomi said, but were only interested in bombed-out buildings. They asked questions but would not believe the answers, especially about the prisoner. They did not believe that she had helped them, that she had existed.

As she talked, Aye's thoughts drifted, always returning to what the policeman had again come to his village to ask. Did his family want to return to Burma?

Then one day, White Paula came to see him. He tried to remember the last time they had met. It was before he joined the labour camp, but he could not remember exactly. She was as beautiful, if not more. Her hair was longer, her freckles still fanciful. When he remembered kissing them, he remembered what he had become. He found himself growing more ashamed in her presence than in anyone else's. It seemed to him that she did not notice. What use was he to her, anyway? What use was he to anyone? When she told him she wanted to leave the islands, he shut his eyes, pretending to sleep. When she leaned over him, to kiss his forehead, he thanked her in his heart, but could do no more.

After she left, he wished to take to the sea. This time, it would be on his own terms, unmoored by anyone else. Had he been waiting for the right wind? Had it come? His family could board the *S.S. Noor* as early as next month. His father could bring his rock. They could go to his mother's village. Aye could learn how to whittle better. His grandfather insisted Aye could do that here—hadn't he? Yes, Aye conceded, but he longed to capture the fluidity of the wind and water in the ancient wood of his true homeland. He wanted to help rebuild his country after the war, with his own hands. He still had two of these. His own country. His own hands. He would use them better than he had used his feet. This is what he wanted.

He tried to speak of it to Nomi, but each time, she would run away, looking as though she had again been tossed off the side of a boat.

Once, she said, 'It's because of the thunderbolt!'

'What?'

'The blood mixing! You promised. We mixed our blood in the bowl but then you spilled it!'

'Nomi.' He sat up. His wound was no longer bandaged and the sight of the puckered stub was so revolting to him that he threw a sheet over the entire leg. 'Listen—'

'I believed you! You *lied*.'

It was the second time she accused him of this. He tried to hop towards her but she ran out of the hut, all the way out of his village, and he could no longer run.

The next morning, he woke up with an excruciating pain in the area where his foot and shin had been. When it would not go away, his mother sent for the nurse, who explained that pain signals were still being sent to his brain. With time, the signals would stop, but he must try not to dwell on them, or the brain would continue to play tricks on him by retaining a memory of pain.

Nomi did not return to his village that whole week. He did not leave his village, to look for her. Nor could he unmoor himself from thinking of her.

In that week, he tried harder to walk. He stepped outside, and his father was there, on the rock. When his father saw him, he stood up. It was the image Aye had seen at the runway, when the father wind had come to him. The man was standing up. Then he began to pace, the way he had paced at Mr Howard's villa, after Aye's surgery. Without looking at Aye, his father was telling him to walk.

Aye hobbled towards him. Together, they walked in silence. After about ten minutes, exhausted, Aye returned to his hut. That night, he lay awake, wondering what his father wanted. Did he want to leave, or to stay?

The next morning, when Aye left his hut, his father again stood up. This time they walked a little longer. 'Nay kaung lar?' Aye asked. 'Are you well?' When there was no answer, he added, 'What should we do?'

His father kept walking in silence. His gait was tentative, but Aye liked to believe that this was so Aye would not be left behind. Then he laughed to himself—how could his father have an awareness of any-one else's feelings?

From the corner of his eye, Aye looked at the cheeks he had never shaved. They were scruffy, but clean. The hair, too, was not terribly dishevelled. How alarming it would be if, after the war, everyone's body but his father's had aged? There was no stench coming off him. His nails, like his beard, were surprisingly trim. His longyi was freshly washed and tied securely at the waist. And his feet! Ah—they were his beautiful own, with *two* high arches!

For the rest of that week, each time Aye stepped outside in the morning, his father was waiting. They walked together a little longer each day.

On the seventh day, Aye appeared with his whittling knife, a towel, a bowl of steaming water, and some soap. It was not the luxurious shaving cream he had used on Mr Howard, but it would do. When his father stood up from the rock, Aye asked him to please sit back down. He would shave him first, then they would walk. He knew his father never let anyone but his mother attend to him, yet he was not surprised that, today, his father listened. Finding another rock, Aye placed it behind his father's. It was with some effort that Aye was able to fold his good leg while protecting the other, after which, he got to work. He tucked the towel into his father's shirt. He scooped out water with his palm and, with his fingers, patted his father's cheeks till they were wet but not dripping. He repeated this motion three times. He lathered the face with his bare fingers. The soap was not as foamy as he would have liked, but he still enjoyed this part. His fingers swept all the way down the neck and along the ear lobes and up, to the arch of the cheekbones, which were prominent. The texture of his father's skin was like his own.

Aye scraped the lather off gently with his whittling knife. Not too slow, not too fast. His father shut his eyes, and sighed. It was almost indiscernible, but it was there. Aye took his time, living only in the fluidity of his movements, as he touched his father for the first time in his life.

Did either of them need to leave this place? Was this island not known to Aye more intimately than any other land? Wasn't it the same for his father, who had observed the moon and the stars worshipfully from his rock? A prisoner had once told Aye that the islands were not evil, even when what happened on them was. He said the islands were born of Rama's desire for a bridge between India and Malaya and, ever since, many gods had come here, and they too would leave. He had been right. The war was over.

Aye rinsed his father's cheek. 'There. You look younger than me.'

That night he was visited by a dream that helped him decide. The dream was this.

He was walking towards the *S.S. Noor* with a cane. A large crowd had gathered to wave goodbye to the first batch of repatriates. How often he had come to this same jetty to witness prisoners disembark from the same ship! He turned around, to face the island instead of the sea. He glanced at the trail leading up to the jail, recalling the way the prisoner had looked at him on her first day. He scanned the jetty for Nomi. He feared she had not come to say goodbye, but then he spotted her in the crowd, a small girl with a crooked haircut and a mouth set in anguish. Her stomach seemed less distended, and he wished he could tell her how glad this made him feel. How could he leave her, without Zee, without a father? Her mother was alive, but in his dream he knew it was not she who could love Nomi the way she deserved to be loved, the way he had tried to love her. What more could he give? Could he continue to love her like a mother or a brother, before loving her differently one day? Could love, like pain, migrate to a different part of the body?

He could hear the sea unburdening itself on the shore. He could hear it speak the truth: he had already begun to love her differently.

He knew, yet still he stepped onto the ship.

He arrived in Burma. At night, he looked up at the sky, the way his father had done on South Andaman Island. There was the moon, being painted by his loving wife, the sun. He remembered how the moon had shone on Nomi's face as he looked over the side of the boat, that night of the first round-up.

He woke up the next morning with a feeling he never wanted again, a feeling of inconsolable regret. If he left her, his brain would keep tricking him into holding onto his loss. There were losses he might recover from. Losing Nomi was not among them.

He walked down to Aberdeen, his longest walk outside his village. Forced to slow his gait, he tried to accept the new body he was in. In the months when he had unloaded cargo for the Japanese, his arms had strengthened, his chest had filled. But all of that was now gone. His right leg had been the stronger one; his left was adjusting to the weight it had to carry. On the days when he woke up cursing the remaining leg for not handling the shift better, it too would ache. Now he paused frequently on his way to Aberdeen, willing his left leg to cooperate, training his brain to move away from hindrance and focus instead on who he wanted and what he wanted. He leaned on the beautiful cane his grandfather had made, and touched the trees. Gurjan, padauk, mahua, chuglam, and the nameless one that wrapped diseased trees in a knotty overgrowth that his grandfather said could be carved exquisitely.

Aye had good hands. He need not go all the way to Burma to use them well.

He found Nomi on the jetty. She was gazing at the sea, as restless as the body of water before her.

He lowered himself, though this was harder than yesterday, when he sat on a rock to shave his father. It was taking too long and he cursed.

When he finally settled next to Nomi, she said, 'I can hear the islands breathe.' She was watching the sun as it dipped towards the sea. Neither had to say it: this was a holy hour, for it had claimed first Zee, and then the prisoner and Lala Ram. Remembering the boat tear into the sky, and the sound of the blast, Aye said a silent prayer.

Nomi picked up the cane between them, examining the design. 'Who is it?'

'Mahagiri Nat. Do you know about nats?' No, she said, she did not. There were good and bad nats, he explained, and he had once believed himself to be a bad nat.

'What kind of nat was Mahagiri Nat?'

'At first, he was just a very strong human boy,' said Aye. 'He could crush elephant tusks with his hands, and the king was afraid, so he had him killed. The boy became a nat. He is worshipped all over Burma, and that is him on the walking stick, on an elephant throne, holding the world in his hand.'

'And now you have his protection.'

'Yes. So do you.'

After a time he added, 'I will not leave, Nomi.'

Sher Sahib and the Fireflies
1945–47

IT WAS THE END OF September and few journalists still came to the island. If they did, it was to ask about the assassination of Mr Martin, and photograph bombsites. But one day, an Australian by the name of Roger Gill saw Nomi arranging fallen flame tree flowers on Zee's grave. He came towards her, saying he had heard talk of building a tombstone. 'A good idea, don't you think, for the war's first casualty?'

No other journalist had heard about Zee. She was pleased with Mr Gill, and pleased there would be a tombstone. Then people would walk by and not see only a lump of dirt.

Mr Gill asked how it happened. He was the first to ask. Last month, when more reporters had come here, children followed them about, happy to oblige with a re-enactment of Mr Martin's killing, and show them places they knew would be photographed. A few of those same children now came towards Mr Gill, some on bicycles left behind by the Japanese. When they heard what Mr Gill wanted to know, Aberdeen Square became a stage upon which they ran around first as chickens, and then as soldiers trying to catch the chickens.

Nomi had never heard anyone tell the story before. It had recurred in her body so incessantly that she was stunned to have the pictures interrupted. They forgot the part when Zee took her up Mount Top. They forgot whose gun it was. They were at that point when Zee was being secreted away from the hut—they did not say he was wearing one half of his mother's green sari—when Nomi noticed that Mr Gill was writing nothing down in his small, rectangular notebook. He had thinning red hair, did not wear a hat, and also carried a pen. He was wiping the sweat that dripped off his forehead. He was about to leave, when Shakuntala passed by, looking herself like a flame tree flower.

For the past month, Shakuntala had been bringing Nomi small gifts—fried snacks, delicious sweets, a plant, even scented lotion for her skin—always asking if she was drinking enough milk, and inviting her to the farm. White Paula had left for Europe. Her father's brother had sent for her when he heard how badly the islands had been ruined by the war. Shakuntala kept her loneliness to herself. Nomi could feel this. She accepted the gifts, but had not been to the farm. Now Shakuntala carried a plate covered in cloth, approaching with a bemused smile. The children were leaping off the ground, to enact fire.

Shakuntala lifted the cloth from the plate and offered first the journalist, then Nomi, and then the other children, four perfectly shaped rounds of sandesh. There was not enough for everyone, so the children had to share, which distracted them from the story. Shakuntala told Mr Gill that there were no pistachios or almonds to complete the dessert, which was milk-based and good for the children. He took a bite and said it was fantastic even without nuts. Soon, Nomi could tell the two were flirting. 'Oh, I *know*!' said Shakuntala, her hand flying up to her ear or adjusting the palloo of her red sari as Mr Gill said 'hard to believe' about something or the other.

The other children were done with the dessert and, sensing a change in their audience, began to get restless. They rode away, ringing their bicycle bells. Shakuntala absently played with Nomi's hair, still talking to Mr Gill. Nomi enjoyed the sensation of supple fingers on her scalp. She squinted up at the pale blue sky with puffs of clouds in the distance. Though her periods had not returned, the last time she was weighed, she had put on six pounds. Maybe the sandesh would give her another pound. She pulled in closer to Shakuntala and the warm afternoon feeling of her touch.

Shakuntala was telling Mr Gill about the round-ups. Nomi had washed up on an island, she said, and been returned to her mother by a woman who was once a prisoner, and by the descendant of another fugitive. Mr Gill smiled as though he had heard the rumours. 'Hard to believe,' he said.

'Oh, I *know*! The fugitives brought food, which the stranded people, I mean, on the other island, they fought over, even killed for. Some survivors say they—' Shakuntala looked down at Nomi, still squinting up at the sky—'they even *considered* eating . . . you know.'

'That I *can* believe,' said Mr Gill, chuckling. 'It wouldn't be the first time. Desperate measures, and all. But a child's memory is full of holes. A runaway, eh? A woman?'

'Well, yes. Tell him, Nomi.' Shakuntala gently nudged Nomi's shoulders.

'She brought bananas for everybody,' said Nomi.

'You see? Her boat exploded in front of them.'

'Well,' said Mr Gill, laughing heartily now, 'that would explain why there's no trace of her to be found.'

'What do you mean?'

'We've checked all the prison records. She never even came to this island. Most likely, she was an islander. Or a figment of the imagination of a starving people. When the body is stressed, you can never trust the mind.'

'But of course she was here!' said Shakuntala, sounding less flirty. 'We all saw her arrive. She was chained to a woman who worked at my farm.'

'And where is this woman now?'

'Dead, of course! She was shot in the second round-up. You must have heard about that. She was the wife of the Ferrargunj headman. They helped end Japanese rule.'

Still laughing, Mr Gill looked at his watch.

'You don't believe me? I have proof that she existed.'

'Proof?'

'I have a letter for her.'

'From whom?'

'I don't know exactly. A not very nice boy by the name of Faris. Seems they were romantically involved, at least in part.'

Mr Gill laughed.

'Would you like to see it?'

'Well,' said Mr Gill, looking again at his watch. 'It's three o'clock.

My ship sails for Calcutta soon. I would like to ask your husband a few questions.'

'My husband?'

'Yes,' he mumbled, finally writing in his notebook. 'I'm short on time, but would like his opinion on an independent India. I must say, I've noticed how people here seem hardly to speak of it, though it seems imminent, wouldn't he agree?'

The children were back. When they heard of an independent India, they grinned.

'Moreover,' said Mr Gill, 'it's unlikely to be a united India. Though my story is about what happened under the Japanese, I would like his opinion on a separate homeland for Indian Muslims.'

'I don't know,' said Shakuntala. 'This is the first I'm hearing of it.'

'Of course!' said Mr Gill, scribbling in his book. When he next spoke, it was hard to know if it was to them or to himself. 'A curious outcome of convict descent. Is the island free of the prejudices of the mainland? They appear not to have heard even of the Lahore Declaration.'

'What is the Lahore Declaration?'

'Right,' and now he looked at her. 'Muslims in west and east India, according to the declaration, should be liberated from Hindu dominance. What about your brothers, surely they know? Will they support it, if you all go back?'

'Mr Gill, I really do not know. I am not even a Muslim. Do you know, Nomi?'

Nomi, who wished Shakuntala would keep playing with her hair, looked now at the lump of dirt before them. She wished to rest with Zee upon those petals she had arranged. She had watched his body being broken, been pushed into the sea, lost their father, almost lost Aye, and was being told her memory was full of holes. Now she was told of a separate Muslim homeland. It was her turn to disbelieve.

She was not the only one. Shakuntala was trying to withhold a laugh. 'But you are speaking of two opposite wings of the same country!'

'Yes,' said Mr Gill. 'Now you see what I'm getting at.'

'But you won't believe me about the prisoner?' She laughed as heartily as he had done, only moments ago. The children pedalling around them were also laughing.

Mr Gill put away his notebook, his face flushed from the heat, or from indignation, it was hard to tell.

After he left, Shakuntala said, 'Oh, Nomi, would he believe that I have no brothers and no husband?'

Nomi pressed closer, and Shakuntala's fingers were back in her hair.

'Will you come to my farm tomorrow? I'll make more sandesh. I'll invite Aye.'

Nomi agreed, smiling shyly.

Nomi was alone with her mother now. She slept beside her on the cot, watching that stomach rise and fall. The skin around her eyes was creased. The right hand clutched prayer beads, and the fingernails were curved like spoons. The white hair was parted to the right, and if she peered closely, she could see the scalp—oddly coloured, almost pink. For some reason, the sight of that scalp embarrassed Nomi, as though she was seeing her mother naked.

Did the woman lying beside her ever laugh flamboyantly, like Shakuntala? Did she flirt? As Nomi studied the face, trying to discover the one buried underneath, she was aware that she now slept in her father's place. She was aware, too, that when not clasping the prayer beads, her mother was clasping Nomi, as a way to stay afloat.

Her mother would not apply for repatriation. Nomi was glad for this, it kept her with Aye, but her mother had other reasons. When she had been sent here, pregnant with Zee, her mother's family had said she belonged to Haider Ali. His mistakes were hers. She could not return to them. Besides, Nomi knew there was a second reason, one which she shared. Zee was buried here. His blood had made a home of this soil, and they were the soil's keepers. It was for this reason that people said he should have a tomb. In the coming months and years, many of those who could leave would do so for only a short time, to bring a little dirt from mainland India and mix it with the dirt here, to stake a claim, finally, to this zameen, this land, as belonging to them. Nomi hoped, one day, to do the same. She would go to Jalandhar, her father's home, bring back its earth, link it with Andaman earth, and their story would, in some small way, be safe.

Till then, she tried to suppress something. Every night, as she sat up in bed, gazing at her mother's face, she wanted to ask. *It was you who heard me in the sea, when I called out, I am Nomi! You who said, Keep kicking! I did—but why then did you leave me?*

If she could only find the courage to ask, her mother would deny it, and this would be worse. She would have abandoned Nomi *and* lied about it.

So Nomi would never ask. She would let her mother have her secret. In this way, the woman whose face she studied would not only be Zee's mother, but also her own.

But in the middle of the night, the memories returned, like the one of seeing her naked.

It happened on the island where they were reunited. Her mother had been too tired to care that when she squatted to relieve herself, men watched. Once, a man approached her. She stood up with the shalwar of her tattered prison uniform still at her knees, and kicked him. After that, she kept a close eye on Nomi. The man died, but one day, while she slept, another man came for Nomi. He was one of those who had fought for the food brought by the prisoner. When he grabbed Nomi, her mother did not only kick him. She sliced his shoulder with an axe, and as the life poured out from him, she pulled Nomi away. She took to sleeping with the axe close by and no one dared to remove it, or to remove her child.

If Nomi's father were here, maybe she would tell him. Then again, maybe not. Maybe she would prefer to go back to the way things were, sleeping on the mat on the floor, while he crawled down from the cot to lie beside her till she fell asleep.

She wished she could have done the same for him, in the water. The horror of not knowing how he died was, on some nights, worse even than the horror of replaying how Zee was killed. *Did* he die, or was he still alive, on another island?

Whenever she told Aye that her father was dead, Aye did not like her using the word. But she used it to convince herself that there could be no more search parties, not since finding two men alive on two separate islands. One had escaped before the round-ups, the other had swum to shore during the first boat campaign. Both had survived, somehow. What if her father was doing the same?

The men who had survived were young. Someone reminded her of this every night, in the same voice that had told her how to stay afloat, that night in the water, tipping each foot upward, keeping both slippers on. *Hush*, the voice said, and perhaps it was the voice of the sea, telling her that her father died in its arms, telling her, too, to store in her breasts all the stories she must one day learn to speak.

When she thought of Aye, Nomi's heart constricted in a different way from how it constricted for anyone else. She could have lost him too. There would never come a day in the life they were to share together when she would not remember this.

The two of them began to develop a ritual. Twice a week, she walked to his village, and then they either walked together to Shakuntala's farm for dinner, or to a different part of the island. In this way, she helped him to get his muscles back, while he helped her to see more of the island. Though Nomi's mother did not like it, she maintained a curious distance from Aye, and Nomi knew why. He had saved her, in the water. Perhaps she was afraid that if she objected to Aye seeing her daughter, he would disclose her secret. Realising that this was the only leverage she had over her mother, Nomi held onto it, and to the secret.

One day in November, as Nomi left Aberdeen Square for Aye's hut, she saw a herd of elephants and two bulldozers being taken towards Chatham jetty, which had been rebuilt by the Japanese before they left. The sawmill on Chatham Island had reopened. The crashing of the forest coming down—a sound that had stopped during the war—had returned. Businessmen flocked to the islands for Andaman padauk, as valuable as Burmese teak. Aye had told Nomi that he wanted his own hands on the padauk. He wanted to open his own workshop, carve his own canes, cabinets, mirror frames and so much else. He wanted to shape the winds that had returned to him by putting his hands where he knew they belonged.

As she walked, Nomi wondered how he would be feeling today. On some days, he was remarkably agile. Other times, he could barely summon the strength to step outside the front door. When it was the latter, his father still walked with him, and Nomi would watch the quiet communion between them. She wondered what it would be today: spry Aye, or father and son.

When she reached his hut, Aye said he wanted to take the ferry to Ross Island, to explore what was left of its buildings. His father was on the rock. They left the village knowing that he would still be there when Aye returned. In her heart, Nomi said a prayer for him, and for her own father too.

The ferry to Ross Island was now called *Sentinelese*, the name of another tribe considered hostile. The *Jarawa* and its captain had disappeared during the war. The boy now at the helm was also Burmese. When they arrived on Ross Island, Aye disembarked first with his good leg, then with the other, and the boat was rocking as Nomi skipped onto shore. They thanked the boy with only a nod, and the boy, who had his back to them, nodded in return.

Before Nomi and Aye lay the buildings that had been dismantled by the Japanese for timber and stone, towards the end of the war, and largely destroyed in the Allied attacks. Among these was the Japanese headquarters, once the British chief commissioner's villa. Other structures, like Mr Howard's villa, somehow remained, at least in part; the study of Mr Howard's villa, where Aye had his surgery, was intact. Neither of them had been back here since then. As they headed towards the building they could see that its exterior was swiftly being claimed by ficus trees and interwoven frills of casuarinas.

At the entrance to the villa, Aye hesitated. The rubble had still not entirely been cleared and his footing was awkward.

'What is it?' Nomi asked.

'I don't remember how I got out of there.'

'Your family helped you,' she replied, though she knew this was not all he meant. How did he get out from under Mr Howard, or the jail, or that murderous island, with all the rotting bodies? How did she? Since Zee's death, time had kept moving strangely. Like the sea, it had sometimes moved forward and taken them with it, or tossed them absolutely anywhere it wished.

Aye hopped forward.

The floor was coated in dust and shattered concrete. The kitchen lay straight ahead. There had been a half-door there, Aye said, most likely used for firewood. There were holes in the walls; the one above the kitchen was large. The gaps helped with ventilation, but also let in the wind, rain and peculiar echoes. The study was to their right. Aye hopped forward again.

The bed on which he had recuperated after his surgery was gone. The photograph of Jack the Sailor that Nomi remembered seeing when she came to him here, while he slept, was also gone. Aye pointed to the area where Mr Howard's desk had been. Behind it had been the cabinet where he found the skull, and there, along the walls, had stood the bookshelves. Like the doors of the villa, these lovely items had likely been used as fuel. The long, meandering staircase to Mr Howard's bedroom was all that was left of the Burmese woodwork of this villa. It seemed it was too beautiful for the Japanese to tear down. Aye told Nomi that he could still remember skipping up the stairs to fetch the superintendent's shaving tools, or to read the newspapers stacked near the bathtub.

As he talked, Nomi walked to the corner of the study, where the rubble had been swept into a high heap. With her toes, she began shifting the broken fragments. She spotted a dusty green corner of what must have been a ledger, and a few bits of paper too faded to read. When Aye saw her uncrumpling the paper, he reminded her that the Japanese had destroyed all records of their occupation, and destroyed many of the jail records too. After the British reoccupied the island, they had taken away whatever they could find. Or so the local inhabitants said. But Nomi said that if the Japanese could leave the staircase, they might have left other things, maybe without even knowing it, things the British too never found. She kept removing the stones, now with her hands. There were scraps in English that had not entirely faded. On one she found written, *the matter is of . . . public interest, I assume.* She decided the missing word was 'great.' On another, *the decision we have most reluctantly . . . take.* The missing letters, she decided, spelled 'felt obliged.' Then she wondered if she might also find things in Japanese, and kept digging.

'What are you looking for?' said Aye.

'Nothing,' she replied. 'I just like looking.' She pocketed the scraps the way she had once pocketed a corner of an Englishwoman's gown, and when Aye came towards her, she asked him if he would like to take them from her, perhaps to feed them to a pig. He laughed, throwing his head back with abandon, the way she had not seen him do, perhaps ever. She wished she could be like Shakuntala and White Paula and know how to flirt. Since she could not, she returned to moving aside the rubble, pocketing whatever she could read. He was watching her, though, and it made her flush. When the natural light pouring through the holes in the wall began to fade, they took the ferry back to South Andaman Island.

The island too developed new rituals. A memorial was built on the site at which forty-four prisoners, including the barely recognisable Dr Singh, had been taken to Homfreygunj by the Japanese, to dig their own L-shaped grave. The memorial had a list of everyone who had been shot that day. Those who came here to pay those names homage brought with them an egg, incense, flowers and a sheet of paper with the name of someone who had hurt them. The flowers were arranged, the incense was lit, the paper burned. Then the egg was cracked, as an offering to the spirits of the forty-four. The people believed that the spirits would serve as mediators, revealing to those whose names had been burned what they had done. The perpetrators had to face their victims. Only then could tranquillity return to the village, and to its damaged souls.

Nomi loved coming to the memorial. She brought her mother, and together they wrote the name of Governor and General Ito. When they did not know the names of everyone who had hurt them, they burned blank paper instead, sometimes visualising the faces of the two men who had broken Zee's body, or those who had pushed them off the boat. They knew their memory was skewed; it had been dark. But they remembered anyway. Because many people who came here were not literate, Nomi helped them write names. And when she had no more names to write, she still arrived with blank paper in her hands, to feel not only the ghosts of Zee, their father, Dr Singh and countless others walk beside her, but also those of Lala Ram and the prisoner. The prisoner had told Nomi of a star made entirely of words, where the right words always found each other. And it struck Nomi that this was similar to what all the people coming to the memorial with scraps of paper in their hands were doing. It was as though the memorial was the star around which they all gathered, to speak what had to be spoken.

'What is your name?' Nomi had asked, before the prisoner left on the boat with Lala Ram. *Kal*, the prisoner had answered—the word for tomorrow, and for yesterday. Did it mean she would have disclosed her name had she returned, had her boat not exploded? The prisoner had exchanged her life for Nomi's, and exchanged Lala Ram's life for Nomi's, too. She had returned Nomi to her mother, but forever separated Lala Ram from his. It had been in Lulu's hut that Nomi had lain unconscious for three days. Lulu, with a face so composed it suspended time, had nourished Nomi with grainy pastes that Nomi had somehow been able to taste, that had been bitter, yet strangely refreshing. For three days, though unaware of pain, Nomi had known so much kindness. But where was Lulu now, without her son?

The smell of burning paper and crushed flowers at the memorial were also a reminder that there were those who never got to share their story, who never got to say the words.

Perhaps it was for this reason that Nomi kept looking for lost words in the scraps in the rubble in Mr Howard's villa.

She continued into the following year, when Aye accompanied

her less and less to the villa, and hardly ever to the memorial. He said there were better ways to seek justice. He had joined an association of Local Borns that demanded compensation for the war. Though reparations had been given to Burma, Singapore, Malaya and other places devastated by the war, the world still did not look here. When the rulers had been British, people had called them Sher Sahib. Tiger Man. When the rulers were Japanese, they had been called the same. Now that more overseers were Indian, when people asked for reparations, all three Sher Sahibs kept sending them away. The people who regularly visited the memorial began burning scraps of paper with the names of Sher Sahibs from all three countries.

And then there was a fourth. Nomi and Aye would watch the unbelievable picture Mr Gill had described back in 1945 come true. India was divided. There was West Pakistan and East Pakistan and now people came to this island willingly, to escape the violence of Partition. They once again left in a hurry, separated from every possession held dear. But what was left of the living with the death of the past? They came in boats that, like the *Darya-e-Noor,* were a bridge between the living and the dead. Sometimes the boats guided them to safety, other times, the boats fed a few bodies to the sea. How could these islands be a haven from violence, after all that had happened here, after all that had still not been seen, or redressed? It was a mystery, but the refugees kept pouring in. And the names being burned at the memorial were increasingly of Sher Sahibs who had caused them to flee their own homes.

When later still the jail became a national memorial, people wanted to know—whose nation, and whose history? Whose freedom fighters, and whose dead? India's or Pakistan's?

See them one last time in the mid-summer of 1947.

Nomi leaves for Aye's village, to bring him to Shakuntala's farm for dinner. It is twilight as Nomi walks for a time along the jetty, the sea churning up silt and mud, the surf crashing on a coastline of anti-aircraft guns. Two bunkers are visible from her perspective. Till recently, there was a mass of bombs nearby, meant to have been dropped on India. She wonders when the bombs were finally cleared. Children were warned to stay away, but she can remember them playing here often.

She turns inland, to a path leading through the forest. Arriving at a lavender-pink flower with three large petals and a pistil shooting up like an arrow from its centre, she halts, amazed. The petals shudder. A shock of insects whirls across her vision. A giant bromeliad drops from the sky. Rain begins to fall with ferocious and blinding impact. Through the noise she can hear the wood crack. Possibly, these trees are older than anything alive. They are trees like those once cleared by convicts, and those being cleared again. They are trees that became the *Darya-e-Noor* and the *S.S. Noor*. Today, they are like geckos in the jaws of the wind. She thinks of Kwalakangne, the southwest wind whose temper brought the monsoons. She thinks of Kwalakangne's mother, Dare, who returned to her home in the sky the day Nomi washed ashore. She looks for signs. She remembers other things the prisoner said.

She waits for the rain to pass. Shadows draw curves, like a woman dressed in different depths of black. Then she sees something else— brief, flickering. By the time there is a gap in the rain, she knows where she has first to bring Aye, before they head to the farm.

She runs to his village. With the help of his grandfather and neighbours, Aye has constructed a workshop behind his family's hut. It began with him carving small things—bowls, flutes, lanterns and especially walking sticks—in exchange for the wood. The businessmen who flock to the island for padauk have come to learn of the beauty of these walking sticks, and his reputation slowly grows. He is carving a cane today, as Nomi enters the shop. At its base is a god holding up a goddess holding up a chain of islands, each a different size and shape. There are those who will see them as Rama and Sita, Adam and Eve, Siddhartha and Yashodhara, or mere mortals stretching their arms to the world in supplication.

Nomi wishes not to disturb him, but disturb him she must.

'How is it?' he asks her, without looking up from his work.

'Beautiful. Of course. But we need to hurry!' she pleads.

He shakes his head. The top of the cane, where South Andaman Island must rest, is not fitted properly, he insists. Perhaps he should also carve, right along there—

He is not only moving reluctantly, he is not moving at all, and they will be too late. 'Hurry!' she pleads again, pulling his arm.

'Nomi,' he says, stomping his good foot. 'Let me be today.'

But she will not.

As they walk, he keeps despairing. He needs a way to indicate the moon and the sun, he tells her, to show how the island looks, when illuminated. How can his hands bring it all alive? The moon and the sun will not fit atop that walking stick! He can still only make the little things!

They arrive at the lavender-pink flower.

'Here,' says Nomi. She remembers how the prisoner had loved to be at the mangrove forest at dusk, and remembers why. The creek towards which she takes Aye is in an indent of the forest, and though she has never taken this detour before, she takes it now, because what she saw had come from there.

After another five minutes, they are stepping over the woven limbs of mangroves, the ground soft and yielding. They look around, and gasp. Fireflies, thousands of them. The night is studded with their choreography of gold and black. Nomi recalls the day two fireflies had trailed the prisoner to her nest, in which Nomi lay. It was the day she told her of the star made only of words. She had plucked the green one, and as it throbbed, she had handed it to Nomi. 'Fireflies are the stars of the forest,' she had said, as Nomi released it. 'They are the pathways through shadow to light. And this movement, this blinking and fading out, it lives in all things. It lives inside our body.'

Nomi repeats this now, for Aye. He drops his cane and takes both her hands in his.

Together they watch. They listen.

ACKNOWLEDGMENTS

The genesis of this book dates back to an accident, some twenty-six years ago, when I chanced upon a quote by a British politician who described a group of islands to which Indian prisoners were banished as a 'paradise.' I had gone to the library to find a book that I did not find. I came away with the one I knew I had to write. Therein lay the problem. The prison colony of the Andaman Islands was, at the time, almost entirely written out of history. Women prisoners, who were also transported to the islands, rarely merited even a footnote. And the Japanese had destroyed all records of their occupation of the islands during the Second World War. These stories had been all but dismissed, even by those who concede that the past and present are part of an entangled, fragile continuum.

I am so grateful that in the past two decades, an engagement with these missing chapters has become available. I am especially indebted to the following sources, without which this book would still not exist. For details of prison life: *In Andamans, The Indian Bastille* by Bejoy Kumar Sinha; *My Transportation for Life* by V.D. Savarkar; *Bina Das, A Memoir* translated by Dhira Dhar. On the Japanese occupation: *Black Days in Andaman and Nicobar Islands* by Rabin Roychowdhury; *Japanese in the Andaman and Nicobar Islands* by Jayant Dasgupta. For details of the islands: *New Histories of the Andaman Islands* by Clare Anderson, Madhumita Mazumdar, Vishvajit Pandya; *The Land of Naked People* by Madhusree Mukerjee; *In the Forest: Visual and Material Worlds of Andamanese History* by Vishvajit Pandya. On prisoner brides: 'Settling the Convict: Matrimony and Domesticity in the Andamans' by A. Vaidik. 'Rationing Sex: Female Convicts in the Andamans' by Satadru Sen. Additional sources: *Feminism and Nationalism in the Third World* by Kumari Jayawardena. *Comfort Women* by Yoshimi Yoshiaki. *Imperial Bodies* by E. M. Collingham. *Legible Bodies* by Clare Anderson. *Forgotten Armies, The Fall of British Asia 1941–1945* by Christopher Bayly and Tim Harper.

The italics on page 30 are lines from the diary of Mr Gwyne, as quoted in *Imperial Andamans: Colonial Encounter and Island History* by A. Vaidik. The italics on page 61 are lines from the diary of Michael Symes, as quoted in *The Land of Naked People* by Madhusree Mukerjee. The quote by Sir Henry Craik on page 98 is taken from *Kala Pani* by Dr L.P. Mathur. The italics on page 115 are from Savarkar's *My Transportation for Life*. The italics on page 146 are the words of the suffragette Sylvia Pankhurst. The quote on page 208 from Rabindranath Tagore's *Char Adhyay* is taken from *The History of Doing: An Illustrated Account of Movements for Women's Rights and Feminism in India* by Radha Kumar. The italics on page 220–21 are from a talk given by Lu Xun, titled, 'After Nora Walks Out, What Then?' Translation is by Wen-Chao Li. The speech given by Subhas Chandra Bose on South Andaman Island, in italics on page 274–75, is from *Black Days in Andaman and Nicobar Islands* by Rabin Roychowdhury.

Although my novel is based on historical events, it is important to stress that the characters and their situations are fictional.

I am grateful to the Marion and Jasper Whiting Foundation Fellowship, with whose support I was able to do research at the British Library, Cambridge University, and Imperial War Museum.

Special thanks to my agent, Laura Susijn, and my editors, V.K. Karthika and Ajitha G.S., with whose care and patience this is a much better book. Deepest gratitude to Will Evans and the Deep Vellum team for steering it across more oceans.

Thank you to my mother, for her abundant faith. To Dave, for showing me every day that paradise is now. And to my father, who taught me to look at power, and never forget. This book is for him.

Thank you all
for your support.
We do this for you,
and could not do
it without you.

PARTNERS

pixel ||| texel

ADDITIONAL DONORS, CONT'D

Mark Haber

Mary Cline

Maynard Thomson

Michael Reklis

Mike Soto

Mokhtar Ramadan

Nikki & Dennis Gibson

Patrick Kukucka

Patrick Kutcher

Rev. Elizabeth & Neil Moseley

Richard Meyer

Scott & Katy Nimmons

Sherry Perry

Sydneyann Binion

Stephen Harding

Stephen Williamson

Susan Carp

Susan Ernst

Theater Jones

Tim Perttula

Tony Thomson

SUBSCRIBERS

Ned Russin

Michael Binkley

Michael Schneiderman

Aviya Kushner

Kenneth McClain

Eugenie Cha

Stephen Fuller

Joseph Rebella

Brian Matthew Kim

Anthony Brown

Michael Lighty

Erin Kubatzky

Shelby Vincent

Margaret Terwey

Ben Fountain

Caroline West

Ryan Todd

Gina Rios

Caitlin Jans

Ian Robinson

Elena Rush

Courtney Sheedy

Elif Ağanoğlu

Laura Gee

Valerie Boyd

Brian Bell

AVAILABLE NOW FROM DEEP VELLUM

FORTHCOMING FROM DEEP VELLUM

MARIO BELLATIN • *Etchapare* • translated by Shook • MEXICO

CAYLIN CARPA-THOMAS • *Iguana Iguana* • USA

MIRCEA CĂRTĂRESCU • *Solenoid* • translated by Sean Cotter • ROMANIA

TIM COURSEY • *Driving Lessons* • USA

ANANDA DEVI • *When the Night Agrees to Speak to Me* • translated by Kazim Ali • MAURITIUS

DHUMKETU • *The Shehnai Virtuoso* • translated by Jenny Bhatt • INDIA

LEYLÂ ERBIL • *A Strange Woman* • translated by Nermin Menemencioğlu & Amy Marie Spangler • TURKEY

ALLA GORBUNOVA • *It's the End of the World, My Love* • translated by Elina Alter • RUSSIA

NIVEN GOVINDEN • *Diary of a Film* • GREAT BRITAIN

GYULA JENEI • *Always Different* • translated by Diana Senechal · HUNGARY

DIA JUBAILI • *No Windmills in Basra* • translated by Chip Rosetti • IRAQ

ELENI KEFALA • *Time Stitches* • translated by Peter Constantine • CYPRUS

UZMA ASLAM KHAN • *The Miraculous True History of Nomi Ali* • PAKISTAN

ANDREY KURKOV • *Grey Bees* • translated by Boris Dralyuk • UKRAINE

JORGE ENRIQUE LAGE • *Freeway La Movie* • translated by Lourdes Molina • CUBA

TEDI LÓPEZ MILLS • *The Book of Explanations* • translated by Robin Myers • MEXICO

ANTONIO MORESCO • *Clandestinity* • translated by Richard Dixon • ITALY

FISTON MWANZA MUJILA • *The Villain's Dance* • translated by Roland Glasser • DEMOCRATIC REPUBLIC OF CONGO

N. PRABHAKARAN • *Diary of a Malayali Madman* • translated by Jayasree Kalathil • INDIA

THOMAS ROSS • *Miss Abracadabra* • USA

IGNACIO RUIZ-PÉREZ • *Isles of Firm Ground* • translated by Mike Soto • MEXICO

LUDMILLA PETRUSHEVSKAYA • *Kidnapped: A Crime Story* • translated by Marian Schwartz • RUSSIA

NOAH SIMBLIST, ed. • *Tania Bruguera: The Francis Effect* • CUBA

S. YARBERRY • *A Boy in the City* • USA